Also by William F. Nolan

Things Beyond Midnight
Dark Encounters
Urban Horrors
Helltracks
Night Shapes
The Winchester Horror
Down the Long Night
Dark Universe
Nightworlds
Death Drive
Ill Met By Moonlight
Demon!
How to Write Horror Fiction

Nightshadows

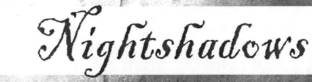

Nightshadows

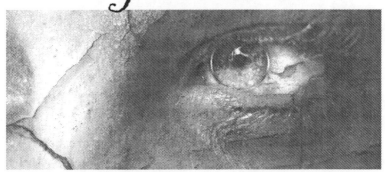

WILLIAM F. NOLAN

The Best New Horror Fiction
by a Living Legend in Dark Fantasy

DARKWOOD PRESS
Bonney Lake • Seattle

Nightshadows

A Darkwood Press Book
December 2007
Copyright © 2007 by William F. Nolan

Darkwood Press
an imprint of Fairwood Press
21528 104th Street Court East
Bonney Lake, WA 98391
www.fairwoodpress.com

Cover and Book Design by Patrick Swenson

ISBN: 0-9789078-4-1
ISBN13: 978-0-9789078-4-6
First Fairwood Press Edition: December 2007
Printed in the United States of America

For Patrick Swenson,
who knows horror publishing
from his head to his talebone

Copyrights

CONTENTS

The Things That Go Bump in My Night
William F. Nolan

The word "new" in the sub-title of *Nightshadows* is quite accurate. Nineteen of the twenty-three stories in this present volume were written in our new century following the release of my retrospective collection *Dark Universe*, which covers almost all of my work into the year 2000. I say "almost" because four stories written in the 1990s were excluded. Why were these earlier tales left out of *Dark Universe*? The answer is simple: at 140,000 words, the book was already overlong (with 41 stories) and I didn't have room for more. The "missing four" are a match in quality for the stories chosen for *Dark Universe*, and I'm happy to see them finally collected here. Thus, my sub-title holds; this is a new collection representing my best work in the genre of shock fiction over recent years right through 2007.

The majority of these stories are first person narratives; I like the immediacy of first person. The reader feels directly connected to the narrator, whether an 11-year-old boy, a lighthouse keeper on another planet, or an accountant-turned-werewolf. An intimate bond is established.

I began reading Dark Fantasy as a teenage boy in Kansas City in the 1940s, buying each new issue of *Weird Tales*——and discovering a writer named Ray Bradbury in its lurid pulp pages. (Remember the thing in "The Jar," or the little girl who never came out of "The Lake"?)

Boris Karloff's edited anthology *Tales of Terror* (1943) introduced me to Algernon Blackwood, Bram Stoker, Ambrose Bierce——and *Great Tales of Terror and the Supernatural* (1944) allowed me to savor the dark worlds of H.P. Lovecraft, A.E. Coppard, W.W. Jacobs, Arthur Machen, H.G. Wells, John Collier, and Henry James (never dreaming that many years later I would be adapting his "Turn of the Screw" for television). Although I have stripped my library of ten thousand books down to a "can't-bear-to-part-with" three thousand, I still have these two seminal anthologies. They set me firmly on the road to horror and, along that road, I discovered such masters as Nigel Kneale, Robert Aickman, Fritz Leiber and, yes, Stephen King and Peter Straub. Not to forget Shirley Jackson and Robert Bloch.

I shivered as a young boy, crouched beside our tall family radio for each episode of Arch Oboler's *Lights Out!* (and will never forget the chills I got from Oboler's "The Chicken Heart" as it slowly covered the world, or the thrills received as I watched Karloff shamble through *Frankenstein* and Lugosi stalk his victims in *Dracula*). Thus, it was only natural that I became a horror writer.

I have multiple credits in the genre in all media: novels (*Helltracks, Demon!, The Winchester Horror*), short fiction (numerous tales in *Playboy, Night Cry, The Twilight Zone Magazine*, and *Weird Tales*, as well as in a variety of anthologies such as *Great Tales of Terror, Best New Horror, Masterpieces of Horror, The Year's Best Horror Stories*, etc), films (*Burnt Offerings, Terror at London Bridge*), television (*The Turn of the Screw, Trilogy of Terror*), the stage ("Dead Call," "Dutch"), radio ("The Party," "The Small World of Lewis Stillman") and comics ("The Underdweller").

I was honored when the International Horror Guild voted me a "Living Legend in Dark Fantasy," and have been pleased to see my horror tales published in a variety of Nolan collections from *Things Beyond Midnight* to *Ill Met by Moonlight*.

Many of my illustrious contemporaries have praised my work. At one World Fantasy Convention, Stephen King approached me to say how much he liked my short story "Dead Call," and Peter Straub told me that my tale of a man trapped in his past, "Dark Winner," was one of the most disturbing horror stories he'd ever read.

Since I've written headings for each of the stories in this collection, I won't go on here. Suffice to say that Dark Fantasy remains a major force in my life, both as entertainment and as a creative outlet. I'm constantly searching my imagination for new horrors to put on paper. Horror fiction is one of our earliest forms of literature, and will always be with us.

Let me end with a poem that reflects my feelings for this genre. Title: "The Horror Writer."

Shadow shapes,
swimming in fogged darkness,
razored teeth,
slicing deep, releasing
crimson heart tides.

Prowling beasts,
within a scything moon,
wild of eye,
lust-hungry for the kill.

Demonic fiends,
claw-fingered, eager
to rend flesh,
in blood-gored midnight feasts.
Specter spirits,
summoned from gloomed grave, risen
from dank coffined earth
to fetid life.

Witch, devil, ghoul,
the tall walking dead,
night companions all,
who join me at the keys,
Welcome!

Welcome to my world!

A final note of thanks to Patrick Swenson for coming up with the idea of a 100,000 word collection of my recent best. His support as publisher is much appreciated.
Will I ever stop writing tales of Dark Fantasy?
I hope not.

W.F.N.
Bend, Oregon
2007

I'd always had a yen to write a full-blown werewolf story, but I was bothered by the tradition that, in all such tales, the protagonist suffers from the "Curse of the Werewolf."

I asked myself: why must it be a curse? Why couldn't someone enjoy being a werewolf? I determined to write a story that turned the curse into a blessing.

Thus, "Wolf Song."

Wolf Song

Late at night, under a full moon,
have you heard the song of the wolf?
——Jules LeGrande, 1876

Oh, yes, I know that rational, sane people do not believe in them. They are something you encounter in a fairy tale, something fanciful and dark that logically cannot be. They don't exist. They aren't real.

Yet I'm real. I exist.

I fingered the long white scar on my neck, remembering that night in the Alabama woods . . . .

I was ten. Little Donny Morgan. Pampered. An only child. Small for my age, with pale colorless eyes and skin that would never tan. Like white wax. Walking home, taking the short cut through Mobile's thick-treed woods. Under a full moon. Whistling. Feeling good after the John Wayne cowboy movie at the Strand. Full of popcorn and iced coke.

Then, with a terrible roar, a creature erupted from the trees. Covered with dark, matted fur. Glowing red eyes. Sharp razor claws. A long snout lined with teeth like a serrated row of glittering knives.

I screamed, began to run, stumbled, falling to my knees. A deep growling, as the foul creature's teeth sank into my neck. A bright burst of pain. Blood. The fetid breath of the beast, like rank steam in my nostrils.

Then . . . from deep woods . . . a sudden shotgun blast. The wolf-creature, howling in anger, badly wounded, retreated . . . fading back into the tree shadows.

A tall figure stood over me. Dizzy. Blood at my throat. I stared up at the man with the shotgun.

"Dunno what in the name of God that was —— but it's lucky for you I come along when I did."

Lucky. Yes, *lucky*.

"You're bleedin' something fierce, son," said the tall man. "Need to get you to a doctor."

Hands lifting me. Swirling stars. An engulfing darkness.

I blacked out.

Fifteen years had passed since that fateful night in the woods. I'm already balding. My face is long and bony. Skinny legs, thick glasses. All in all, not much to look at. I've lived in Mobile all my life. Until recently, I held a boring job as an accountant for the Gulf, Mobile, and Ohio Railroad. Eight dull hours each day, perched on a high wooden stool, wearing a green plastic eyeshade, working with endless figures in a small dusty cubicle next to the downtown post office.

My salary was modest and would never be substantial. But that was fine because I knew I was something more than an overworked, poorly paid railroad accountant. I was *special*.

I vividly recall the first transformation.

It had not happened right away. I didn't even know that I was infected, or exactly what kind of beast had attacked me. My parents said it was most likely a wild dog, and they had me checked for rabies. The checkup was negative, with the doctor assuring my parents that once the neck wound healed I'd be okay. My parents were greatly relieved.

I knew that the thing I'd seen in those dark woods was no dog. But what exactly *was* it?

A month later, under a grossly-bloated full moon, as I was returning from a late-night visit with my only friend, Bobby Wilkes, it happened.

The transformation.

I felt my body begin to reshape itself. Bones bending, twisting, flesh stretching, a dark thick matting of fur spreading over my skin, daggered teeth lining a long wolf's snout, a deep, gutteral growl rising in my throat —— and a sudden lust for blood.

Human blood.

Afterward, with the sun shimmering golden in the sky the next morning, I awoke in my parents' apartment. My clothes were tattered and streaked with crimson. Bits of flesh adhered to my teeth, and the rusty taste of blood was on my tongue. My breath was foul and I smelled of death.

I could remember everything that happened the previous night. Vivid images. Screams. The odor of fear. I had attacked a seven-year-old girl in the woods, ripped her throat open, and devoured parts of her body. I felt no guilt. On the contrary, I felt renewed, refreshed, satiated. A dark appetite had been appeased. I had enjoyed a satisfying meal of tender young flesh.

Over the months that followed, prowling the dark woods, I'd struck again and again under the pale yellow circle of the moon, feeling no regret over my actions. What transpired in those moonlit woods by night left me buoyant and pleasantly light-hearted by day.

Deny not the beast!

I read that somewhere. I was doing extensive research on the subject of werewolves, surprised at what I'd uncovered. Werewolf lore extends back into the dim past. For centuries, people in many parts of the world have accepted the werewolf as reality. Not a thing of myth and folk tales, but a real, three-dimensional creature who stalked and killed under the full moon.

Reports of such beasts could be traced far back in prehistory.

In the fifth century B.C. the Greek historian Herodotus reported on the Neuri, a wild tribe that transformed themselves into wolves for a given period each year. It was also believed that Nebuchadnezzar, the fabled king of ancient Babylonia, was a victim of lycanthropy. Lycanthrope derives from the Greek words "lykos" (wolf) and "anthropos" (human).

Lycanthropy was said to have flourished during the Middle Ages. Between 1520 and 1630, some 30,000 individuals, men and women, were condemned as loup-garou in France and burned at the stake. (Loup-garou: French for werewolf.)

In 1767, a creature identified only as "The Beast of Le Gevaudan," was proclaimed to be a werewolf and was killed in the French countryside by bullets made from a blessed chalice.

Under a full moon.

In fact, the full moon figured as an essential element in every account, ancient or modern, concerning a werewolf. Etheric energies in the Earth are at their peak when the moon is round. At the full, this cold, lifeless heavenly body, close companion to Earth, affects the oceanic tides, stimulates worldwide unrest, and is said to produce startling changes in the human form. Police around the world have reported that under a full moon crime increases tenfold.

Much has been written or dramatized concerning the werewolf, and a large proportion of what I had encountered in my research proved to be lurid trash. Outlandish novels and stories, a host of obviously fallacious studies, and countless motion pictures featured myth over reality. For example, the idea that it takes a silver bullet to slay a werewolf is pure Hollywood hokum.

I recalled a dark chant from one such film I'd seen as a child:

> *Even a man who is pure of heart*
> *and says his prayers by night*
> *may become a wolf when the wolfbane blooms*
> *and the moon is clear and bright*

Utter nonsense, of course! Wolfbane is a poisonous flower of a variety mainly grown in Nepal. Warriors used the poison from this flower to tip their arrows, but it had nothing to do with an actual transformation of man into beast.

Again and again, throughout my research, I encountered one universal element —— that those who survived the teeth of the beast became its victims. Under a full moon, they suffered "the curse of the werewolf."

I reject this idea. I am certainly no victim; I have been given a strong new identity, a life beyond anything I could ever have imagined. What I have undergone is no curse. It is a blessing. A gift of fate.

Without this gift, without that transforming night in the woods of Mobile, I would be no more than a plain-faced, bored accountant toting up figures for the railroad, a dull speck of humanity, one of billions of colorless little men laboring like ants on the planet, who live and die without notice or regard.

Oh, how I have savored this new existence, how grateful I am for having been chosen by destiny to be unique among my fellows. Never had I felt stronger, healthier, more fulfilled.

Then *she* entered my life.

My employer had posted a HELP WANTED — SECRETARY sign in the office window, and she had come in to apply for the job. Edith Anne Hartley, twenty-five, single, supple-bodied and beautiful.

My parents had divorced by then and had moved to California. This was no great loss to me since we had never been close. My mother and father are cold, emotionless people. They never abused me, but lacked the capacity or desire to express their love. We exchange cards at Christmas, and that's it. No phone calls or letters — just impersonal Christmas cards each year.

I was living alone in a cramped one-bedroom rented apartment just two blocks from my workplace. Had no friends. (Bobby Wilkes had gone away to college in Boston and we had lost contact.)

I've never had an emotional relationship with a woman. In fact, women found me aloof and unattractive, and I had long since reconciled myself to living alone.

Until I met Edith.

She was the first girl I'd ever yearned to be with, but I didn't know how to approach her.

One morning, a week after she'd come to work in the GMO office, I left a limerick on her desk. Edith giggled, reading it:

> *I sit at my desk and ponder*
> *about the new girl over yonder.*
> *Would she possibly agree*
> *To have lunch with me?*
> *I'm sure if I asked her, I'd flounder.*

The limerick worked. Edith laughingly agreed to meet me in Walgreens at noon. This initiated a cycle of daily lunches. Despite my shyness, our relationship progressed rapidly. Edith overlooked my obvious physical shortcomings. She was, in fact, charmed by my awkward manner. Many handsome men had paid court to her over the years, but she had rejected all of them. Good looks were not a concern to her. She sought depth and sincerity in a man, and she felt that I had both. She understood me in a way no one else ever had.

We made love in my apartment that same month. It was an incredible experience, my first real sexual adventure.

In a rented Ford, I would drive from town each evening after work to see Edith at her home on the outskirts of Mobile and we would sit together, holding hands, on a stone bench in the garden behind the tall, white-pillared mansion, talking quietly for hours . . . facing the woods.

Streamers of hanging moss draped the trees like white confetti, lending an incongruous carnival atmosphere to the area, but, to Edith, the woods represented blood and death.

She told me about her early life in Shreveport before her father, Thomas Hartley, bought the big plantation house in Mobile. He had been a very successful trial lawyer in Louisiana, and had now retired at fifty.

"Daddy spends most of his time these days watching football on TV," Edith declared. "He'll never have to work again. We have lots of money."

"A beautiful young girl with lots of money." I smiled. "How come you haven't been snapped up by now?"

"Because I happen to be very particular about who does the snapping," she replied.

"Must be nice, having all that money."

She nodded. She'd been spoiled, Edith admitted. Daddy's girl. Given everything she ever wanted. She was now driving a new Mercedes, a gift from Daddy for her twenty-fourth birthday. And her mother was equally indulgent.

"I don't think you're spoiled."

She was sweetness itself, her voice like soft music. I was stunned when she told me, just a month after we had met, that she had fallen in love with me. By then, of course, I adored her.

I found it curious that she never asked me why I never visited her under a full moon, but we did talk about what the local Mobile papers were now calling "The Full Moon Murders."

"It's so horrible," she declared. "All those murders. Old folks. Young children. Who could be doing such awful things?"

"People seem to think it isn't a man doing the killings," I said. "More likely a wild beast of some kind."

She drew in a quick breath, trembling. "I used to love walking in the woods under a full moon. When I was a young girl just after we moved here from Shreveport. It was one of my favorite things to do. I never felt in any kind of danger. It was exciting—all mystery and magic. But now . . ."

"Now it's not that way anymore," I said, taking her hand. "I want you to promise me something."

"Yes?"

My eyes locked to hers. "I want you to promise me that you'll *never* walk in these woods after dark."

She laughed. "That'll be an easy promise to keep. I'd be terrified to go walking there at night."

"So you promise?"

"I do."

"Good girl."

The slaughter continued —— a mounting series of gruesome deaths in those moss-draped Alabama woods under the pus-yellow face of a full moon. Brutal, bloody, savage deaths. Half-devoured corpses with throats ripped open. Children. Women. Old men.

The authorities were baffled. Some ravenous animal was loose in the area. But no victim survived to describe the killer. Traps were set. Armed police patrolled the woods. To no avail. They found nothing.

The slaughter continued.

Then there was an evening in late fall when I asked Edith to be my wife. She happily accepted. We were married a week later by a local justice of the peace. Her parents attended, pleased that their daughter had chosen a solid, feet-on-the-ground working man. That I lacked money of my own was of no consequence.

"Remember, Don," Thomas Hartley had told me, "you'll always have my money behind you. I don't want my little girl to miss any of the good things in life. Don't ever hesitate to ask me for extra funds. Whatever you need."

"I'll remember."

No one from my side of the family attended the wedding. Mother wrote a brief note of congratulation; I got only silence from my father. When I tried to phone them, no one answered.

But I didn't mind. Nothing mattered beyond Edith. She became my personal universe.

I was elated, overwhelmed; I felt myself to be the luckiest man in the world to have won this lovely girl as my wife. Which was when I made the vow: to never again venture into the night woods under a full moon. The beast within must not be allowed to emerge for further carnage. I owed that to Edith. My willpower was strong, and I was certain that I could keep my vow.

The decision had been difficult. I would miss that marvelous feeling of euphoria and well-being experienced on the languorous mornings after my moonlit kills. I had never suffered guilt. Why should I? The only person on the planet I cared about was Edith. I had no brothers or sisters, and if I met my mother and father in the woods under a full moon I'd have no qualms about ripping their throats out.

Death comes to claim everyone. What matter that strangers died in the woods? Death would have taken them eventually. Death was universal.

Yes, in all the world, only my sweet wife mattered. And, for her sake, I would sacrifice the joys of my moonlit adventures. She must never know the truth about that long-ago night in the woods when I was a boy . . . about what I then became under a full moon.

Edith must never know.

As a wedding present, Thomas Hartley gifted us with a handsome two-story stone-and-stucco home not far from the family plantation. I was grateful to escape my cramped apartment. The new structure had just one drawback: it faced the woods.

Our lovemaking was intense. As if a sexual dam had broken.

I never imagined that I possessed such wild passion.

Edith was shocked, but not displeased, at my sexual boldness, and once had ironically called out: "Oh . . . you beast!"

I had smiled.

For the first year of our marriage I somehow managed to keep my vow. It was always a struggle When the round pocked face of the Alabama moon flushed the sky with its sickly yellow radiance, I'd draw the curtains tight at each window to stifle the light, to keep it at bay.

I must never go out to it. Its terrible rays must never touch my body!

Yet, incredibly, the "Full Moon Murders" continued, as fresh victims were slaughttered in the woods of Mobile. Tourists, unaware of the danger. Locals, unwilling to bow to personal fear.

Could it be that my dark side had surfaced on those nights without my conscious knowledge? Was I losing my battle with the beast?

On each night of the full moon the hunger to kill, to maim and feast, increased — building, becoming all-powerful. I could not sleep on such nights. I roamed through the house, sweating, shivering — and still Edith, the perfect wife, never questioned my bizarre behavior, leaving me alone in my agony.

Tortured and alone.

Summer in Mobile. A hot, sticky southern summer night a year and six months after the marriage of Donald Morgan and Edith Hartley.

A full moon.

Edith gone from the house. I was alone. Sweating. Shivering.

Deny not the beast!

I walked to the front door, opened it — and entered the woods. Each tree and bush was alive with sulfurous light. Reflecting the moon's eerie glow, fingers of hanging moss, white and stark, laced the looming trees.

I stood in the middle of a wide clearing, my head tipped upward toward the sky, hands fisted, drawing in the transforming rays of the round yellow giant above me.

Awaiting the change.

I felt the beast-power rising within my body. My bones and muscles stretched and altered; my skin prickled with a spreading mat of dark fur. Soon I would be stalking, killing, feasting.

Then, from the inked tree shadows, a dark shape surged toward me. I twisted about to face a roaring, swift-running beast. Fangs bared. Eyes blazing red. My God!

Werewolf!

I felt the stunning weight of the creature as it smashed me to the ground. Its blade-sharp paws were buried in my chest. Blood spurted from ravaged veins. I screamed.

Razored teeth flashed in the moonlight.

There was one fact that I'd not encountered in my research: that the bite of a werewolf was not the only way to activate the human-to-wolf transformation, that sexual intercourse with a werewolf was equally infectious.

This was the case with sweet Edith as she lowered her beast's head to rip my throat open.

How can I be telling you this story if Edith killed me? Well, of course, she *didn't*. I survived her attack. Perhaps she *allowed* me to live, to function as her night companion, to share the joys of severed flesh.

We are closer than ever as we prowl the woods together under a full moon.

Beast-woman and beast-man.

A perfect union.

This story began as an original screenplay, written for director William Friedkin—just before he left to direct The French Connection. *Suddenly I had an orphan script on my hands and decided to turn it into a short story using the same basic plot and much of the dialogue.*

"DePompa" is based on the life and death of screen icon James Dean. I had met Dean at a sports car race in California, and had written several pieces about him. Dean became the perfect character to fit my dark plot. The small fishing village of San Felipe, at the edge of the Gulf, really exists. I drove down there with Friedkin to scout locations for our aborted film.

As described, it's a spooky place at night, and (like Dean) exactly fits my bizarre plot. Yeah, bizarre is the word for "DePompa."

DePompa

The year is 1960.

His name is Terence Rodriguez Antonio DePompa, and he is on his way to death.

He is dressed in casual, wine-colored sports slacks and a white polo shirt. He wears doeskin driving gloves and a black leather cap. A knitted silk scarf, imported from India, whips out behind him like a white flag.

The winding Mexican highway he moves over runs to a dizzy height above the Gulf of California, with the water spreading to the horizon in a rippled sheet of sun-dazzled gold.

The car he drives is an open-cockpit Mercedes Benz 300 SLR. Its 3-liter, eight-cylinder fuel-injected engine generates nearly 300 horsepower. At 7,000 rpm, this machine is capable of 170 mph. In a near-identical model, the legendary British ace Stirling Moss won the 1955 Mille Miglia, Italy's thousand-mile road race.

Terry had purchased the car directly from the Mercedes factory in Stuttgart after flying to Germany in his private jet. The tooled-leather bucket seat, in fire-engine red, was custom fitted to his five-foot-eight-inch frame (he looked much taller on the screen), and he had the Benz painted in U.S. racing colors: white, with a metallic blue stripe running along the hood and back deck. In the late 1950s, with this car, he'd competed during Speed Week in the Bahamas, winning the Nassau Trophy over a potent trio of Ferraris driven by the prime American racers, Phil Hill, Dan Gurney, and Carroll Shelby. Terry's best friend was killed during this event when a tire blew on the back straight, but the loss was minimal. Best friends were easy to come by.

Following the event, a fat banker from Chicago offered DePompa a million in cash for the Benz. Terry declined politely. That same weekend, over a rum punch in Blackbeard's Tavern, he was offered a factory ride in Europe with Ferrari, which he also declined. A reporter for the *Nassau Blade* asked him why he chose to risk his life in a racing car. Why didn't he just stick to acting?

Terry smiled for the camera (the smile that had fired the hearts of a million young women) and told the reporter: "Well, you see, I'm not sure whether I'm an actor who races or a racer who acts." It was a line he'd often used in the past to explain his passion for motor sport.

Of course, there were many other passions: bullfighting in Spain, bobsledding in Switzerland, big-game hunting in Africa, mountain climbing in Colorado — and beautiful women everywhere. (He'd tried a man once, at a gay bar in Detroit, but that had been a fiasco.)

Margaret, Terry's ex-wife, was working as a top fashion model when they met in New York at a cocktail party for Howard Hughes (who never showed up). She'd been gorgeous, and still retained her slim figure. She also retained their mansion on the Riviera, Terry's custom-designed white Cadillac, their lavishly furnished apartment in Bel Air, three million in diamonds, and their five-bedroom town house on Fifth Avenue. Terry had called her "a greedy bitch" in court, and she had called him "an egotistic bastard."

They understood each other.

DePompa ended up giving Margaret almost everything her lawyers asked for. Since he was now paid over half a million for each of his films, he felt no loss. Keep the bitch happy. Get her (and her lawyers) off his back. At least she was sterile, with no kids to muddy the water.

For Terry DePompa, the Benz is sheer joy to drive, ballet-gliding the tight curves and devouring the long straights. He savors the raw power of this swift metal beast, all his to control, to dominate (in a way he could never dominate Margaret).

Terry smiles into the flow of the heated wind, pressing his booted foot down harder on the gas pedal, feeling the engine surge. Control. Power and control.

He touches the slight scar along his left cheek, remembering the violent fight with Margaret in their Bel Air bedroom last Christmas when she'd raked his face with her sharp nails.

It is nearly dark now, and an approaching truck flashes its headlights at Terry — reminding him of the spotlights shining into his eyes at Grauman's Chinese in Hollywood for the premiere of *Pain World* when he'd placed his hands and shoe prints in the wet square of cement, with the sensual redhead from Vegas pressing her soft, tanned body against his.

He snaps on his high beams, illuminating the chalk white ribbon of cliff road stretching ahead. He enters a mile-long straight with a wickedly sharp U-curve at the end. Terry knows this road, has driven it many times.

His foot jabs harder on the gas pedal and the Benz responds. Roars. Bullet fast. And faster. Eating up the road at 100 . . . 120 . . . 130 . . . 140 . . . 150 . . .

The straight ends. The curve is here.

Terry smiles.

He doesn't slow down.

In his small New York apartment, twenty-five-year-old Dennie Holmes sits in his frayed pajamas on the faded rose throw rug in front of the television set. His dark eyes are intent on the screen as he leans forward to adjust the volume. The voice of newscaster Morley Purvis is now sharp and clear:

". . . dead at twenty-four in the twisted, charred remains of his fast German sports car. Life had tragically ended for the young screen idol, cinema's new golden boy, who was —"

Dennie switches to another channel. This time the newscaster is a woman:

". . . with the cause of the crash shrouded in mystery. No tire marks were found on the cliff road, proving that DePompa did not brake for the deadly hairpin curve. Could he have suffered a sudden heart attack? His family physician, Dr. Mark Kalman, claims that DePompa's medical history shows no evidence of heart disease. However, an autopsy is not possible, since the actor's body was —"

A third channel.

Margaret DePompa, in her early thirties, is being interviewed at her New York town house. Slim, bottle-blonde, and cat-featured, she dabs at her eyes with a dainty lace handkerchief. Her voice is strained: ". . .but our silly little quarrels meant nothing. Like any couple, we didn't *always* agree — but we adored each other. Had Terry lived, I'm certain we would have remarried. He was (sobbing) the . . . the whole world to me."

The interviewer, anchorman Len Lawson, moves the mike closer to her. "Do you believe that your ex-husband *deliberately* drove to his death?"

The reply is fierce and direct: "Never! Terry loved life far too much." And she continues to sob.

Lawson turns to the camera. "The life he loved so much and lived so fully began in poverty for Terence Rodriguez Antonio DePompa . . ."

The scene shifts to a small, squalid Mexican village. The camera moves along the dusty street to enter a crude adobe hut and center on a timeworn old woman. Her head is bowed, as she rocks listlessly back and forth in a wicker chair.

Lawson's voice-over tells us: "Little Terry DePompa grew up here, in this poverty-ridden Mexican village after the boy's father, an Irish-Italian bricklayer, deserted the family when Terry was three. His mother, Maria, mourns her famous son."

The interviewer's voice is soft and gentle: "What was he like, Mrs. DePompa? Can you tell us about your Terry?"

"He . . . don't like play . . . with other boys. He . . . many times run away . . . like burro . . . My Terry . . . he never happy here. Run away to Mexicali for job . . ."

The scene now shifts to DePompa himself, speaking directly into the camera during an earlier interview:

"At fourteen I was working in a coffin maker's shop in Mexicali and spending all my free time at the local movie house, dreaming that someday I might be up there, on that silver screen. Two years later, at sixteen, I got a job on a lemon grove in Chula Vista, on the U.S. side of the border. The owner's wife took what you might call a 'personal interest' in me." A knowing grin for the camera. "She paid my way into Dave Corey's acting class in New York — and that was the start of everything."

The screen features DePompa in class, enacting a scene, fists clenched, eyes blazing.

The documentary now centers on Dave Corey.

"He was a natural," says Corey. "Terry utilized his inner pain as a weapon. Watching him was like being struck by lightning. He shocked you. I knew he'd be great. From the moment he walked into my class, I knew he'd be great."

Lawson's voice-over again, introducing Sidney Shibinson of Universal Pictures.

"Me, I got an instinct for talent," says Shibinson. "When I spotted DePompa doing a scene in Corey's class, I right away knew for a fact that he could be the next Brando. We signed him for Universal that same week and put him into *Drive the Blade Deep*, *The Black-Leather Boys*, and *Restless Rebel*. And bingo! —— he becomes famous overnight and makes himself a ton of money."

The voice-over: "Money and instant fame opened many doors for young Terry DePompa, allowing him to experience life on a multitude of exciting levels . . ."

Action photos flash across the screen: Terry on a bucking bronco . . . executing a veronica with a bullfighters cape . . . speed-jumping a wide ditch on a dirt-bike . . . whipping down a vertical ski slope . . . dueling with a masked opponent . . . firing a shotgun from a duck blind . . . mountain climbing in the high Rockies . . . blasting a tennis ball over a net . . . skydiving in from a private plane . . . surfing the crest of a massive wave . . . taking the checkered flag in his 300 SLR —— always with a beautiful woman in the background.

Lawson once again: "No screen idol since James Dean has ever touched the lives of so many young people . . ."

A nervous teenage girl stands in front of a DePompa poster in the lobby of a movie theater, wearing a T-shirt bearing Terry's smiling face.

Her voice is intense: "My girlfriend and me, we saw *Restless Rebel* fourteen times." She fumbles for words. "Terry was like . . . like a religion to us . . . He *was* us!" A tear rolls down her cheek. "Why did he have to die? Why?"

Lawson speaks directly into the camera: "Indeed, there are many unanswered questions regarding the tragic death of Terry DePompa. But one thing is certain: His bright image will continue to burn forever in the hearts of those who ——"

Dennie snaps off the TV. He begins to pace the room, hands fisted, his face flushed. "Damn!" he says under his breath. Then, louder: "Damn! Damn! Damn!"

*   *   *

The girl moves back from the table, eyes wide, betraying her fear. She keeps moving away from Dennie as he advances on her.

"Dennie, I —"

"Shut up, bitch! Didn't I tell you to shut your lousy trap?"

"But you lied. You didn't keep your word."

Dennnie slaps her hard, across the mouth, bringing tears to her eyes.

"You cheap little tramp," he snarls. "This is the last time you'll ever —"

"Hold it! Hold it!" Dave Corey mounts the raised platform, shaking his head. Several other young men and women, all aspiring actors, are seated on folding wooden chairs, forming a half-circle around the platform.

"What's wrong now?" Dennie demands.

"You're doing him again," Corey declares. "The way you walk, the angle of your head . . . even the way you slapped Susan. All him. All DePompa."

A strained silence.

"True art in acting is never achieved by using borrowed emotions. Each actor must find that individual truth within himself or herself. Imitation is not creation."

Dennie stars at him. "You figure I haven't got it, right?"

"I never said that. You possess genuine talent, but you're blocking it. You are walking in Terry DePompa's shadow. The trouble is, you won't —"

Dennie cuts in, his voice edged with anger. "The trouble is I've wasted my time listening to you spout a lot of useless crap. I don't need you to tell me what I am — and Terry didn't, either. So I don't happen to fit your mold. Well, to hell with your mold, and to hell with you!"

And he stalks from the room, slamming the heavy soundproof door behind him.

Margaret DePompa's town house is alive with a babble of voices, the chiming of cocktail glasses, the tinkle of iced scotch, and the muted cry of a jazz trumpet.

"Some people think that New Orleans jazz is outdated," Margaret tells the mayor of New York, "but I find it liberating."

The rotund little man nods. "It's part of our native culture, and native culture is never out of date."

A servant approaches, hesitant to break into the flow of conversation. Margaret turns to him. "What is it, Jenson?"

"A young gentleman to see you," says Jenson. "He is presently waiting in the foyer."

"And what does this young gentleman wish to see me about?"

"He did not say."

"Name?"

"Dennis Holmes."

She frowns. "Never heard of him."

"He seems quite . . . intense."

She turns back to her guest. "You'll excuse me, Mr. Mayor?"

"Of course, my dear." He glances toward the bar. "I'll just have another glass of your excellent Chablis. Good for the digestion."

And Margaret follows Jenson to the foyer.

"I saw you on television," Dennie is saying, "in a newscast about Terry — and I just had to meet you." He hesitates, nervous and uncertain. "I know this is an intrusion, but Terry . . . well, he meant a lot to me."

"Did you know him?" Margaret asks.

"Not personally. I mean, we never actually met. But I've watched all his movies, and I've read everything about him...the cover story in *Newsweek* . . . the interview in *Life* . . . I even saw him race once, at the airport in Palm Springs. He's been kind of . . . a role model for me, if you know what I mean."

"Yes, I know. Terry affected many young people that way." She regards him intently. "Your hair . . . you wear it exactly as he did. And that red jacket you're wearing . . ."

"Just like the one he wore in *Restless Rebel*," Dennie says. "I got it from a novelty store in Hollywood. They had it in the window — along with posters from *The Ravaged One*, *Dawn Is For Dying*, and *Fury on Friday*. I got 'em all."

"You're taller than Terry," she says, "but you have his eyes."

Dennie smiles. "Thanks."

". . . and his smile."

He's embarrassed. "Well . . . guess I'd better be going." Dennie extends his right hand. "Been great meeting you, Mrs. DePompa."

Margaret takes his hand, clasping it firmly. Her fingers are warm. "Don't be in such a hurry," she says softly.

After lovemaking, they talk quietly in Margaret's bed, fitted together, flesh to flesh, her naked hip against his leg.

"Tell me about him," says Dennie. "I need to know what Terry was really like." He hesitates. "Was he . . . a good lover?"

"At first he was overwhelming. It was like making love to a panther. But that didn't last. Everything had to be fresh for Terry, new and fresh. And that included sex. He was never satisfied for long with any one woman, and I was no exception. When he grew bored with our lovemaking, he substituted violence and pain for sex. That's when I knew it was over."

"But didn't you love him? On TV . . . you seemed so broken up over his death."

She smiles. "Quite an act, huh? I was just giving the public what they want." She pauses. "Did I love Terry? Sure, at first, with that smile of his . . . those eyes." She traces a slow finger along Dennie's jaw. "You're incredibly like him — the way he was in the beginning, four years ago."

"Why did . . . I mean, I have to know. Why did he —"

"— kill himself? It was inevitable. Terry was an addictive thrill-seeker, always pushing closer and closer to the limit. When he made *Hell Run*, the film on bobsledding in Switzerland, he broke both ankles when the sled clipped a tree. In Madrid, he was gored by a bull with the horn barely missing a main artery. He'd never let them use a stand-in. Did all the stunts himself. Used to drive the producers crazy. Terry fractured his left shoulder on a dirt bike running a motocross at Indio. Then, just two months ago, his plane crash-landed in the San Bernardino mountains. It burned, but Terry got out in time."

"You're saying he had a death wish?"

"Damn right I am. No question about it. All of the other thrills finally wore off until only death itself remained. He *had* to taste it, savor it, experience it. The ultimate thrill. So he did."

Her fingers ran erotically along Dennie's naked spine. Her voice is soft. "Would you like to see where he died?"

"In Mexico — near the Gulf?"

"Yes. Just above San Felipe, his favorite hideout. Ratty little fishing village. No one ever goes there. When things got too stressed, he'd drive down there from L.A." Her eyes burn into his. "I could take you . . . in Terry's white Cadillac. It's garaged in Beverly Hills. Would you like to go?"

"Oh, yes," says Dennie. "Christ yes!"

The flight from New York to Los Angeles is smooth. Perfect weather all the way. In Beverly Hills, the white Cadillac is serviced and made ready for the trip into Mexico. Dennie is hyper. For him, this is a dream come true; he can barely contain his excitement.

On the morning of their departure, Margaret appears in a trim white pantsuit, wearing a white straw bonnet to keep off the sun. ("I don't tan, I burn.")

She takes the wheel for the trip down 99 to Calexico. Jokes with the uniformed border guard who waves them through, then takes Dennie to what she terms "the only halfway-decent restaurant in Mexicali."

He doesn't like the noisy border town with its garish purple facades, peeling wooden storefronts, and dirt-blackened neon signs.

"Why are we stopping here?" he asks. "Why can't we eat later, on the road?"

"I thought you'd want to talk to old man Montoya. At his coffin shop."

Dennie brightens. "Where Terry worked when he was fourteen?"

"Right," she says. "If the old bastard's still alive, you can ask him about Terry."

"Terrific!"

They order grilled sea bass with stewed pinto beans, which is served with a large basket of corn tortillas, topped off by two bottles of warm Mexican beer.

Next on the agenda: the coffin maker's shop of Carlos Montoya.

The shop's exterior is painted in funereal black in keeping with the owner's trade.

Lettered on the door: COFFINS MADE TO ORDER.

As they enter, Montoya steps forward to greet them. He is toothless, the color of worn leather, needing a shave and a new frame for his taped glasses. He wears ragged coveralls.

"You require the services of Carlos Montoya? A loved one to bury, perhaps?"

"We came to ask you about a boy who once worked here," says Dennie.

"Ah!" The old man chuckles, a dry, rasping sound. "You wish me to speak of Antonio. Many others have come here to ask of him. My fee is fixed. If you pay, I talk."

Margaret hands him money, and he leads them to the rear of the musty shop, past coffins of all sizes, many unfinished. Uncut boards, smelling of sawdust, lean against the walls.

In his dark office Montoya gestures them toward a pair of cane-bottom chairs, seating himself behind a desk cluttered with hammers and saws.

"The world knew him as Terry," says the old man, beginning a speech he obviously delivered many times, "but I knew him as Antonio. He came to me as a boy of fourteen, eager to learn the trade of coffin maker."

Montoya opens a desk drawer, removes a photo, and hands it to Dennie. In the photo, Terry DePompa is lying in a coffin, posing as a corpse, eyes closed, hands folded across this chest.

Montoya continues: "I gave him shelter, an honest wage, and shared my knowledge with him. Antonio was quick to learn. I taught him many things."

Margaret cuts in: "You taught him, all right. To lie and swear and steal. He told me all about you — about your cheating ways and your filth and your foul women." She gestures toward a standing coffin. "You'll soon be in one of these yourself, and when you are, who will come to your funeral, eh? Ask yourself that, old man."

And she herds Dennie from the shop.

Back in the car, the boy is silent. He looks stunned and shaken.

"Well, what did you expect?" asks Margaret.

"I thought . . . that he . . . would be different."

"Different? He's a corrupt old fool. Terry despised him."

Silence. Then Dennie asks: "How long will it take us to reach San Felipe?"

"Four or five hours," she replies. "It's at the edge of the Gulf where the highway dead-ends. We should make it before dark."

With Margaret again at the wheel, threading their way slowly through streets jammed with overloaded fruit and vegetable trucks, bicycles, ancient taxicabs, and sweat-crowded buses, they finally clear the border town and roll onto the long stretch of open highway leading to the Gulf.

Out of Mexicali, they pass the high green arch of the Funeraria Santa Elenaz with its irregular rows of pink-and-blue gravestones. As the sun descends in heated slowness down the western sky the Mexican scenery is spectacular. Rolling hills thrust up like vast brown fists, separated by wide plateaus and dry lakes. Endless sand dunes and spike cactus line the highway to either side. A dead cat lies sprawled on the road shoulder.

A sudden sharp report. Like a gunshot. The white Cad swerves as Margaret fights the wheel, braking to a stop on the gravel verge. "We just blew a tire," she says.

"I thought all the tires were checked before we left."

"Yep, and they were perfect. Obviously we hit something on the road."

They get out with the doors automatically locking themselves behind them. A long sliver of blue bottle glass has penetrated the side wall of a rear tire. Margaret turns to get the keys for the trunk. "Damn!"

"What's wrong?"

"All the doors are locked, and I left the keys in the ignition." She sighs. "But it's okay. I keep a spare set taped inside the front fender."

Crouching, she fumbles for the extra keys, using them to open the driver's door, then retapeing them back inside the fender. "In case we ever lock ourselves out again."

She removes a jack and a tire iron from the trunk. "You any good at changing tires?"

Dennie shrugs. "Dunno. I've never had to."

"I'll do it. No big deal."

She jacks up the car, removes the damaged tire, and puts on the spare. Checks her watch. "Close, but I think we can still make it before dark."

Hurriedly, she tosses the jack and tire iron into the rear seat. "And away we go," she says, gunning back onto the highway.

Hours pass as the sun dips lower in the sky. Ahead of them, a jagged rise of black mountains lends a luna texture to the land: raw, alien, hostile.

The Cad is now moving along the winding mountain road above San Felipe.

"There's a long straight about a mile ahead," she tells Dennie. "That's where he sailed off into the blue, at the end of the straight."

Dennie sits rigid, excited, wanting and not wanting to see the spot where Terry died.

They enter the straight. Dennie is silent, tensed, waiting.

"Here's where it happened," says Margaret, stopping the car a few yards short of the tight U-curve. "This is where he went over the edge."

They stand at the lip of the cliff, looking down. "It's a long drop," says Dennie, shivering at the mental image.

"With lots of sharp boulders at the bottom," says Margaret. "When he hit, the gas tank split and his car burned."

"Was he dead when he hit bottom?"

"We'll never know."

They get back in the car and motor on to San Felipe.

The white Cadillac, now gray with dust, reaches the small fishing village — a scatter of rude shacks along a short main street (unpaved), boasting a half-dozen paint-blistered storefronts. The village is nearly deserted. A few local residents lounge in shadowed doorways, staring out at the strangers.

The sun is almost down along the horizon. A dozen small fishing boats ply the red-gold sunset waters, bobbing like corks, their nets out for the evening's catch.

"It's getting dark," says Dennie. "Is there a motel here?"

"One. Just one. But I'm sure they have a vacancy. First, I need a drink."

They leave the locked car, walking to the village cantina located at the end of the street in a weathered two-story building. A rusted Coca-Cola sign is tacked to the front door.

Inside a drift of guitar music reaches them from a cobwebbed ceiling speaker. Three young fishermen are hunched over cards in a far corner of the room. The air is hot and musty, retaining the heat of the day, smelling of sour beer and strong Mexican tobacco.

The owner, a stout little-red-faced man in a stained apron, takes their order. Over two Carta Blancas and a plate of stale pretzels, they talk.

"I don't see why Terry would ever come to a dumb place like San Felipe," says Dennie, sipping his beer; it's sour, but cold. "There's nothing here."

"That is exactly what he wanted to find — nothing," says Margaret. "Terry came here to get away from the spotlight."

"It's a hellhole," says Dennie.

"Gotta pee," declares Margaret. "Hold the fort."

As she passes the table where the three young Mexicans are playing cards one of them reaches out to grab her leg. She stops, says something in soft Spanish. The fisherman laughs, lets her go.

Five minutes later she's back with Dennie.

"What was that all about?"

She grins. "Just a friendly pass."

"He had his hand on your leg."

"Yeah, that was nice. He has soft hands."

"You liked it?"

"I didn't mind."

Dennie stares at her.

She smiles. A cat's smile.

The motel mattress is thin and lumpy. Coil springs jab sharply into Dennie's back as he sleepily shifts position. He opens his eyes, reaching out to touch Margaret. She's not there. He's alone in the bed. It's 3:00 A.M. by his watch. He gets up to check the bathroom.

Empty. Where is she? Where could she have gone at this time of night in a place like San Felipe?

Dennie slips into a pair of pants, pulls a sweater over his pajama top, and leaves the motel. He pads barefoot through the milky sand. The waters of the Gulf lap softly against the beach, and a gull cries out in the night like a lost child.

Then: rough male voices. Laughter. *Margaret's* laughter. Coming from a nearby tarpaper shack, its lighted window a pale yellow square in the darkness.

Dennie reaches the shack, peering through the glass. Christ! Margaret is inside, in bed with the three fishermen from the cantina. Naked. They are all naked.

She looks up as Dennie appears at the door. Glares. "Go away! Get the hell away!"

The three Mexicans grin at him. One has a gold tooth.

Dennie takes a step toward the bed. "God, but you're rotten."

Her mouth twists in anger. Her eyes are afire. "I *said*, get the hell away!"

Dennie looks agonized. "Why are you doing this to me?"

"To you?" snaps Margaret, scorn in her tone. "That's a laugh. Don't you get it? You walk like him, wear his clothes, even try to make love like him. But it's all a joke. You're not real. You don't exist. You're just a reflected image from a broken mirror."

Her words cut and stab at him. Dennie reels back under their verbal assault, swings around, and stumbles from the shack.

He staggers down the beach, tears clouding his vision. He's numb, directionless, running blindly toward the center of the village. The area is tomb-quiet, dark as spilled ink, with the moon hidden in a clouded sky.

Now Dennie pauses, blinking up at a dusty façade ringed by broken, time-blackened marquee bulbs that long ago spelled out a name: CINEMA JIMINEZ.

Dennie listens. Sounds echo faintly from within the ancient movie house. Someone — or something — lives in the time-haunted interior.

Peeling a loose board from the door, Dennie pushes his way inside, drawn to the sounds. The main auditorium is a shamble of broken seats, discarded trash, and buckled cement.

But the screen is alive:

Dennie gasps as Terry DePompa's head fills the screen. The actor's eyes blaze down at Dennie. Then the mouth gapes wide in a flow of manic laughter. Insane, cacophonous laughter.

Dennie claps both hands to his ears, squeezing his eyes shut against the frightful apparition. When he opens them, seconds later, the cracked, dust-hazed screen is blank and silent.

As if pursued by demons, Dennie runs from the theater, thrusting himself along the main street. He enters a wooden graveyard filled with the decaying corpses of abandoned fishing boats, beached like dead whales, their ruptured hulls black and flaking from wind and sun.

Dennie stumbles forward, falling weakly against the side of *La Ordina*. The boat's interior is gutted, with a rusted engine housing, like a surreal coffin, buried within the rotted hull.

Dennie blinks, staring downward — and now there is an *actual* coffin inside the hull. Fourteen-year-old Terry DePompa lies inside, eyes closed hands folded across his chest — exactly as he appeared in the photo at Montoya's shop.

Then . . . a change. The body of the actor slowly ripple-dissolves into the corpse of the adult DePompa, with half of his face torn away and broken bones protruding obscenely from his charred, crushed body.

Frozen in shock, Dennie continues to stare downward — but the horror has not ended. The corpse-figure changes once again, and it is now Dennie himself who lies in the dank coffin, his body broken and charred.

"Oh, God!" the boy cried out in agony, wheeling away from the boats to stagger up the beach — back to the shack of the three fishermen.

He bolts inside, grabs Margaret by one arm and drags her naked and screaming, along the sand to the parked Cadillac.

"I know what you want now," he sobs, "what you brought me down here for. Well, I'm going to give it to you. I'm going to play your sick little game to the end."

He retrieves the spare set of car keys from the fender well, yanks open the passenger door, and pushes Margaret inside. Firing the engine, he roars out of the village onto the mountain highway in a cloud of dust and gravel.

"You're crazy!" shouts Margaret. "Stop the car. Let me out!"

"No, this time *I'm* in charge."

The Cadillac rapidly gains speed, high beams slicing the dark, unraveling the road ahead. The speed is now far too great for Margaret to risk jumping from the passenger seat.

Dennie powers around the serpentine turns, finally reaching the long straight leading to the final curve. He floors the gas pedal — and the car leaps forward . . . 70 . . . 80 . . . 90 . . . 100 . . .

"You want it, and you'll get it," Dennie shouts.

"Want what?" Margaret's voice is frenzied. "*What?*"

"You want to die. You want to share Terry's death, experience it for yourself, share the horror of it, the thrill of it — to end your jaded, empty existence. That's why you brought me here, for *this!*"

They are now almost to the end of the straight, with the white Cadillac bulleting the road, a ghost-rocket heading for destruction.

Margaret twists around to snatch up the tire iron from the backseat, lunging forward to slam it against Dennie's skull. As he slumps sideways, his foot slips from the gas pedal. She jams her foot hard down on the brake, gripping the wheel for control.

The car whips madly across the road as its speed drops to 80 . . . 70 . . . 60 . . . slower, slower. With the U-curve rushing at them, Margaret claws open the passenger door and jumps.

The rolling impact stuns her; road gravel lacerates her bare skin, but she survives, staggering to her feet, bleeding from a dozen cuts. Numbly, she watches the still-moving Cadillac reach the end of the straight and dip over the edge of the cliff road, tumbling down to explode on the rocks below.

Margaret walks slowly to the drop-off point, looking down. Flames illumine the darkness, and smoke swirls around her from the burning machine.

I didn't have the guts, she tells herself. *I wanted to die, just the way Terry did, to achieve what he achieved — the ultimate thrill — but I didn't have the guts. Now I've lost the chance. And I'll have to live with that . . .* she continues to stare down at the flaming wreckage . . . *for the rest of my life.*

The idea of a corpse that won't stay dead has haunted me as a writer longer than I can remember. I finally came up with a way to handle this idea. As comedy. I've done several readings of this story at various conventions and was gratified by steady bursts of audience laughter. Proving, to me at least, that I took the correct approach with "Killing Charlie."

I think you'll agree that Charlie is a pretty nice fellow. Persistent. Patient. Loving. But, as his wife discovered, not an easy man to kill.

Killing Charlie

The first time Dot killed Charlie was in Oakland, across the Bay Bridge, at an amusement park. They had an argument and she pushed him out of their seat on the Ferris wheel. Charlie went crashing through the roof of the ticket booth below, and there was a lot of screaming, with people running around like headless chickens.

A week later, when Dot (back from a trip to our local Sure-Save store) opened our apartment door, there was Charlie, sitting on our big overstuffed sofa. He smiled at her.

"Hi," he said. "Hope you brought home some of those yummy frosted cinnamon rolls for me. I'm really in the mood for a frosted cinnamon roll."

"I thought you were dead," my wife said. Her legal name is Dorothy, but I've always called her Dot.

"Nope. Still alive and kicking," said Charlie.

"But I saw you smash through the ticket booth." She was staring at Charlie, standing there kind of frozen, still holding the sack of groceries.

"Yeah, that was quite a shock," said Charlie. "Kind of hurt when I hit the roof."

"I thought you were dead," my wife repeated.

"I *was* shook up," Charlie admitted. "Had me some busted bones. Broke my nose." He touched his face gingerly. "But everything healed fast and here I am, fit as a fiddle, back in my happy home."

"I don't want you here," Dot said. "This isn't your home any-more."

"Hey, now . . . let's us try to get along," said Charlie. He shrugged his shoulders in a way that had always irritated her. "I forgive you for pushing me off that Ferris wheel. What the heck . . . I'm willing to let bygones be bygones."

"Well, *I'm* not," said Dot.

She put the groceries down, walked over to the desk, took out a loaded .38, and shot Charlie in the head. He fell off our sofa onto the rug. There was a lot of blood.

"Have to buy another rug," Dot sighed. "This one will never clean properly."

She dragged Charlie out through the kitchen and pitched his body off the fire escape. He landed with a *plop* in the alley.

Another week passed —— and when Dot opened the driver's door on our Buick Roadmaster, Charlie was in the back seat, curled up and snoring.

"Wake up, you bastard!" shouted Dot. "And get the hell out of my car!"

Charlie sat up, blinking. He scrubbed at his eyes and yawned big, the way a cat does. "I didn't have the apartment key," he said. "Must of lost it when I hit the alley."

"I shot you in the head," Dot declared. "And it's a three-story drop from our fire escape."

"Yep," nodded Charlie, rubbing the back of his skull. "Bullets messed up my head for sure, and I broke both legs in the fall. Took a while for things to mend, but I feel all chipper again."

We lived in San Francisco, a few miles from the Golden Gate, and Dot drove out to the middle of the bridge and made Charlie jump. From that height, hitting the bay water is like going head-on into a concrete wall. Charlie sank fast.

Dot watched until she was certain that he didn't bob back up again.

Then she drove home.

Everything was fine for another week —— and then Charlie sat down in the aisle seat next to Dot in the AMC Multi-Plex where she was watching a new war movie starring Tom Hanks.

"Hi," he whispered, patting her knee. "How ya doin'?"

"This is crazy," Dot whispered back. "I *saw* you hit the water. You never came up."

"I know," nodded Charlie. "And boy, was it ever *cold*! *Brrr*! I get the shivers just thinking about how cold that water was. Freeze the balls off a brass monkey." He chuckled at the old saying.

"How did you get here?"

"The tide washed me ashore," he said, keeping his voice low. On the screen, Tom Hanks was killing Nazis with a machine gun. "Had to buy a new suit. My other one was ruined, being in the salt water so long. My shoes, too. Had to pay for a new pair."

"I don't understand any of this," said Dot. "I keep killing you, and you keep showing up again."

"Guess I'm just mule stubborn," Charlie said. "Or maybe I should say I'm like a rubber ball. I keep bouncing back." And he chuckled again. "But I harbor no hard feelings against you."

"I don't give a damn about your feelings," Dot told him, causing the woman seated next to her to protest. The woman couldn't hear the dialogue with all their jabber.

Dot stood up. "C'mon," she said to Charlie. "We're leaving."

They walked out of the Multi-Plex and Dot pushed Charlie in front of a bus on Market Street.

"Dear God!" cried the distraught bus driver. "I tried to miss him, but he just popped up, right in front of me. I just couldn't brake in time."

Charlie was crumpled under a rear wheel.

"He's dead, that's for sure," said a sleepy-eyed cop who was on the scene.

The bus driver shook his head. "My first accident. Wow! I really clobbered the guy. This is not going to look good on my record."

"A lousy break," agreed the cop. His eyes were almost closed.

Dot was watching them from the doorway of Mel's We-Never-Close Drug Store. No one had seen her push Charlie in front of the bus, but her stomach was rumbling.

She bought a packet of Tums for her tummy from Mel, walked to the garage where she'd parked the Buick, and drove home.

Charlie was sitting on the apartment steps when she got there. He looked pretty beat up. His new suit was ripped in several places and the left coat sleeve had been torn off.

"How did you get here so fast?" Dot asked him, plainly vexed.

"Took a taxi," said Charlie. "Woke up in the meat wagon, and when it stopped for a red light, I hopped out and found me a cab. Lucky I had enough money to cover the tip."

"I don't want you here," said Dot.

"But I *live* here," he said.

"Not anymore," she declared.

Charlie looked sad. "Getting whacked in the street by a bus is no fun," he told her. "I need to lay down for a while."

"It's *lie* down," she corrected him. Then she sighed. "All right, come on up and I'll fix you some hot chocolate."

"Great!" said Charlie, following her inside.

Dot put a saucepan of milk on the stove to heat, then got a box of rat poison from the top shelf in the pantry. She poured it all into the saucepan, then followed up with a couple of heaping tablespoons of cocoa mix.

"Whew! This stuff is *bitter*! exclaimed Charlie, making a face. He held out his half-empty mug. "What'd you put in there?"

"Rat poison," said Dot.

Charlie convulsed, then collapsed on our new rug. No blood this time. She checked his wrist.

He was dead, all right.

She dragged the body out to the stair landing, and was about to pitch Charlie over the rail when he sat up.

"Look," he said to her. "I've ignored a heck of a lot from you lately, but this is the last straw. That stuff tasted *awful*."

"I put in enough poison to kill a whole house full of rats," she said peevishly. "How come you're still alive?"

"Simple," said Charlie. "I'm immortal. Seems to me you'd of figured that out by now."

"What makes you immortal?"

"About a month ago I was down in the Marina district, kind of kicking back," he said. "Then I spotted this funky shop, just off the main drag. Dark little place. Musty. Full of cobwebs. With all kinds of weird stuff inside. Run by a freaky-looking humpbacked guy with one eye and a club foot. Asked me if I wanted to live forever, and I said sure, that would be swell. Cost you ten dollars, he said. Okay, that seems fair enough, I told him. Once I'd handed over the cash, he went to the back of his store and came back with a beetle."

"A *beetle*?"

"Scarab, actually. He told me that scarabs guarantee immortality. An ancient fact, discovered by some Egyptian guys. Took a dirty pestle, ground the scarab into powder, dumped the powder into a cup of root beer, and — Pow! — I'm immortal. All for ten bucks."

"That's ridiculous," said Dot. "I don't believe anything like that could ever happen in San Francisco."

"Well, it did," nodded Charlie. "But lemme get back to what I was saying — about that rat poison being the last straw and all."

"Go ahead," said Dot.

"My patience is exhausted," said Charlie. "I don't think you love me anymore."

"I *hate* you," snapped Dot. "Absolutely loathe and despise you."

"That's pretty darn obvious," said Charlie. "But the point is, I can't let you go on killing me the way you've been doing. It's ruining my clothes. And bottom line, it's really annoying me. So . . ."

"So? So *what?*"

"So I'm going to have to put a stop to it."

That's when I drove my pocket knife into Dot's heart. She gurgled and slumped forward, sprawling out along the landing like a big rag doll.

She was dead. And my wife is not like me. She'll *stay* dead.

I pulled the knife out of her chest, wiped it off against the leg of my pants (they were ruined anyway), and put the knife back in my pocket. It has nostalgic value — Dot gave it to me on my thirtieth birthday.

By now, I'm sure you know who I am. Well, gosh, isn't it plain as pie? I'm Charlie. Been playing a little word game with you. Just to prove I haven't lost my sense of humor, despite all that's happened to me. And since I'm going to live forever, I *need* a sense of humor.

I thought about me and Dot. Strange how quick a good marriage can go sour. I'd been convinced that, deep down, she still loved me. But I was wrong. Dead wrong. Ha! Ah, well . . .

I left our apartment building and took a cab back to the AMC Multi-Plex on Market. Bought a ticket to the war movie with Tom Hanks. I'd liked the part I'd seen with Dot.

Worth another look.

Like most youngsters of my generation, I grew up reading fairy tales, but I was deep into adulthood before I got the idea to write one of my own. In "Once Upon a Time" you'll meet Snow White (who isn't so innocent) and a wicked witch named "Old Meg," along with some other unsavory fantasy folk.

Here's my take on a modern fairy tale. Dark. Very dark. Disney it ain't.

Once Upon a Time

My name is Snow White and I'm writing this from my house in the woods. Of course, you won't be able to read these words because after you meet me you'll be dead. Guess I'm just a silly goose for putting all this on paper, but it's a way to pass the time while I'm waiting for you.

If I explain, very carefully, why I have to kill you, then maybe somebody else will come along, after we're both gone, and read this and say, "Golly, Snow White wasn't such a bad person. She just did what she had to do. It was Old Meg's fault, not hers — from the world beyond the meadow."

Whoops! I'm getting ahead of myself. Can't talk about another world until I explain what I'm doing in this one. First things first. I'm trying to be very organized about what I have to tell you. The Seven Dwarfs are organized — as a *group*, that is. Individually, they wouldn't impress you. But I don't want to write about them. That's way off my subject.

If I ramble from time to time, hey, I'm no writer. Never tried to tell a story before in all my days. So bear with me, huh. Give me some goddam slack. That's an Earth expression, from your world, this one I'm in right now. I read it in one of your magazines. People who've come here, to my home in the woods, bring all kinds of things. Food. Toys. Sun hats. Sleeping bags. Tents. Fishing poles. And magazines. Even a book. I tried to read it but it didn't make much sense. About cowboys in something called The Old West. Whatever that is. I figured a cowboy is half-cow and half-boy, and that I can understand. Like our centaurs. I put down the book at the end of the first chapter. Anyhow, one of you came with a magazine that had a man saying, "For Christ's sake, give me some goddam slack!" And the woman was described as being "plenty pissed." I was able to figure it out, but I don't know who Christ is. Doesn't matter. There's a lot about your world I don't know.

Maybe I should tell you about my house and the ones I live with here in the woods. I built the house myself, mostly using my teeth. I have very strong, sharp teeth. They can bite right through wood, real easy. I made the house out of trees, with a nice grass roof. I bit in holes for the windows so I could look out to see who's coming. Maybe I'll see *you* from one of the holes!

I live here with Ben. He's a unicorn, all muddy-brown-reddish colored. And with Angelbird, who is all white with big wings and an orange beak. (There's another bird who comes to visit, and likes to drink from the stream next to our house, but she can't talk the way Angelbird can.) Then I have Irma and Willie who are kind of grumpy. They look a little like your lizards with lizardy tails, but they're actually snarbs because they're from *my* world. When Old Meg — and I'll get to her in a minute — sent me here to your world she sent along Ben and Angelbird and the two snarbs to make sure I had some company. At least, that's what Meg told me. But I know the real reason. The *real* reason is they're supposed to keep an eye on me and make sure I don't go running off somewhere. As soon as I finish doing what I have to do here on Earth they'll disappear — Poof! — and I'll be able to —

Whoa! (That's what the book said they say to horses in "The Old West" from the first chapter.) There I go again, getting ahead of myself with what I want to tell you.

As for running off, where would I run, looking the way I do? Nine feet tall with a big bulgy green eye in the middle of my forehead and with a mouth full of real sharp teeth and four hairy arms that drag on the ground when I walk. In this world of yours, if I ever left the woods, I'd be locked up in a cage like some kind of terrible beast. Yet, all the time, here I am, Snow White, beautiful and slender and waiting for Prince Charming. Well, I *was*. But not anymore. Not now. Oh, no, now I'm big and ugly. You can blame Old Meg for that. She made me look this way.

Maybe I'd better tell you about her. Old Meg lives in a thatch hut deep in the forest and she eats live rats and hates me. Always has. Once she offered me a poison apple, but I was smart enough to say no thanks. It looked delicious, all ripe and plump and shiny, but I knew I shouldn't bite into it, and I didn't. That made her mad. She even stomped on her hat, which gave me the giggles. Then she flew off on her broom.

She's a real witch, all right, and you wouldn't mistake her for anything else. Hook nose with a big wart on the end of it. Pointy chin. Red-glowing eyes. Wears a tattered smelly black dress and black slippers with curled-up toes. Long fingers with rotty nails on them, like claws. And she loves to cackle.

So that's Old Meg.

As I said, she's never liked me. You know, the mean old witch who hates Snow White because of her beauty. And I am beautiful. Was beautiful, that is. Inside, I still feel beautiful, and I'll be again once I finish what I have to do here in your world. (And I'm de-pending on you to get the job done!)

Well, let me tell you how I got here, so you'll be clear on things. It started when I turned down the apple. The next morning, when I was in front of my mirror brushing my lovely hair (100 strokes, never less!) Old Meg made a broom-landing outside my little cabin. Stormed in, glaring. Said she was going to put a spell on me as punishment for refusing her apple.

She took me to her smarmy hut in the forest where she had this big iron pot boiling in front of the fireplace. Cackling, she poured in some stinky powder, some snake's entrails, some crocodile tails, a toad's liver, and lots of other awful items and stirred them all up and then dipped a cup into the pot and swallowed what was in the cup. Eck! It *had* to taste foul, but being a witch, this gave her the power to cast her spell. I recall her exact chant:

> Rigga do and rigga dee,
> Thy body will no longer be!
>
> Agga dee and agga day,
> Snow White vanishes away!
>
> Igga op and igga yee,
> To Earth I herewith banish thee!

Which is when I turned into this one-eyed ape creature and ended up here in the woods.

Before I left, Old Meg gave me a Sheet of Basic Instructions, telling me what I'd have to do in order to regain my true body and return to my world. On the sheet are a list of things I have to get in order to break the spell. Different things. All under the heading: FEMALE (Human).

All right, I know you're confused. So let me tell you the whole story in the proper sequence. I just wanted you to know about Old Meg.

Odd thing: I used to worry about Prince Charming finding me. Kept looking for him to show up on his big white horse and ride off with me as his blushing bride. But now I have a lot more serious things to worry about because Old Meg hasn't made it easy for me to break this spell. For instance, there's a time limit. If I don't get all the things on the list within thirty Earth days then I'll be stuck there forever on your world in this ugly one-eyed ape body.

Thirty days. That's all she gave me.

Angelbird says I'll never make it. Ben is more open-minded. The two snarbs won't even talk to me. They just sit around on the rocks eating red berries and getting into arguments with each other. (I'm glad Meg didn't turn me into a snarb!)

"Why *me*, Angelbird?" I ask.

"It's obvious," she says, ruffling her feathers. "Meg is jealous of you. The old 'mirror, mirror on the wall' routine. She can do a lot with her spells, but she can't make herself beautiful. So she made you uglier than she is. And that's going some."

"Angel's right," nodded Ben. "But just hang in there, Snow. You're getting the stuff on her list."

"But I'm running out of time," I say.

"At first, I didn't think you'd make it," Ben admits. "I was wrong." He taps me on the shoulder with his horn. "I'm proud of you, Snow."

That cheered me. Feels good to have a unicorn backing you up. I didn't think I would, but I truly like Ben. He's turned into a real pal.

To get here, you take I-50 all the way to the Tuskaroot Turnoff and then go left on Stanhope Road for about ten miles into the woods and here I am at my tree-house, waiting.

So far I've been very fortunate in having people drop by. First it was the Rickmans, who were looking for a quiet place in the woods to pitch their tent. A honeymoon situation.

I bit off her right leg and then had the snarbs dispose of the two honeymooners. A good start!

Then, about a week later, the girl runner shows up. She was training for some cross-country race and her name was Norma. Got her left arm. Angelbird buried her. (Used her beak to do the digging.)

Next came a long-time-married couple, Grace and Harley Gibbs. On vacation. Looking for a nice spot to have a picnic. They thought my house was a wonderful structure. That was Harley's phrase: "My goodness! What a wonderful structure."

When they saw *me*, however, they didn't think I was so wonderful. Especially when I bit Mrs. Gibbs in half to get her torso.

Young kid on a bicycle shows up two days later. Teenager named Sally. Outdoor type, all tan and supple. I bit off her right arm — and felt I was making some real progress. Ben ran her through with his horn and we cremated her. The fire was nice. Gets cold at night here in the woods.

Then I got lucky again. A Girl Scout who'd wandered away from her troop and was lost in the woods. Got her left leg. One quick, clean bite. Toes and all. She's buried by the stream, next to the Gibbs. The snarbs wanted to eat her, but I said that was disgusting. They grumped around for a whole day over that.

Things seemed to be going my way. I was in a really good mood, kidding around with Angelbird and teasing Ben (pulling his tail) when along comes the Sutter family. Bob and Beth and little Jane, who was nine.

Jane wasn't afraid of me, which was nice. She said I looked like something out of one of the fairy tales in her books, which is when I found out that on Earth fairy tales are *not* true! I was astonished.

She told me about Little Red Riding Hood and Cinderella and Rapunzel with her long golden hair and Jack and the Beanstalk. Of course I know all of them personally. In *my* world they're all quite real, like I am. We take dragons and giants and wizards very seriously. If we didn't, they might eat us up!

In that one talk little Jane gave me a whole new insight into what Earth is like.

Naturally, she was no good to me. Female, sure, but too young to bite into. So I had the snarbs deal with her and Bob while I took Beth inside and bit off her left leg. Chomp! Right down to the toes.

And we had another warm fire that night.

Hey, maybe by Earth standards this is upsetting you. Telling about these body parts I'm biting off females who come by my house. But they're all on Meg's list: two arms, three legs, one torso. Et cetera. If I miss getting any of them then I'll never be rid of the spell.

I admit I'm a little worried now. A *lot* worried, really. Because twenty-nine-and-a-half days have gone by and I still need the last item on my list. In less than twelve hours the time will be up and I'll never get home.

Never.

Oh, great! I SEE you! Headed this way — straight for my tree house. Here you come. Hooray!

It's all over now. You're dead and buried and I'll soon be on my way to the meadow to meet Old Meg and she'll be forced to take me back home. Where I'll be Snow White again, all young and lithe and beautiful. Meg's going to be really surprised that I got all the things on her list in time to meet the deadline, but she's got to play fair, by witch-spell rules. Angelbird and Ben and the two grumpy snarbs have already vanished, so that's a step in the right direction. (Though, I'll miss Ben.)

You saved me. When you arrived on your shiny motorcycle I was about ready to give up and just accept having a bulgy green eye and four arms.

But there you were. In a metal-studded leather jacket with "Hell's Bikers" stitched on the back, and boots, and a big black helmet with orange stripes on it. You didn't see any of us around and you were hungry so you went inside my house to look for food. Which is when I jumped on you and got the final item on my list: "One female head, with neck."

This all would have gone much faster except that, under the rules of the spell, I could only keep what I get on my first bite. One major body part per female. And since I needed *two* arms and *three* legs and torso and a head-and-neck combination to complete the list it was really rather difficult. Old Meg figured I'd never get them all in thirty days, one at a time the way I had to do it. But I proved her wrong.

Hooray for me!

Well, that's my story. As I wrote, right at the start, with you dead you won't be reading these words, but that's okay. Maybe somebody else will. I hope they understand that I'm really a good person. I did only what I *had* to do. I really didn't have any choice.

I feel happy now. I met the deadline.

It was actually kind of fun.

Got to go. Old Meg's waiting.

And I bet she's going to be . . . plenty pissed!

One of the most frightening aspects of being a major film icon is that you often end up attracting a stalker, one of those nut cases who becomes fixated on a celebrity and follows that person everywhere day and night. A stalker is not simply deranged; he or she can often turn violent when iconic worship spins out of control. In the story that follows I pose the question: what if this is not an ordinary stalker? What if the stalker really is . . .

Really is what? Read "Mama's Boy" and find out.

Mama's Boy

Following her again. Told not to. Warned not to. Restraining order on me. Can't get within a thousand feet of her. Can't talk to her. Can't go near her house. Can't do a lot of things I'd like to do. But we'll see what I can do. Don't let shitty cops tell me what I can or can't do.

She knows me. Oh yes! Scared of me. Thinks I'm crazy. Told the cops I was crazy. Got roughed up by them. Lousy damn cops! Weekend in jail. Smelly. Toilet backed up. Homos in there. Almost raped in the shower. Had to yell for a guard. Cold. Heater broken. Nearly froze my ass.

Promised I'd stay away from her. Did for a while. Now following her again. But being careful. Staying far enough away so she doesn't know I'm there. Watching her at night.

Standing on the grass outside her window. Watching her talk. Eat. Watching her laugh. Beautiful teeth. White as snow. Watching her tits.

Watching.

Following her to the studio in my car. Staying well back in traffic so she can't see me in her mirror. Going to her pictures. Sitting in the dark watching her on the screen. Feeling close. Smiling at her in the dark. So beautiful. So very beautiful.

Shrine to her in my Hollywood apartment. That's what the landlord called it once. A shrine. Posters from all her movies. Hundreds of glossy photos. Magazines with her in them. Lots of times with her on the cover. Once with her in a thong bikini. Showing what she's got. Interviews with her. Some where she talks about her marriage. Divorced. How she never sees her ex-husband anymore. He lives in Kansas City with another woman.

Went through her garbage. Found notes she'd written. Lists. Letters to her she'd thrown away. Best of all, a pair of her torn panties. Black silk, with lace at the edge. Keep them in a plastic bag. Special.

See her movies over and over. Every one of them maybe ten or twenty times. Never get tired of watching her.

We're very close. Meant for each other. Destiny.

Found out what studio she was working for now. Article in the paper. Followed her from the studio. To her new house. Big place in Brentwood. White with a red tile roof. Climbed up there one night. To see her undress in her bedroom. Exciting. Neighbor reported me. That's the first time the cops grabbed me. She told them to keep me away from her. Has a loaded gun in her house. Threatened to shoot me. Awful. Hurts to hear things like that. Why does she hate me? All I ever do is love her.

Second time the cops came was when she got home from the studio and I was on her porch. Waiting for her. I love you I told her. You are so beautiful. And I love your tits. To jail that time. Gave the cops a phony name. Have fake I.D. Don't give my real name. Ever. To anybody.

Judge puts restraining order on me. My picture in the papers. Said I should be in a mental ward. Treat you like shit in those places. On probation.

Changed myself since then. Cut my long hair real short. Now wear sunglasses. All the stars wear them. Shaved my beard. Makes me look different. Stare at my face in the mirror and it's like somebody else is there inside the mirror. Hello, stranger!

I'm thirty. Not old. Feel like a kid, in fact. Don't feel thirty. Used to live with Mama after Daddy left. Just the two of us. Slept in her bed. It was neat until I had to go to school. Always hated school. Didn't fit in. Grade school terrible. High school terrible. Got punched a lot. Blood on my clothes. Called me a mama's boy. What's wrong with being that? Always loved my mama. Maybe too much. Had a psychological exam once. Guy told me I was obsessed. Obsessive personality potentially psychotic. And other bullshit. That's all it is. Doctor's bullshit. What do they really know about me? Just sit there spouting their crap. Can't see inside me. Nobody can. Deep inside. Real me.

No friends. Nobody to talk to. Don't trust people. Wouldn't understand the way I feel about her. Don't really mind. Like it being alone and thinking about when I'll see her again. Bet she thinks about me too. Whether she wants to or not.

Have a hunting knife. Long blade. Real sharp. After jail, for a little while, I was pissed. Ran the knife right through her photo. One where her tits show. She shouldn't of called the cops on me. But I forgave her. Don't hold a grudge. Not in my nature. Usually keep the knife in a locked drawer. Don't carry it when I follow her. Can't. Not smart. If the cops found it on me I'd probably go back to jail.

Went into a Hollywood store where they sell movie stuff and bought this statue of her. Just her head and shoulders —— no tits. Put it on a little platform and got some colored lights to go around it. Looks great with the apartment dark with just her statue and the colored lights making it glow. Almost like she's there with me in the room. Intimate.

She made a record from one of her movies. A musical. Has eight songs on it. Real nice soft voice. Like an angel would sound. Know all the words to each song by heart. Play them over and over.

Hot today. Middle of August. She came out to her car wearing a light summer dress. Yellow, with flowers printed on it. Tight around her ass and tits. Exciting.

Followed her home. Had the knife in my car. Took it with me when I walked into her back yard and used it to pry open a window. First I cut the alarm wires. Know where they are. Don't want the cops coming to grab me again.

She's inside. In the den. Fixing herself a drink. Hate it when she drinks. Her face goes puffy and her hair and makeup get messed and she doesn't care.

Kicks off her shoes. Settles onto the couch. Snaps on the news. Sits there in her tight yellow summer dress with her drink, watching TV. Nobody else in the house. Maid's day off.

I go up to her. From behind. Put the tip of the knife blade against the faint blue vein in her neck. (*My* blood!) Smile at her as she jerks her head up, spilling the drink. Her eyes are round. Scared. She's really scared.

Love you, Mama, I say.

I happen to believe in UFOs. I'm convinced that they are no mass illusion. Too many reputable pilots and astronauts have seen them. Did one actually crash at Roswell? I think it did.

"Scotch on the Rocks" is one of only two of my stories to deal with the UFO phenomenon. It's also my first story set in Bend, Oregon, where I moved here from Los Angeles in 2004. UFOs and Bend, a workable combination. I had fun with this one. I hope you will too.

Scotch on the Rocks

*N*ormally, he was not a drinker, but today, on this particular afternoon in Bend, Oregon, he felt the need for a stimulant. Surely one drink wouldn't hurt. It would calm him, soothe his nerves, help him adjust — a stranger in a strange town.

He pushed open the door of *The Happy Hours*, underneath a sign proclaiming it to be "The Best Damn Bar in Bend." The bartender was polishing a row of already spotless wine glasses. It was three o'clock of a winter's afternoon and *The Happy Hours* was nearly deserted. Only one other customer: a small, bald-headed old man in a faded fleece jacket, hunched over his beer in a corner booth.

"I'll have a glass of Scotch whiskey with ice cubes in it," he told the barman.

The bartender had dark, melancholy eyes which were set into a long, thin-lipped face. Lugubrious. Yes, that was the word for him.

The barman reached for a bottle. "One Scotch on the rocks comin' up," he said. And, as he poured the drink: "New in town?"

"Indeed I am. Arrived this morning."

"From where?"

"Well, I was in Los Angeles for a time . . . then San Francisco. Now I'm here in Bend."

The lugubrious man extended his hand over the bar. "I'm Eddie."

"I'm Martin."

They shook hands.

"We've got us a neat little town here," the barman said. "In the old pioneering days it was called 'Farewell Bend' —— the last stopping off place for the wagon trains before they tackled the Cascade Mountains."

"Uh-huh," nodded Martin. Local history bored him.

"Lots to do around here," said the barman. "River rafting, fishing . . . there's skiing and golf . . . most everyone hikes, and a lot of people climb the rocks. You can take your pick."

"I'm not much of an outdoors man," Martin admitted.

"So . . . what line'a work are you in, Martin?"

"I'm a doctor."

"Hey, no kiddin'! Mind if I call you Doc?"

"That's perfectly agreeable."

Eddie turned toward the cash register. "Wanna run a tab?"

"Beg pardon?"

"You wanna pay now, or pay me after more drinks?"

"Oh, *now!*" said Martin, producing a wallet and paying for his Scotch. He put down money for a modest tip on the counter. "One drink will suffice."

He sipped delicately at the Scotch. It burned his throat going down.

"You're not much of a drinker, huh, Doc?"

"Correct." Martin nodded toward the glass in his hand. "This is an exception for me. I felt the need for a stimulant."

"I getcha," said Eddie.

Martin coughed. "This is quite potent."

"Top grade," said Eddie. "Aged to perfection. I serve the best Scotch in town, and that's a fact."

"I believe you," said the doctor.

Eddie hesitated, then leaned across the bar, closer to Martin. "You believe in UFOs?"

Martin blinked.

"Unidentified Flying Objects," said Eddie. "From some other galaxy way out in space. Flying saucers."

"I'm a practical man," said Martin, "and I must say that I consider such things as flying saucers to be pure hokum."

"Hokum?" Eddie frowned over the word. "Then ya don't believe in 'em?"

"Afraid not."

Eddie sighed. "Well, I didn't either, 'till they showed."

"I don't follow you," said Martin.

"The Weirdos from the saucers," said Eddie. "They been takin' me up in their ship."

Martin shifted on the stool, a skeptical expression on his face. "Are you telling me you have been abducted by an alien species?"

"Damn right! That's exactly what I'm telling ya. Been up there four times so far, them comin' for me." He stared into Martin's face. "You figure I'm tellin' ya a tall one?"

"Oh, no. Not at all," said the doctor. "I understand that it's a fairly common delusion, this abduction scenario. I've read magazine articles about it."

"Delusion, my ass!" said Eddie. "It happened! And I haven't told anybody, not even my wife. But I just gotta tell *somebody* or I'll go bats. When you walked in, I said to myself, here's a guy who'll listen to my story."

"I'm flattered by your trust," said Martin. "Of course, I'll be happy to listen. Just don't expect me to —"

"—believe it's real, eh, Doc?"

"Precisely."

"Okay, maybe after I've finished you'll change your mind."

"Please, go ahead," said Martin, taking another small sip of the whiskey. Already he felt more relaxed. "Tell me about what you believe happened to you."

"Well, it all began about a year ago," Eddie declared. "I was alone, out at my cabin in the pine woods, doing some fishing. My wife was here in town, tending bar. She can mix drinks almost as good as me."

"A rare talent, I'm sure. Proceed."

"Well, I was out on the river. The sun had just set and it was getting dark. The fish weren't biting, so I was ready to haul in my line and call it a day when this beam of light stabs down at me. Bright as all hell. Lit up half the river."

"Coming from the sky?"

"Yep. I look up, shading my eyes, and I see this big silver saucer hovering there. No sound. Just kind of *sitting* in space. Had a row of lights, all different colors, outlining it.

"What did you do?"

"I rowed like crazy for shore, with the light beam following me all the way. When the boat beached, I jumped out and ran for my cabin. I was going for the shotgun I keep there."

"Were you able to reach it?"

"No way! Suddenly there I was, floating above the shore. That damned light beam was pulling me up, into the saucer. I was so spooked I crapped my pants on the way up."

"I can understand your fear," said Martin.

"A kind of round trapdoor popped open in the belly of the saucer and I was taken aboard. By aliens. Little guys, with big balloon heads and slanted black eyes. No nose, and just a slit for a mouth."

"Did they talk to you?"

"They didn't need to. I could read their minds."

"Telepathy," said Martin.

"Yeah, *that*," said Eddie.

"What happened inside the ship?"

"They walked me to this circular room. All sterile looking, like a hospital room. They made me take off all my duds and laid me out on my back on a shiny metal table. I was yelling for them to lemme go, but they just went right on with their business."

"Which was?"

"One of 'em kept poking me with a long, glasslike thing that kept changing colors. Another one kept running small machines round me that clicked a lot. And a third guy did sex stuff to me."

"Sex stuff?"

Eddie looked down at the bar. His jaw tightened. "I don't wanna go into what he did, but it wasn't anything I'd ever done before. Then they put in a 'tracker.' I heard 'em call it that."

"I don't know what you mean."

"It's about the size of a pea, and they used some kind of air tool to put it inside of me. Just kind of floated it into my skull is the best way I can describe it. Didn't hurt, really, but my stomach felt cold when they did it. Like the things we put into animals to keep track of them in the wild. That's why these aliens always know where I am when they want to take me aboard their saucer again. Which they've done four times already. Each time I wake up back where I was, before they beamed me into their ship. I wake up with a lousy headache each time."

"Why do you think they keep abducting you?" the doctor asked.

"Don't know for sure, but I guess I'm some kind of lab animal to them. They like to poke and prod me."

"If you knew they had this implant inside your skull, why didn't you have it removed?"

Eddie gestured in despair, his eyes haunted. "Heck, I tried to. I went in for an MRI, and there it was, right there on the picture."

"So?"

"The hospital said that no operation was possible without 'severe brain damage.' Coulda turned me into a vegetable, so there wasn't nothing I could do but just learn to live with it inside me."

Martin finished his drink. He felt mellow and cool. The Scotch had done its job.

"Anyway, that's my story." Eddie looked uneasy. "Do you believe it?"

"I believe that *you* believe it," said Martin. "But I don't think anything you've told me really happened."

Eddie listened with mounting frustration.

"What you've described," Martin said, "is a product of pure fantasy, supplied by your subconscious mind. Interesting, but totally unreal."

"Then how do you figure I was able to describe aliens like so many other people have described 'em?"

Martin smiled. "No mystery here. You heard about these other descriptions and you simply followed they same pattern. By now, everyone is aware of how the big-eyed aliens are supposed to look. But they don't exist. It's all delusion."

"You're full of it, Doc," snapped Eddie, his thin lips set tightly. He swabbed the bar in angry circles. "I know the difference between what's real and what ain't. And this was *real*!"

"To you, certainly," said Martin. "But all the business about aliens zipping through Earth's skies from other galaxies is sheer nonsense."

"*Hell* it is!" declared the bald-headed man in the corner booth. He spoke in a thick-tongued, drunken drawl. "I oughta know, 'cuz I'm one of 'em."

"One of *what*?" asked Martin, turning on his stool to face the drunk. The old man was rail-thin, unshaven, and reeked of stale beer.

"One a'them," he slobbered. "I'm from Venus."

"You mean the *planet* Venus?" asked Martin. His eyes glinted with amusement.

"You betcha," nodded the old drunk. He stood up shakily, wobbled over to Martin, and poked a sun-wrinkled finger into the doctor's chest. "I come direct here to Oregon in my own friggin' big silver spaceship. Yessir, all the way from Venus!"

"And your parents were aliens? From Venus?"

"Well, *sure* they were. Jus' like me."

"You don't match Eddie's description. Big black eyes, slit for a mouth, head like a balloon. That's not you, old timer!"

"So what?" The drunk wavered and clutched the bar rail for balance. "There's all kinds of aliens. Them bigheads is jus' one kind. Me, I'm the other."

"I suggest you go home and sleep it off," said Martin. "You've been putting away too much alcohol."

Eddie nodded agreement. "Time to go home now, Mr. Abernathy."

"Home?" muttered the old man. He smiled, revealing two missing front teeth. "Yer right! I need me some sleep so I'm strong enough to get drunk again tomorrow."

He struggled for a moment to stay upright, then staggered out of the bar.

"Don't pay him no mind," said Eddie. "Mr. Abernathy, he comes in here every day, starts out sober, ends up soused. Regular as clockwork. Once, I heard him claim to be a leading ace in World War II. Said he shot down eighty Nazi plans." Eddie chuckled. "Another time, he told me he was the ex-president of France."

"Just a harmless drunk," said Martin.

"Well, *I'm* sober," Eddie declared. He gestured toward the row of bottles along the wall behind him. "Never touch the stuff. So when I tell ya about aliens, I'm talkin' from a clear mind. I'm just damn sorry you don't believe me."

"I wish I could," said Martin, "but on a rational basis, there has never been any verifiable proof of aliens from space coming in UFOs to visit Earth."

"Yeah, well that don't mean it never happened," said Eddie.

"Where is your proof?"

"The tracker inside my head. You can see it plain as day on an MRI. It's damn well *there*!"

"Oh, I'm sure something is there," said Martin, "but it's no alien artifact. Possibly a blood clot, or a plaque of calcium which formed. In any case, it's not from outer space."

"Okay," shrugged the sad-faced barman. "I give up. Truth is, I never expected you to believe me."

"I'm not laughing," said Martin. His eyes radiated sympathy. "I know you think you actually experienced these alien abductions. It's all very real to you."

"I'm nuts, is that it?"

"Not at all," said Martin. "You've simply become part of what is, unfortunately, a widespread delusion." He stood up. "I must be going. It's been very interesting, talking to you. I hope you'll find your own inner peace somehow."

"So long, Doc," said Eddie.

He looked tired and defeated.

Outside *The Happy Hours* Martin shivered and turned up the collar of his coat. The sky was heavy with massed clouds and the air was suddenly chill and biting. He smiled to himself, thinking: the next time I enter a bar, I must remember to order Scotch on the rocks, not Scotch whiskey with ice cubes. Otherwise I'll sound . . . *alien.* He chuckled at the word.

Martin scanned the passing pedestrians, focusing in on a blonde teenager who was just leaving the drug store directly across the street with a purchase.

Her, he thought. *She's perfect.*

Martin followed the girl to her home, where she greeted a joyfully barking dog, then handed the plastic drug store sack to a woman she called "Mom."

Have to get her when she's alone. Maybe late tonight, after her parents are asleep.

Right at the moment, though, he had to get back to the ship. He had an appointment to install a tracker in a construction worker in Portland who'd been abducted earlier in the day.

Martin carefully checked the area in all four directions. No one in sight. He pressed a button hidden beneath his coat.

The bright beam found him and he floated skyward — toward the saucer-shaped UFO waiting for him above the winter clouds.

I was stunned to receive an enthusiastic letter regarding this story from no less a personage than Literary Lion Norman Mailer (author of such classics as The Naked And The Dead, Armies Of The Night, *and* The Executioner's Song). *Mailer liked the story, commenting that it "took me by surprise—and it does have one hell of a smack at the ending."*

This is one of my newer tales, set in the area of my apartment complex here in Bend. It was first-drafted as a crime story; then I got the idea for my twist ending — and the story became Dark Fantasy. Moral: be careful about picking up strangers on the road. Or should I say, be careful about who might pick you up? Confusing? Read the story and you'll see what I mean.

An Unlucky Encounter

Sure, I've read the Bible. I don't believe it's God's word. No sir. It's the work of several hands, down the centuries. An anthology of tall tales. Is any of it true? Who knows? Maybe. Maybe not. Me, I long ago rejected all traditional religions, whether based on the Bible or Buddha or what have you. People have all kinds of beliefs around the world. It's their crutch, what they lean on for moral support.

Me, I'm anti-belief. I believe in myself, and I have my own ideas of morality. But if I hadn't read the Bible I would never have called Bracker a "Good Samaritan."

I'm jumping ahead. Let me lay it all out the way it went down. First, you have to meet Bracker. Sitting behind the wheel of his Dodge, talking a blue streak, telling me more about himself than I cared to know.

"I've spent half my life in jail," he said. "Did time from when I was just a kid. I'm thirty, and been fifteen years in the slammer. You ever been inside?"

I shook my head.

"Hell, jail ain't no hassle for me." He grinned, but there was no warmth in it. His eyes were obsidian, dark and glassy, without visible pupils. "I don't mind doing time. Even kinda like it. No temptations is what I mean. No booze. No broads. No poker." He glanced at me. "You play poker?"

"Afraid not," I said. "I don't know much about cards."

"Me, I play poker," Bracker declared, violently twisting the wheel to miss a pothole in the street. It was early December, and we'd had snow the week before. The sun had melted most of it, leaving piles of ugly brown slush along the curbs.

Bracker was unshaven, with a ragged growth of beard and two teeth missing in his lower jaw. The rest were badly discolored. A faint, unpleasant odor emanated from his armpits.

We were in his '66 Dodge Dart, paint-flaked and rusting. A large dent scarred the door on the passenger's side, and the trunk lid was tied down with a twist of rope.

"Hell, I'm just plain unlucky at poker. In Vegas, they got these poker machines. I dropped a hundred a day in 'em for six days straight. Seems like I always lose."

"Then why do you go on playing?" I asked him. We were on the way to my apartment, and I was anxious to get there. Being with Bracker was nerve-wracking. We lived in different worlds.

"I play poker because I *like* playing poker," he replied.

"You're obviously addicted," I told him.

He glared at me. "You're *full* of it! I ain't addicted to *shit*! I can quit poker same way I can quit booze if I damwell feel like it. Same as I gave up smokes. I got will power that way."

"Okay," I said. I didn't want to argue with him. You don't argue with a man like Bracker.

"You wanna know my first name?" he asked, grinning again.

"All right," I said. I really didn't want to know his first name; all I wanted was to get back to my apartment.

"It's Kingsley," he said. "After Norman Miller, that war writer guy."

"You mean Norman Mailer — the man who wrote *The Naked And The Dead*?"

"Yeah, *him*," said Bracker. "His middle name is Kingsley. Norman Kingsley Mailer. My Ma, she thought that middle name was real fancy, so she stuck me with it. Kingsley Bracker. Fancy, huh?"

I nodded.

"Well, I purely hate the goddamn name," he said, his tone hard-edged. "Had a smartass son of a bitch in the slammer call me Kingsley, an' I made me a shiv outa'a butter knife and stuck him good. Didn't kill the bastard, but he spent a month in medical."

"What did they do to you?"

"I claimed it was self-defense, that he came at me with the shiv and we wrestled some and the shiv ended up in him. They bought my story, an' he got all the blame." He looked at me. "You ever stick anybody?"

"You mean have I ever used a knife on someone?"

"Yeah, that's what I mean."

"No, never. I'm not the violent type."

"You sayin' *I* am?" His tone was hard again.

"Oh, no, not at all. I was just answering your question."

We were now only four blocks from my apartment. Off Green-wood, down 27th to Forum, then straight into the unit. "Turn left when you get to Forum Drive," I said. "The apartment complex is just behind Safeway market."

"You shop at Safeway?" Bracker asked.

"Sometimes. Not always."

"They got them little red plastic Safeway cards. Save a bundle with them cards. You got one?"

"Yes, I have a club card."

"Bet you save a bundle, huh?"

"It adds up," I said.

"Damn! If I lived here in Bend like you do I'd have me one a' them little red plastic cards."

"Where *do* you live?"

"Wherever the road takes me. I jes' keep movin'. A rollin' stone, that's me."

After an awkward silence between us, I said: "Just want you to know how much I appreciate your helping me out this way."

Bracker shrugged. "Fella stuck outa town with a busted wheel, least I can do is give him a lift."

"It was very kind of you." I smiled at him.

"Yeah, that's me, Kindly Kingsley." He chuckled. A dry, rasping sound. "I'm like one a' them ginks from the Bible. Know what I mean?"

"A Good Samaritan," I said.

"That's it. Got me a heart as big as all outdoors." He scratched at his chin. "Ma, she plain loved her Bible. Usta quote from it over supper. Called me a 'stained lamb.' Said I'd never amount ta nothin'." Another chuckle. "She was dead right about that!"

"I'll have a tow truck take my car in to the garage," I said. "I think it's a broken front axle. Metal fatigue."

"Some cars'll do that," said Bracker. "Specially them dinky little foreign suckers. What's yours called?"

"An MG-TC," I said. "Wire wheels. Original leather and paint. A classic."

He snorted. " A classic pieca shit, I'd say! Hell, this here Dodge a'mine, it'd never break no axle. Built like a goddam tank!"

"You're fortunate," I said.

"Ya oughta dump that freakin' little buggy a'yours an' get yerself a Dodge Dart. I found this baby in Cincinnati. Ever been to Cincinnati?"

"Regrettably, I have not. Afraid I'm something of a homebody."

"Where you from?" he asked.

"California originally. I'm a native of Los Angeles. I moved here to Oregon after . . ." My voice faltered.

"After what?

"After the death of my wife and children. A boy and a girl."

"How'd they kick off?"

"I . . . I'd rather not talk about it," I told him.

"Kinda painful, huh?"

"Yes . . . painful." I drew in a long breath. "I think a lot about Claire and the children."

"Me, I never been hitched," he said. "Don't need no broad tellin' me what to do . . . tyin' me down. No ball an' chain for me. Wham, bam, thank you ma'am. That's my style. And I never wanted no kids."

"They can be a trial," I admitted.

More silence between us. Then . . .

"You'd probably like to know what put me in the slammer," said Kingsley Bracker.

I shook my head. "It's none of my business."

"It was a girl. Name a' Cindy. One wild bitch she was! Cindy liked rough sex, so I got rough with her — an' she ended up dead."

I drew in a breath, without response. A block more to go, then I'd be home.

"Hell, Cindy *asked* for it," said Bracker. "She wanted it rough so I gave it to her that way. It was all her idea."

He seemed to be waiting for my reaction. "Uh-huh, I can see how something like that could get out of hand."

"Shit, I ain't no woman killer," he declared. "Nigger lawyer got it reduced to manslaughter, so I done my time an' now I'm free as a friggin' bird."

"You paid your debt to society."

"That's it." He chuckled again. "Paid in full from what I done to that little bitch."

A silence between us.

"I like to drink," said Bracker. "You drink?"

"On occasion," I said.

"Me, I like my booze. Partial to Irish whiskey. They took away my driver's license after I slammed inta the back of a laundry truck. I was swacked. Drunk as a hoot owl. Can't even remember the accident."

"Liquor will do that," I said.

"Judge suspended my license an' impounded my car. Chevy Impala. But I went right out an' bought me this here Dodge. Got it for a song."

"Then, currently . . . you are driving without a license?"

"Sure I am. No fat-assed judge is gonna keep me grounded."

"What if you are stopped for a traffic violation?"

"I won't be." He winked at me. "I'm real careful."

"Do you still drink and drive?"

"Hell yes. But I can handle the booze. I won't be hitting no more laundry trucks, that's for damsure."

I nodded.

"My pop liked his booze, same as me," said Bracker. "The two of us, we usta get loose-assed drunk together. That was after Ma kicked off with the T.B. and Pop got lonely. Replaced her with a bottle. Hell, I was drunk afore I was seven. Whoeee! A six-year-old drunk. Oh, but we had us some *times*, me an' Pop."

"You've led a colorful life," I said.

"Yeah, colorful, that's me." He looked over. "You bein' here in Bend and all, you fish an' hunt?"

"I'm not the sports type," I admitted. "But I do like to be out on the water. I'm a Pisces. The water sign. But I don't fish. Let them be, I say. Why put a steel hook in their throats?"

"Cuz fish is good eatin' is why," said Bracker. He scratched his chin, squinting. "Me, if I lived here I'd be out catchin' me some fish an' killin' some game. I'm a damn good shot."

"I've never used firearms."

"Well, you're a helluva case, you are," Bracker declared. "What *do* you do?"

"Not much, I'm afraid. I read. See European films. Rented. We don't get them here in Bend. And I like classical music. Bach is my favorite."

"Jeeze, what a drag!" said Bracker, pulling the Dodge to the curb.

"Why are we stopping?" I asked.

He cut the engine, turning to me with his cold grin. Bracker drew a small black automatic from his coat. "I'll need your wallet," he said.

"What?" I was startled.

"I happen to be a little short'a cash, an' I figger you must carry plenty, dressed all slick the way you are, and with that nifty little sporty car you drive." His tone was ice. "So gimme your wallet."

"You're . . . robbing me?"

"Call it a loan." Again the dry chuckle. "To a Good Samaritan." He brought up the gun, holding it rock-steady in his right hand. I noticed that his nails were ragged, caked with grime.

I looked down at the weapon.

"I'm not afraid of a gun," I told him.

"Well ya damnwell *better* be!" he snapped. "You don't hand over your wallet I'll blow a fuggin' hole right through you!"

With snakelike speed, before he could react, I clamped my fingers around his right wrist, crushing the bone. He let out a sharp cry of pain and the automatic dropped from his nerveless hand. I relaxed my grip on his wrist, smiling at him.

"That's better," I said.

He'd flinched back in the seat, staring at me. "Who the hell *are* you?

"It's not who I am, but *what* I am," I replied.

"I don't ——" He fumbled for words.

"You have made me angry," I told him. "I would have left you alone, but you have made me angry with your clumsy attempt at robbery."

He was holding his shattered wrist with his left hand, breathing heavily. Blood seeped between his fingers.

"Look, mister," he began. "I never meant to ——"

I smashed a fist into his face, breaking his cheek bone. He cried out in agony as I picked up the fallen automatic.

"Don't," he pleaded. "Don't shoot, mister. Christ knows I never meant to ——"

"I don't intend to shoot you," I told him.

He looked vastly relieved.

"It was a joke . . . about my wanting your money."

"You have a strange sense of humor," I said, holding the gun loosely in my hand. I applied pressure, and the metal twisted like black taffy.

I tossed the discarded weapon out of the car window.

Bracker was staring at me, eyes wide.

"We possess great strength," I said quietly.

"*We?*"

"My kind. Oh, there's much that has been written and said of us that is not true. That we cower before crosses . . . that we sleep in coffins . . . that we fear sunlight and can turn into bats . . . All untrue. But we *do* possess great strength."

Bracker snatched at the door handle, hoping to escape from the car, but I struck him again, a chopping blow that rendered him unconscious.

Cars were passing along the highway, but their drivers ignored us. I had plenty of time.

Bracker was slumped over the wheel. I leaned toward him, sinking my teeth into his neck.

His blood was refreshing.

As I was enjoying him my thoughts turned to Claire and the children. Of course, when I married her, she had no idea of what I was. She was shocked, to say the least! I left her drained body in the back yard . . . with our two dead children.

I was almost finished with Bracker. His heartbeat was erratic, slowing. To a stop. I felt him die.

A great sense of fulfillment. A sense of utter peace. I drew in a long, relaxed breath. Then I left the car and walked back to my apartment.

Kingsley Bracker, Good Samaritan, had been unlucky at more than poker.

I wrote this one for a Dennis Etchison-edited anthology. Dennis told me he wanted a story that had a "savage" impact, that was direct and uncompromising. With all stops out.

I gave him "In Real Life," an experiment in form and structure that met all of his requirements. My goal: to see just how far I could push the stylistic envelope.

This, I truly believe, is one of a kind.

In Real Life

She came into the room raving as usual in that shrill voice of hers. Like a train whistle. Or nails on a blackboard. Called me a fucking loser. Said I wasn't worth cat shit. Raved and shouted, waving her hands around. Swearing like a mill hand. Eyes blazing at me, like two hot coals.

She made it easy, killing her. Like the end of that Mickey Spillane book where Mike Hammer shoots the evil bitch in the belly. I just walked into the bedroom and took the gun from her vanity table where she always kept it for protection. Paranoid. Afraid of intruders, of being raped. As if anyone would want to.

What are you doing with my gun? she yells. Always yelling. Mouth like an open sewer. I said I took the gun to shut her up for good. You're gonna kill me? She laughed her hyena laugh. Real unattractive. You couldn't kill a fucking fly, she tells me. Oh, no, that's not true . . . I can kill you okay, I said. No problem. My voice was icy calm. This was the Big Moment.

That's when I fired point-blank at her: Bang, bang, bang.

She flopped over like a big rag doll. Kind of comical. But she really messed up the sofa, falling across it with all that blood coming out of her. Ruined it, really. You can't ever get blood out of a white sofa. That was when Bernie said, in his quiet way: cut and print.

How was I? Linda asked him. Did I fall the right way? You were perfect, darling, he told her. They hugged. Directors always hug their female stars. Treat them like children. That's because

every actress is insecure. They need a lot of attention. Best I get is
a pat on the shoulder. Good job, Chuck.

He held that gun too close to me, Linda complained. The wads
from those fucking blanks *hurt* me.

Linda was like the bitch in the movie. She liked to say fuck.
Tough broad. One of the boys. Never liked her. Third picture with
her and we still didn't get along. Strong mutual dislike from the first
day we met. None of the crew liked her either. Always complain-
ing. Didn't approve of the way her hair was fixed: too short on the
sides, too rigid on top. The pale make-up made her look like a corpse.
Her dress didn't do her figure justice. The sound man was an asshole,
didn't maintain her modulation level. The head grip smoked too
much on his breaks. His clothes reeked of stale cigar smoke. Always something to criticize.

But she saved her prime complaints for me. I blocked her key
light. Stepped on her lines. Hogged the camera. Wouldn't stick to
the script. (She hated improv because she couldn't handle it herself. No flexibility.)

Killing her had been a pleasure. Wouldn't mind doing it in real
life. Not that I would. I'm no psycho. Don't go around killing foul-
mouthed females. But getting paid for faking it was satisfying. I got
to kill Linda in two of our pics together. Strangled her in *The Dark
Stranger* and stuck her in a food freezer in *Wake Up to Death*.
Fun. A flat-out pleasure.

Ralph handed the pages back to me. "I don't believe it," he
said, a nasty edge to his voice.

"Why not?" I demanded. "What's wrong with it?"

"Everything," said Ralph. He seemed to take special delight in
hurting me. "You just don't know how to get into the male mind. It
takes a man to write about another man."

"That's crap and you know it," I snapped back at him. "Women
have been writing successfully about men for three thousand years."

"Okay." Ralph shrugged his scarecrow shoulders. "Maybe they
have — but these pages fail to convince me that you're one of them."

"This is my fifth novel for Christ's sake," I protested. "If I'm so
lousy, then how come Viking keeps buying them?"

"Hey, Linda! Get real. Your other books all had female pro-
tagonists." Ralph had that know-it-all grin on his face. "You wrote

them from a feminine perspective. A man is different. It's obvious that you can't handle the male viewpoint."

"That's your opinion," I said. "I know exactly what I'm doing. *I'm* the writer, chum."

"And I'm your best editor!"

"Yeah, and my *worst* husband."

"Then why did you marry me?"

"Damned if I know. Guess I figured you'd be a step up from my first three. But I was wrong. You're a step *down*."

"You're a stupid cunt."

"And you're a stupid prick."

I looked him straight in the eye. "I want a divorce," I said.

And that's when I killed her.

Killed the character in my novel, I mean. This is as far as I got. Thing just wasn't working for me. No flow. Jagged. I was forcing it. And it wasn't truthful. For example, women can write beautifully about men, they do it all the time. Look at Joyce Carol Oates. She writes men that breathe on the page. Eudora Welty. Shirley Jackson. And lots of others.

So that part was all wrong. Yet if I had Linda's husband *approve* of her scenes then my structural conflict would be missing. I could do it over, but I just lost heart. And this novel-within-a-novel stuff is tricky to bring off.

There was something else. Using my dead wife's name for the female character was a bad idea. I should have called her something else. Any name but Linda.

Maybe I'm not cut out to be a novelist. Maybe I should just stick to directing other people's scripts. That's what I'm really good at. Hell, in France they think I'm another Jerry Lewis. Not that I do comedy; I don't. But the Frenchies love me. Edgar Price is a genius. That's what they say. In Frogland, I'm a hot property.

Writing about my dead wife was painful. Bitter memories. Linda drove me nuts during our marriage. We were never compatible. People still believe she died of "natural causes," I made sure about that. Used a poison you can't trace. My little secret. Her family was convinced of my grief. Kept my head lowered at the funeral, dabbing at my eyes. In the cemetery I leaned down to plant a kiss on her coffin. And the single rose I tossed into the grave was a lovely touch.

Guess I shouldn't be admitting it all here, in this diary. But no one will read it. Who'd ever think of looking for a floor safe in a garden shed? Ideal hiding place. That's where the diary goes each morning before I leave for the studio. And I keep the safe's combination in my head. Never wrote it down. I'm not fool.

Well, at least Linda's gone. I'm damn well rid of her. No more arguments about money, or my drinking, or my women. That loud mouth of hers is shut forever. Comforting thought.

Oops, a horn outside. The limo is here, so I've got to wind this up. End of entry.

Off to the daily grind.

Killing him was easy. Big shot director. Bit *shit* is more like it. With all his fancy clothes, and his foreign cars, and his big house in Bel Air. Claims he saved my ass. Said I'd be nothing if he hadn't come along. Probably be waiting tables at Denny's. Bull! I've always had talent, even as a little girl in Kansas City. Mama used to brag about me to all the neighbors. I'd do those little skits of mine, dancing and singing, and Mama would clap like crazy and tell me I was another Judy Garland. (But I could always dance better than Judy Garland.)

Edgar Price, the big shot director. Discovered me, he always said. Well, *someone* would have. He just happened to get a hard-on during that dumb little theater play in Pasadena when I showed a lot of leg. Came backstage after the curtain to tell me that I demonstrated "genuine talent" and that the studio was looking for talent like mine. Yeah, sure. *He* was the one looking——at my tits, not my talent.

He did get me into pictures, if you can call the kind of crap he directed a picture. Cheezy horror stuff, with me playing the nude corpse in the first one. Not a frigging line in the whole movie. *The Blood Queen's Revenge.* Yuck.

Then he had me doing bare-ass scenes in a shower for that crappy film of his about women in the Air Force. I was supposed to be a Lesbian jet pilot. A nothing part. I had maybe five minutes of screen time and I was butt-naked for most of that.

Next, he put me in his wrestling thing, where I was this female wrestler who gets her clothes torn off in the ring. Just the pits.

And then there was the one where I played a doomed prostitute with lung cancer. God! How I hated the scene where I died in the bathtub. They got worried when my nipples stayed erect, which they said should not happen when I was dead. But that bathwater was frigging *cold*!

Edgar was a ten-carat liar. All the time, while he was putting the blocks to me off-camera, he kept saying what a great star he was going to make out of me. But all he wanted was my pussy. I wasn't born yesterday.

Finally, I'd had enough. He comes to the studio in his custom stretch limo and the first thing he wants to do is screw me in his trailer before the morning's shoot. Told me he needed to release sexual energy. To relax his creative drive. Creative, my ass!

He'd been directing this moronic vampire flick. *The Devil Bat's Daughter*. I was the daughter, but natch I got snuffed in the first reel with my boobs hanging out.

I was really pissed. When we were inside his trailer that morning I put some stuff in his coffee. Gave him a heart attack. When he keeled over I started screaming for help. Terrified maiden with a dead director on her hands. Great scene. I was wonderful. Academy Award caliber.

Naturally, the doc wouldn't do anything for Edgar. I sobbed up a storm. Big-time tears. The whole bazonga. The doc was so concerned about me that he gave me a prescription to calm my "severe emotional state." Hah! All the time I was giggling inside. The lecherous, lying bastard was dead.

I don't feel any guilt. Not a twinge. Hey, he killed his wife, didn't he? Poisoned her. That's where I got the idea for the stuff in his coffee —— from the diary I fished out of the garden shed. When he was loaded one night in bed he kept mumbling the combination, over and over again, like a mantra. Didn't have any memory of it the next day —— alcoholic blackout —— but by then I'd written the numbers down. I'm very clever about things like that. God a good head on my shoulders. Mama always said so.

And she was right about my talent. When Edgar had his "unfortunate heart attack" I started moving up the industry ladder. Took a while. I'm no spring chicken. And recently, as a "mature" actress, I started getting some fat parts with the likes of DeNiro, Stalllone, and Sean Connery. (I was Connery's doped-out mistress in *Kill Me Sweetly*. A plum role. Won me a Golden Globe! Hotcha!)

They're calling for me on the set so I'll quit writing, but my journal is real important. Me writing to me. Very healthy. This no-bullshit stuff is supposed to flush out the emotions. Gets me ready to emote in front of the cameras.

In this one, the picture I'm doing now, I'm a bitchy killer. I drive an icepick into my boyfriend. The producer told me I was perfect for the part. He was right. Fits me like a second skin. I could grab an Oscar for this one. Oh, yeah! Little Linda is ready for stardom! (Funny thing, me having the same name as Edgar's dead wife.) Anyhow, I'm ready for the big icepick scene. Killing my boyfriend in this one will be a pleasure. Easy. No problem.

After all, it's not real life.

This one is "fantastic," but it is certainly not Dark Fantasy. Yet "Hopping for Abe" offers a relaxing change of pace from the more serious tales in this collection. I've written two novels and four other short stories about the protagonist of this tale, my wacky Mars-based private eye, Sam Space. He represents, in combination, my passion for both science fictional and hard-boiled literature. He's a direct descendent of his namesake, Sam Spade. However, his manic adventures through the solar system transcend anything that Dash Hammett ever imagined. Sam has to deal with three-headed clients, robot dragons, talking cars, and aliens from God-knows-where. All in a day's work for my rock-fisted detective. In "Hopping for Abe" I have Sam bounce back from an abortive love affair, all the way back to a certain fateful night at Ford's Theater. . . And if my admittedly irreverent portrait of our former President shocks some Lincoln fans, well, folks, it's only fiction!

Hopping for Abe

I was in love.

That's right, me, Sam Space, the toughest private op on Mars, hitherto impervious to the Wiles of Women, hard-souled and hard-fisted, able to handle any crisis in the system. Yet here I was, daydreaming like some half-baked Earthbrat.

It was windy in Bubble City, with sand rattling against the vents. I was in Albert, my hovercar, headed for my beloved's lifeunit on Twin Moon Avenue. I began to sob with joy at the thought of seeing her again.

"Shape up, Space," the car growled. "You've gone soft as a soaked doughnut. What the freeb's wrong with you?"

"I'm in love," I told the car. "For the first time in my life I'm deeply and truly in love." My voice throbbed with emotion.

"You make me want to puke," declared the car. "It's bad enough, what you've been doing to your liver with the booze, but now you're all starry-eyed over some lousy dame."

"She's not a lousy dame," I protested, "she's the most delightful creature in the system."

"A triplehead from Venus?"

"No, she's got just one head. From New Old New York. Her name is Ginevra."

"Got a big set of bazongas on her, right?"

"Yes, she's amply endowed, but that's not why I —"

The car snickered. "How'd you get tangled up with her?"

"None of your beeswax," I snapped. "You already know too much about me."

I popped out in front of a tri-deck plasto complex. Gin lived on deck two. "Go on home," I told the car. "If I want you I'll buzz."

"Okay," said Albert. "Give my regards to the broad."

And he snapped back into traffic.

"Dearest!" said Ginevra, clasping me in her arms after I'd un-zipped her unit door. "Darling! Sugarcake! Precious!"

Her lush lips smashed into mine.

"Wow!" I gasped. "You're driving me bats, the way you've been withholding yourself from me. I can't wait any longer to make love to you. Let's run off to Jupiter and get married. I know a mouse preacher that will unite us."

"That's just not possible, sweetums," she said. Her face glowed, and her supple body was pressed against me.

"What isn't possible?"

"Getting married. A machine can't get married."

I stared at her. "A . . . machine?"

She gave me one of her dazzling smiles. "Yep, that's me. I'm an android."

"But you don't have a turn-off switch behind your ear!"

"I'm a newer model. You turn me off by pressing my belly button." She giggled, driving her twin thrusters into my chest. "But it tickles."

Numbly, I slumped into a dozechair. "I've fallen for a damn robot!"

"Is that so terrible?" she asked.

"Yeah . . . it is. I can't screw a machine." I glared at her. "You played me for a sap. All this time I thought ——"

She rubbed her flat tummy against my round tummy. Her tone was little-girl sweet. "Don't you still love me?"

"How can I? I'm a human and you're . . . a bunch of nuts and bolts."

She pursed her full lips. "Kiss me, snookums, and let's forget I'm an android."

"No way, babe. It's over. Finished. Kaput. Done. And I'm outa here." I got up, put on my classic hat, and left her unit.

Then I buzzed Albert.

* * *

Back in my office on Red Sands Avenue I was in a foul mood. My outdated plug-in secretary tried to cheer me up.

"What you need to do is a good deed," she said. "Doing a good deed will cheer you up."

"Suggest one."

"Why not hop back to 1865 and save Abe Lincoln?"

I raised an eyebrow. "That's not a bad idea," I admitted. "But how do I get back there?"

"On that Timebike you rescued Matilda Scratch with . . . when you saved her from the Mukluks."

"They were Meekluks," I corrected her.

"Whatever. Anyhow, Daddy Arnie probably still has the Timebike at his joint. You can use it to go back to 1865."

"Yeah," I mused. "He'll still have it. Arnie is too cheap to get rid of anything."

"You'd better unplug me before you leave," Edna told me.

Arnie's joint was seedy, shabby, and stank of stale nearbeer. Arnie was the same: seedy, shabby, and stinking of nearbeer. He met me downstairs without his wheelie. I'd never seen Arnie walk before.

"I put on my protolegs just for you," he said.

"I'm flattered. Looks like you have *both* arms. What happened?"

"I got to a doc who fed me a dose of Regrow. Brand new on the Market. Grew my missing arm back."

"Neat-o," I said. "Will it work on your legs?"

"Dunno. I'm gonna try it this week and see."

Arnie had lost both legs and an arm on Antar III during the Zeeb war. But that didn't slow him down. He was one tough cookie.

"You still got that Timebike I used to fetch Matilda back from Magna V?"

"Yep. In the back room."

"I want to borrow it."

"For what?"

"To save Abe Lincoln from being assassinated."

"Okay. I'll rent it to you for six creds."

Arnie was cheap. He never missed the chance to hook a profit.

"I'm flat," I told him. "Got stiffed on my last caper. I still owe my apartment for last month and it won't let me back in. I've been sleeping at the office."

"That's no skin off my ass," said Arnie. "I don't get six creds you don't get the bike."

"You tight-fisted son of a bitch."

"Go ahead, call me names. But all that counts is the moolah."

"It's okay, pop," said a velvet voice from the doorway. "I'll pay you the six."

It was Matilda, stunning as ever. A bosomy blonde darling. And certainly no android. I'd forgotten how chesty she was. Her twin thrusters poked deliciously out of her globlouse.

"You've got an ulterior motive for doing this," I said to her.

"How very perceptive of you, Sam," she said, smiling. "I've always wanted to go back to 1865 and meet Abe Lincoln. His beard is *so* attractive!"

"Nertz on that, sister," I snapped. "Me, I travel solo."

"Not this time," she said. "Either I go with you or no six creds. Deal . . . or no deal?

I sighed. "Deal."

It was close. We got to Ford's Theater just as John Wilkes Booth was raising his weapon to shoot the President. I zapped him with a charge from my quickgrip Sheckley-Ellison .225 and he yelped like a stepped-on pup. Then he jumped from the balcony down to the stage and shook his fist at me, yelling something about death to tyrants.

"Who the hell are you?" asked Lincoln.

"My name is Samuel T. Space," I said. "I came here from the future to save your life."

"Well, I'll be damned!" said Lincoln.

"I never knew you swore," I said. "None of the history books mention it."

"Screw the history books," said the President. "Written by pussies who don't know crap about me."

"I'm glad you're okay," I told him. "I feel as if I've done a really good deed in saving you and it cheers me up."

Lincoln turned to Matilda, taking her right hand in his. "And who is this charming young cunt?"

"Boy, Mister President, you *do* use rough language," I said.

"She's Matilda Scratch and she's very attracted to your beard."

"It's so sexy," murmured Matilda. "And I love your mole too."

"My wife Mary and I don't get along worth shit," said Lincoln. "For one thing, she's flat-chested."

Matilda giggled, rubbing her thrusters against his beard.

"Ummm," said Lincoln. "What I'd like to do is to go back to my place and see what's under that tight little outfit of yours."

Matilda gasped. "You want me butt naked?"

"That's the idea," nodded Lincoln. "How about it?"

Matilda giggled again. "How can I resist a beard like yours?"

And they got it on in Lincoln's office.

When I climbed back on the Timebike with Matilda in the saddle behind me the lousy thing wouldn't start.

"Let me have a gander at it," said Lincoln. "I have a knack with machinery."

And he fiddled with the powerpak. "Ummmm . . . looks like your solenoids are corroded. I can clean 'em for a price."

"A price?" I raised an eyebrow.

"Yep. I want to go back with you . . . see what the future looks like centuries from now."

"I don't think the bike can handle three," I told him.

"Sure it can," enthused Matilda. "I'll scrunch up against you and Abe can ride behind me."

The thought of Matilda "scrunching" up against me with those marvelous thrusters led to a quick agreement on my part.

Abe Lincoln would see the future.

When we Timebiked back to Arnie's joint on Mars he was sacked out upstairs full of nearbeer. Lincoln was like a sweet-toothed kid in a candy shop. He devoured everything, eyes bugging.

"I *like* this future," he said. "It's just goddamn wonderful!"

"You're coming here is going to have a huge effect on history," I told him. "I'm not so sure it was a wise move on your part."

"Wise, my ass," said the President. "I'm having fun."

And he reached for Matilda, squeezing her left thruster.

Then his face darkened.

"What's wrong, Abe?" asked Matilda.

"I'm given to fits of deep melancholy," said Lincoln. "Suddenly I feel terrible."

"What can I do to help?" asked the girl.

"Let me take the bike back to Ford's," said Abe. "I'll let John Wilkes Booth shoot me."

"You mean you want to go back there and be assassinated?" I asked.

"It's the only way to end these damn fits of depression," he said. "The Civil War was shit. *Very* depressing. I'll never get over it."

Matilda rubbed herself against Abe's beard. "Can't I *do anything* to end your depression?"

He shook his head. "Afraid not, my little crumpet," he said. He removed his stovepipe hat and handed it to me. "Take this, Sam," he said, "as a souvenir."

I accepted the stovepipe. "I don't know what to say."

"Just say I can have the Timebike," Abe mumbled, holding his head. "I have a killer headache. Get 'em all the time. I just want to end things." He gave us a painful smile. "Hey . . . nobody lives forever."

"Go ahead, take the bike," I said.

"Arnie's gonna be pissed," said the President.

"I'll explain things to Pop," said Matilda, giving Lincoln a deep-tongue kiss. "Bye, Abe darlin'. I'll miss your lovely beard."

"And I'll miss your ample chest," said Lincoln as he climbed aboard the Timebike.

"Have a safe trip," I said.

And he disappeared in a shower of timesparks.

So that's the story of my good deed gone bad. Abe's going back to be shot restored my foul mood.

The red sand was blowing in Bubble City. A wicked storm had moved in, and some of the sand got down my neck.

It was a lousy afternoon.

All this happened seven Marsmonths ago.

I still have Abe's stovepipe hat under a belljar on my desk.

Warning: I reveal a pivotal plot device in my heading for this story, so I strongly suggest you read "Listening to Billy" first and then read the following comments.

This one was written a the request of an editor who was assembling a collection of original shock tales, all of which were set in bars. He liked my "Billy," but rejected it, telling me he had a firm policy: no ghost stories. "But this isn't a ghost story," I told him — and then explained that yes, I did have the character talk about ghosts, suggesting that he himself was one. But this was done to make Billy seem to be a ghost — to throw off readers. Billy is actually a mental projection of a disturbed killer, inspired by the western décor of the bar, and created to mask the killer's guilt. (Had he been a real ghost the bartender also would have seen him.) It was impossible to change the editor's opinion, and to this day I'm sure he's convinced that he rejected a ghost story.

The murder as described here is factual. This is exactly what happened to the husband and wife who lived next door to our family in Kansas City. (I even used their real names.) Arthur ended up cutting his throat. And they did own a lake house that fueled their final argument. I spent many happy summers there as a boy.

By the way, there is a ghost story in this collection, but it's not "Listening to Billy."

Listening to Billy

*A*fter he'd killed her, Arthur decided he would cut his throat, but he had plenty of time for that. There was no hurry. First, the roses in the backyard needed watering, so that was what he did next. He watered the roses, making sure the hose pressure wasn't too strong. You can damage roses if you use too much hose pressure. He was wearing only his blue-striped boxer shorts and a pajama top, but no one noticed him out there in the backyard, watering his roses.

After he'd finished, he turned off the hose and coiled it neatly, putting it back on its proper hook in the garage. Everything in the garage was clean and orderly. Arthur Joergens was a very orderly man. All of the tools were in their proper places and the 1954 family Chevrolet (only a year old!) was under a dust cover. Even in a closed garage, he knew, dust can eat into body paint. He didn't drive the Chevrolet much anymore, now that he'd turned sixty. I guess sixty isn't that old, he told himself, but he just didn't feel that he had the reflexes of a young man anymore when it came to driving in heavy traffic.

And, of course, Adele never drove the Chevrolet. She kept telling him that she was a licensed, fully capable driver. She thought his strict prohibition against her driving was ridiculous, but he didn't trust a woman behind the wheel. When they bought the Chevy he told her he would do all the driving. Later, after they'd had the car for a couple of months, he thought about letting her drive. She smiled (sweet smile) and said that would be nice, but nothing came of it.

Last Thanksgiving, when he turned sixty, he thought maybe he should let her drive the next time they went to the lake house, but when they got there, he changed his mind.

However, the matter of her driving or not driving was now settled. With Adele lying in the kitchen, two bullets in her head, she definitely wouldn't be driving the Chevrolet to the lake house.

The lake house.

The lake house.

Back in the kitchen, the words were constant drumbeats inside Arthur's head as he washed blood from his hands at the sink. The lake house had been the reason he'd killed Adele. That, and what Billy told him in the tavern.

"Kill her, Art. It's the only thing makes any sense. Ya really hafta kill her."

The first time he'd gone into the tavern to have a cold beer in the afternoon — to get out of Missouri's summer sun, which can boil a man's brains — Billy had taken the stool next to him at the bar. Back in the 1800s, Kansas City had been the starting point of the old Santa Fe trail, and — in keeping with the city's history — the tavern had been decked out in Old West décor. The walls were filled with faded sepia photographs of old-timers and wagon trains on their way to California and other points west. Billy fit right in, dressed like he was, Western style.

"I'm Billy," he said. "What's your handle?"

"I'm Arthur Joergens."

"Howdy, Art!" They shook hands. Billy's grip was soft, like a young girl's. A soft handshake.

"So . . . whatcha do fer a livin', Art?"

"I put in concrete basements," he told Billy. "I pour concrete, cover the dirt floor and walls with it, smooth it out and they pay me for that."

"You married, Art?"

"Yes, I am. To a fine woman. Adele. Met her at a church picnic. She let me take her home on the back of my motorcycle. Of course, that was when I still had one. I don't own a cycle anymore."

"Me, I ride a horse," said Billy. "You can always depend on a horse. A horse can be a real friend."

"I suppose that's true," said Arthur. "I've no direct experience with horses."

"My daddy had me on the back of a horse practical a'fore I could walk," said Billy. "Me and horses, we get along."

"I'm sure you do," said Arthur.

"This woman a'yours . . . ya really love her, right?"

"Yes, I do. Indeed I do. Adele is a perfect wife. She respects me. Knows her place. I'm the boss. I make all the decisions."

Billy narrowed his eyes. They were narrow to begin with. Kind of squinty. "You *trust* her, Art?"

"Absolutely," said Arthur Joergens. "I trust Adele absolutely one hudred percent."

"Well, ya better watch out for her," Billy had told him on that first afternoon. "You can trust a horse, but you can't trust a woman."

Arthur sipped his cold beer. When he looked back at the bar stool next to him, it was empty.

A week later, after watching Adele very closely, Arthur was back in the tavern.

Billy was on the next stool, wearing a plaid shirt (out at one elbow), and scuffed leather chaps, with a heavy Colt jammed into his belt. He took off his battered sombrero and ran a hand along the sweat-stained brim.

"Gotta get me a new hat," he said. "This one's all wore to hell."

"It's very weathered," said Arthur.

"Yeah," nodded Billy, staring down at the hat. "Weathered is what it is." He placed the sombrero on the bar.

"Do you still ride a horse?" Arthur asked.

"Yep," nodded Billy. "Always have. Always will."

"Does your horse have a name?"

"Nope." Billy shrugged. "I just call him horse. Whoa, horse. Giddyup, horse." He snickered. It was not a pleasant sound.

"Where do you keep the animal?"

"Out back." Billy jerked a thumb toward the rear of the tavern. "Got him hitched out back."

Arthur noticed that Billy's nails were ragged and encrusted with dirt. He wondered when Billy had last taken a shower. His hair was thick with grease and looked matted. Hadn't been combed in a long time. Arthur prided himself on his personal hygiene, and was quick to note the lack of it in others.

"May I ask why you wear a gun?"

"Protection," said Billy. "Lotta folks want my hide. Hafta defend myself. Galoot comes in, all hot an' bothered, lookin' to get a rep for killin' me, I hafta kill him first."

"Have you killed many people?"

"Sure have," said Billy. "One fer each year'a my life. I'm twenty-one, an' I've killed me twenty-one."

"That's a lot of killing."

"Yep, but it's like I said, I hafta defend myself." He patted the Colt's worn handle. "Old Judge Colt here does the job."

"Any regrets?"

"About what?"

"About shooting twenty-one people."

"Naw. They had it comin' ever'time." He put one of his soft hands on Arthur's shoulder. "Look, Art, shootin' somebody is no big deal. Let's suppose you shot Adele. That would be no big deal."

"Oh, Lordy, I'd never do a thing like that," declared Arthur. He smiled, shaking his head at the thought.

"Got an iron at home?"

"An iron?" Arthur looked onfused. "Adele has one. She irons all my clothes."

"Naw. I mean a shootin' iron. A gun. You got a gun?"

"Well . . . yes. My grandfather was a police officer in Chicago at the turn of the century. Played the stock market on the side. He invested unwisely, and died penniless. All he left behind was his old service revolver, which I inherited. I keep it in the roll-top desk in the den."

"Still work?"

"I suppose it still works," nodded Arthur. "Of course, I've never fired it. I've taken it apart from time to time to clean it."

"Good fer you!" said Billy. "Me, I do the same for this here one." He took out his Colt and flourished it. Arthur noticed that the gun seemed to have been well cared for.

"Got bullets?"

Arthur nodded. "Yes, I have a box of rounds in the same top drawer. I assume they're for grandfather's weapon, but I've never attempted to insert them in the chamber."

"Gun's no good without bullets —— just like your pecker," Billy said, snickering again. He took his sombrero from the bar, whacked it against his chaps to knock off some dust, then put the hat back on. The brim flopped loosely, giving him a lopsided look. "You been watchin' Adele?"

Arthur was embarrassed to admit that he had.

"She been spendin' yer money?"

"Well . . . she buys things, of course. Adele sure does like gloves."

"How many she got?"

"I've never counted."

"Got a dozen pair maybe?"

"Yes, easily that. I'd say more."

"Wastin' yer money, Art. Nobody needs all them gloves."

"Adele thinks otherwise," Arthur stated. "She has different colors to go with different outfits. Several pairs of white, because she says that no matter what a woman does, white gloves get dirty and must be changed. That's why, when she's wearing white, she always has a spare pair or two along in her purse. In case they get dirty and have to be changed while she's out. Then she says she needs at least two pairs each of black and gray, plus a pair of navy blue to match her good coat, and a special, long pair to wear to weddings and such. And last winter she bought a pair of red gloves, just because she liked the color. Said wearing them made her hands feel warmer when it was freezing outside."

"That's a lotta crap, if you ask me," said Billy. "Ya gotta put yer foot down, Art. Tell her flat —— no more damn gloves."

"But I can't ——"

"No buts about it," declared Billy. "Tell her flat."

Arthur frowned. "I think you're right. I'll tell her."

"You do that, Art. An' keep a sharp eye on her. Remember, ya can't ever trust a woman."

Then he was gone.

Two weeks later Arthur was back in the tavern. Tired and sweaty. He'd just put in a concrete basement over on Paseo for a woman who couldn't speak English. Big Italian woman who shouted constantly, thinking that if she just kept yelling, Arthur would understand what she was saying. He needed a cold beer.

The tavern was deserted when he'd walked in. Arthur sat down on his favorite stool at the bar, alone. When his beer arrived, and he turned to pay the bartender, there was Billy, perched on the next stool. He looked dusty.

"Hiya, Art."

"Hello, Billy." Arthur didn't know the youth's last name, and never asked. None of his business.

"You look kinda bushed," said Billy.

"I am. Exhausted, really. Pouring concrete is rough work. Maybe I'm getting too old for the job."

"How's the wife?"

"We had a bad argument last night. She wasn't speaking to me when I left the house this morning."

"Whatcha argue about?"

"I did as you said," Arthur told him. "I put my foot down about the gloves. She bought another pair last week — said she needed them to match her favorite summer dress — and so I said no more. No more damn gloves."

"That's the stuff!" Billy grinned at him. A stupid grin. Arthur had to admit that Billy actually looked retarded, but what the young man said seemed logical.

"She blew up," Arthur related. "Told me I had no right on God's green earth to dictate how many gloves she could buy. Said she got the new pair on sale, and she had a right to something special for herself if she used money she'd saved from her food budget. I told her the food budget was for *food*, and if she had enough money left over to buy gloves from it, then I needed to cut her allowance because I was obviously giving her too much. We had a bad argument."

"Bet ya felt like killin' her, right?"

"Oh, no," said Arthur, shocked at the idea. "Nothing that severe. I admit that I was very angry at her, but I guess all married couples have their squabbles. It was just a family squabble."

"Ya have many?"

"Never used to," said Arthur. "Now we seem to fight quite a lot. Just lately." He sighed. "We've been fighting a lot lately."

"Mind if I ask a real personal question?"

"No, go right ahead."

"What in tarnation keeps ya together?"

"I don't follow you."

"What's the glue that keeps you an' her stuck together?"

"Uh, well . . ." Arthur hesitated. "Adele has always been very loving toward me. Very considerate of my feelings. At least that's the way she used to be. But . . . things have changed. Don't know why, but they have."

"Got any kids?"

"No." Arthur shook his head. "No children. Always been painful to me, not being a father. I was raised in a big house full of brothers and sisters. I wanted children, but Adele didn't. She grew up an only child. Thinks children are messy, that they can't be properly controlled. Always underfoot. Better not to have them. Know what she used to say?"

"Tell me," said Billy.

"Adele used to say there are enough children in this world without us adding to the number. Not up to us to help populate the human race."

Billy grunted, saying nothing.

"Adele was quite firm in her viewpoint — how she felt about not having children. I went along with her. I didn't pursue the matter."

"So I guess you're not the boss after all," said Billy. "It's Adele who really calls the shots."

"I've never thought about it that way," said Arthur.

"She's a sly one," declared Billy. "Usin' you like a puppet. Adele pulls the strings, an' you jump."

"Oh, no, that's not the case," said Arthur. "Adele abides by my decisions."

"Sure — long as they fit what *she* wants to do." Billy spat on the tavern floor. Ugly habit. "You own any property, Art?"

"Why, yes, we do," nodded Arthur. It was cool in the tavern, in contrast to the day's searing heat, but Arthur tugged at his shirt collar. His clothes felt restricting, tight against his skin. "We own our house on Harrison," he told the youth. "Two bedrooms, with a den. I put in the basement myself. And we're buying a small summer place at the lake."

"What lake would that be?"

"Tapawingo," said Arthur. "We go there in August, when it gets really hot and humid in the city."

"Yeah, gets dang hot in New Mexico, too."

"I take a couple of weeks off each August and we drive out to the lake. To Tapawingo."

"Like to fish, Art?"

"Yes, I do, and I'm a fair hand at catching trout. My father used to take me to the Lake of the Ozarks. He taught me how to fly cast. We were very close. Died of cancer."

"I did me some fishin' once," said Billy. "Kinda bored me, tellya the truth. Me, I like action, an' ya don't get much out of fishin'."

"Well . . . to each his own," said Arthur.

A silence between them as Arthur Joergens sipped his beer.

"Want me to put a head on that?" asked the bartender.

"No, no. I'm fine," said Arthur.

"Ya believe in ghosts?" asked Billy.

"I suppose they *could* exist," said Arthur. "Never thought much about them, one way or the other."

"Me, I believe in 'em," declared the youth. "But not ever'body who kicks off becomes one. Just them with a job to do back in life."

"That's an interesting theory," said Arthur.

"Yeah," nodded Billy. "I sure as heck believe in ghosts."

Again, the conversation trailed off into silence. Finally, Arthur spoke in a low monotone.

"Adele thinks I'm spending too much on the lake house. Had to put on a new roof last year because of winter snow damage. Then the boat's engine went on the fritz and I had to buy another. An engine, that is. Plus new lumber to fix our dock. The boards were rotting. Since I'm a basement contractor, I got the lumber at discount, but it still cost a lot more than I expected. The rock chimney needs repair, too. Adele says she's having trouble with the wood cookstove in the kitchen, and next year the county's going to force us to put in a cesspool. They say the lake is being poisoned by outhouse seepage. The house is beautiful, but it was built back before the turn of the century. It's starting to fall apart, and that's a fact."

"Place means a lot to ya, huh?"

"Yes, it's my only refuge." Arthur smiled at the phrase. "I mean, I look forward to going there all year long. Just thinking about those two weeks in August makes me feel good. Nights at the lake are really peaceful, with the water lying all quiet under the moon. The air's so clear you can see every star. I really *relax* at the lake."

"But Adele, she resents it, huh?"

"I wouldn't go that far. She just thinks it costs too much, keeping it up properly, making the payments, and all."

Billy shook his head. "Adele don't want ya to have the lake house, Art. Plain as shit on a stick. She'll find a way to make ya give it up."

"That's simply not true," Arthur countered. "Adele enjoys herself out at the lake."

"Ever say so?"

"Say *what*?"

"That she enjoys bein' there."

"Well . . . not exactly. Not in so many words, but I can tell she likes it."

"Yer kiddin' yerself, pardner," said Billy. "She hates it."

That August, at the lake house, Arthur asked Adele if she was happy being there.

"Happy?" Her eyes were vague. "I suppose so."

They were sitting out on the porch, facing the water. The sun was setting and a motorboat, far out on the lake, made a tiny insect buzz. To Arthur, it was a comforting sound.

"You don't *seem* happy."

"Well, I have a lot of things to do back home," Adele said.

"This *is* our home. For the next two weeks it is."

"Not our *real* home," she said.

"It's real to me," he told her.

"You like to fish and swim," said Adele, "and I don't. So I just sit around here, waiting for you with nothing to do."

"Can't you just enjoy the beauty?" Arthur asked. "It's like a little piece of paradise out here."

"What's so wrong with Kansas City?"

"It's hot and muggy and jammed with people," Arthur said.

"There's nothing to do out here," she said.

"You used to make butterscotch ice cream," Arthur reminded her. "When we first came here, you made wonderful butterscotch ice cream."

"Uh-huh," she said listlessly.

"Why did you stop?"

"Too fattening," she said. "I have to watch my weight."

"I *loved* eating your butterscotch ice cream," said Arthur.

"Uh-huh," said Adele.

When Arthur told Billy about the ice cream the youth slapped his battered sombrero against the bar. "What'd I tell ya!" he declared. "She resents yer having the lake house. She won't even make you ice cream, even when she admits she doesn't have anything better to do."

"Adele keeps talking about how high the mortgage payments are," Arthur said, staring into his beer. "Last week, after we returned from Tapawingo, she said we should think about selling the place. Let somebody else worry about paying off the mortgage."

"There ya are," nodded Billy. "Tryin' to take away the one thing that means somethin' special to you. Oh, sure, it's just dandy her buyin' all them gloves she don't need, but when it comes ta what *you* want . . ." He let his voice trail off.

"I told her, damnit, I'd never sell the place," declared Arthur. "That there was no room for discussion."

"But ya argued about it, right?"

Arthur nodded wearily. "Yes. Another bad argument. Adele said some nasty things."

"Kill her, Art," said Billy. "It's the only thing makes any sense. Ya really hafta kill her."

"I could never do a thing like that," Arthur declared.

"Hey, it's real easy," said Billy, pulling the heavy Colt from his belt. He aimed it at the bartender. "Bang!" he said. Then he gave Arthur another stupid grin. "Easy."

That was a week ago. Early this morning, they had another bad argument. In the kitchen. Arthur and Adele kept the front rooms for holidays like Christmas and Easter, when relatives came by. The rest of the year they lived in the back of the house: kitchen, bedroom, bathroom, and den. Arthur kept his collection of antique clocks in the basement. (Adele claimed that all the ticking kept her awake at night, but she never chided him about the cost of the clocks, and he appreciated that.)

She was adamant, though, about the lake house. Adele told Arthur he would have to sell it because —— now that he was sixty, and his concrete basement business was slowing down —— they couldn't afford such a major expense anymore. Either he sold the house, or she would leave him. Simple as that. No more mortgage payments.

He yelled at her. She yelled back at him. Then Arthur walked into the den, to the roll-top desk, opened the top drawer, took out his grandfather's gun, loaded it from the box of bullets, walked back to the kitchen, and shot Adele twice in the head.

When he got to the tavern that afternoon, after deciding not to cut his throat until he'd talked to Billy, he found the place deserted. Just him and the bartender, whose name was Jake. Big man, tall and beefy, with a front tooth missing.

"Where's Billy?" asked Arthur.

"Billy who?"

"The young kid I talk to all the time when I come in here," Arthur said peevishly. "The one in the sombrero."

"I never saw you talk to nobody," said the bartender. "You always come in alone, drink a beer or two, argue with yourself, mutter a lot of stuff about your wife —— and then you leave. Period."

"What?" Arthur drew in a sharp breath. "Are you *blind*? Billy comes in here all the time. We have good talks. He understands my problems. With my wife, Adele. The problems I have with her." His voice became heated. "Billy really *understands*. He's the only one who does. He really understands."

"Look, mister," said the bartender in a patient tone, "it's like I said. You been in here alone every damn time."

"Told me he was twenty-one," murmured Arthur. "Has an old gun in his belt. Wears a dirty sombrero. Keeps his horse out back."

"*Horse*?" snorted Jake. "Nobody around here rides a horse. Maybe all them beers have gone to your head."

Arthur suddenly pressed forward against the bar, pointing. "That's him. In the photo. That's him!"

It was Billy all right. With the brim of his hat all loose and lopsided. And with those squinty eyes and that stupid grin on his face.

The bartender swung around to look at the back wall of the tavern. At a framed portrait which hung next to a big photograph of a Santa Fe Trail wagon train.

The big man smiled broadly. "You really had me goin' there for a minute," he said. "Fella in that picture hasn't been talking to you or anybody else for a mighty long time. Not since he was shot by Pat Garrett back in 1881. That's Billy the Kid."

Arthur Joergens didn't move. He continued to stare at the framed photo of the young outlaw.

"You want a beer?" asked the bartender.

This one is based on my childhood in Kansas City when, each Halloween, I would prove my bravery by entering our neighborhood's "haunted" house. Scared myself silly on these holiday excursions.

When writer/publisher Rich Chizmar asked for a Halloween short to feature in his massive anthology October Dreams, *I sat down and rapped out "Year of the Witch." I double-dare you not to enjoy it.*

Year of the Witch

I was twelve that year, and enjoying a carefree life in Kansas City with Don Miller and Jack Morgan, my two closest buddies. Don was kind of shortish and red-haired, with a ton of freckles. Jack was tall and thin as a bean stalk, with dark eyes and a great smile. We'd play Cowboys-and-Indians in Troost Park, shoot marbles "for keeps" in Don's driveway, attend the Freddy Fox matinees at the Isis Theatre, break old whiskey bottles with bricks at the corner lot, swap issues of super-hero comics (we liked Dollman the best because that little guy could really kick butt), and hide out in the treehouse we'd built in Jack's backyard. (We were hiding from an army of terrible purple aliens from Mars who were invading the Earth, starting with our neighborhood.)

In early October of that year I made my folks proud by winning first place in the big, all-class spelling bee at my grade school. I even beat out Joanne Haake from seventh grade, which nobody had ever been able to do before.

Anyhow, Don and Jack and I had special plans for Halloween. Three blocks from our neighborhood, on Paseo, there was this old vacant, boarded-up house that other kids at school swore for sure was haunted. A long time ago, the story went, a scuzzy old witch moved into the house and cast awful spells on anybody who came near her, so people stayed clear of the place. She finally got into trouble with the law by luring little kids into her house with raisin cookies and then boiling them (the kids) in a big pot for supper. After her meal, only tiny bones remained. According to the story, the cops broke in one night and shot her in the heart. After that, the house was boarded up and left to rot.

But she didn't go away. Her ghost lived upstairs on the second floor and if you crouched in the yard next door and listened hard, you could hear scary thumping noises up there. It was the witch, all right, and that was a known fact.

So that year, when I was twelve, Jack and Don and I decided to challenge the witch-ghost on Halloween. It took a lot of courage for us to do what we planned, but we'd all double-dared each other to face the ghost that night, so of course we *had* to go. You can't chicken out on a double-dare.

We didn't tell our parents or anybody else. It was our secret. For us, there wasn't going to be any going from house to house for trick-or-treats. And that night we wouldn't go to bed with stomach aches, or have our own brown paper sacks filled to the top with all kinds of candy sold at Radaker's Market. Nosiree, not *this* Halloween.

So on Halloween night there we were, all dressed in costumes our moms had bought for us. I was a pirate, Jack was a clown, and Don was a scarecrow. (Straw kept falling out of his pants.) We tossed away our unused candy sacks and trudged up the long hill to Paseo.

At last we reached the witch house. We stood close together in the weedy, abandoned front yard and stared at the place. It towered above us like a dark castle. We strained our ears, but could hear no ghost noises.

"Maybe she's sleeping," Jack said hopefully.

"Naw, ghosts don't sleep," Don said.

"How do *you* know?" Jack demanded. "You don't know nothin' about ghosts!"

"Do too!" said Don. "I read up in a book about them. The books said ghosts just float around all the time. They don't sleep."

"Yeah," I chimed in. "They just keep floating around."

"I got me a bad feeling in the pit of my stomach," said Jack. "What if she don't like us coming into her place? What if she tries to kill us?"

"The book said ghosts can't kill people," Don said authoritatively. "They're made out of stuff that's sorta like smoke. They don't have real bodies like us."

Jack shook his head. "I just got me a bad feeling," he repeated. "We shoulda gone trick-or-treating."

"Fooey!" I said. "You're chicken. You're *scared* to go inside."

"Am not!" Jack muttered, but his denial wasn't very convincing.

"Well, *I'm* not afraid," declared Don. "Let's do it."

The truth was, we were all plenty scared, but you can't go back on a double-dare.

Slowly, we moved up the weathered porch steps to the front door. It was nailed shut.

"Over here," I said, after shuffling carefully along the dark porch. "Look! This window's got a loose board. We can get in here."

So we did.

There was a full moon that night and it cast an eerie yellow light over the sheeted furniture in the living room. An oil painting of some old Civil War guy in a blue uniform was hanging over the fireplace. He had big whiskers and mean eyes.

"C'mon," I whispered. "We gotta head upstairs."

Our images rippled past us in the dusty wall mirror as we moved into the hall that faced the main stairway.

Suddenly, horribly . . . a *thump* from the second floor!

We all gasped.

"That's her!" Don's voice was quavery. "She's up there for sure."

"I'm leaving," said Jack, but I caught him firmly by his clown collar.

"No, you aren't," I said. "We're all in this together ⸺ like the Three Musketeers."

"Maybe Jack's right," said Don, losing more straw as his body shook. "Maybe this wasn't such a great idea."

"No chickening out," I said, pushing them forward. "Up we go."

We crept up the creaking stairs. *Creak* . . . step . . . *creak* . . . step . . . *creak* . . . step . . . all of us huddled close together, our eyes bugged, our hearts beating in unison like Indian tom-toms.

We were within three steps of the top when Jack yelled: "Yikes!"

The ghost had suddenly popped into sight. It was a tall pale figure in gray rags who shook a bony finger at us and shouted: "How *dare* you come into my house! Curse you! Curse the lot of you!"

That's all it took. We tumbled crazily down the stairs, reached the open window, and got the hell out of there.

*   *   *

A week later things started going bad. Don's parents received a letter from Illinois telling how Don's grandpa, on his mom's side, had fallen into the town ravine in Waukegan and died of a heart attack. That meant Don's dad had to take over the old man's lumber business, so the whole family moved to Illinois and I never saw Don again.

Bad things kept happening. An old-fashioned horse-drawn ice wagon serviced our block in those days and, just a week after Don's family left for Waukegan, Jack slipped on a pile of horse manure in the street and broke his ankle. The local doctor set it, but it didn't mend right, so Jack's parents took him to a special hospital in St. Louis to get it fixed. They never came back to K.C., and that was the end of my friendship with Jack. A new family, who only had girls, moved into Jack's house and soon after they took down his backyard treehouse. Suddenly I had no one left to help me defend our neighborhood from Martians.

Then, without warning, I couldn't spell anymore. I just lost the ability overnight. Finished dead last in the next spelling bee at school.

"It was the witch," I told my dad. "She put a curse on the three of us, and that's why I can't spell anymore."

My folks never believed in ghosts or curses so they failed to share my view of things. They blamed my spelling lapse on "stubborn laziness," which my mom was sure I'd inherited from my father's side of the family. (She never liked Dad's relatives.)

Two months later Dad brought me the morning paper and pointed out a news article. "Read that," he ordered.

The article said that the body of an unidentified woman, probably somewhere in her late eighties, had been found dead on the second floor of a vacant house on 3625 Paseo. She was a hobo who, unknown to anyone in the neighborhood, had been living in the house for approximately the last three years.

"You see," said Dad, "there's your explanation. No witch. No ghost. Just a poor lady down on her luck."

I didn't argue with him, but I was certain he was wrong. I know a witch when I see one, and that awful figure at the top of the stairs was no hobo. She was an honest-to-God witch.

Why did Don's grandpa fall into the ravine? Why did Jack slip on the horse manure? Why did I suddenly lose my ability to spell?

I knew it was the curse. The curse that old gray witch put on us. And I double-dare you to prove me wrong.

This story is an example of truth wrapped in fiction. In it, I reproduce, almost word for word, an actual conversation I had with another patient during a brief stay in the hospital. (Unlike my protagonist, I was not involved in a car crash. I was there for a totally different reason.) Only the climax of "Behind the Curtain" is fiction.

Sometimes, when strangers talk to us, it pays to listen. This was one of those times.

Behind the Curtain

The city at night. Dark. Menacing. Dangerous. I've always equated a big city with a fatal disease: it can eat you alive. Muggings in dark alleys. Stoned teenage punks ready to cut your throat for the price of a fix. Serial killers on the prowl for fresh victims. I've never been mugged, or had my throat cut, or been stalked by a serial killer —— but on one dark, rainswept Friday night the city finally nailed me.

I was driving home alone from a late movie at the local multiplex. I'm usually alone (divorced, no kids), so it was a normal night for me. The streets were slick from the storm, and my windshield wipers were barely able to keep up with the steady downrush of rain pelting the glass. Visibility was poor, so I didn't see the black Chevy Corvette until it hit me. Drunk driver. He'd run a red light and slammed broadside into my Mazda pickup. Twisted metal. Sirens. Cops.

The drunk went to jail and I woke up in the Manhattan Medical Center.

Which is where this bizarre story really begins . . .

I spent the first thirty-two hours after the accident in a coma. Everything was surreal. I'd sleep, have wild dreams I couldn't recall, then wake up to a nurse or doctor probing me with needles or adjusting electronic sensors.

Finally, on the morning of the second day, I came out of it, clear-minded and wide awake. "How am I doing?" I asked the nurse, who had a plain honest face and very direct eyes.

"How do you *think* you're doing?" she countered.

Aside from a few large bruises and a bandaged cut on my forehead, I seemed to be unhurt. The Mazda's airbag had saved my life.

"I feel okay," I told the nurse. "No pain." I flexed my arms and legs. "No broken bones. So why am I still here?"

"You're under observation until the results of the final tests come in," she said. "You could still have internal injuries."

"But I feel all right," I said.

"The doctors have to make certain," she said. Her hospital name tag read ANNA. "Maybe you'll be able to leave later today," she added, as she took my temperature. "Your car is a total wreck. You're lucky to be alive."

I nodded.

"Just relax. Need anything, press the call button."

"Thanks, Anna," I said.

She exited through the hanging blue linen curtain that circled my bed.

"She's right, Buddy Boy. What that nurse said about you being lucky."

The voice came from a patient in the adjoining bed, who was hidden behind the blue curtain. A male voice. Probably late twenties, early thirties. But not happy. A sad voice.

"Me, I *never* been lucky," the man said. "All my life, I've never had no luck. The early days, when Ma left me on my uncle's farm, those days were okay. My Uncle Ned was real good to me. Treated me like a blood son. But I got itchy feet when I was sixteen. Lit out for the bright lights. Wanted to be a big city boy, and that's where all my bad luck started. Joined a street gang. Stole hubcaps and radios. Got in trouble with the law. I shoulda stayed on the farm with Uncle Ned."

"What about your mother? Didn't she ——"

"Crap on my mother!" The voice was angry, laced with a cold hatred. "After she ditched me, dumped me on Uncle Ned, I never saw her again. She's probably dead by now. Who cares? She was a worthless bitch."

"And your father?"

"Never knew my old man. Ma said he was a bum with a hard-on. She met him in a bar. Ma drank like a fish."

"So what are you in here for?" I asked him.

"I got AIDS," he said. His voice took on a harder edge. "Can you friggin' *believe* it? Me, Davey Leland, with AIDS!" A pause, then a deep sigh. "It all started when this big dude broke my jaw."

Obviously, he needed to talk, so I let him. Why not listen? I had nothing better to do and he had a lot to say.

"This guy was maybe six three," said the man behind the curtain. "Two hundred fifty pounds, easy. Me, I'm just five eight. Hundred and thirty with rocks in my pocket. When he popped me, it was like getting hit by a concrete slab. Fractured my jaw. They had to wire my mouth shut. Ever try eating with your jaw wired? Everything I ate had to be put into a blender so I could suck it through a straw."

"What was the fight about?" I asked.

"I was working the ramp for Acorn Furniture," he said. "Helping unload stuff from the big rigs that rolled in. I was strong back then . . . strong for my size, anyway. Strong shoulders, strong arms. Not like I am now." I heard him sigh heavily. "Anyhow, this guy —— name of Eddy Freez —— he was the shift foreman and we didn't get along. Never liked me from the day I signed on. So he kept saying I wasn't working fast enough, that I was dogging it. And that made me sore, because the truth is, I was busting my butt on that ramp."

"And what he said to you —— *that* started the fight?"

"Yeah, if you can call it a fight. I told Eddie he was full of shit, and bang! He popped me one on the jaw, and I went down like cut timber. Hit my head on the deck. Broke my jaw. And that was the start of the damn AIDS."

"What has a broken jaw to do with AIDS?" I asked.

"Well, first I got me a case of double pneumonia in the hospital, where they wired my jaw. Took me a while to get over the pneumonia. After I left, I looked up Eddy and hit him from behind with an iron pipe." He chuckled. "Gave him a nice concussion. Cops came along and threw me into the slammer. For aggravated assault."

"I see."

"Jail was a real bummer. I got raped by this other dude —— in for armed robbery —— and he gave me AIDS. See, the drugs they gave me for the lousy pneumonia had blown my immune system all to hell. Which is why I got the AIDS. Later, I started losing weight, and some bad-ass, freaky sores were spreading around my body, so I went to the hospital again and they said I had full-blown AIDS."

"Tough break," I said.

"It was my lousy luck," he said. "It's like all my life I been cursed. Once I got the bad word, I thought of offing myself, but I just didn't have the guts."

"Suicide isn't the answer," I said.

"Hell it isn't! Who's kidding who? I'm dying. Only thirty-four and I'm dying. Damnit, I'm still young!" His voice was strident. "I should have maybe forty or fifty years ahead of me. But not now. Not with AIDS. I'm on the road out."

"That's a pretty grim way to look at it," I said. "You should fight it. See yourself beating this thing."

"Easy for you to talk," he snapped back at me. "You bend up your car and walk out clean, while I *die* in here."

"I'm sorry."

"Don't be. I don't need people being sorry for me." He stopped to cough. The sound was weak, like his body was all used up. "It wouldn't be that bad if it wasn't for Amy."

"Who's Amy?"

"My lady. We been together for a few years. When I got the news about the AIDS, I quit sleeping with her. The docs say you can use protection, but I didn't want to risk passing it on to her. So we just quit having sex."

"Did you tell her why?"

"No. Tried to, but I was chicken. Guess I was ashamed. When I stopped screwing her, she thought I didn't love her anymore. She took a powder. Left me flat." He coughed again. "I was wrong. I should of trusted Amy, told her the truth. She would of stuck with me. Letting her go was a big mistake."

"At least you see that now," I said.

"Hell, now I see a lot of things. When you're dying . . . it makes you think." He paused. "After Amy left, I got so weak I couldn't take care of myself any more. So here I am, in the frigging hospital, waiting to die."

"There's a lot of research being done on AIDS," I said. "Plenty of people working on it. They could find a cure any day." I spoke forcefully. "Use the power of your mind. Imagine all of your infected cells healing, one by one, and see the AIDS leaving your body. Miracles can happen."

"Not to *me* they can't," he shot back. "Not with my lousy luck."

Before I could say anything else the nurse came back, ducking through the blue curtain with a smile on her face.

"Good news," she said. "No internal problems." She handed me a release form signed by a doctor. "You can get dressed now; you're free to go. They'll check you out at the front desk and call you a cab so you can get home."

I thanked her, got out of bed, and put on my clothes. Then I decided to offer one last bit of encouragement to the poor guy in the next bed. Grasping the edge of the curtain, I pulled it aside.

The bed was empty. Mattress rolled up over the metal frame. No sheets or pillows.

"Nurse!" My voice was shaky.

Anna came through the curtain. "Yes?"

"I don't understand . . . in that bed . . . I was just talking to the man in that bed, but . . . he's gone. How could that be?"

"You've been in a bad accident," she told me. "It was traumatic, and your brain may take a while to completely clear. Hearing voices is not uncommon in your situation."

"But this was *real*," I protested. "The man was real. He told me his name was Davey."

Anna frowned. "That's odd," she said. "There *was* a patient in that bed named David, but he died a week ago . . ."

I stared at her.

". . . of AIDS."

On a lighter note, this story is a joyful reflection of my boyhood passion for comic book superheroes, extending back to my early teens in Kansas City when I avidly collected Batman, Captain America, Sandman, the Human Torch, Hawkman, and the Flash, along with dozens of others.

"The Clown's Daughter" is my homage to Batman and, in tone and style, it's straight out of a comic book. I make no apologies for its wild plot and lurid dialogue. (On a more subtle level, it's also a tragic love story!)

I'm sure that young Billy Nolan, back in Kansas City, would have loved this one. Therefore, I dedicate "The Clown's Daughter" to him.

The Clown's Daughter

From Nightboy's Casebook:

It was a solo night job.

Nightman had gone to Washington in his public persona as Brad Brockton to deliver a lecture on economic affairs at a business convention, and had asked me to stay here in town. My job was nailing the Tomcat, a really sharp jewel thief who'd been hitting all the big west side mansions in the hours past midnight. One by one, he'd been cleaning them out, and his loot amounted to millions. The insurance companies and a lot of very angry citizens were demanding his arrest, but the police had never been able to catch sight of him, let alone arrest him. Nabbing this wily fellow, with Nightman gone, was my responsibility.

"As you know, Dick, a prowling cat tends to follow a prescribed route," Brad had reminded me. "So all we have to do, in order to figure where our Tomcat will prowl next, is to counter-triangulate the area of his robberies, feed in the fixed coordinates of his probable strike area, and we'll have it narrowed to a one-block target."

When Nightman pulls off stuff like this he reminds me of Sherlock Holmes —— but ole Sherlock never had a directional computer to work with. Ours produced a one-block-area readout, mansion to mansion, so all we had to do was set up a stakeout in that area and wait for the Tomcat to show.

Then Brad got word from Washington and I was left to do the job alone.

"Up to you to nail this Tomcat's tail to the fence," Brad told me.

"Don't worry, I'll make him yowl," I promised.

So here I was on my solo night job. I'd come in the Nightmobile, but had sent it back to the Nightcave. Didn't want the Tomcat to spot it. The directional computer took it back with no problem, like sending a smart horse back to the stable.

I was on the hunt, hugging the tree shadows along Forest, using the Nightscope to scan the buildings for possible Tomcat activity. A full spring moon rode above the city, painting roofs and sidewalks with glimmering silver. A lovely night for action.

It was good to be out here on the hunt instead of being stuck in Washington the way Nightman was. Despite all the years of crook-chasing, the thrill of the hunt hadn't diminished. My blood raced and my body was on alert, every muscle tensed and ready for combat. For a true crimefighter, what else was there to live for?

That was when I saw him —— the Tomcat —— clawing his way up a vine toward the roof of a lightless mansion, a big Victorian structure set well back from the street and almost buried in trees.

I muttered, "Gotcha!" Adjusting my cape and mask, I headed for the mansion's black iron fence. I was up and over, sprinting for the tall side of the house, riding ahead of me like a silver iceberg under the moon. I glided over the grass, shadow-quick, without a sound. The Tomcat had no idea I was closing in on him.

I scrambled up the roof, reaching it just in time to spot Mr. Tomcat crouched next to a skylight, trying to jimmy the lock with a crowbar. He was a tall stringbean of a guy, all in black, sporting a stove-pipe hat and leather gloves, and he had a sharp, beaked profile. Apparently he figured nobody was home since he sure wasn't trying to be subtle about getting inside.

I padded across the roof, grinning, sure of my game. Bagging this cat was going to be a cinch.

Wrong. When I was just two feet away from him the Tomcat whipped up his head, let out a venomous hiss, and lunged at me with the crowbar. Which wouldn't have given me any trouble if my right foot hadn't snagged on a loose shingle, throwing me off-balance.

The Tomcat's crowbar slammed me across the chest, and I went crashing, head first, through the glass skylight. I felt myself falling through space. Then a big smash —— and darkness.

Total darkness.

What I saw next was a delicate white face floating above me, the face of a beautiful young woman with round, dark, startled eyes, like the eyes of a fawn in the forest.

"Hello," she said, in a voice as soft as her eyes. "Does your body flesh hurt?"

An odd question. "My . . . body flesh?" Things were coming into focus around me. I was in a large bedroom, hers most likely, since it was all pink and flouncy. The young lady was also in pink, wearing the kind of wide-skirted lacy Victorian dress you'd see at a costume ball.

I tried to sit up. "Ouch," I groaned, clutching my side. "It *does* hurt!"

"That's because you have ribs," she said, "and my friends think you broke one when you fell through the skylight. They put a bandage on you."

Which is when I realized I was wearing white silk pajamas. My cape and mask and other clothes were gone. This was serious, since no one in the city was ever supposed to see Nightboy without his mask. Nightman was going to be plenty sore at me for this. Not to mention for losing the Tomcat.

"Who are you?" I asked.

"Sue Ellen," she said softly. She made the name sound like music.

"Sue Ellen who?"

She flushed. "I don't have a last name. Sometimes I don't even feel like a real person. I mean, real people have last names —— and Father has never told me what mine is."

"It would be the same as his," I pointed out.

"But I don't know that either. I just call him Father." She blinked at me. What's *your* name?"

"I . . . I'm not authorized to reveal my true identity."

Her eyes were wide. "Are you with what they call the FBI?"

"No. But I *do* fight crime."

"Is that why you were wearing a mask?" She had long blonde hair framing the oval of her face; the moonlight from the window made it shine like a halo.

I adjusted the pillow, sitting up straight. "Haven't you seen my picture in the papers?"

"Oh, I don't ever see newspapers. Or magazines either. Father won't allow them in the house."

She'd caught me in full costume —— and Nightboy had been on TV plenty of times. "You must have seen me on television."

"We don't have any television," she said. Then she smiled for the first time. Her face was radiant and her skin glowed, as if lit from within. I was stunned at her pale beauty.

Our surreal conversation was going nowhere. It was time to end it. "I must leave now," I told her. "How long have I been here?"

"About ten hours. But you can't leave. Nobody ever leaves this house but Father. And he's away now. Far, far away."

"No, really," I insisted. "I must go. Just get me the clothes I had on when you found me."

She shook her head. "I want you to stay here with me. You're the first flesh person I've ever known, except for Father."

"Look, Sue Ellen," I said, sliding my legs over the edge of the bed. "I certainly appreciate what you've done for me, fixing up my rib and all, but I *must* leave now." I stood up. "Even if I have to walk out of here in a pair of silk pajamas."

"Gork will stop you," she declared. "I told him that you should stay." And she snapped her fingers.

A huge seven-foot figure appeared in the bedroom door. He had a flat gray face and eyes without pupils, and wore a seamless gray uniform. He looked strong —— but I was sure I could handle him. I'd handled bigger guys.

"Sorry," I said, "but I'll have to clobber your pal if he gets in my way. Tell him to move back from the door."

"Gork does what I ask. He won't allow you to leave."

I was in no mood to argue the point. I lowered my head and charged. Wow! Hitting him was like slamming into a brick wall. And trying to punch him was hopeless. My blows had no effect. They just bounced off him.

Then Gork put his hands on me. Like two steel meathooks.

"Don't hurt him, Gork," said the girl. "Just put him back in bed."

The big lug did that. He tucked me in like a two-year-old. All without a change of expression.

"You can go now," Sue Ellen told him.

He shambled out.

"He's not human, is he?"

"Of course not," she replied. "No one in this house is human, except for me. And Father, when he's home."

I shifted in the bed to ease the twinge of pain from my bandaged rib. "What *is* Gork?"

"He's made of durrilium. That's a special metal Father invented. From the time I was very young Father's been interested in the science of robotics. He began to experiment with metal people. Robots. That's what Gork is —— and he's identical to a dozen others Father has constructed to take care of me. But Gork is the only one I really like."

"How can you tell him apart from the others?'

She giggled like a schoolgirl. "He has a little dent on the left side of his head. That's how I tell." She leaned very close to me. "May I touch your face?"

"Uh . . . sure, I guess so."

Sue Ellen reached out with tentative fingers to explore the planes of my face.

"It's warm, just like mine. The robots have cold faces, like wet fish." She gave me one of her radiant smiles. "I'm a flesh person, too. Just like you are."

The situation was totally wacko; I couldn't figure it out.

"I need to communicate with a friend in Washington," I told her. "Could I use your phone?"

"We don't have any phones," she told me. "Father says they'd just distract me, that I might use them to call other flesh people." She giggled again. "But that's silly, because I don't know any —— except you, and you're right here in the house. I don't have to phone you."

I looked at her intently. "Is it true . . . that I'm the first boy you've ever met?"

"I said so, and I never lie."

"Where did you go to school?"

"Here. In this house. The robots taught me."

"You mean that you've never been to an outside school?"

"I've never been to an outside anything," she declared. "I've always been here, in Father's house. For my whole life."

I was shocked. "Are you saying that your father has kept you prisoner?"

"Prisoner?" She frowned. "No, I'm not a prisoner. I'm Daddy's girl. This is where he brought me as a tiny baby after Mother died giving me a flesh life."

"Didn't you ever feel like running away?"

"Why would I? Everything I need is here. And Father truly loves me. He told me I was too precious to have the outside world 'pollute' me. That's the word he used."

"Did you get to play with other children?"

"Oh no, not flesh children. Father had robot children made for me to play with. I never saw any real ones. So . . ." She smiled. "I just grew up with metal people. I've even learned to make robots myself now. I'm very good at it. When Gork got one of his arms crushed I made him a new one!"

I stared at her. "Who *is* your father?" Anger boiled up inside me for what this man had done to his daughter.

"As I've told you, I don't know his name. He's just Father."

"You must have a picture of him. I want to see his face."

"Father doesn't like pictures. There aren't any."

"What does he do for a living? How did he earn the money for all this?"

"He works in the circus. As a clown. I guess he always has. That's where he is right now, with a circus way off in Washington, the D.C. place. Far, far away."

"That's where my friend is," I told her. "The one I need to contact."

She nodded. "Maybe Father will see your friend there."

Something was very wrong. I sensed it —— a rushing chill along my spine, a prickly feeling that this crazy father of hers was a threat to Nightman. I had no evidence to back it up, just a gut feeling.

I *had* to find out what was happening in Washington.

"When you found me," I said urgently to Sue Ellen, "after I fell through the skylight . . . I was wearing a wrist chron."

"I remember," she nodded. "It was funny looking. The robots took it away with your other clothing."

"I *need* it, Sue Ellen. Badly!"

"All right, I'll have Gork fetch it."

And she did. Two minutes later the big guy handed me the wrist chron, then shambled out again.

Among its other features, the device functioned as a mini-TV. I punched in the coordinates for Washington and a worried-looking newscaster flashed to life on the tiny screen. He was speaking with gravity: ". . . and the shocking attempt on the President's life was averted by the caped crimebuster known known as Nightman who threw himself in the path of the killer clown, managing to wrest a deadly dart-weapon from his grasp. Had just *one* of the lethal venom-coated darts struck the President he would have expired instantly. In the subsequent melee the killer escaped, but local police are . . ."

I switched it off. Sue Ellen looked stunned.

"That clown . . . on the newscast," she said slowly. "They only showed him from the back, but I'm *sure* it was Father."

"Then your father attempted to assassinate the President of the United States."

"I'm sorry," murmured Sue Ellen softly, head down. "That's very wrong, isn't it?"

"Very," I said.

"I wonder why he'd *do* a thing like that," the girl said. "But then, he's really not a very nice man. I have tried to return his love, but I just can't. Gork has been much kinder to me than Father."

I was beginning to suspect a terrible truth about Sue Ellen's father. But I needed to have her verify it.

"Describe him to me. What does your father look like?"

"If you mean his features, I'm not sure. He's always in clown makeup. I've never seen him without it."

"What about his *hair*? What color is it?" My voice was intense.

"It's purple," she said. "An ugly purple color —— and he always wears red on his lips."

I was right. Sue Ellen's father was none other than our old enemy, the Clown. The King of Crime.

"Surprise!" A familiar voice rasped from the doorway.

I looked up and he was standing there, with a demonic smile distorting that dead-white face, the face of total evil.

"So it's *you*," I said, glaring at him.

Sue Ellen drew back, as if from a poisonous snake. The Clown ignored her, his eyes blazing into mine.

"Ahhh," he rasped, "Dick Peyton. The known friend of Nightman."

"And proud of it," I said tightly.

"Well, it seems that your dark friend foiled me yet again," said the Clown. "But I intend to make him pay for what he did to me in Washington."

We were face to face at the bed. His breath was foul, like rotted meat. "You're big at making empty threats," I told him. "But when the chips are down you always lose. Nightman and Nightboy have defeated you time and again — and one of these days they'll put you permanently out of business."

"Never! My brain far surpasses that of normal men."

"At least we both agree on that," I said. "You're anything but normal."

During this entire exchange, from the moment her father had appeared in the room, Sue Ellen had been silent, intent on the play of heated words between us. Now she spoke firmly, her small chin raised in defiance.

"Father, you are being very unkind. This is my first flesh friend, and I don't like the mean way you've been talking to him. I think you should apologize."

"Apologize!" The Clown's laugh was bitter. "I'll apologize to no friend of Nightman! That caped fool has been a plague in my life, continually thwarting my plans."

"If you have acted as wickedly in the past as you did in Washington," declared the girl, "then your plans *should* have been thwarted."

The Clown glared at her. "What do you know of good or evil . . . of profit and gain . . . of besting authority . . . of the sheer power and joy in being a master of crime?"

"I know it's nothing to be proud of," she snapped. "From what I've learned here today, I would say you belong in jail."

"If Nightman were here you'd see how he'd deal with your father," I told Sue Ellen. "He'd put him out of action fast enough."

"Oh, he'll be here," smiled the Clown. "I'll see to that. I'll lead him to this very house." A fiendish cackle. "I don't know what delicious twist of fate delivered you into my hands, Dick Peyton, but I shall make good use of you. When Nightman arrives he shall find his young society friend awaiting him . . ." Another fiendish cackle. ". . . with a cut throat!"

And he held up a long-bladed knife. Light trembled along the razored edge.

"And you, my dear daughter," he said, turning to Sue Ellen, "shall slit his throat neatly from ear to ear. Then we'll leave him for his night friend to find." His eyes glowed hotly, and his smile was hellish. "It will be a true delight, watching Nightman's shock when he encounters Peyton's corpse!"

"How utterly *horrible!*" exclaimed Sue Ellen. "You're a monster! You can never make me do such a . . ."

Her voice faltered. The Clown was standing close to her, staring into her eyes. His tone was soft and commanding: "You shall obey your father. You will do exactly as I command. You are Daddy's girl . . . Daddy's girl . . . Daddy's girl . . ." And his eyes burned like hot coals in the dead white of his face.

"I . . . am . . . Daddy's . . . girl," Sue Ellen murmured in a drugged voice. Her hands fell to her sides; she was blank-eyed and rigid, a victim of his dark hypnotic power.

That's when I jumped him, leaping from the bed to drive my right fist into the white of that grinning face, but before I could strike a second blow I was jerked violently backward. Two gray-clad house robots held my arms in a literal grip of steel. I was helpless.

"Don't try to resist them," said the Clown. "They are far more powerful than any human." The crime king reached into his striped coat and brought out a small jelled capsule. "When she uses the knife on you," he said, "you won't feel a thing."

And he popped the capsule under my nose. A wave of sleep-gas spun me into darkness.

From Nightman's Casebook

I had just returned from Washington, more enraged than ever at the Clown. His vicious attempt on the President's life was yet another act of total madness. I was grimly determined to run him to ground.

When no word from Dick awaited me upon my return I became concerned as to his whereabouts. Cruising the west side in the Nightmobile, I scanned each section of the street, but found no sign of him. Where could he be?

Then, abruptly, the Clown's grinning face appeared on the side of a building directly ahead of me. The image was being beamed down from the inked sky above me, from the Clowncopter. I peered upward to see him at the controls as he hovered there with his mocking devil's smile. He fired a burst from his laser cannon, blasting a large crater in the road; I veered sharply left to avoid it. (More work for the street deparment.)

I quick-punched the copter-conversion panel and a gyro blade unfolded from the Nightmobile like a dark flower, whisking me skyward in pursuit of my old enemy.

It was a short chase. The Clown brought his machine down on the roof of an ancient Victorian house on Forest Avenue, and I followed, exiting the Nightcopter to scamper after him through an open roof door.

The house was silent and lightless. The Clown was hiding somewhere inside this gloomed structure, and I was determined to root him out. The silence seemed to deepen as I moved through the darkness, checking each room, then gliding down the main staircase.

I padded softly along a dimly-lit hallway toward an open door just ahead. This turned out to be the main ballroom, immense and ornate, moonlight tinting its polished oak floor.

Then I gasped. A figure was spread-eagled on a table in the middle of the cavernous chamber. I moved closer . . . and fell back in agonized shock. It was Dick! Unmasked, and wearing white silk pajamas spattered with blood. His head was twisted at a sharp angle — and his throat had been cut from ear to ear!

I staggered back as a searing white cone of light stabbed suddenly down from the ceiling. An amplified wave of ghoulish laughter filled the room. The Clown's laughter: Taunting, demonic, triumphant.

"He's dead, Nightman. Your meddlesome little friend, Dick Peyton, is no more."

"Damn you, Clown, I'll tear you apart for this!" In a red rage, fists doubled, I swung around, raking the darkness for a glimpse of him. My fingers itched to close on his windpipe; I wanted to choke the life out of his foul body, to see his eyes bug and his tongue protrude from his swollen red lips . . .

"No use looking around for me," boomed the voice. "I'm in my second-floor study, enjoying this splendid show on my monitor screen."

I looked upward. A shielded scanner rotated with my movements, providing the Clown with the image of my agony. Then the tall entrance door to the ballroom banged shut like an exploding cannon. I heard an outside lock click into place.

"You're trapped, Nightman!" the Clown informed me. "There's no way out. The door is steel-ribbed and the walls are reinforced."

"What's your game, Clown?"

"Simple. I intend to leave you with your dear friend. No food. No water. Just you and a slowly-rotting corpse." Fiendish cackling.

"I shall savor your death, Nightman, like a vintage wine. A *delightful* show!"

Again, the cackle of demonic laughter from the wall speaker.

I sprinted for the door, throwing my full weight against it, but it held fast. The Clown was right; I was trapped like a fly in a web.

I slumped to the floor, the full horror of Dick's death assaulting me. Tears ran down my cheeks. Indeed, it seemed the Clown would have his show.

Then, just beyond the view range of the scanner, from the deep corner shadow, I saw a small white hand beckoning me.

I didn't want to alert the Clown, so I put on the act he was hoping for: I groaned aloud, turned in a hopeless circle, then staggered to the corner to beat both fists against the wall.

A young woman with frightened eyes was crouched there. Looking up at me, her words tumbled out in a desperate whisper: "Your friend is alive," she told me. "The figure on the table is a robot, to fool Father. He thought I was hypnotized, but I just pretended to be. Gork helped me. He's my metal friend. We modeled the robot to look like Dick Peyton. I made the face myself."

A vast sense of relief flooded through me. I leaned closer to the girl. "Who are you?"

"I'm Sue Ellen, the daughter of the man you call the Clown. He tried to force me to kill your friend, but I could never kill Dick. I *love* him!"

"Where is he now?"

"Gork carried him to the basement. He's still unconscious from Father's sleeping gas. The two of you can get away through a secret passage leading to the street."

"But how do I get out of this room?"

"There's a trapdoor in the floor behind you. It was bolted shut from below but I got it open."

"Where are you, Nightman?" The Clown's taunting voice boomed from the speaker. "Come, come, this will never do. Step back into the light or I shall be forced to send in some of my metallic companions to drag you out of that corner. And they won't be gentle. Now, do as I say. Step forward!"

Sue Ellen was gesturing to me. Her voice was urgent. "Quickly! He'll send his robots if we don't hurry."

She tugged open the trapdoor, revealing a square of pale yellow light from the basement below. A twist of sagging wooden stairs led downward.

"This way," whispered the girl. "Follow me."

I slipped through the opening, closing the trapdoor behind me, and followed her rapidly down the stairs.

From Nightboy's Casebook:

I woke up, blinking, acrid fumes in my nostrils. Nightman was leaning over me. He'd used a reviver vial from his utility pack to bring me around. "You okay, Dick?"

"Yeah . . . a little dizzy is all." I gripped his arm. "How did you get here? And where's Sue Ellen?"

The girl stepped toward me, taking my hand. Her grip was warm and strong. "Here I am." She was smiling sweetly —— my personal angel.

"I don't understand," I said. "I thought the Clown had ——"

"No time for talk," snapped Nightman. "By now the Clown knows that his daughter tricked him. He'll be sending down his killer machines." He reached out a gloved hand. "On your feet. We need to get out of here."

I stood up, a bit shaky, but otherwise fine.

Then: WHAM! The basement door crashed open.

Sue Ellen screamed: "They're here!"

A dozen giant, gray-faced robots poured through the door, straight at us.

"This should slow them down," shouted Nightman, tossing a nitropellet at the advancing tinmen. They fell back as the pellet exploded into orange fire.

"This way!" cried Sue Ellen, taking the lead down a narrow, rock-walled tunnel. I made out a faint glow from the far end.

"That's the street light from the corner of Forest and Troost," Sue Ellen told us. "We're almost out."

But "almost" wasn't good enough. The robots were gaining fast. In scant seconds they'd catch us for sure.

"*Do* something, Nightman," I pleaded, "or we're goners."

The caped crimebuster spun around and tossed back another nitropellet. WHOOM! The whole tunnel roof caved in behind us, burying the tin guys in rocks and mud.

Then we were outside on the street. Sue Ellen stepped forward. "Go quickly," she urged.

I hesitated. "But we're taking you along."

"Oh no, you're not!" rasped an oily voice —— and the Clown leaped toward us, a gleaming .357 Magnum in his gloved hand.

Nightman didn't say a word. It was time for action, not talk. He ducked under the Clown's gun arm to deliver a smashing blow to the fiend's pointed chin.

The Clown staggered back, dropping the Magnum. Then he pressed a button on his chest —— and the Clowncopter, blades whirling, dropped to the pavement between us like a giant cat. Instantly, the Clown hopped aboard, roaring the chopper skyward. It whipsawed away over the trees.

My voice was intense: "Can we catch him in the Nightcopter?"

"Afraid not," sighed Nightman. "I left it on the roof. No doubt our purple-haired friend disabled it. He wouldn't risk a pursuit."

"He'll show up again, and when he does we'll be ready for him," I said.

We turned to Sue Ellen. She had withdrawn back into the tunnel, and peered at us from the darkness.

"Come on, Sue Ellen," I said, "we have to go."

She shook her head. "No, I can't."

I moved quickly to her. "But why *not*? You've said that you love me."

"I do," she declared. "I really truly do. But . . ."

I stopped her words with my lips.

"A kiss!" she gasped in delight. "I've never had one before."

"I want you with me," I told her. "To share my life. I've never met a girl like you. I want to marry you."

Tears ran from her eyes. "Oh, that sounds so wonderful. But it can't happen. Because . . ."

"Because why?"

She stepped forward into the light from the street lamp. "Because I'm dying."

She was pale, and her hands trembled. A crimson thread of blood ran from the corner of her mouth, staining the white lace at her throat.

"I . . . I don't . . ." I groped for words.

"Father made certain that I'd never be able to go out into the world," she said softly. "He gave me . . . an injection. So long as I stayed indoors, in the house, I was all right. But the injection altered the chemistry of my body. I can't survive on the outside. My coming out here to the street . . . it set off a kind of chain reaction inside my body, and nothing can save me now." Her eyes glimmered with tears. "Not even your love."

"But . . . there must be an antidote," I gasped.

"No . . . too late . . ." She was moaning out the words. "Father made sure that I'd always be . . . Daddy's girl."

She reached out slowly, to clasp my hand. Her fingers were already turning cold. "Goodbye, Dick Peyton," she whispered. "Goodbye, my love."

And she was gone.

I lowered her body gently to the ground.

Nightman gripped my shoulder. "Dick, I . . . I'm sorry."

I'd lost the sweetest girl I'd ever known.

I loved her. Very much.

And I always will.

Many years ago, long before I began to sell my fiction as a professional, I wrote a very bad story I called "Poetic Justice." Naturally, I never submitted it anywhere. However, I have always liked the title — which is why I have used it here.

This story concerns the violence often encountered in today's young people. Restless, frustrated, looking for a rush, they are willing to ignore the dire consequences that result from their impuslive actions.

I don't expect you to like any of the characters I've created in "Poetic Justice," but perhaps you will understand them.

Poetic Justice

"Let's kill someone tonight," said Amber.

They were sitting in Amber's Honda (it was her brother's but he was away in college), on a rural side road that was flanked by deep Missouri woods. Both seventeen. In their senior year at high school. Amber and Michelle. It was midnight.

"That's sick," said Michelle. "Trash talk. Talking like that is sick."

"Well . . . we could kill Mike Rickard and get away with it. No way to connect him getting dead with us. Nobody would ever know."

"Why Mike?"

"He's an asshole. You said so yourself after the Vice Versa last month."

"So he's an asshole. So are most guys. Doesn't mean he deserves to be murdered."

"All assholes deserve to be murdered," said Amber. She smiled, and the Glo-gloss on her lips sparkled in the moonlight.

"You're really spooky sometimes," said Michelle. "All of a sudden you'll go Goth on me, and then I just never know what you're going to do."

"That's why we hang together. You get off watching me do wild stuff. It *excites* you, and God knows we *need* some excitement in this town."

"Not true. I hang with you because I like to borrow your clothes." She smiled. "Besides, everybody else I know besides you is boring."

"I told you! You hang with me because I'm never boring. Right?"

Michelle grinned. "Okay, so you're never boring. But you scare me sometimes."

"Like?"

"Like when you called that police officer a son of a bitch for giving us the speeding ticket."

"*Me*, not us," said Amber. "I got the friggin' ticket, all by myself. And he *was* a son of a bitch."

"You can't say stuff like that to the police."

"But I did. And I got away with it. Cops expect to be insulted when they give you a ticket."

"He could've arrested you, if he wanted."

"For what? I signed his fucking ticket."

"You're wild, Amber."

"The only way, dude . . . the *wild* way." She lowered her chin and stared into Michelle's eyes. "What about it? How 'bout we kill Mike Rickard?"

"Quit shining me on."

"I'm serious!" She smiled crookedly. "*Dead* serious."

"He *is* a real asshole," mused Michelle. "Dumped me for Cindy-the-boobs at the Vice Versa, and then told me he couldn't take me to the prom like he *promised* because he was going with *her*. That really pissed me off."

"You had a right. Mike needs to be put out of his misery. And we're just the two who can do it."

"How?"

"What?"

"How would we . . . *do* it?"

"Go to his house when he's asleep. Climb through that dormer window he leaves open and ——"

"How do you know he leaves a window open?"

"I hooked up with him, stupid! That's how I know!"

"In his bedroom?" Michelle's eyes were wide with amazement.

"Yeah. His parents went up to Des Moines for a funeral. Left him all alone for two whole days and nights. So we got it on."

"You never told me!"

Amber shrugged. "Didn't seem important. Didn't mean much to him . . . or me. Thinks he's God's gift. Hah! Stoners suck, big time."

Michelle's eyes darkened with anger; she had no idea that Amber and Mike had hooked up. Cindy-the-boobs *and* Amber! Her stomach spasmed. "Maybe he *does* deserve to die."

"Yeah. It'll be easy. We climb the elm tree outside his bedroom window, go inside, and do him."

"With a gun?"

"You crazy? We'd wake up the neighborhood. We use a knife." She unzipped her backpack. "*This* knife."

Amber took out a slim switchblade. Pressed the end. A long blade clicked out, glittering.

Michelle's voice was unsteady as she stared at the knife. "Have you ever . . . I mean, have you . . ."

"Used it on anyone? Yeah. Remember that weird kid in grade school? Willie Evans?"

"The one they found in the woods?"

"Yeah. The one with his throat cut. I did that."

"Why?"

"He saw me take a couple of dollars from Mrs. Parson's purse and told her. They almost kicked me outta school for that. So I did him. In the woods. With Junior here."

Amber turned the blade in the moonlight.

"Jeez!" said Michelle, softly.

"Everybody figured it was some road bum, did him in 'cause he wouldn't put out, or maybe for his money. Always carried a twenty, just to show off. I took it. Knew everyone would think the killer stole it. Got me a Hot-Bi-Babes CD — and my mom never knew. She never let me buy anything by the HBBs because they were X-rated, but I got their best CD anyway — thanks to Willie."

"You really did him?"

"Yep. Screamed to holy hell, but we were in the woods, and it *wasn't* hunting season. Nobody heard a thing."

Amber reached over and squeezed Michelle's shoulder softly.

"What about Mike?"

"If you . . . I mean, if we . . . uh, when do you think we would do it?"

"Tonight," said Amber. "His mom and dad are in St. Louis for some business thing. Mike'll be alone in the house. What time you got?"

Michelle checked her cell phone. "Twelve twenty."

"Perfecto. It'll take us maybe ten minutes to reach his place. If his lights are off, he's probably asleep."

Michelle shook her head. "I've never . . . stabbed anybody."

"It's easy," said Amber. "I'll show you how. It's *where* you stab that counts. You gotta go for the heart or the lungs."

"What if someone sees us?"

"They won't. We'll be real careful and quiet. In and out fast ⸺ and there will be one dead asshole left behind us."

Michelle's voice trembled. "I dunno . . . this is murder."

"So was what I did to that nerdy kid in the woods. And nobody ever traced it back to me. Remember American Lit? Just think of it as what Miss Lewis called 'poetic justice.' One less asshole in the world."

"Yeah. Mike *is* a real scumbag," Michelle admitted. "Probably cheated on me with lots of girls."

"Then you're game?"

"Okay," Michelle nodded. "I'm game. Let's do it."

The Rickard house stood at the end of the block on Madison ⸺ a big, white, two-story with a pool in back and a wide front porch for Missouri summer nights. It was dark and silent.

Amber and Michelle climbed the old elm tree to the slanting red-slate roof outside Mike's bedroom.

Sure enough, the window was open. It was a warm spring evening. There was no screen on the window, and it crossed Amber's mind that Mike used it as a way to get out of the house so his parents wouldn't know he was gone.

They slipped easily over the window sill. Amber pulled the switchblade from the back pocket of her Levi's and gently touched the button that opened it. She held it tightly in her right hand. The two stepped to the bed.

It was empty.

"He's not here!" whispered Michelle.

"I can see that, stupid," said Amber softly. Her eyes flashed. "Maybe he's in the john."

"If he's awake . . . he won't be so easy to kill."

"Leave that to me," said Amber. She moved silently across the room. "Once I've stabbed him, I'll hand over the knife. You can finish the job."

But the bathroom was empty.

So was the rest of the house.

Every room.

Empty.

"Now what?" asked Michelle.

"Now nothing," said Amber. "We'll do him some other time. Could be he went out tonight." She clicked the blade shut and put the weapon in her back pocket.

"Shit," she said.

When they got back to the Honda Mike was lying across the back seat.

His throat was cut.

"Jeez!" said Michelle. "Somebody else did him."

"Yeah," nodded Amber. "Assholes have lots of enemies. Maybe another girl he hooked up with. Maybe even Cindy-the-boobs."

"Somebody did it while we were inside his house."

"Yeah," murmured Amber.

"What're we going to do?" asked Michelle.

"We can't take him back into the house. His blood's all over the back seat of my car."

"Then . . . what?" Michelle's voice trembled with fear.

"We can take him into the woods and sink the Honda in the lake," said Amber.

"But when they find it — with Mike dead inside . . . I mean, it's your brother's car. It couldn't be your brother because he's away at college, so won't they think you did it?"

Amber shook her head. "Nobody's going to go fishing for a car in Barker Lake. At least, not for a while. And if they find it, I'll just say that whoever killed Mike stole my brother's car."

"You think the police will believe you?"

"Why not? First thing tomorrow morning I'll go down and report the Honda stolen. There'll be nothing to connect me to Mike."

"I guess you're right."

Amber slid behind the wheel and started the engine. "The only thing that pisses me off," she said, "is that I didn't get the chance to cut his throat."

They took the rough fire road inside the woods beyond town. When they reached Barker Lake, Amber drove out onto the abandoned boat dock. The air was full of the throbbing hum of insects mating in the tall wildgrass. A thin night mist hovered over the lake, and the darkness was like draped velvet around them.

Amber put the Honda in neutral and they got out. "Help me push," she said.

Together, they rolled the Honda off the edge of the dock, into the black water. The car splashed briefly, then sank slowly in a froth of bubbles.

"Well, one less asshole in the world," said Amber.

"Not quite," said a familiar voice behind them. Mike was there, his clothes dripping, a .38 in his hand. "I got out and swam under the dock," he said.

Michelle stared at his throat. Only a faint trace of red still remained on the skin of his neck.

"Ketchup," he said. "But it sure as hell fooled you, right?"

"Sure as hell did," said Amber.

He glared at her. "You're some cold-hearted bitch, Amber."

"And you're a cold-hearted bastard."

He chuckled. "Birds of a feather."

Michelle was trembling with fear, her eyes locked on the .38 in Mike's hand. "What . . . what are you going to do?"

"First thing, kill Amber," said Mike.

Amber snarled. "That gun will never fire," she said. "Not after being in the lake."

"Sure it will," he said, pulling the trigger. The gun fired.

Three times. Amber toppled down to the warped wooden planks of the dock. She twitched. Then her eyes glazed over and there was no further movement.

Screaming, Michelle ran towards the shore end of the dock. She made it into the woods, but Mike caught her easily when she stumbled over a tree root.

"You were ready to help her kill me," he said, holding the .38 on her.

"How . . . how did you find out?"

"Easy. UHF cell phone transmitter. Every word you said in her car, so long as the cell phone was there, transmitted to me. It was just like sitting there, with both of you, in the Honda."

"I didn't want anything to do with this," protested Michelle. "It was all her idea."

"I never heard you say no."

"I was afraid . . . of what she might do to me if I didn't agree to go along."

"Bullshit!" Mike snapped. "You wanted to kick ass." He grinned. "And now you're going to pay for it. Biggest kick of all. You're going to off yourself."

"No! I won't!"

"Hey, I'll do it for you. Remember biology, and how Mr. Creech told us about when he was on his college karate team. I just press that spot below your ear and you'll black out. Then I wipe my prints off the gun and put it in your hand. Then I put the gun barrel to your head, press my finger over yours on the trigger and . . . Bang! All done. Your finger on the trigger, and powder burns on your hand. After you shot Amber, you went into a panic and killed yourself. Murder and suicide. Foolproof."

As he talked, Michelle's right hand closed around a jagged rock buried in the forest loam. As Mike reached for her, she struck at him with the full force of her body. The rock smashed against Mike's skull. He looked at her in shocked surprise for a split-second, then slumped to the forest floor. Unconscious.

Michelle nodded to herself. Mike was right. His plan *was* foolproof. She wiped her prints from the gun, placed the .38 in his hand, and put the barrel to his head, her finger over his on the trigger.

"Bang," she said.

The next day it was on the TV news. Two bodies found near Barker Lake. Amber Stevens shot to death by her friend (and rumored boyfriend), Mike Rickard, who police said had run in panic into the woods, where he took his own life. A gash on his skull testified to the lovers' death struggle.

A teenage romance turned tragic.

Michelle switched off the set. She smiled. Amber *was* a murderer. And Mike *was* an asshole.

After all, it was nothing more than poetic justice.

I have taught Creative Writing at college Adult Education level, and I always tell my students to keep notebooks in which to record odd facts, possible story titles, bits of dialogue, film reviews, travel notes, dreams, plot ideas, character sketches and whatever else pops into their minds. Notebooks provide grist for the writer's mill. They are essential. Of immense value. You never know what might develop from a scribbled entry in your notebook. In one of mine, I wrote:

"She had luminous blue eyes, honey-gold skin, pouting lips, full and sensuous, and a spill of blazing red hair. Her legs, in black stretch pants, were long and coltish. She knew the effect she had on men. All she had to do was walk into a room and every male eye was on her. She was hot. The drifting scent of her perfumed body could stoke a furnace. If you were a man, and she asked, you'd kill for her. That's what started it all. She asked, and I killed. For her. I killed a man because Linda asked me to. It was just that simple."

When I wrote "Silk and Fire" I was obviously inspired by this description from my notebook. My story is built around the seductive power of a beautiful woman — all silk and fire. It is set in the 1930s.

Silk and Fire

She was a walking cliché.

How can I describe her? The kind of face and figure you see featured in shampoo and toothpaste advertisements in the newspapers, in glossy movie magazines like *Photoplay*, and in the calendars hard-working men pin up in their back storerooms, or maybe hide from their wives at home. Perfect hair, perfect eyes, perfect teeth, perfect skin, perfect lips, perfect breasts, perfect legs . . . and a sweet little bum that was beyond perfection.

She'd poured herself into a full-bosomed red silk dress, extra tight across the hips, with red stiletto heels, a skimpy little red feather hat, soft red doeskin gloves, and a red silk purse. Red and hot, like she'd just stepped out of the Ziegfeld Follies of 1938. Her flowing hair was Harlow blonde, and as alive as a star-white flame. She was beaming out a radio message, and I was receiving, loud and clear.

That's how she was that morning — all silk and fire.

Her smile could blind you, it was so dazzling. She moved like a ballet dancer, or maybe more like a jungle cat, kind of gliding across the floor of my office, comfortable, in command, enjoying her female power.

I was bug-eyed, but no doubt she was used to this reaction from the male sex. My jaw agape, sweat beads forming on my upper lip, my eyes wide in delighted shock, I didn't say anything to her.

Couldn't say anything.

She did all the talking at the start, and my first big mistake was in listening to her. But what man could have resisted such a vision?

Certainly not me. Not then. Not ever.

Oh, *now* sure. *Now* I could tell her to go take a flying jump off the Empire State. But now is now, and then was then. And never the twain shall meet.

"My name is Alicia," she said in her perfect warmed velvet voice, as she took a chair in front of my desk and crossed her perfect legs. Her silk stockings gleamed up at me, caressed by a shaft of sunlight through my office window. "Alicia Luann Sinniger." (Already I liked the "sin" part.)

I nodded, trying to compose myself, trying to look calm and professional — and not having any luck at it. A faint smile told me she didn't mind.

"I need to hire a private detective, Mr. Thornton, and I was given your name. I came right over from my apartment. I live in the Glenwood Garden Estates on Wilshire."

I nodded again, swallowing with difficulty. My throat was dry. My God, but she was gorgeous!

"I assume your fees are reasonable. I'm single, and I live on a rather slim inheritance from my late father, Timothy Baines Sinniger. Perhaps you've heard of him?"

This time I shook my head. No, I hadn't.

"He was a prominent investor. Bought commercial lots in downtown L.A., back before the boom. They're worth plenty these days, even at Depression prices." She sighed. "Unfortunately, my mother died of pneumonia when I was eight, so Pops raised me. I was his only child, and he adored me . . . treated me like a little princess." She smiled, displaying her perfect teeth. "I *should* be a very rich woman today — but, unfortunately, Pops was also a gambler."

"Cards?" I asked.

"No, horses. He lost most of his money, and all of his property, playing long shots across the board. Said it was more exciting when the odds were against him. He didn't know shit about horses."

It was something of a shock to hear her use a four-letter word. She seemed too . . . ethereal . . . too pure for such language. Of course, as I was soon to discover, she was *anything* but pure. But I couldn't see straight back then; my eyes had been blinded by silken fire.

"I hope you're not a gambling man, Mr. Thornton," she said huskily. "Or an alcoholic. My mother was an alcoholic."

"I'm neither," I said. My voice was a trifle shaky, but the words were coming out okay. "I never gamble, and I confine my drinking to a glass of wine at social events." I grinned. "I don't attend many social events."

She sniffed the air. "But you *do* smoke?"

"A pipe, from time to time, but I'm not a regular smoker. Actually, I'm a man of very few vices."

"That's good to know," she said. "I need someone who is entirely reliable."

"Who referred you to me?"

"A man at the bank where I have my account. Robert Cashman."

"Good name for a banker," I said.

"Do you know him? He seemed to suggest that you were a friend."

"I did a job for him last year. Helped him obtain some evidence in a personal situation. I wouldn't call him a friend, but it was nice he gave you my name." I leaned forward and my desk chair creaked. "Just what is it you want to hire me for?"

"Are you like other private detectives?"

"I wouldn't know. What are other private detectives like?"

"Hard and tough. They carry big automatics and drive fast cars. Like James Cagney."

"I don't think Cagney has ever played a private eye," I told her. "He *did* play a G-Man in '35." I tried not to look tough. "As for me, I'm soft and easy. I don't own a gun — and I drive a '36 Dodge that needs work. My clutch keeps slipping."

Somehow she found this amusing; her laugh was deep and throaty. "I've never hired a man with a slipping clutch."

Despite the sheer pleasure I got from drinking in her beauty I felt a tinge of frustration. When would she level with me? Why was she here? I asked if she'd mind getting to the point.

"Well . . ." She pursed her full lips and then quickly licked them with the tip of her tongue. I got a flash about kissing those lips. They'd be warm and smooth and wet and resilient . . . yielding . . . perfect. "I'm not trying to be evasive," she said. "I wanted to find out what kind of man you are."

I shrugged. "I'm just what I appear to be — a reasonably well-dressed private investigator with a reasonably clean office in Santa Monica. And I charge reasonable fees. Satisfied?"

Her face darkened; a shadow invaded the blue of her eyes, deepening their color. "Have any of your cases involved murder?"

I hadn't expected such a question.

"No," I said. "I generally do insurance investigation, or prepare evidence for law firms . . . that sort of thing. No murders. That's for those Warner Bros. movie detectives — the ones who are hard and tough and carry big automatics."

She ignored the wisecrack, frowning at me. "The man I've come to see you about is a murderer." She lowered her eyes. "But I'm the only one who knows it."

"Uh-huh. So who did he kill?"

"It started with the cats. When he lived in New Jersey he had seven cats. Then, when he decided to move to California, he took each cat out into the woods behind his house and shot it in the head. One by one . . . all seven."

"That's not murder," I said. "It's a lousy thing to do, but you can't —"

She cut into my words with angry ones of her own. "Then, when he moved out here to Los Angeles with his wife, he killed her pet dog, a cocker spaniel named Sparky. With poison."

"Okay," I nodded. "So this guy is a real scumball — but has he ever killed a human being?"

"Yes," she said flatly.

That stopped me cold. I stared at her. "Who? Who did he kill?"

"His sister, Gracie. Sid — his name is Sidney Marsh — hated Gracie from the time they were little kids. They never got along. When Gracie followed him out here from New Jersey last July, and begged him for enough money to hold her over until she could get a job, he refused to help. Told her didn't want her in his life, that she should get the hell away." Alicia hesitated, drawing in a long breath. "Gracie died later that same month."

"How?"

"She was struck down on Sunset Boulevard, just after midnight," said Alicia. "There were no witnesses, and the police had no way of tracing the car that killed her. But I know that it was Sid who drove the car. He murdered his sister because she wouldn't stop pestering him for money. He just waited until she was walking back to her hotel from the bus stop, and then he ran her down in the street — killing her in the same cold-blooded way he'd killed Sparky and those seven cats."

"How do you know for sure that Sid Marsh was the hit-and-run driver?"

She began nervously twisting the thin strap of her red silk purse.

Her breathing had quickened; this was apparently tough going for her. "I'm close friends with Patrice, Sid's wife. We were roommates in college together, before she moved to New York and met him."

I shrugged. "So . . . what has your friendship to do with the murder?"

"I still visit with Pat. She and I were able to resume our friendship after she talked Sid into moving here to Los Angeles. I was at her house the day after Gracie was killed and I saw a red stain on the front fender of his car. And the fender was dented. Sid had it straightened out and painted that same week. Took it down to Tijuana to have the work done."

"Why haven't you gone to the police?"

"With what? The car has been repaired. The blood is gone. I wasn't an eye witness when it happened. What could I bring to the police? I have no evidence to give them."

I leaned back in my creaking chair. "What I don't get is how I fit into this. What is it you want *me* to do?"

"I'm worried about Pat," she said. "Sid beats her. She has bruises and cuts all over her body; he even broke her arm once. And the beatings are getting worse. But she won't do anything about it. She's afraid he'll kill her if she tries anything — and I think he would. He's a prime bastard."

"So what can I do about it?"

"I want you to follow him, find out where he goes and who he sees."

"How will this help your friend?"

"I'm sure he's having an affair with another woman," declared Alicia. "If I can prove it, then show the proof to Pat, maybe then she'll have enough courage to leave him. She just couldn't allow herself to believe me when I told her that he killed Gracie — but the *one* thing Pat will not abide is another woman in Sid's life. I'll take whatever you're able to find to Pat."

"And what if you're wrong? What if he's out bowling, or playing cards with his pals?"

"I'm not wrong. I'm convinced he'll lead you to the other woman. Just follow him. You'll see."

I nodded. "Okay, I'll take the job. I get twenty bucks a day, plus expenses, and I'll need a hundred up front. Non-refundable. Which means that if the case takes less than five days, I keep the entire deposit."

"Fine," she said. "I knew we could work together." And while she was fishing out five twenty-dollar bills from her purse she gave me a heated look.

A look with a lot of erotic promise in it.

Silk and fire.

That was how it all began. My agreeing to follow Sid Marsh turned out to be the worst mistake of my life.

I was the fly —— and I was headed straight for the web.

I'm a good shadow man. I know how to follow somebody —— anytime, anywhere —— and not get spotted.

I first learned about shadowing people from Dashiell Hammett. You know, the hotshot writer who published *The Maltese Falcon* and *The Thin Man*. He was a Pinkerton detective before he quit to become a writer, and when he was with the Pinks he earned this rep as an ace shadow man. He worked out four basic rules:

Keep behind the subject.

Never attempt to hide.

Act naturally, no matter the situation.

Never meet the subject's eye.

Hammett claimed that even a clever criminal can be shadowed for weeks without suspecting it. He'd once tailed a forger for three months without arousing suspicion. Hammett taught me that you don't worry about a suspect's face. His carriage, the way he wears clothes, his general outline, his individual mannerisms and physical habits are much more important to a shadow man than faces.

I used to practice on my mom, when I was a kid. I'd follow her around when she went shopping, and back then I was sure she never spotted me. Now, I'm not so sure. She knew I was into this private operative stuff so maybe she just *pretended* not to see me skulking along behind her. I guess I'll never know; Mom died three years back.

Once I got into the detective game I became an accomplished shadow. I have a natural gift for it. But I'd never followed a murderer, so I was more than a little nervous waiting in my Dodge a half-block up from the home of Sid and Patrice Marsh. Alicia had provided the address: a white two-story Territorial-style in Hollywood. She'd described Marsh as being tall, with a skinny neck and jug ears. And she told me what he drove. A dark green 1937 Packard.

The Packard was parked in the driveway in front of the house when I drove past there late that afternoon. Once I'd spotted his car I parked under a big pepper tree at the far end of the block. The Marsh house was on a cul-de-sac, so he'd have to pass me going anywhere.

I dug out my pipe, fired it up, and waited, puffing away contentedly, thinking about Edward G. Robinson. He smokes a pipe in the movies. A lot of the kids I knew in high school took up smoking cigarettes, but I held out for a pipe. Gives a certain dignity to a man, I always thought. Like Robinson.

An hour crawled by before the green Packard slid past me, driving toward Franklin. A skinny-necked character with jug ears was at the wheel. Who else but Sid Marsh?

He turned left on Franklin, and followed that to Western, with me three car lengths behind him. He turned right down Western, passed Hollywood Boulevard, and turned right again on Carlton. He pulled over, parked, got out, and walked to a modest, one-story, dun-colored frame house, where he keyed open the front door and went inside.

A black Ford coupe was parked in the drive. I eased over to it and looked inside. The registration slip wrapped around the steering wheel bore this Carlton Way address and the owner's name: Lanie Harris.

Ha! The other woman? If so, then this job was a piece of cake. Inside the house Sid Marsh could be in the sack with Miss Harris — or getting there fast.

It was almost dark. The sun had taken a dive toward the ocean and the street lights were blinking to life.

I waited for full darkness before leaving the car. No one was on the street so I was not observed as I walked along the gravel drive at the left of the house to the rear window that threw a yellow square of light into the darkness. I could see plenty, and there was plenty to see.

Sid Marsh was buckass naked on a narrow bed, pumping away like one of those Long Beach oil derricks. The panting female beneath him just *had* to be Lanie. She had a trim little figure, from what I could see, and a tiny nose which was probably sprinkled with freckles. A genuine redhead, I saw, and all redheads have freckles. The bedside radio was playing Guy Lombardo, sweet and low.

I had my camera with me and took a few choice shots of the action. It was nice of them to leave the light on because I didn't have to use my flash. They were both grunting toward a climax when I walked back to my car.

I congratulated myself. I was smug and self-confident, grateful for the easy hundred I'd earned.

I was also a damned fool.

The pictures turned out fine. Developed them myself. Clear and explicit. Sid Marsh in some very compromising positions with his lady love. Hotcha stuff.

The next morning, when I handed the package over to Alicia at her apartment on Wilshire she was delighted. We were sitting together on a big overstuffed silk sofa and she was literally smacking her lips over the evidence I'd brought her.

"You did it, Ray!" she said with a real note of triumph in her voice. (I'd told her to call me Ray. "Mr. Thornton" was just too damned formal.)

"You really think this will cause your friend to leave that creep?"

"I really do," she said, scanning each shot with obvious relish. "They'll drive her nuts!"

It was rough, sitting here next to her, talking about the case, when I felt like grabbing. Body heat seemed to radiate from her, and the rich, sultry smell of her gardenia perfume enveloped me like a dense cloud.

It was early morning, and she was wearing a pale pink satin robe, loosely belted at the waist, over some filmy lace thing that she'd slept in that night. The image of her lying in bed kept popping into my mind . . . her hair tousled . . . her shoulders bare . . . begging me . . .

I stood up abruptly from the sofa.

"What's wrong?" she asked.

"I have to go," I said, not meeting her eyes. "If I don't, something might happen."

"Like what?" There was a teasing lilt to her voice.

"Like my kissing you, for one thing."

I looked into the heated blue of eyes; her gaze was direct and inviting. "Hey, you *deserve* a kiss for these snapshots."

She stood up, looping her arms around my neck. The front of

her robe had fallen open and I got a good look at those perfect breasts. Crimany!

We kissed. Her lips were as hot as a branding iron; at least they seemed that way, or maybe it was her steamy breath as she pressed her body into mine.

The point is, this wasn't just a kiss, it was the beginning of the most intense sexual experience of my life.

In bed, she was incredible. She took me away from this world, anticipating ever desire, matching my intensity with hers. She wove a spell, taking me up and down, up and down, over and over again. My orgasm was so shattering I almost blacked out. And at last we lay side by side, our bodies immobile and our breathing still labored, like two exhausted sailors after a typhoon.

"Was that good for you?" Alicia finally asked, the blue of her eyes a banked fire.

"Is a 90-pound robin fat?"

She giggled and all her curves rippled. "I think you like sex."

"I think I like *you.*"

"Same thing," she said. She rolled away from me on the bed. "You'd better get dressed and leave now. I have things to do."

"Like taking my pictures to Patrice Marsh?"

"Yeah, that's top of the list."

I slipped from the warm, scented bed, hating to leave her. "Call me at the office. Let me know what she says —— and when I can see you again."

She reached across the sheet to take my hand. Her fingers were warm and firm. "You'll hear from me soon."

I got dressed and, with great reluctance, left.

Late that afternoon the office phone rang. My heart jumped at the sound. "Thornton," I said.

"It's me."

And it was. Hearing Alicia's voice was like listening to fine music.

"How'd it go?" I asked.

"Not well." A note of regret darkened her tone. "Pat was very upset over the pictures, but instead of getting mad, she got depressed. Said it was all her fault, that if she'd been a better wife Sid would never have taken up with another woman."

"Then she's not going to leave him?"

"Nope. Pat thinks she can lure him back to her. She's going to buy new clothes, have her hair restyled, try some new makeup and perfume." Alicia sighed. "The whole thing's a washout."

"I'm sorry."

"She's even going to tell Sid that she knows about Lanie Harris. Thinks it will bring them closer."

"How will Sid react to that?"

"He won't like it. I said that if she told him what she knows about the Harris woman it would be a big mistake. He'll think she's been spying on him."

"And you can't talk her out of telling him?"

"Not a chance. Pat's a stubborn mule when she sets her mind on something. She was that way in college. No, I was wrong. She just won't listen to me."

"What do you think Sid will do when she tells him?"

"Probably beat the hell out of her," said Alicia. "Or worse."

"Worse? What could be worse?"

"He could kill her." A cold finality in her tone.

"C'mon, you must be stretching it."

"You don't know him, Ray. I *do*. He's quite capable of killing her. Don't forget what he did to his own sister."

"But the police would — "

"Oh, he'll make it look like an accident. Sid's a very clever fellow. The cops won't be able to lay a finger on him. He'll see to that."

I shifted uncomfortably in my chair. "We should do something."

"I've been thinking exactly that," she agreed. "Can you meet me at four in Hollywood? I'll park a block east of Pat's house."

"Well, sure, but — "

"I'm going in there and take Pat away. I'll have her stay with me at my place. At least until I can talk some sense into her head."

"And you want me along in case Sid gets violent?"

"You got it. You'll be my body guard. And bring a gun."

"I don't have one, remember?"

"Then buy one. I'll pay for it. To be on the safe side."

"Guns are never safe."

"Just do it, Ray. For me . . . okay?" Her voice had turned sultry again and I could feel myself melting inside. My God, I wanted this woman!

"Okay," I said, "but it's against my principles."

"Which reminds me ... " Now her voice was husky. "You have very *nice* principles."

The sexual innuendo was plain, and it aroused me. Hell, if purchasing a handgun was all it took to get back between the sheets with her then I'd do it without question. Alicia was a fire running in my blood.

"All right," I said. "I'll have a gun with me when I get out there."

"Can you still make it by four?"

"Sure. Getting the heater won't be that tough. I know a gent I can contact."

"Great! Then I'll see you at four."

And she ended the call.

I drove into downtown L.A. to a pawnshop on Broadway. Some shabby characters ambled the streets, clutching paper-sacked wine bottles. A panhandler approached me as I got out of the car, a rag-haired crone toting a burlap sack stuffed with rotted clothing and yellowed newspapers.

"Hey, mister," she croaked, thrusting out a grimy palm. "Help a starvin' old lady an' the good Lord'll bless ya forever!"

She looked like a plucked chicken, and very likely she *was* starving. I gave her a buck. She closed her claw hard around the bill and skittered off. There was a bar two doors down. She darted inside. My dollar would buy several shots of rotgut. And, well, maybe she needed it as much as I needed Alicia.

I walked into Eddie Fletcher's place. The air was close and musty and thin bands of sunlight from a slatted window barely penetrated the dim interior.

The store was a jumble of second-rate merchandise typical of a musty downtown pawnshop. I picked up a fake-gold wristwatch; the band fell off. I was stooping to pick it up when a frog-voiced man behind me said, "Whatcha doin' messin' with that?"

It was Eddie, and when I turned to face him he lit up like a Christmas tree. "Cripes, Ray, it's been a lousy century since I've seen ya!" He came over to give me a bear hug. He smelled of sour sweat and nickel cigars.

"I don't get downtown much anymore," I said.

"Want a drink? I got some good hootch in the back."

"I could use some hot coffee," I told him. "Got any?"

"Yeah, I got coffee. Hell, I *always* got coffee."

We walked through a swinging bead curtain into an even mustier room with a chipped cot, a teetering wood table, a dirty washstand, and a leaking toilet. Ed's living quarters. The coffee was simmering in a dented enamel pot atop a rusted stove in one corner. Ed poured me a mug, filling his from a bottle of Wild Turkey.

"Mud in yer eye," he said, taking a deep swig. I took a sip of black coffee so strong it could have revived a corpse, and then we sat down at the oilcloth-covered table.

"You want somethin', an' I got what you want," said Eddie. "Am I right?"

"You're a mind reader, Eddie," I said, grinning at him.

Fletcher looked like an overage pirate — with a frayed leather patch covering his left eye and several teeth missing. His denim shirt was ripped, and stuffed into a pair of ragged work pants that badly needed to see a washtub. He was barefoot and his toenails were dirty.

"What can I do you for?"

"I need a heater. I've got the cash," I said, taking out my wallet.

"You want the untraceable kind?"

"Yeah. Just in case something should go wrong."

"Cost you more."

"Fine."

"Gonna shoot the mayor, are ya? Hell, he's nothin' but a goddamn crook! Never trust an Italian, I tellya."

"I don't intend to shoot anybody, but I need the rod today." I stood up. "Show me one."

"Just hold your horses! Sit back down and wait here," he growled. "I'll go fetch what I got."

He shuffled over to a rusted metal cabinet and brought out a large pine box that was missing a hinge. He placed the box on the table, opened it, and shoved it toward me.

"Take yer pick," he said.

Inside the box, set into badly-worn black velvet, were three hand weapons: a .45 automatic, a .38 Smith & Wesson Special, and an old-fashioned Colt six-shooter.

"They're all oiled an' loaded," Eddie declared. "Fine stock. Dependable."

"How much for the automatic?" I weighed it in my hand.

He named a price. It was worth maybe half what he asked, but I paid him and slipped the gun into my coat.

"You want more rounds? They're extra," he said, shutting the box.

"No, I'm fine." I stood up again, anxious to get out of the place. I needed to breathe some air that didn't reek of sweat and cigar smoke.

"Ya oughta come down here some Friday night and get into a poker game with me an' the boys . . . Like ole times."

"Yeah, maybe I'll do that," I said, thinking, sure, when pigs fly.

Outside, I saw the old lady again. She started toward me, then realized that she'd already put the squeeze on me. She swung around sharply in the opposite direction and hobbled off.

This was a good place to get away from.

I made a quick stop in Santa Monica for a late lunch. Then, with the loaded .45 in my coat pocket, I took Wilshire all the way into Hollywood. It was a crisp October day and the rolling hills were a rich brown, like burnt toast. There wasn't much traffic, so I made good time, even with my slipping clutch.

It was just four when I met Alicia, right where she said she'd be, a block up from the Marsh house. She was waiting inside her car. She waved when she saw me, got out, and walked back to my Dodge. Her provocative, hip-swinging gait seemed to be a preview of future delights, and I counted myself as one lucky gent.

Actually, my luck was about to run out.

Once she was seated next to me in the Dodge I showed her the .45 automatic. She nodded. "I don't know anything about guns," she said, "but this one looks potent enough."

"If need be, I can wave it at Sid to scare him off," I declared. "Maybe he'll be reasonable and let your friend go with you."

"I wouldn't bet on it," she told me.

"So what's next?"

"Drive down the block and park in front of the house. You stay with the car and keep the motor running."

I grinned. "You make it sound like we're Bonnie and Clyde. I thought I was supposed to go in with you for backup."

"I hope I won't need you," she said. "If things get out of hand I'll give a yell. Okay?"

I shrugged. "Sure, if that's how you want to play it."

I parked where she told me to, directly in front of the Marsh place, and she went inside. There was a queasy feeling in the pit of my stomach. I had a hunch that things might, indeed, "get out of hand."

And I was right.

First, there was silence from the house. And silence on the street. No other cars were moving. The engine of my Dodge, purring like a big cat under the hood, was the only sound I heard — until the scream.

A woman's scream, piercing, desperate. Alicia or Pat? I couldn't tell. And it didn't matter.

I jumped out of my car and ran for the house. The front door was ajar. I dived inside, the automatic clutched in my right hand.

Alicia was halfway down the stairs, looking as if the Devil himself was after her. Obviously, the scream was hers.

"What happened?"

"Sid!" she gasped, her breath coming in short bursts, her face tight and flushed. "He swore he'd kill us both!" She jerked her hand toward the second floor. "Pat's up there with him."

"I'll handle this," I said, quickly mounting the stairs. "You stay here."

"He's got a gun," she warned me. "Be careful!"

"I'm no hero," I said. "I'll be *very* careful."

My heart was doing a tango inside my chest and my mouth was parched. I could barely swallow. This kind of action was totally alien to me.

I found them in the main bedroom.

Pat was backed against the far wall, next to French doors which led to an outside deck. She was wild-eyed and shaking. "He . . . he tried to *kill* me!" Her voice was strained and the words were delivered in a terrified half-whisper.

"Where's Marsh?"

"There!" She pointed toward a short inner hallway connecting bedroom and bath. Marsh was on the garnet-colored rug, sprawled on his stomach, unmoving.

"He was . . . going to shoot me," she said brokenly. "I hit him with a chair."

A carved-wood chair from Pat's dressing table lay overturned on the rug. One of its legs had been splintered.

Marsh groaned softly, beginning to regain his senses.

"He's still got the gun!" wailed Pat. "*Shoot* him!"

"I can't do that. He's only half-conscious. I can handle him without —"

She darted across the room to snatch the .45 from my hand. "If you won't . . . I will!"

She aimed the weapon directly at her husband, triggering it three times, the shots like triple thunderclaps in the room. All three bullets found a home in Sid Marsh.

He wasn't groaning anymore.

"Jesus!" I muttered, staring at the fast-spreading pool of wet crimson staining the rug.

"Here!" She tossed the .45 to me and, instinctively, I caught it in mid-air. "Let's get out. *Now!*"

"But we can't just *leave* him here," I protested.

"Sure we can. Sid won't mind." She was suddenly icy calm, her face an emotionless mask. "Let's go."

I knelt down to check his pulse. Nothing. Marsh was dead.

"Come on," she urged, pulling me up. "Alicia is waiting."

"Let her wait. I'm calling the cops."

She smiled at me. "Go ahead, if that's what you want. Tell them you just murdered Sid Marsh. I'm sure they'll be interested."

I glared at her. "I didn't kill him, *you* did!"

"The shots all came from your gun," she said, her voice like edged steel. "And you're holding it. Your fingerprints are on it."

For the first time, I noticed how she was dressed. As if she were going out shopping: a smart afternoon frock, a little matching hat . . . and gloves. She was wearing *gloves*.

"And besides," she continued, smiling at me. "I'm an eye witness. I saw everything. I tried to stop you from killing my husband, but I was helpless."

"She's right," said a familiar voice. "You're a killer, Ray."

Alicia was standing in the bedroom doorway. "You shot an unarmed man."

"Unarmed?"

"Sid never owned a gun in his life," said Pat. "Roll him over. See for yourself."

Alicia smiled. "I'd say you're in big trouble, Ray. Big, big trouble."

I've been writing all this from the cell where I'm being held without bail, which the judge refused because the charge is first degree murder. I couldn't raise money anyhow. My lawyer, a guy I don't much like, advised me to plead temporary insanity when we go to court.

"The jury probably won't go for it," he told me. "But it's the only chance you've got."

According to the cops and the D.A.'s office, the basic facts are crystal clear:

     1: I tried to rape Patrice Marsh in her own bedroom.

     2: Her husband came home and attempted to stop me.

     3: I shot him to death.

Just like that, one . . . two . . . three . . . Poor Sid's wife was a horrified witness to this brutal killing. And according to a signed and sworn statement, Alicia Sinniger had driven over there that day to visit her friend. She was stunned to encounter me upstairs, the gun still in my hand, Sid Marsh dead on the floor. Patrice was hysterical with shock and grief, so Alicia had phoned the police after I left. Pat's afternoon frock was torn where I had pawed at her in my lust-crazed rape attempt.

Naturally, as expected, I denied everything, swearing that Pat had shot her husband with my gun.

Except that only *my* prints were on it. I told the cops she'd been wearing gloves, but they never found any. Just my fingerprints on the murder weapon.

I also brought up the fact of motive: Pat had one. Her husband had been brutally beating her over a long period of time.

Ridiculous, Pat had countered. "Sid loved me deeply," she told the police, tears running down her cheeks. "He was a very gentle, caring man. He'd never lay a hand on me. Never!"

She went on to claim that I'd made up a "crazy story" to try and cover my attempted rape and the murder of her beloved husband. She'd never forget Sid's courage, coming to her rescue bare-handed against a gun-wielding rapist-killer.

It was a great job of acting. Academy Award all the way.

A court-appointed doctor examined Pat's body minutely, head-to-toe. No evidence of beatings. Not a mark. Not the tiniest evidence of fracture, past or present.

Obviously, according to the police, this grief-stricken widow was telling the truth.

Newspapers headlined the case, branding me as a "vicious murderer" whose story of innocence was laughable. They found a grim, unsmiling photo of me (God knows where) and darkened the area around my eyes before they printed it. I looked like Jack the Ripper.

The *Times* ran a photo interview with a neighbor of mine, Ed Morgan, who described me as "moody and reclusive." Morgan went on to say that he had always felt there was something "kind of spooky" about the way I talked, and that he knew for a fact that I enjoyed reading "dirty books."

Actually, I've never said more than hello to the man, and I never knew his name until I read it in the paper.

The *Times* also reported that the grieving widow would receive a substantial amount of life insurance, thanks to her husband's prudent foresight in taking out a number of hefty policies on his own life. Not that the money could make up for the crippling loss of her husband, of course, but it might help ease her pain and allow her to begin life once again.

I'd been a pawn in this game from the moment Alicia had walked into my office. I'd played right into her hands (and her bed). Everything she'd said to me had been lies. Sure, Gracie Marsh *had* followed her brother out to California, but Sid hadn't run her down on the street. That, I was certain, was Alicia's doing; it was surely *her* car that had killed Gracie, not Sid's. She had hoped that Pat would blame Sid for killing her sister and leave him — but that didn't happen. Pat had no money of her own; she was financially dependent on Marsh and wasn't about to give up what she had.

Then Alicia and Pat put their heads together and came up with the bright idea of setting up someone as Sid's killer so they could share the insurance money. I was the someone they picked. A lust-happy private investigator who'd go for Alicia like a cat goes for fresh cream.

What a prime sap I'd been!

More lies to me about wife beating. And as for Sid's affair with Lanie Harris — hell, Pat knew all about that and didn't care. She refused to have relations with him. He wasn't what she was interested in.

I found out about that when Alicia came to visit me, Pat Marsh with her.

"Everything was so easy," Alicia told me, looking gorgeous in her tight red silk dress, the same dress she'd worn that first day in my office. "There was only one problem — having to go to bed with you." She grimaced. "That made me sick."

"Yeah," Pat nodded. "Poor Alicia."

They told me they're thinking about moving to Hawaii. Or maybe France. Since college, they said, they've both loved Paris. So *sophisticated* there. They giggled.

They left the jail together, hand-in-hand.

My trial starts next month.

I have long been fascinated by the idea of being able to return to the past and meet myself as a child. "Dark Return" was written out of this fascination, although I have projected a much darker past than one might expect to find in such a return journey. Of course, as you'll discover in the reading, there is a reason for this darkness.

I don't believe in demons and I'm sure time travel is, and will remain, an impossible dream. Yet I utilize both in this fantastic little tale. That's the job of every good writer — to utilize the stuff of his or her imagination. Here, with "Dark Return," I feel I've done my job.

Dark Return

I'm David Neville, and I'm a paranormal investigator. I deal with all aspects of the occult world. Do I personally believe in devils, ghosts, ghouls and demons? Certainly in the past I didn't; I was smugly confident that such bizarre entities did not exist. But all that has changed since my encounter with Thorgon . . .

Thorgon the demon.

I was born thirty-nine years ago, in March of 1968, in Oak Hill, a small farming community in Southern Missouri near the Arkansas border. Population six thousand. Quiet streets. Tree-shaded houses. Neatly trimmed lawns. Kids on bicycles. Everybody knew everybody else.

Oak Hill had never gone modern like the big Missouri towns such as Kansas City and St. Louis.

Growing up in Oak Hill was like living back in the 1930s and '40s.

I have very fond memories of my home town — despite what happened to Mom. I never bonded with my father. I retain vague images of a very tall, smiling man who liked to pick me up and spin me around in the air. A heart attack killed him before I was five. All I know is that he was a fire insurance salesman, and that Mom loved him very much. She never quit grieving for him.

I have vivid memories of the folks in Oak Hill . . . near-sighted Miss Abernathy with her bottle-thick glasses, who was my grade school teacher (we had only one grade school in town) . . . Tommy Norliss, my best chum, who lived at the corner on Forest, three houses away from ours . . . Old Man Hennessey (never knew his first name) who owned the local funeral parlor in his starched collars and black suits (he'd let me and Tommy watch him work on corpses!) . . . Police Chief Jerry O'Connor, with his fat, foul-smelling cigars, who claimed there were no criminals in Oak Hill . . . the town spinster, Miss Liddy Pearl, always in white lace, who sold me nickel jawbreakers behind the candy counter at Ray's drugstore . . . and the Isis, Oak Hill's "movie palace," where Tommy and I faithfully attended Freddy Fox matinees on Saturday. All the kids got free popcorn at each matinee from rotund Mr. Hastings, who owned the theater. And I remembered Harley Michaelson, the town banker, wearing his polka-dot bow ties . . . and Mayor Stanbridge, pompous and boring.

I left Oak Hill at the end of March, 1980, a week after my twelfth birthday — on the afternoon following Mom's funeral. I was on a plane for California that night.

Mom's death was a terrible shock. The police report stated that it was an accident, that she'd lost control in the rain and hit a tree at fifty miles an hour. The crash was fatal, but she had lived long enough to scribble seven words, in lipstick, on the inside of the shattered windshield.

As I die he dies with me

The police could make nothing of it, but I knew what these words meant. It was suicide. In killing herself, she'd finally managed to kill the grief that had never left her. For her, Pop was finally dead.

For the next nine years I lived with Martha and Lyle, my fraternal grandparents, in Chula Vista, California, not far out of San Diego. (Never liked San Diego; too many drunken sailors.) My grandparents had a lemon grove in Chula Vista and I'd help them set up smudge pots under the trees when frost set in.

I told myself, after losing Mom, that I'd never go back to Oak Hill again.

I *did* go back — and that's what I want to write about — my return to Oak Hill.

*   *   *

Until he died last year of cancer, Tommy kept me up on all the latest news from home. Told me they'd chopped down the town oak and leveled the hill — converting the area into a big parking lot for the new shopping mall. Told me that Chief O'Conner had retired and that Miss Abernathy had moved to central Oregon (I think the town was Redmond), that Old Man Hennessey had shut down the funeral home, and that Miss Liddy Pearl had passed away from pneumonia. Harley Michaelson had left the banking business, and Mayor Stanbridge had been voted out of office. The Isis had been torn down after Mr. Hastings sold the lot and left for Chicago. New multiplex there now. According to Tommy, a great deal had changed in Oak Hill in two and a half decades.

Let me start with the blood circle.

You must understand that I grew up in a house crammed with occult volumes. My mother was a fanatic regarding every aspect of the paranormal, and it's because of her and books I was exposed to in my childhood that I became what I am today. The basic difference between my mother and me was that she was a devout believer in the supernatural while I was a cynical skeptic. One of my principal reasons for becoming a paranormal investigator was to debunk the same beliefs my mother embraced — the way Houdini went after phony psychics in his day. Of course, I never told her the real reason I chose the occult game; she would have considered it a betrayal.

All of which leads me to the blood circle.

Occult lore states that a demon may be summoned from the netherworld by certain incantations, and once summoned, contained within a circle of human blood.

Naturally, I deemed this utter nonsense, and set out to prove it. I went to the local blood donor center and had a liter of my blood drawn. I took the blood home with me and sprinkled it around the floor of my study to form a large circle. I then delivered an incantation from one of Mother's books on demonology, convinced that such a ritual was the stuff of fantasy.

Instead, I was stunned as I ended the incantation to see a horrific form materialize within the circle. A demon! An actual, honest-to-god red-eyed demon, was standing there.

"I am Thorgon," the creature declared in a rasping voice. His lizard eyes blazed, and his face and body were covered with green scales. "Why have you summoned me?"

I was unable to speak. My throat was locked, and my heart was hammering my chest. I kept telling myself that this could *not* be happening.

Desperately, I fumbled through the pages of my mother's book, seeking the words to send this dread creature back to the netherworld.

Too late! When Thorgon realized what I was attempting to do, he reached out with his taloned claws and pulled me inside the blood circle.

Everything darkened around me. My eyes closed — and when I opened them I was back in my home town, back in Oak Hill, standing in the central square with a full moon riding the night sky. The hill was there, facing me, with the tall oak tree topping it. No shopping mall. No parking lot. Just the same town square I'd known as a boy.

It was well after sundown, and the oak and maple shadows were thick and somehow menacing. Odd. I'd never been afraid of shadows as a child.

What of the demon? Had I really seen one or was it an illusion? The blood circle . . . Thorgon . . . was it all a dream?

I was totally confused. The concrete sidewalk I stood on was real and solid. The courthouse across the square with its bronze statue of a Civil War soldier was no illusion. A real moon lit the sky, and a breeze ruffled my hair, bringing the trees to life.

I was truly back in my home town. How I'd arrived here was a mystery, but I *was* here.

I staggered down Main, looking stunned, and the townspeople on the street stared at me as I passed them. Probably figured I was drunk, the way I was walking. A police vehicle rumbled past. Chief O'Connor's official car. He gave me a hard look around his cigar as the car continued along Main. Guess he didn't favor strangers in town.

At 6th and Main, there it was, with the big sign out front just the way I remembered it:

HENNESSEY'S FUNERAL PARLOR
"We Understand Your Loss"

Not closed, as Tommy had reported. Open for business. Dead bodies welcome! And with Old Man Hennessey himself, in a starched collar and black suit, out on the front lawn watering his roses.

"Mr. Hennessey," I said to him, smiling. "It's been a long time."

He scowled at me, saying nothing.

"I know this may seem impossible to you, but I'm David Neville. Davy . . . the boy who used to —"

The scowl darkened. "I *know* who you are, and if you value life you'll get out of Oak Hill. Fast."

I didn't reply. Something in his eyes, in the harsh tone of his voice, caused me to move on down Main.

A block farther, reaching 7th, I stared at a familiar red-brick building: the Isis! Large black plastic letters on the marquee spelled out the current attraction: JAMIE LEE CURTIS in THE FOG.

My God! I recalled seeing that movie about the dead ghost pirates at the Isis in 1980, on my twelfth birthday! Mom was with me, and she'd bought me gumdrops and a Coke in the lobby. And yet the Isis had been torn down according to Tommy. A multiplex was supposed to have been built here.

I fumbled dizzily for some change and obtained a newspaper from the corner vending rack. Opened it. *The Oak Hill Star*, dated March 23, 1980 — the day before my eleventh birthday.

This wasn't possible. It was 2007. How could I be here, in Oak Hill, in 1980?

Mr. Hastings, as heavy and full-jowled as I remembered him, was sweeping out the lobby when I walked in.

He raised his head to glare at me as I spoke. "I . . . I'm very confused. When . . . when I lived in Oak Hill . . . I used to come here to see —"

His harsh voice cut me off. "Leave town if you don't want to be damned."

I took a step back, rocked by his cold words.

What was happening? I was trapped in some kind of insane dream. This *couldn't* be real. Not any of it.

I turned away from Mr. Hastings and moved along 7th to Flora Avenue — to the Oak Hill Grammar School. At the bottom of the weathered stone steps leading up to the entrance I hesitated.

It was Sunday, and the school was closed. Could Miss Abernathy be inside? (She had often worked there on Sundays, grading papers.) I mounted the steps and tried the door. It was unlocked. I walked down the narrow hallway, over the scuffed linoleum floor, to

Miss Abernathy's office. Yes, she was there at her desk, hunched over a stack of student papers. Same pinched face, eyes behind thick glasses, dressed in a baggy gray sweater patched at the elbows, and a plain gray woolen dress.

She looked up at me as I stood in the doorway.

"So you're here," she said in an icy tone.

"You know who I am?"

She ignored the question. "Better get out if you can," she said tightly. "Or don't you care what will happen if you stay?"

"And what's supposed to happen to me?"

"You'll find out soon enough." Her face was a rigid mask, with no trace of the warmth I remembered.

I walked back down the hallway, dazed, thinking: *why can't I wake up? This dream is too intense. I don't like it, I don't want it to continue.*

Mayor Stanbridge was waiting for me at the curb when I left the school. He was in the back seat of his dark blue limo with the window rolled down.

"Hello, David," he said in a flat tone.

I nodded uncertainly. "Mr. Mayor."

"Just arrived in town, eh?"

I nodded again.

"Want my advice?"

"I can guess what it will be."

"Then guess," he said coldly.

"You think I should leave town."

"Yes, if that's possible," said the Mayor.

"Everyone I meet says the same thing. They all want me to leave."

"We don't wish to see you . . ." His voice trailed off.

"I don't know what you're talking about — any of you."

"Of course you don't. But you'll know by midnight. Unless you leave before then."

"How can I leave? I'm in the middle of a dream."

"No dream, Davy. This is real."

And he rolled up the window while the gleaming blue limo purred away into the darkness; its tail-lights dimmed, vanished.

I kept walking.

At the town drugstore, the same thing was said to me by Liddy Pearl, that I should leave Oak Hill at once. I told her I couldn't and she smiled, a twisted, chilling smile. "Have it your way, David."

And she turned her back to me in a disturbing bird-like motion.

Harley Michaelson was sitting on a stool at the end of the marble fountain counter sipping a chocolate malted. He looked just as I remembered him: gaunt turkey neck, leather skin, deep-sunk eyes. He adjusted his polka-dot bow tie and nodded toward the silver shaker of malted in front of him. "Want some? There's too much for me."

"I don't like chocolate," I said.

"Suit yourself."

"This is all insane," I said. "I don't know why I'm here. Nothing makes sense."

"You don't have much time left," Harley said.

"This *is* March 23rd, 1980, right?"

He nodded. "It is."

"Then my mother is still alive."

"Yes."

"I need to talk to her."

"Then go," said Michaelson.

I started for the door.

"See you at midnight," said Harley, and his tone was mocking.

I staggered down the hill from Main to Forest, ran unsteadily along Forest through inked night shadows to my old home, a white, one-story, wood frame house near the end of the block.

Young Davy was on the wooden porch, winding the prop of a tissue-and-balsa wood model airplane. *Me!* Me with freckles across my nose, wearing my old red sweater, a day away from twelve!

He looked up, his eyes — *my* eyes — hard and fixed, like the eyes of a predatory bird.

"Is . . . is your mother home?" I asked, my voice faltering. I was sweating and my hands shook.

"She's inside, but you'd best stay away from her," Davy said softly.

"I need to see her," I said.

"What you need to do is leave this place. Stay here and you'll be sorry. Real sorry."

I pushed past him to rap on the pitted screen door.

My mother opened it. Her face was expressionless.

"Mom!" I said. "It's *me*, Davy!"

She looked at me calmly. "Roll up your right pants leg," she said, "and show me your knee."

I did, revealing a long white scar extending from my right knee-cap halfway to my ankle. I'd fallen from my bike into some broken glass when I was eleven and the scar was still there.

"Come inside," said my mother, pushing open the screen door. I entered the house.

Everything was the same inside the small living room . . . the big, overstuffed chair by the TV set, the faded red sofa with two of Mom's hand stitched pillows on it, the antique clock on the mantel that chimed the hour . . . everything was exactly as I remembered it.

"Sit, Davy . . . or should I call you David now that you're a grown man?"

I eased down on the sofa, bone-tired — yet with a vast sense of relief. "Then you *believe* me?" I said. "You believe that I'm really your son?"

Her eyes darkened with concern. "You're in great danger."

"I was pulled into a blood circle," I told her. "By a demon. He said his name . . . Thorgon."

"I know," she said.

"How can I be here . . . in 1980?"

"Thorgon is a demon of great power," declared my mother. "Such demons can alter the time continuum. Thorgon sent you back here to destroy you. Once you're dead he'll have your soul."

"But that's . . ." I hesitated to use the phrase, but I blurted it out. "That's *crazy!*"

"Not at all," said my mother. "In order for a demon to claim a soul the adult self must be absorbed by the younger self — to render the soul complete. That's why you were sent back here, to accomplish this transformation."

"I don't believe that such a thing is possible."

"What you believe is not important," my mother told me. "You must be returned to 2007. Once this is done, the demonic pattern will be broken and you'll be free again."

"The townspeople . . . Old Man Hennessey, Chief O'Connor . . . Mr. Hastings . . . they all seemed so hostile."

"They are all under Thorgon's control," she said.

"What about you? Why aren't *you* under his control?"

"Because I have protected myself with certain rituals of which you know nothing. I'm immune from his power — the only person in this town who is."

"Look, mother, all this is —"

She pressed a finger to my lips. "Hush, David — and do exactly as I say. We have very little time. It's almost midnight. They'll come for you at midnight."

"Who? Who's coming for me?"

"O'Connor, Hastings, Stanbridge, all of them. And my Davy. He's the vital one, the one Thorgon will use."

"How do you know all this?"

"Call it psychic vision. I can't explain it, but I know we must act quickly." She gripped my shoulder. "Now, no more questions. Trust me, David?"

"I trust you."

"Then come with me."

She cleared a large space in the kitchen, pushing aside table and chairs. Then, with a stick of chalk, she began to execute a pentagram on the floor. "This will take you into 2007. You must step inside and —"

The living room clock chimed midnight.

The kitchen door banged open, and young Davy was there. Behind him: Chief O'Connor, Hastings, Liddy Pearl, Michaelson, Miss Abernathy, Stanbridge, and Old Man Hennessey. They stood in dark silhouette, back-lit by the moonlight, their glistening eyes fixed on me.

"Take him," said Hastings.

My mother lunged forward, screaming. "Leave my son alone!" Mayor Stanbridge gave her a violent shove. She struck her head against the sink, slumping to the floor.

"You've killed her!" I raged.

"I said *take* him," Hastings ordered.

Strong hands gripped me. There was no chance to resist, to escape. I was pushed roughly into the street and propelled along the root-cracked sidewalk toward . . .

And suddenly I realized where they were taking me — to Miller House, where old Mrs. Miller was found hanging from a rafter in the attic. Others had also died there under dread circumstances. People claimed that Miller House was evil. The place was boarded up and left to rot.

I knew that's where Thorgon was waiting to take my soul. I tried to break free, but O'Connor's clubbed fist struck me to the pavement.

"Don't try to get away," a piping voice warned me. "You belong to Thorgon now." It was Davy, my young self, leaning above me, his cruel eyes reflecting the moon.

"We don't want to have to hurt you, David," said Liddy Pearl. "We're only doing what he wills us to do. He commands, we obey."

I'd been to Miller House only once, on Halloween night when I was ten. Tommy Norliss had double-dared me to climb through an open window (where the glass had been smashed out) and mount the staircase to the second floor. To prove I got there I had to wave from a second-floor window as Tommy waited below on the sidewalk in front of the house.

I recall how terrified I was of encountering the ghost of old lady Miller on the stairs, with her head all crooked and broken-necked, and her claw hands reaching for me. I made it in and out of the place without meeting her, but when I reached the sidewalk I was sweating bullets, with my heart drumming my chest.

"Was it scary?" Tommy had asked me. And I remember my answer: "Piece 'a cake."

So here I was, back at Miller House, about to confront something far worse than a ghost.

The house loomed high like a dark castle against the moonlit sky, surrounded by towering oaks and maples; the night wind stirred their branches, creating a flickering shadow-pattern over the cob-webbed porch.

Mr. Hastings pried a loose board away from the entrance, kicking the door open. "Upstairs!" he ordered.

We climbed the creaking staircase with my heart beating fast, just as it had done on that long ago Halloween night. The area smelled of mold and decay. Dead leaves, blown in from the shattered windows, crackled beneath my feet.

Halfway to the upper landing I stopped, turning to Old Man Hennessey who'd always been my friend. "Why are you doing this?" I asked, with a tremor in my voice.

"We have no free will, Davy," he said. "Thorgon is all powerful."

Mayor Stanbridge prodded me. "Keep moving."

Upstairs, I was taken to the main bedroom. All of the furniture had been removed, and only dust and cobwebs remained. A plump rat scurried across the floor as we entered. The window curtains had rotted to dust, and the wash of pale moonlight cast an eerie glow in the empty room.

No, not empty. Thorgon was there, slithering out from a dark corner, a great scaled lizard, eyes blazing red coals in his skull. The demon's voice rasped like rusted iron hinges: "Welcome home, David."

"Damn you to hell!" I snarled.

Thorgon's laughter was chilling. "No, it is *you* whose soul will be damned."

Young Davy stepped forward to stand rigidly between me and the demon; his face was emotionless, mouth tight set, eyes glazed, totally under Thorgon's power.

"Now!" commanded the demon. "Boy and man . . . become *one!*"

I knew what would happen. My younger self would blend into my adult body; his child's soul would join my adult soul, making it complete. Then Thorgon would claim his prize.

I swung toward the window. A possible escape route? Could I twist free and jump to the roof from the second floor window? It was my only chance. I tensed my muscles, then desperately attempted to break away, but Harley Michaelson threw his right arm across my throat, forcing my head back. I was helpless.

"Don't make us hurt you, David," he said.

"That's right," added O'Connor. "Just accept your destiny."

"Accept," intoned the others. "Accept."

Davy was less than a foot away, reaching out to me, when my mother rushed into the room, planting herself directly in the boy's path.

Thorgon's red-coal eyes blazed. "Stand aside, bitch!"

"You hold no power over me," she told him; her tone was calm and steady.

And she began to chant in a language I didn't understand. Each word of the incantation was like a knife stroke to Thorgon. He reeled back, mouth writhing under the verbal assault.

"I command you . . . Enter!" my mother said in a tone of steel. "Enter my body!"

"No! No!" Thorgon gasped, fighting her words.

"Again, I command you . . . Enter!"

His scaled body slowly flowed into hers, melding, lizard flesh to human flesh.

"It's over, David," said my mother. "Go to the pentagram. It will free you."

With Thorgon's passing the others in the room had ceased all movement. Old Man Hennessey, Stanbridge, O'Connor, Miss Abernathy, Davy, Liddy Pearl, Harley Michaelson, and Hastings. They stood immobile, like carved statues, totally devoid of life.

I faced my mother. "I want you to return with me."

"No." She shook her head. "My place is here. I have a vital mission to perform. You must return alone, David. Now . . . go."

We embraced. I kissed Mom's cheek, feeling her warm tears against my lips.

"*Go!*"

I stumbled from the room, down the stairs, rushing through the gusting dark toward my boyhood home.

The house was dead quiet when I stood in the kitchen, staring down at the pentagram. Could it really propel me into the future?

(*Trust me, David*)

I stepped into the chalked pentagram . . .

. . . and out — into my study in 2007.

For the first time, I understood the real meaning of the words my mother had left in the smashed wreckage of her car.

As I die he dies with me.

I knew there was now one less demon in the netherworld.

When writer/editor Chris Conlon told me he was putting together an anthology by various authors with each story to be an extension of an unfinished Edgar Allan Poe fragment, "The Lighthouse," I jumped at the chance to participate. I took Poe's concept and moved it into deep space, to an imaginary planet I called Capella Septime, using Mr. Poe's lighthouse as a warning beacon for incoming spaceships.

Read it and find out what happens when a malfunction causes one of the great ships to crash. I direct your attention, in particular, to Neptune the alien. He's not quite what he seems.

The Tragic Narrative of Arthur Bedford Addison

Jan 1. The first day of the New Year, and the beginning of my second year at the light-house. I have decided to keep a journal from this point forward. A New Year's resolution. To get my thoughts and feelings down on paper. As regularly as I *can* keep this journal I will, but no one can tell what may happen to a man alone.

"You are not alone," said Neptune, reading over my shoulder. "I am with you, master. I shall always be with you."

Neptune seemed to be smiling, yet he is a most serious creature. He is incapable of understanding the concept of humor and his "smile" is, of course, an illusion created by the odd configuration of his dog-like features.

How to describe Neptune?

He's a native of this planet we share —— of Capella Septime —— the last of his species to survive the Plague. He has been with me for nearly a year now, having staggered into my light-house during my first month as Keeper, sick from the Plague and on the verge of death.

I fed him, protected him from the cold fog, and slowly nursed him back to health. He has been with me, night and day, ever since.

But I want to continue my description, for whoever may discover this journal after I am gone.

The body of Neptune is covered with a dark brown fur which seems to thicken rapidly. I must trim him on a regular basis, and he appears to enjoy the process. His eyes are quite large for his

head and very black, without visible pupils. His nose is also black
— and moist — like an Earth dog's. That's why I cited his dog-
like features. He reminds me of a collie dog I once had when I
was a boy growing up in Chicago. Although Neptune lacks a tail,
his ears are pointed and possess such an intricate musculature
that they are quite expressive. He will cock his head to one side
when he listens to me, and often he seems to smile. As I have
stated, this smile is not real. And like Earth dogs, I don't believe he
has the bodily parts which would allow him to indulge in what we
humans call laughter.

Earth dogs walk on four legs, but Neptune stands erect on two
furry ones, like a human being. He is shorter than I am, with the top
of his head coming to the level of my shoulder.

And, of course, he talks. He learned to speak English in just
under a month, and to read from the books I have here in even less
time. (I have never been able to learn how to speak Capellan flu-
ently, so we never converse in his native language.)

He told me his real name, but I cannot pronounce it, so I call him
Neptune. He calls me master. A rare good fellow, withal.

I grew up on Earth before the Great Impact. Before Harvey
wiped all life from the planet. It is amusing, calling an asteroid Harvey,
but that was the name of the scientist who initially charted the
asteroid's course. Professor Elwin H. Harvey of Yale University —
the first to warn everyone to leave.

Many of us did. Many more didn't. You had to have money to
buy your way aboard one of the Ships. My family had ample funds,
and therefore I am still alive. For a time after the exodus I felt guilty.
Me surviving when so many were dead. But then I came to believe
that some of us are fated to die sooner than others. We *all* pass on
eventually, so feeling guilt at a temporary reprieve from death is a
useless emotion.

I hold many good memories of Earth. The way the wind bent
the trees (we have no wind on Capella Septime) . . . the way the sky
turned colors at sunset, flushed with orange and purple as Old Sol
dropped below the rim of ocean . . . the way the sea water turned to
plum-red wine under the moon . . .

Capella Septime has no moon. We do have a sun, however, a
distant burning star which delivers a pale yellow light for periods
which last forty-eight hours, with equal intervals of darkness.

Odd, how I ended up here. I never expected to, although my

ancestors for many generations were all light-house keepers. On Earth, each light-house was built atop a high rise of coastal ground, sending out its revolving beacon of light to warn ocean ships away from the shore. My father was a light-house man. So was my grandfather, and *his* father before him. I swore that I would never serve in such a lonely position. I wanted to be a Ship's pilot, and when a boy, I read every book I could find on Deep Space. I would go inland to the rocket port on Sundays to watch the Moontugs blast off on their weekly Lunar runs. I thrilled to the way those metal beasts shook the ground with their powerful jets, climbing skyward on a tall plume of white-hot flame.

I never piloted a Ship. The Space Academy rejected me because of substandard eyesight. I could see well, but not well enough to be a space pilot. Perfection was required.

So I have ended up here, at the light-house, doing what my father and grandfather did before me, sending out a warning finger of light to alert the Ships.

The ocean of Septime is not made of water. It is composed of alien fog. Thick and treacherous. A limitless mass of floating particles of opaque gas that hangs over the planet like a shroud and never dissipates.

The light-house stands atop Baltimore Peak, the only mountain on Capella. This tower was built to warn the galactic Ships when they fire in on their scheduled supply runs for the colony.

Although all of the natives are dead now (except Neptune, of course), a small Earth colony still functions here, conducting mineral research. Perhaps twenty or thirty humans, working with a scattering of aliens from the Cluster. I never see any of them. I never leave the light-house.

I grow my own food here. Hydroponics. Luckily, Neptune is able to eat what I do, his digestive system appearing remarkably similar to my own.

Water is no problem. The tank next to the tower has enough in it to last a lifetime.

I live here, and I will die here. In the light-house.

My reward? The knowledge that I am saving the lives of countless Spacers who might have driven their Ships straight into the mountain without my beacon to warn them off. I take an odd pride in doing the job my ancestors have done.

The light must never go out.

We need, each of us, to find our ultimate place in the Universe. Mine is here, on Capella Septime, at the light-house.

Jan. 8. Life at the tower is not as bleak as I may have portrayed it in my previous journal entry. In truth, I simply do not fit into normal society and never have. By nature, I am a solitary soul and prefer, for the most part, to be isolated from other humans. As a child, I would shut myself away in my room for long hours each day and become lost in books and spacegames. This, to the despair of my parents, who urged me out of doors with Orndoff, my adventurous brother. A wearisome, ongoing clash of wills.

Neptune is, of course, a great blessing. Would to Heaven I had ever found in "society" one-half as much faith as exists in this poor creature. He is my soulmate. Asks nothing and gives everything. The perfect companion.

What still surprises me is the difficulty my father had in getting me the appointment here as a Keeper of the Tower — and I of a highly influential family. It is not that the Galactic Council doubted my ability to manage the light. They simply felt that my brother should accompany me, that I should not be alone.

Certainly, Orndoff wanted to come, Lord knows why. He begged to share these duties with me, but it would never have done to let him do so. Being shut away with him, here in the tower, would have been nothing less than maddening. For one thing, I should never have been able to progress on this journal while Orndoff hovered nearby with his constant, intolerable chatter.

At my age now — past sixty — I wish to be left alone, having had my fill of my fellow human beings. There is a comforting sense of peace within these sturdy walls.

Jan. 15. I have been standing on the top deck of the tower, gripping the cold guard rail, staring into the endless ocean of fog— my ears protected against the periodic, penetrating blast of the great horn.

I have not written about the horn. Of course, the tower beacon is designed to be seen from space, slicing through the fog with its laser-bright beam, but the light is augmented by the foghorn — an incredible sonic burst strong enough to penetrate a Ship's metal shell and alert the pilot to potential danger.

The inner walls of the light-house have been insulated to muffle the horn while I am inside, but on the outer deck I must always wear ear isolators to deaden the killing sound. I would go stone deaf without them.

The deck is an ideal place for remembering. I often stand here, high above the rocks of Carter Peak, staring out into the pale wash of hanging fog, thinking about my boyhood on Earth, of dreams unrealized, hopes unfulfilled. Yet I am not unhappy in such ruminations. My sense of duty sustains me, my pride in being chosen as a Keeper of the Tower.

"What are you thinking about, master?"

Neptune glided up beside me, noiseless as always, his head canted for my reply.

"Of Earth," I told him, stroking the thick fur along his neck. "I was thinking once again of my life on Earth. Oh, Neptune, I wish you could have seen it before the Great Impact . . . savored its lush beauty."

"You have shown it to me in many books, master."

I shook my head. "Pictures can never convey its majesty. They called it the Blue Marble. Seeing it from space, with its white clouds and swirling blue oceans, it was true magic, a sight to steal the breath away."

"It is my misfortune that I was never witness to such a sight," said Neptune. His eyes were dark and luminous.

"Earth was a marvelous place for a growing boy," I said. "Lakes to fish in . . . hills to climb . . . meadows rich with wildflowers . . ."

Neptune was silent, allowing my thoughts to achieve verbal life.

I sighed. "The asteroid destroyed it all. The cities, the mountains, the people . . . all destroyed. Now Earth is simply a dead ball of clay hanging in space."

"You were fortunate to have escaped, master," said Neptune as he wrinkled his nose. "As I survived my species, you have survived yours. In this, we are united."

"Yes," I nodded. "We are both fortunate."

*   *   *

Jan. 23. A calm day, as always, on Capella Septime. Towards evening, the fog — like a vast sheet of glass — reflected the setting sun, as the mild heat of the afternoon dissolved into the cool of the evening.

Ascending from the lower floor of the tower, where Neptune and I eat and sleep, to the top deck is an exhausting endeavor. A distance of at least 180 feet. The winding stairs seem interminable — yet they *do* provide me with daily exercise. I must keep my body in prime condition in order to properly perform my duties in the lighthouse. Good health is crucial.

We experience occasional planetary ground quakes here on Capella that cause the tower to sway rather violently, forcing me to grip the rail tightly if I am on the top deck. However, I'm never concerned about the collapse; the walls are four feet thick and the foundation of the tower extends for a full twenty feet beneath the ground surface. Thus, I feel perfectly secure within these solid, iron-ribbed walls.

This is not, however, true of Neptune. He cringes against me during a quake, and I can feel his heart pounding. I assure him that he is quite safe, but he doubts my word. His ears twitch, and his large black eyes go wide with fear.

"I do not like the ground to move, master," he will say to me. "It is not a natural thing."

"On Earth we had far greater quakes," I tell him. One of these, in ancient times, destroyed an entire city that was called San Francisco."

"Yes, you have shown me pictures of its Golden Gate Bridge," said Neptune. "It must be a fine thing to see an ocean of blue water. I should like to have seen such an ocean."

"We had two of them book-ending our land," I told him. "One was called the Pacific, and the other the Atlantic. I saw both in the time before the Great Impact."

"How I envy you, master."

And, in a drift of silence, the conversation ended.

Feb. 2. Tonight a terrible thing happened — the nightmare of every Keeper. A short in the main power cable caused the system to fail. The beacon dimmed to black, and the voice of the great horn ceased in mid-cry. We were suddenly engulfed in silence and darkness.

I worked frantically to repair the cable, knowing that a supply Ship was due. Could I make the repair in time to warn its captain?

I could not. Within minutes, as I struggled with the cable, I heard the scream of jets, followed by a mind-stunning explosion as the massive spacecraft slammed into the solid rock face of Carter Peak.

"Dear God!" I shouted at Neptune. "We've lost a Ship!"

I exited the light-house at a dead run, scrambling wildly down the mountain trail, with Neptune close behind me. We each carried medkits, in case there were any survivors. Which I doubted. The Ship had disintegrated against the mountain, and pieces of its metal corpse were strewn over a wide area at the base of the peak.

I checked the bodies that had been thrown clear in the crash. Dead. All dead. A gruesome sight. Then . . .

"Over here, master!" Neptune called out to me, gesturing toward a kneeling figure among the rocks. Human. A young female attired in the dark blue-and-gold uniform of Service.

She was stunned and badly hurt. The right leg of her uniform pants had been ripped away and her leg was bleeding steadily from a deep cut. The skin of her face was slashed in several places, and her blood dripped steadily onto her white blouse.

Neptune and I helped her to stand.

"Are you in great pain?" I asked, opening the medkit.

She ignored my question and blinked at me, attempting to focus her eyes. "What about . . . the *others*? Captain Baxter . . . the crew members?"

I shook my head. "You're the only one to come out alive." I hesitated, aware of the import of my words. "I'm sorry."

"Who . . . who are you?"

"Arthur Bedford Addison," I answered. "Keeper of the Tower here on Capella Septime."

At her questioning look, Neptune shyly introduced herself.

"Why did we crash?" the young woman asked. "I don't understand why we crashed."

"The system failed," I said. "A rare malfunction. Everything shut down — and with the Ship coming in . . . well, I couldn't effect the repair in time to warn your captain."

Her head lowered and she moaned, deep in her throat, as I worked to staunch the flow of blood from her wounds.

"You need surgical help," I told her. "I'll vidphone the colony and have them send out a Medship."

"No!" Harsh and final. "I don't want anyone to see me . . . not like *this*." She touched her face. "Surely you can take care of me?"

"I can stop the bleeding," I told her, "but I can't repair the damaged tissue."

"That doesn't matter," she said. "It's my father . . . he works here at the colony. I don't want him to know about this . . . about the crash . . . or my injuries. He has a heart condition. Seeing me . . . like this . . . could kill him."

"But that's no reason to ——"

"It's reason enough!" she declared. Her voice became intense. "Please! I don't want him to know."

"I will do as you wish," I said, "but I think it extremely unwise. You require expert medical care. I am no doctor, and cannot do much for you."

"Do what you can," she said softly. "That's all I ask. Just do what you can."

March 3. Anna — this is her name — has been with us in the light-house for a month now, and her wounds are healing well. She'll have scars, of course, but they can be erased with plastosurgery back at her base on Arcon Three. Her father will never know about the crash that nearly killed her.

Anna is marvelous company — filling in the long hours with the music of her voice. I had not realized just how lonely I had been until Anna appeared. Her glorious spirit has brightened my life. I walk the tower, now, in a haze of joy.

"My grandfather came from your home planet," she declared. "But he would never tell me about his life on Earth. I know that he lived in a great city called the New York. Have you heard of it?"

I smiled. "Yes. I have been there many times."

"My grandfather worked in this city on what he called a wall street. Do you know the place of walls?"

"There are no walls," I said. "Wall Street was an early histori-cal name, and the area where it existed later became a district of commerce. Your grandfather obviously functioned in what they called the stock market."

"In a commissary?"

"No. This market had to do with financial instruments: stocks and bonds."

"That sounds very strange," she told me. "Tell me about these stocks and bonds."

And I did. Just as I had explained many other Earth things to her. About animals. Plants. Oceans. And so much else. She was fascinated, drinking in my words and poring over the books from Earth I gave her to read.

Neptune also seems to enjoy having her with us at the light-house, although my talks with the alien have been greatly curtailed. I spend many hours each day with Anna. Like an eager child, she is hungry to learn even the smallest fact about her ancestral Earth.

March 6. I kissed Anna. At sixty-odd years, I had deemed myself too old for love, but that is precisely the emotion I am feeling for Anna. I have grown to love her, and I think she now loves me in return. When we kissed, it was a thing of passion and meaning.

Will our kiss lead to sexual bonding? I do not know.

I dare not hope.

March 24. Anna does not want to leave the light-house. Her wounds have healed, but she does not seek a return to Arcon Three. She swears that her life is now complete.

With me. *Only* with me.

We have made love. It was wondrous. Her body is warm and smooth. Vibrant. Liquid fire.

I am young again.

Today I climbed the tower stairs with Anna to the top deck. We stood there together at the rail, hand in hand, sharing the evening's slide into darkness. The beacon blazed and the horn cried out across the sea of fog.

"I don't ever want to leave," she told me. "I want to stay here always, with you."

I could not speak. The words of happiness were locked in my throat. The thought of having Anna beside me for the rest of my life is a joy beyond belief.

April 7. A day of incredible agony. I am in the midst of deep shock.

Anna is dead from the quake.

Yes, my dear girl is gone. I had left her on the top deck and had descended the stairs to fetch a special picture book I wanted her to see when the quake began. The tower swayed crazily as I fought my way back to the top. When I arrived, wide-eyed and panting, Anna was gone.

Neptune was there, his body quivering with emotion. "A dreadful occurrence, master. Your lady has fallen! The quake began and she lost her grip on the rail. I tried to reach her . . . but I was too late."

Numbed with shock, I leaned over the railing. The fog obscured my view of the rocks below. I could see nothing.

When I was able to descend from the tower to find her, I fell to my knees in agony. Lifting Anna's broken body, I held her against my chest and sobbed uncontrollably.

I shall never forget that moment.

April 10. Neptune and I are once again alone in the light-house. I am no longer content to be here. Anna's loss is a stabbing pain that never leaves my heart. I stood today on the deck, in the exact spot from which my beloved had fallen, and stared endlessly into the gray wall of fog.

"A tragedy," I said softly to Neptune. "Anna . . . my poor darling. Oh, God, Neptune, I feel so alone."

"You are not alone, master," said the alien. "I am with you. I shall always be with you."

And as I looked at him, he seemed to be smiling.

As this story clearly demonstrates, it is not easy to become immortal. On an outer level, this is a mad comedy, but it has a below-surface darkness that becomes apparent by the climax.

Whenever I write about ghosts or vampires or werewolves or demons I try to avoid the conventional, to strike out for something fresh and unique. After all, such creatures have had thousands of tales written about them. My only justification for revisiting them lies in being able to provide a new approach, new twists. I don't think you've ever read anything like "On Becoming Immortal."

On Becoming Immortal

*H*ey, it's not easy. Becoming immortal, that is.

It all started with an argument. Between me and Letricia. I called her Tris — but she never looked like a Tris. I mean, when you think of Tris, you think of a bright, happy young girl. Like a high school cheerleader. With a perky smile, long, tanned legs, and saucy hips. Not to mention a full rack. The kind of girl you see in soap ads and shampoo commercials. Well, my Tris is dark and dour. (In fact, until much later in our relationship, I never saw her smile.) Average legs, with not much topside. Short black hair and a thin mouth. And no fashion plate — unless you consider Goth fashionable. Always dressed in black, to match her hair. But compelling. Definitely compelling.

We met in a sports bar in Westwood. I'd put away three margaritas and was feeling no pain when I saw Tris, sitting alone in a corner booth. The bar lights flattered her — softened her features, made her look more attractive. I sat down across from her and we began to talk. Just like that. I don't remember what we said to each other that night, but she ended up giving me her phone number. I called her the next day.

We went out together for five months before I put a serious move on her, which was a risk on my part. Thought sure she'd think I wasn't interested in her, but I've never been pushy with women, and Tris let me know, right away, that she didn't appreciate being hit on. So, for five months, I kept my distance.

One night I decided I'd waited long enough. It was time to

make my move. It was late —— almost closing —— and we were sitting side by side on the big sofa in her apartment in Brentwood, not too far from Los Angeles International Airport.

The room was dim, with just the flickering glow from some candles Tris had going. There was the scent of jasmine in the air. (Tris favored incense, and jasmine was her incense of choice. Me, I can take it or leave it.) The candlelight reflected off a bronze shield which hung on the far wall. Tris was hot for old Chinese stuff. Fans and scrolled lamps and long, pale watercolors in a group of three. The effect was like being in another century. Nice, if you're hot for Chinese.

That night, I was hot for Tris. Up to then, I'd never laid a hand on her. I leaned close to her, we kissed, and I ran my fingers lightly over her breasts. (Not her *naked* breasts, God knows; she was laced into some odd kind of Chinese black silk blouse.)

Tris flinched back, her dark eyes flashing. "Don't touch me," she said flatly. "I don't like to be touched."

"We've been dating for five months," I said. "Don't I even rate a *feel* after five months?"

She moved away from me on the sofa. "You're gross," she said, frowning at me.

"Well, *excuse* me, Your Highness," I snapped back. "I think a little 'gross' is in order at this point in our relationship."

"I assumed we were friends," she said, an iced edge in her tone. "I guess I was wrong."

"Friends evolve," I said, trying to control my feelings. "Friendship evolves into something deeper."

"You mean sex."

"Of course."

She sighed, her eyes dark and brooding. "If we get it on, you're going to be hurt."

"Hey, I'll risk some hurt." I was trying to humor her, but it didn't register. I reached out to take her into my arms but she slipped away from me, stood up, and began adjusting her black leather skirt.

"You don't really know me," she declared. "If you really knew me, you'd never want to get it on with me."

"I'll take my chances," I told her. "I can't really get to know you until ——"

"Until we have sex."

"Yeah. Exactly." I reached for her again.

She moved back, pointing at the door. "Leave now. Please. Our friendship can no longer continue."

I stood up, glaring at her. "You want me to just walk away?"

"As you put it, yes. It's best for you. I'm doing you a favor."

Further discussion was useless. "Hell," I said, "maybe you *are* doing me a favor. Five months is long enough to waste on a no-where relationship."

"Just go," she said.

I went.

That's how it started — this business of becoming immortal. I felt as if I'd wasted five months of my life in pursuit of Tris. But five months, to an immortal, is less than a single drop in the ocean of eternity. I considered the possibilities. Living forever would give me the chance to make it with *thousands* of young women. A pleasant thought. A marvelous goal to strive for.

So, as I drove back to my apartment in Westwood, I made my decision. I would become immortal.

The problem was: How?

I'm a life guard on the beach in Malibu, so I get the chance to meet a lot of women. They get caught in riptides, or swim out too far and can't get back to shore, or they get hit by a big wave they can't handle. Then it's up to me. I dive in and rescue them, like *Baywatch*. Me in my Speedos and them in their thongs. They're always grateful to me for saving their lives, and one thing should normally lead to another.

Only it hasn't. I've always been too shy to follow up on my rescues. I keep telling myself I just need more time to get over my shyness, and that's exactly what I'd get if I became immortal. All the time in the world.

I thought about this a lot. There was only one sure way I knew to become immortal: I needed to be bitten by a vampire. Once those fangs sank into my neck, I'd have it made. I'd become a vampire myself and live forever.

There *were* a few disadvantages.

I wouldn't be able to go out in daylight — which meant I'd have to give up my beach job.

I wouldn't be able to eat garlic — but other than shrimp scampi at Alessio's, I didn't like it anyway.

I'd have to avoid crosses — but since I've never been a church goer, that was no problem.

I'd have to sleep in a coffin — which was okay; I could get one at cost from an ex-life guard I knew who was now a funeral director in Newport Beach.

I could keep my apartment. Just have to replace my bed with a coffin. I'd make sure to order one with extra padding under the satin lining for maximum comfort.

I'd also have to give up going to afternoon Dodger games, but that was no big deal. I didn't like the drive to Chavez Ravine much anyway.

But I did have one *big* problem: In 2007, where was I going to find a vampire to bite my neck?

You just don't see members of The Undead around much anymore. Back when they were making all those Dracula movies, there must have been some real vampires lurking near the sets, just to make sure everything was authentic. Vampire consultants. Bela Lugosi probably knew a few, but he was long gone. (Obviously, none of them bit him on the neck, or he'd still be here.)

Then inspiration hit me. I got on my computer and sent an e-mail to Anne Rice, the chick who turns out all those blood-sucking bestsellers, asking her how I could contact a vampire. She never replied. Guess she figured me for some kind of nutcase.

I Googled vampires on the net, but came up empty. A ton of stuff *about* vampires, but nothing about how to *contact* one.

It was frustrating, trying to become immortal. I checked the Yellow Pages, then consulted a fortune teller in Santa Monica named Madame Spartacus (her ad said she specialized in "the unusual") and asked her if she saw a vampire in my future.

She lived in a small, stucco-and-brick frame house two blocks south of Wilshire. Her living room windows were draped with black velvet — old and dusty, with cobwebs clinging to the tops — and inside her living room it was like being in a musty cave. She used a Middle Eastern kind of table, with a clouded crystal ball on top, which was placed near her chair. She was maybe six feet tall, skinny as a fence post, with spiky white hair and skin like dried out parchment. And she wore a lot of purple eye shadow, which didn't improve her looks.

Madame Spartacus gazed into the crystal ball for maybe five full minutes, muttering to herself. Then she smiled. Since she had a wiry black mustache and several of her teeth were missing, it wasn't an engaging sight. "Yep. Yep. Yep." She finally nodded. "I see one."

"A vampire?"

"No doubt about it," she told me, adjusting the stained white lace which surrounded her turkey throat. "Got a cigarette on ya?"

"I don't smoke," I told her.

"I oughta give 'em up. Damn cigarettes gonna ruin my looks."

"You do see a vampire in there, right?" I asked, pressing the point.

"Righto," she said. "I do. There is most certainly a vampire in your future."

"Great!" I said. "When do we get together?"

"You askin' me for a *date*?" She smiled again and I winced.

"Eh, no . . . I meant . . . when do I get together with the vampire?"

She clucked an age-blackened tongue against her remaining teeth and bent low over the crystal ball. "Nope. Nope. Nope."

"What does 'nope' mean?" I asked.

"Means I can't give ya a time or a location," she said. "It's all pretty smoky in there, but I did spot one vampire for ya." She held out a mottled hand. "That'll be ten bucks."

I handed her a ten dollar bill and she gave me a receipt.

When I left Madame Spartacus, I was more frustrated than ever. It was nice to know that I was due to meet a vampire —— but *when* and *where*?

I drove to downtown L.A. to check out some of the scummier areas where I figured a vampire might hole up. Cheap bars. Seedy hotels. Dark, dank places. The wino I met in a scuzzy alley off Spring Street looked up from his bottle and squinted at me with rheumy eyes when I spoke to him. He didn't question my need to contact a vampire. Nice guy, actually, who tried to help me as best he could. Told me to talk to the desk clerk at the Bright Hawaii Hotel. The wino was sure that at least one vampire lived there.

And one was all I needed.

The Bright Hawaii was not bright, nor was it, of course, in Hawaii. It was on Broadway, directly across the street from a boarded-over porno theater which was still advertising *Debbie Does Dallas* on its marquee. The hotel was in a sleazy, weathered-brick building, and its cramped lobby reeked of rot and mildew. I walked over the threadbare carpet toward the desk clerk. He was a bald little man with no chin, and the bright red spots on his nose proved that he drank too much.

His name, according to the soup-stained tag on his shirt, was Clarence.

"Clarence, I'm going to ask you an unusual question," I said to him.

"Go ahead, fella," he told me in a rasping voice. "I been asked every kind of question there is." His eyes were boiled eggs above a thick pair of dirty glasses perched on his sweaty nose.

"I would like to know, do you have any vampires staying here?"

"Vampires?" He spat into a wad of toilet paper. "Ya mean folks who fly around at night and suck blood?"

"Yeah. I was told you may have one or more of them residing here."

Clarence shook his bald head. "We got us all kinda freaks stayin' at the Bright Hawaii — but no vampires. An' I'd know if we did. I sure would."

"Do you have any idea where I might find a vampire?"

"Try Transylvania," he rasped.

"A hotel?"

"Naw, it's a place. Somewhere over in Romania. Where that writer fella said Dracula come from. They got vampires out the ass in Transylvania."

"An excellent suggestion," I said. "My profound thanks."

I laid a five dollar bill in front of him on the desk. His claw-like hand closed over it. "I always try to help folks," said the little man. "My wife, Alma, she calls me a natural helper. 'Clarence,' she'll say to me, 'you're a born natural.' Makes me feel like I'm worth more than spit on a stick in this crazy world."

"As indeed you are," I agreed, moving for the exit door.

The air outside was brown and dense with smog, but after the lobby of the Bright Hawaii, it smelled like rain-freshened roses.

I found a travel agent in Burbank who booked me on a flight to Romania. Southeastern Europe. The colorful tourist brochure said that Transylvania contained most of Romania's mountains, and that's where Dracula's castle is located — in the high mountains.

I landed in Bucharest, the capital, and hired a car and driver to take me to Brasov in the Transylvanian Alps. My driver's name was Niculescu, but he said everyone called him Nick. He was skinny and undernourished (most everyone I saw in Romania was, but he spoke English pretty well and was a jolly sort of guy and good company for the long journey to Brasov). When I told him I wanted to go to Dracula's castle, he told me that the people around there believed that Dracula's ghost still haunts the place.

"A ghost won't do me any good," I said to Nick. "Ghosts can't bite." He laughed, and said that was a good title for a film.

After a tiresome night drive on very bad roads, the sun finally dawned over the eastern crest of the high mountains that surrounded us. Nick stopped the car and pointed upward to a dark stone castle which loomed over the top of a thickly-forested peak. "That's where Count Dracula lived. He ordered the castle built with extra big cellars for all of his coffins. Sucked blood from a lot of people up there, or so they say."

"How do I get there? I don't see any road."

"Climb those steps cut into the side of the mountain," Nick said, as he waved his arm to the right to show me. "They'll take you up to the main courtyard."

"Anyone live there now?"

"The Protopopescu family," he answered. "They're famous in Romania."

"What kind of people are they?" I asked, hoping he'd tell me they were vampires.

"Quiet folk. Hard-working. They export wine from grapes grown in the valley on the other side of the castle. Goes out from Brasov to all over the world. Brings in much money to Romania."

I paid him his fee, and added an over-generous tip. Then I began climbing the stone steps up the steep mountainside.

It was a long way to the top.

Castle Dracula (or, to be currently accurate, Castle Protopopescu), was impressive: multi-level battlements, a high water tower, what looked like a Gothic chapel, and cobbled walkways and courtyards.

I was met at the castle door by Mrs. Protopopescu, probably in her late eighties, who wore a floor-length, embroidered dress that looked like it came from a Hollywood studio prop department. She was short and dumpy, with apple-red cheeks. Long black hairs were growing out of both of her ears.

She immediately sized me up. American. Jet-lagged. Starving because of the long overland trip from Bucharest. (My last meal had been on the plane.)

"Come in to eat," she said. "You need a good Romanian breakfast."

At a large wooden table in the huge castle kitchen, I chowed down eggs with olives, home baked bread fresh out of the oven, and a lot of small, fried meat balls. When I finished, both my stomach and my courage were full again.

"Thank you for breakfast," I said. "I definitely needed that. And I've been wondering, how do you come to speak English so well?" I asked.

"It was my favorite subject in school," she said. "When I was in secondary school, Romanian students competed in national examinations of English, and I scored the highest in the country in my year." Her eyes shone with the memory as she looked directly at me. "Where are you from?"

"Los Angeles," I said.

She nodded knowingly. "My brother was there, in the last big war. He jumped off the top of your City Hall."

I was shocked. "That's terrible," I said. "What caused him to ——"

"He was convinced he could fly." She shrugged. "He was wrong."

"Terrible," I repeated numbly, thinking that if he'd been a vampire, he could have actually flown off the building. Providing it was dark outside, of course. If he was a vampire, he wouldn't have been able to fly in daylight.

"Why did you come to Romania?" she asked.

"I'm looking for a vampire. I'd hoped to find one here at the castle."

She chuckled. "Then you've had a long trip for naught."

"For naught?"

"We have no vampires here," she declared. "They were quite plentiful in the thirteenth century, according to our local legends. But you never know about local legends. There are a lot of crazy people in Romania."

I could feel my face fall. "But this castle was——"

"Oh, yes," she nodded. "This has been identified as Count Dracula's castle, but that's just hogwash. The castle has always been in our family. That writer who did the book on Dracula —— Mr.

Stoker —— he came here once, searched for a likely castle, and decided that this one was frightening enough for a vampire to live in." She shook her head. "But that was ——"

"Hogwash," I said.

"Yes," she said.

I thought for a moment. "If there are no vampires here, where do you think I might find one in your country? Surely in some of the small, out-of-the-way areas . . ."

"You might try the village of Basarab, at the end of the Borgo Pass," Mrs. Protopopescu told me. "Things haven't changed much there in the past eight hundred years. If any vampires are left in Romania, that's where they'll be."

"Terrific," I said. "I'll try there."

And I did.

I'd seen enough vampire films to know that Dracula's coach traveled regularly through the Borgo Pass, so Mrs. P's lead was a good one for me. Of course, much had changed since Dracula's time. The winding dirt road which cut through a thick forest of dark trees in his day had given way to a paved mountain highway that snaked crazily through a thousand twisting curves. The bus trip along the Borgo Pass was nothing short of a nightmare, as I peered from the window at the thousand-foot drop awaiting us at the highway's edge. The bus driver was a bored scarecrow with haggard eyes who seemed half-asleep at the wheel as he barely negotiated the hairpin turns. My stomach churned with anxiety all the way to Basarab.

Once I'd reached the village, a pudding-faced peasant dressed in a sheepskin vest and a shedding fur cap directed me wordlessly to a local tavern. There I was served stuffed cabbage, sauerkraut, brown Romanian bread, and a mug of wine by a mournful hunchback with a milky cast over one eye who spoke just enough half-remembered school English for us to communicate.

Basarab was a small village of crude stone huts, surrounded by unpaved streets which smelled of raw sewage. I asked the mournful hunchback if there were any vampires in the area. "No more. Long time ago, yes. Young girls show bite marks on neck." The hunchback sighed deeply.

"What happened to the vampires?"

He shrugged. "Who know? Go to Bucharesti, maybe. Them who survived the stakes."

"Stakes?"

"Villagers did not want necks bitten by vampires, so found sleeping vampires in cemetery, where they sleep during day. Bang! Drove wood stakes through the every one."

"And now?

"No vampires left in village. Too bad. Vampires bring tourists, tourists bring hard money. No vampires in Basarab."

I nodded.

His good eye winked at me. "If you interested in werewolf, we have here. Every full moon, they howl in woods. Bad wolves. Tear throat out of several people." He looked mournful again. "Tourists not care about werewolves. No 'charisma,' one man from New York City, United States, tell me." He fixed me with his good eye. "You like werewolf?"

"Afraid not," I told him.

"Too bad," he said, humping mournfully off towards the kitchen.

My belly was rumbling when I left the tavern. Everything I'd eaten there had been cooked, but I was really worried about the sewage water which had probably been used to wash the dishes in the kitchen.

The trip had been a total bust.

Back in L.A., I placed an ad in the L.A. WEEKLY:

VAMPIRE WANTED
Man seeks immortality. Requires member of Undead
for neck-biting purposes. Will pay for service.

I listed my hotmail address. No telling what crazy person might decide to check me out for their own deviant purposes.

I didn't actually believe that my ad would attract a vampire, but it was worth a shot. I'd tried everything else. Maybe this would work.

A week passed. No incoming e-mail from my Hotmail account. I gave up, figuring that I'd never become immortal, and then a message *did* arrive. It was my only shot. I was desperate, so I did the unthinkable: When I answered back, I included the address of my apartment in Westwood.

At almost midnight, on Friday the 13th — a prime night for bloodsuckers — my doorbell chimed. I opened the door to a cowled figure in a long black cape, who stood silhouetted against the hallway lights. A hand reached out to display a copy of my ad. The vampire's bona fides.

Madame Spartacus had been right. I had found my vampire.

"Step inside," I said, swinging the door wide.

The vampire entered my apartment.

I was nervous, and about to offer my guest some wine, when I recalled that vampires didn't drink . . . wine.

The bloodsucker sat down on my living room sofa. I peered at the creature's face under the head cowl and realized it was a female. Her features were lost in shadow, but it was a female for sure.

She spoke in a low, whispery voice: "How may I serve you?"

"Well," I said, "to get right to the point, I want to become immortal. Which means I'd appreciate your sinking your fangs into my neck and sucking my blood. I'm prepared to pay you two hundred and fifty dollars for the neck bite. Is that satisfactory?"

The vampire nodded.

"Then . . ." I grinned nervously. "Shall we, uh, get to it?"

I popped the top button on my shirt, loosened my collar, and bared my neck. "Where do you want me?"

The vampire patted the pillow next to her. I sat down on the sofa and tipped back my head for easy access.

She leaned towards me, with a kind of hungry hissing, and I got a good close look at her.

"Holy shit!" I gasped, jumping to my feet. "You're Tris!"

She threw back her cowl. "You know I've always preferred being called Letricia," she said. And for the first time in our relationship, she smiled. She had two long teeth, sharp as needles, at each side of her upper jaw.

Vampire fangs.

"Now you understand why I couldn't become intimate with you," Tris said. "I didn't want to turn you into one of *us*." She chuckled softly. "Until I saw your ad, I had no idea you actually wanted to become . . . undead."

"Yeah, well . . . so now you know." My voice was shaky. The idea of Tris being a vampire blew my mind. I was still trying to adjust to it when she grabbed me, pulled me into her arms, and hissed: "Let's get intimate!"

She sank her fangs into my neck. There was a split second of what I later identified as pain, followed by a total feeling of full-body ecstasy.

There's no more to tell. Except to end this with a slightly re-worked version of an old cliché . . .

And they lived happily *forever* after.

When "Blood Sky" was chosen for Volume Three of Best New Horror, *the editors described it as "a terrifying glimpse into the mind of a serial killer, made all the more disturbing by the author's matter-of-fact treatment of the subject."*

From Ted Bundy to John Wayne Gacy, the serial killer invisibly walks among us. Their crimes lack the motivation of the average criminal. The fact that their victims are randomly chosen makes such killers extremely difficult to apprehend. There is no distinctive "type." The guy next door could be a serial killer, or that clean-cut fellow who's dating your teenage daughter. No way of knowing — until they make a mistake and are captured. But how many more are out there that may never be caught?

Blood Sky

Note: The following excerpts are from the notebook
of Edward Timmons, known as "The Big Sky Strangler."
Mr. Timmons was shot to death near Lewiston, Montana,
on October 15, 1990 by Sheriff John Longbow of
Fergus County. It has not yet been determined how
many victims Mr. Timmons assaulted and killed, but
it is known that he favored young women with long hair.

ometimes, sleeping here alone in these strange Montana motel rooms, I have some weird dreams, so I figured I'd put
some of them down in my notebook to give insight into them.

Like the carnival dream. I'm a kid in the dream, maybe ten or
eleven, and my grandpa (on my mom's side of the family) takes me
to this carnival. It's one of the cheap road shows, run-down and
seedy, with holes in the tents, and with most of the rides in bad
shape, and with the Ferris Wheel all rusted and unsafe looking. The
clowns look sad and the hoochy-koochy girls have sagging bellies
and dead-fish eyes and wear lipstick like slashes of blood across
their lips. They try to look sexy, but they're just pathetic. They make
you sick.

Gramps says let's try some of the games and he buys two tick-
ets for us to try the shooting gallery. I miss most of the painted
ducks but Gramps hits every one, knocks them all down, and the
guy in the booth, real fat and mean in a dirty white shirt all stained
under the armpits, hands Gramps his prize. It's a live chicken. (In
dreams, I guess you can win prizes like that.) Gramps takes the bird
under his arm and we go into this water ride called the Tunnel of
Terror. You get in this creaky dark green boat and it takes you
around corners in the dark where things jump out at you, and horns

blare and you hear people screaming. (I hate being confined in dark places.)

Suddenly, in the middle of the ride, the boat stops dead still in the water and we're sitting there alone, just me and Gramps. It's real quiet. Just the water lapping at the sides of the boat and the two of us breathing there in the dark. Gramps takes the chicken and holds it out in front of him. Then he starts to chuckle and next thing in the dream he's got his hands around the bird's neck and he strangles it. Then he hands me the dead chicken, with the head lolling loose. The chicken is wet and mushy, and I tell Gramps I don't want to hold it. Worms are coming out of it.

I throw the dead chicken into the water and when I turn back to Gramps his face is all lit in red, the Devil's face, and he has fur on his tongue and his eye sockets are empty, like in a skull. He puts his hands around my neck and begins to squeeze.

Good boy, he says, my good, good boy.

And I wake up.

Now what does a dream like this really mean?

A week later . . .

Another bad dream. Really bad. In fact, I'm writing this entry at 6 a.m. in the morning (there's a blood sky outside my motel window) because the nightmare woke me up and I can't get back to sleep, thinking about it. So I might as well write it down.

It started real ordinary. The scary ones all seem to start that way, easy and natural, and they gradually slip into the awful parts, taking you along into the dark area you don't want to get into, that you get terrified of, and would never go to if you weren't dreaming.

This one began in warm yellow sunlight, with me walking along a road that cut through this piney wood. (There were other kinds of trees there, too, but I don't know much about different trees so I can't say what they were.) Anyway, there were plenty of trees, with a mass of pine needles under my feet, and with thick green foliage everywhere.

There was the crisp smell of sunlight and the church smell of the pines and the cheeping of birds. All straight out of a kid's picture book, and that's what I think inspired this part of the dream, because I remember when I was seven, that Gramps bought me this picture book of forests around the world, and I just got totally lost in that book, trying to imagine what it would be like to walk through those magical-looking forests, with the tall trees all around me.

And that's how it was in this dream — just me alone at the age of seven, in this pine forest, enjoying the peace and quiet. But then it started getting dark. Fast. A lot faster than in real life. All the birds stopped singing and the sun dropped out of the sky like a falling stone. The path I was on narrowed, and the trees seemed to be pressing in closer. And it got cold. A wind had come swirling up, with voices in it, crying Run, Eddie! Something bad is coming, Eddie! Better run, boy! Catch you if you don't run fast. Run!

And I took off like a wet cat. Started booting it along that path with tree branches whipping me, slashing at my face and cutting my shirt like swords. I was crying by then, and really scared, because the whole forest seemed to come alive and the trees all had mouths full of sharp teeth, like daggers, and now they were leaning over to bite at my flesh. I felt pain, and blood was running into my eyes, blinding me.

Then I saw a cabin. Just ahead, with the path going right up to the door. It was open. I ran inside, slamming the door behind me and leaning against it, sobbing and shaking all over.

Suddenly I wasn't a seven-year-old kid anymore. I was me, now, at my age, and I was buck naked. My flesh (no cuts or blood!) was puckered with the cold as the night wind sliced through the cracks in the cabin's roof and walls.

Then I realized (the way you do in dreams) that a big deeply-upholstered chair (we had one back in Kansas) was directly in front of the fireplace and I hunched down in that chair, pressed against the cushions for warmth, shivering, with my arms crossed over my chest. There was no warmth from the fireplace — only dead black ashes.

That's when I heard the sound of something coming out of the forest toward the cabin. Clump, clump, clump. Heavy footsteps. Heading for me. Coming for me. Something awful.

And getting closer every second.

I was sweating. As cold as it was, I was in a sweat of fear. My eyes searched for escape. There was no back door to the place, no windows. What could I do? Where could I go?

Then the door bulged. Like it was under a terrible pressure. Something was bending it inward. A deep voice, old and raspy, cried out. Let me in, Eddie! Open the door!

I jumped from the chair and ran to the far wall, pressing my back against the rough wood, my eyes bugging as the door just *exploded* open.

And Gramps was there. Just like in the carnival dream. Only instead of carrying a chicken he had a long dark green coat over his arm. He was smiling at me.

Nothing to be afraid of, boy. It's just me an' your mom.

And that's when I saw that it wasn't a coat over his arm. It was my mother's body, loose like a sack and dark green with grave mold. Dark green rotting.

Your mama's hungry, boy. I brought her here for a feed. She needs to eat.

And he walked over and grabbed me by the neck and kind of draped my mother's body around me, with her rotted arms hanging over my shoulders and her moldy legs pressing against my naked skin. The stink that came off her was the stink of the grave, of deep earth and things long dead.

I was helpless. Then, slowly, her head raised itself and her dead face was right in front of *my* face, maybe an inch away, and she was smiling a broken-toothed idiot's smile and her eyes were filmed with red, wormy veins, and I could see her tongue moving like a fat dark snake inside the rotted cavern of her mouth.

Eddie . . . my little boy. Didn't I always take care of you, sweetie? Now it's your turn to take care of your Mommy . . .

And she buried her teeth in my neck, ripping out a huge gobbet of my flesh and starting to chew . . .

Which is when I woke up here in the motel, covered with cold slimy sweat. My muscles were twitching and I could hardly breathe.

It was one of the worst nightmares I've ever had.

Now, why would I ever have a dream about being devoured by my mother's corpse? She's not even dead, for one thing. Why should I dream of her being dead? There's no reason on earth I should have a dream like this. No reason.

The science people tell us that if we don't dream every night we go crazy. That our minds need to let off steam, as it were, and that dreaming is natural for everybody. Maybe. But I hate having dreams I can't control and being a victim to them. Having dreams is supposed to keep you from going nuts, but what if they *make* you nuts? I mean, if I had dreams as bad as this every night I'd go insane.

I had the dream about my mother two days ago and I think I've figured it out. For one thing, I consider myself on the level of a professional shrink (which is why I'd never go to one). I've always been able to study people and what makes them tick, and I am quite good at reading beneath the surface of a person.

So I analyzed my dream in relation to my inner self. I think there must be a deep-buried part of me that thinks my mother was kind of smothering me, that she fed off me emotionally after my father began treating her so bad, beating her up and everything. Not that she was the huggy-kissy type. Not at all. I've mentioned in this notebook before how she didn't like any open affection, no outward displays. But, inside, I think she turned to me as a kind of replacement for my father. It was subtle, but it was there, and I sensed it somehow, even as a kid.

For example, she didn't like sharing me with anybody. When Gramps would come over (even Mom called him that) and he'd want to take me home with him for the weekend, take me to the park for ice cream and a ride on the merry-go-round they had there, she always said no, I couldn't go with him to his house because I had to do chores over the weekend. Once every summer she did let me go out to a cabin Gramps had rented near a lake in the woods (the cabin in my dream looked a lot like it) and I had some great times swimming out there and eating the fresh peach ice cream that Gramps made himself.

I have one bad memory connected with the lake. It was what I did to a litter of pups, six of them. I put them all in a cardboard box and then took them to the edge of the wooden dock and then pushed them under the water. When the bubbles didn't come up anymore I knew they were dead. I can't remember exactly why I did that except for the power feeling it gave me, that charge I get as I'm taking a life, that's still with me, even today. When I strangle someone, when I drive my thumbs deep into their neck, when I feel them kick and struggle and then go limp like a loose sack in my hands, it's a very satisfying thing. Fulfilling, really. It's not a sexual thing, not like the wet dreams I used to have as a kid, and it doesn't give me a hard-on. It's more like what I've heard from people who take drugs — a sudden high, a rush of pure pleasure. You kind of tingle all over.

Killing has always given me that. Which is one reason it's so hard to quit.

But getting back to the dream . . . I suppose it came from my subconscious, based on that deep-down feeling that Mom used me as a kind of emotional *food* when I was a kid. The dream makes some sense on that basis.

I feel better now, having figured it out. It was still terrible, having it, and I hope I don't have any more like it, but at least I've got it analyzed.

And I'm proud of myself for that.

There's a feeling in Montana that you're back in the Old West. Lots of the men wear cowboy hats and walk around in fancy cowhide boots. Every town you go to is full of Western artifacts and every area has its Western ghost town. It's kind of like the Civil War is in the South. You go there and it seems the Civil War just ended about a month ago. People still talk about it and there are souvenirs and Confederate flags and banners. In Montana, it's the Old West which is very much alive. Real John Wayne country. Including a lot of rodeos.

There was one going on here in Conrad, just a mile or two beyond the main part of town, and I decided it might be fun to go see it. Get my mind off what the papers were saying. I'd never been to a rodeo. Had read about them and seen movies. In fact, I remember one with Steve McQueen in it. He played a guy named Junior somebody and I enjoyed watching that one.

I found out that rodeo was a lot like going to a circus. Everything is noisy, with bucking horses and cowgirls in flashy spangled outfits and bright-painted clowns for the bulls to chase and big grandstands full of people eating popcorn and drinking Cokes. (Is there anywhere on this whole planet where people don't drink Coca-Cola? I've seen photos of Coke signs in the deserts of Arabia and the jungles of Africa — and you can bet that when they build a city on Mars the first thing they'll be shipping in is truckloads of Coca-Cola. Me, I'd like to have just a tiny percentage of the profits from these zillions of Cokes they sell all over the world every day. I'd be a rich man for sure.)

I got a pretty good aisle seat in the main grandstand and nibbled on some roasted peanuts and watched those whooping cowboys get tossed off these fierce-looking bulls. They'd roll their eyes, these big bulls would, with white froth looping from their mouths, and just shake off the riders like water off a dog's back. The second a cowboy hit the dirt a clown would jump out to lure the bull away from the fallen rider — and when the bull went after the clown he'd jump into a barrel and the bull's horns would bang into the wood while the cowboy got up and limped back to the chutes. Not all of them limped, but most did. I couldn't figure why anybody would want to try riding a bull or a wild, crazy-eyed bucking horse. Even when you won, the prizes weren't anything to write home about. There are plenty of broken bones and skull fractures in a rodeo. Dumb way to make a living.

I read somewhere that they use a real tight strap around the balls of the bull to make him jump harder and higher. And they do other things just as bad. This article I read told all about it. I like getting the inside scoop, because there's always more to everything than you see on the surface. (There's sure a lot more to Yours Truly than most people ever guess at!)

The calf-roping was fun to watch — and these boys could ride and rope like the rest of us breathe air. It was something to see the way they competed against the clock, making every move count. Makes you realize how much time we waste in our lives. What I need in my life right now is a goal to work toward. Not just getting control of the compulsion, I mean having a solid future in mind. But when I try to think of the future it's all blank, like a sheet of white paper. Like getting a fortune cookie in a Chinese café and breaking it open to read your fortune and finding out there's no little slip of paper inside. Just an empty cookie. That's how my whole life seems these days. Like that cookie.

I was thinking such thoughts when I felt a hand touch my left shoulder.

Hi, pardner, you look a mite thirsty. How 'bout a beer?

I looked up at this attractive cowgirl in a short, fringed skirt, white boots decorated with silver stars, a spangled blouse and red bandanna, topped by a wide-brim Western sombrero. A beer tray was balanced from a strap on her shoulder. I don't like beer, I told her.

That's okay. I've sold enough today. Mind if I sit? I'm kind of tuckered.

I don't mind, I said.

And I moved on the wooden slat seat to give her some room. She sat down, slipping the tray from her shoulder and letting it rest against her booted leg. The skin between her skirt and her white boot tops was very tan. A real outdoor Montana type.

You got a cigarette?

I've given up smoking, I told her. Cigarettes can kill you.

Lotta things can kill you, she said. I also drink Scotch whiskey and that can kill me. When I visit my sister in California I could get killed by an earthquake. Or a dog with rabies could bite me. Hell, I could even meet up with the Big Sky Strangler — but right now, I just want a cigarette.

Her remark about meeting the Big Sky Strangler seemed almost surreal. The last thing this woman figured was that she was talking to him right this minute. Strange. Life can be strange.

It wasn't easy for me to quit cigarettes, I told her. It's something I really had to work at.

What do you want from me? she asked sharply, a Boy Scout merit badge?

You can make fun of it if you want to, I said, but I'm proud of what I've done.

She patted my shoulder. You're right, I was just being a bitch. Didn't mean to put you down, darlin', but I get a little testy about this time of day. This is no sweet job lugging heavy cans of beer up and down these lousy grandstands, and getting my fanny pinched by drunken cowboys who think I can't wait to climb into the saddle with 'em. Lotta creeps in this world.

I can see how it's a rough job, I told her.

She took off her big white hat and pushed at her hair. It was the same color hair as the one that I killed in Butte, a kind of sandy brown.

I'm gonna take off early, call it a day, she said. Do you like fish?

I blinked. Oh, I guess they're all right. I neither like nor dislike them, I said. I never had one as a pet.

She let out a hoot and slapped her hat against one knee.

No, no. What I meant is, do you like *eating* them?

I had to laugh at myself on that one. I'd taken her question in a literal sense. Her personality was throwing me off. I'm never much good with direct women.

My boyfriend, bastard that he is, just rode off into the sunset, leaving me with a fridge full of trout and no one to feed 'em to. So what do you say to a free fish dinner?

I say great, I told her. In fact, I appreciate the offer.

Good. You may be straight arrow, but I think you're cute. She shook my hand and her grip was firm.

I'm Lorry Haines, she said.

Ed Timmons, I said back to her.

I didn't want to eat alone tonight, she said. Now I won't have to.

Lorry Haines drove me to a small cream-colored frame house trimmed in blue with a neat little fenced yard.

I met Bobby at a rodeo in Billings, she told me as she started dinner. He was a bronc rider, top of his class. Tall and hunky with muscle in all the right places. We hit it off and he asked me to leave town and tour the circuit with him.

Is Billings your home town? I asked.

Yeah, I grew up there. When I met Bobby, I was working in a clothing store. Went to the rodeo that weekend with a girl friend and there was ole Bobby, tall in the saddle, with a glint in his eye. Before the weekend was over I'd agreed to quit my job and follow him around the circuit.

That's when you started selling beer, eh?

Yeah. They always need people in the stands. It was easy to get work.

What happened between you and Bobby?

Oh, it was great for awhile. He was Bobby Superstud, knew just about everything there is to know about giving a girl a good time in the sack.

Uh huh, I said, beginning to feel a little uncomfortable.

But we fought like a couple of bobcats. Over all kinds of stuff. Then, last night, I came home here to this house and found a note from the bastard. A kiss-off note. He just up and took off. Probably with some bimbo he met in town.

Then this place isn't yours?

Nope. I never owned me a house. This belongs to a friend of Bobby's, a retired rodeo rider. He's out of town this weekend, so we got it. I'll be leaving tomorrow.

Where will you go?

Who knows? I'm just a rolling stone these days.

Funny, I told her. That's what a lot of people have called me.

She'd been fixing dinner as we talked, bustling around the kitchen while I sat at a small Formica table in the dining nook. She asked me to help her fix the salad, so I stared cutting up the lettuce she'd washed.

You could always go back to Billings, I said. Aren't your folks still there?

Sure, but we never got along. We're not on what you might call the best of terms. Mom's a real bitch, if you want to know the truth. And Dad's no bargain, either.

So what *are* you going to do?

She turned from the trout, which were browning in the pan, and grinned at me. I dunno, she said. Maybe I'll join a convent.

I grinned back at that. Yeah. I can see you as the praying cowgirl nun!

I know one damn thing, she said. After tomorrow, I'm finished with rodeos.

The food was ready and she laid it out on the table. We sat down and began eating. The trout was great — covered in cornmeal, all brown and crusty, just the way I like it — and I told her so.

Thanks, pardner! she said.

We ate in silence for a while, then she canted her head and gave me a little cat-grin.

Anybody every tell you how cute you are?

I knew it was coming, but it still shook me. This direct sexual approach. Like the older woman in Butte. I didn't know how to handle it. I never have.

You're the cute one, I said. Bet a lot of guys have been after you since you grew up.

She bit into a dinner roll. Then she took a swallow of coffee. Then she looked at me again.

You like oral sex? she asked.

I woke up the next morning alone in bed. Lorry was already dressed and packed.

You better get your butt in gear, darlin', because ole Jeeter, who owns this place, is due back today. And that man can be mean as a snake in a sock. We'd best be gone.

She was right. It would be hard to explain just who I was if this Jeeter guy showed, so I took a quick shower, got dressed, gobbled down the breakfast Lorry fixed for me (great little cook!) and got out of there.

We'd talked in bed after we had sex. About the future. About us pairing up on the road. Just two rolling stones. It sounded good to me at the time, since the sex with Lorry had been real fine and I needed somebody like her to help me straighten out.

Naturally I didn't tell her about the compulsion, or that I'd ever killed anybody.

The thing is, and I know whoever reads this will get a big laugh out of it, but the thing is I was in love. For the fist time in my whole life. Truly in love. They say that love can strike like lightening, that one minute you're not in love and the next minute you are. And that's how it happened with me and Lorry. There was something about her that just ignited my blood. I don't mean just the great sex we had, I mean her whole *being*. She gave off a kind of wondrous aura. I don't expect you to understand because I don't myself. But it happened, and a fact is a fact.

Lorry owned an orange VW — a Volkswagen bug. I'd never driven one before and I was not impressed with its performance. It had so little power that it was almost impossible to pass other cars on the Interstate.

A bug's not supposed to be fast, she told me with a grin. This is no sports car. VWs were made to *last*. This one's twenty-five years old.

She told me she'd had it for the last three years and it had never given her any mechanical trouble.

I don't like it, I said. Ted Bundy drove a Volkswagen.

Who?

The guy that killed all those coeds, I told her. Cut their heads off, on a lot of them. He drove a gold VW.

So he drove a bug, she said. So what? It's not going to turn you into a mass murderer.

I blinked at that. Talking to her about Bundy was stupid. I had to avoid that kind of talk.

I want you to sell it, I said.

Sell it! Her voice jumped up a couple of octaves. You gotta be nuts. I'm not selling my bug.

I didn't look at her, just kept driving. I'd made her angry. Our first day together and already we were fighting.

When we get into Great Falls, I said, I want you to find a dealer and get rid of this car.

You're *serious*, aren't you?

Yes.

But Eddie, we need wheels. If we're gonna travel around to-gether we need a car.

Fine. Buy another. Just so it isn't a VW.

A silence. Then she said, hard-toned: And what if I say no?

Then we split, I said.

Over a car! Her brows were lifted in astonishment.

I took the next off ramp for I-15 and pulled to a stop on an access road under a big tree. Then I turned off the engine and reached for her. She came into my arms smooth as butter. I kissed away the frown between her eyes. She kissed me back. Things were a lot better.

I'm really not trying to give you a bad time, I said. It's just that whenever I'm in this car I'll be thinking of Ted Bundy and what he did to those coeds — and I don't want to do that.

She nestled her head against my shoulder.

Okay, she said, if it bothers you so much, I'll sell the VW.

Then she raised her head and looked at me. You know, Eddie, you're a strange guy.

I nodded. I never said I wasn't.

I'm not going to let what we've got go to hell over a car, she said. Already, you're very special to me.

When I came to Montana, I said to her, I never thought I'd get into a heavy relationship. It's kinda spooky.

I think I love you, she said.

I think I love you, too, I told her.

She nestled deeper into my shoulder. It was a fine fall day, cool and crisp. A slight breeze ruffled her hair against my cheek. I had my arm around her and I guess we looked like something out of one of those Norman Rockwell paintings.

I want to know all about you, Lorry said. I don't know anything. What was your childhood like?

I don't want to get into that kind of stuff, I said. Not now.

She didn't argue, just closed her eyes and let the breeze blow over us under that big Montana sky.

I sat there in the silent VW with her head pressing against my shoulder wondering if this was the karma that Kathleen Kelly told me I'd find here in Montana. Was this the answer to my problem? Was this what I came here for? And what about the future? Could I have a real future — a loving future — with Lorry Haines? A man like me?

Could I.

I started the engine of the VW, then headed back for the Interstate. We would have to live the future hour by hour, day by day.

And the compulsion. What about the killings? Maybe, with Lorry in my life, I could find a way to stop.

Maybe.

As a native Montanan, Lorry knew Great Falls. She was my own personal tour guide, telling me things as we drove.

Got its name, she said, from the Lewis and Clark Expedition when ole Meriwether Lewis walked out of camp one summer morning in 1805, following the sound of a tremendous roar along the river. That's when he discovered what he called The Great Falls of the Missouri. Big dam is there now.

Is it still worth looking at? I asked Lorry.

You bet, she said. It's a sight, lemme tell you.

You know, I told her, I've always had a yen to go white water rafting down the Colorado River, along the Grand Canyon and all.

Sounds like fun. We can do it together, she said.

The scenery around us was postcard perfect. Off to the west the Rockies took a hike into the sky and to the east were vast wheat fields and rolling prairies.

How big is Great Falls? I asked.

Pretty big, for Montana, she said. More than seventy thousand, last time I heard. People just like the location, the way it's set between Glacier and Yellowstone. And the winters are not all that bad here, because of the chinooks.

The what?

Warm winds that blow down off the slopes of the Rockies. You never heard of 'em?"

Never, I said.

Now we were into town, with Lorry pointing out various sights as we drove past.

That's the Russell Museum, she said. You know, the famous western artist, Charles M. Russell. He lived here in Great Falls. His paintings are worth a fortune.

I think I've seen some of his stuff, I said.

This would be a nice place to raise kids, Lorry said.

I never wanted kids, I told her, my voice taking on a sharp note. If you're looking to have kids by me, you've got the wrong stud.

Hey, don't take everything so personal, she said. I was just talking about what kind of a place this is. It's a *family* kind of town.

What about you, I asked. Did you ever want children?

I guess every woman wants children at some time — but I don't think I'd make a very good mother, she said.

Maybe not, I said.

We found a motel with a long wooden hitching rail in front and three big plaster horses hitched to it. The place was called (you guessed it) The Hitching Post. Another touch of the Old West.

We booked a room there and spent most of the afternoon having sex.

Lorry was great in bed. I'd never felt so free before when I'd been with a woman. With her, everything was different. Easier. More comfortable. And a whole lot more fun.

We had a TV in our room and Lorry was watching the news when I came out of the bathroom, rubbing my head with a towel. They had a picture of the Big Sky Strangler on the screen. I threw the towel aside and sat down on the bed, staring at the composite drawing, asking myself, does it really look like me? How *much* does it look like me?

I don't know how they expect to catch the guy from that sketch, Lorry said. It could be any of ten thousand guys. What they need is a big scar on his cheek, or a harelip, or something.

I was calm. Inside me, there was no feeling of connection with the news story.

The anchorwoman was talking about how police throughout Montana were looking for the killer.

How do they know he's still in Montana? I said. The guy could be halfway across the country by now.

Lorry didn't reply. She was listening as the woman reported that authorities figured that the same killer was responsible for another murder. The police had discovered the strangled body of a 12-year-old girl in Dodson, not far from Malta. She'd been dumped in a trash bin behind a drugstore.

When they showed the little girl's photo I jumped from the bed, walked over and snapped off the television set. I was furious and my heart was pumping fast.

Lorry complained. Hey! I was watching that. What's wrong with you? Why did you turn it off?

My hands were fisted. I was half-shouting at her. Because they're lying! That . . . guy they're after . . . he'd *never* kill a 12-year-old.

Lorry stared at me. How do *you* know?

I hesitated. I realized that my sudden anger had put me in a tricky spot with her. I took in a couple of deep breaths to steady myself.

Well . . . because . . . his other victims were all much older. Why would he start killing children? It doesn't fit his pattern.

Lorry shook her head. Who knows what a crazy person is going to do next? she said. I can't understand why you're so upset.

I . . . I just get emotionally involved with this kind of thing. I don't like the way they exploit these deaths.

Murder is news, she said. When a serial killer is on the loose, people deserve to know. They *need* to, for their own self-protection.

What are they going to do — carry guns around? I asked.

People deserve to know, Lorry insisted. Now can we watch the rest of the news?

Sure, I said, slumping into a chair. I felt exhausted, drained of energy.

I'd have to be more careful around Lorry in the future.

That night I had another dream. Another nightmare. About being down in Mexico (where I've never been) and walking naked over this landscape of dead trees and broken brush — like after an atomic blast, and having one tree look like its head had been ripped off. It had long, clutching arms with dead bark clinging to them like pieces of black skin and one arm had a hand on it, like one of my hands. A strangler's hand. In the dream I stumbled over a rock, and the tree's dead hand closed over my neck. I could feel it tightening around my windpipe and I could feel the sharp-edged bark digging into my skin like razor blades.

And that's when the dream ended.

The next morning we went out to sell the VW. Lorry had a pretty fair idea of what the car was worth, even as old as it was, and she didn't like what the first two used car lots offered her for it.

These VWs can run forever, she told me. This one's in real sharp condition. Engine had a complete overhaul last year. Got another hundred thousand miles in it at least.

Then we saw this lot with big colored banners and a blinking neon sign:

FRED FARLEY IS FAIR!
TOP DOLLAR FOR YOUR CAR!
YOU CAN TRUST FAIR FREDDY!

Pull in here, Lorry told me.

I did, and by the time I'd cut the engine a tall skinny guy in a dark business suit topped by a white ten-gallon hat comes out of this wooden shack to look at the VW. He's all smiles.

Howdy there, folks! I'm Fred Farley. They call me Fair Freddy.

He didn't impress me much. Just another cheap huckster.

I wandered around the lot looking at the cars he had for sale while Lorry talked to him about the VW. Some of the cars looked okay, but there were plenty of junkers. When I got back to Lorry she was shaking hands with Farley. They both seemed satisfied.

We've made a deal, she told me. Mr. Farley says he'll swap even — my VW for the red Mazda pickup. What do you think?

Okay with me, I said.

As she was filling out the paperwork inside the shack I sized up the Mazda. I didn't like the bench-type front seat. Her legs were shorter than mine, which meant that when she drove, my knees would be in my face. And there was a big dent in the front right fender, and quite a bit of rust along the bottom of the driver's door. But I didn't complain. Anything was better than driving Ted Bundy's VW. That's how I thought of it, as *his*. If she'd traded it for a hay wagon I would have kept my mouth shut.

We were moving along the Missouri River and Lorry was driving the pickup. It had more snap than the bug but it was still sluggish. And the front seat *was* uncomfortable.

You look kinda sour, Lorry said. I hope you're not gonna tell me the Boston Strangler drove a Mazda.

I grinned. Lorry could be pretty funny and I admired her sense of humor.

It's not the pickup, I told her. There's nothing wrong with it.

Then what's bugging you?

I'm hungry, I said.

I was, but that wasn't what was bothering me. I'd been fighting back the compulsion all morning. It was spreading inside me, growing like a kind of dark fungus, getting more intense with each passing hour. I guess that's the way a heroin addict feels when the need for a fix begins to take over his body. The feeling just kind of overwhelms everything else.

What worried me — and still worries me as I write these words — is that instead of lessening after each kill, the compulsion was coming back stronger than before. As if each time I killed someone I was feeding it, making it grow.

For the first time since I came to Montana I wondered if I *could* control this disorder of mine.

Which is really frightening to consider.

We found a cheap, family-type steak house and Lorry ordered a T-bone while I ordered a tuna salad.

Is that all you're going to eat? she asked me. I thought you were hungry.

I am, I told her, but I decided just this week to quit eating dead animals. That's what steak is, you know. A dead cow.

That's crazy! she snapped. Tuna is *fish*. They're animals, too. And they're dead as any cow right there in your salad.

It's not the same, I said. They fill cows with all kinds of chemicals in their food. You can get cancer and heart trouble and all kinds of other diseases from eating meat. And the animal fat is almost pure cholesterol. It's a scientific fact that vegetarians have the best health of anybody. I've been giving the whole thing a lot of thought lately and I've decided not to eat anymore steaks or hamburgers or bacon or ham. It's a decision I made.

You're a weird dude, Eddie, she said.

There's nothing weird about not eating meat, I said. A lot of people are becoming vegetarians now. It's in the magazines and newspapers and on the news and everything. I just want to be healthy and live to be a hundred years old.

Don't we all? she said. Well, she added, not actually a hundred. That's too old, and nobody wants to be a walking corpse.

She ordered strawberry ice cream for dessert. As she was eating it she looked up at me. You don't trust me, do you? she said.

Why do you say that?

If you trusted me, you'd tell me what's been bugging you. Ever since we got to Great Falls, something has been bugging you. I got rid of the VW, so it can't be that.

I'm just a little tired, I said. Then I grinned at her, trying for some lightness. I've been in bed a lot, I said, but I haven't been sleeping much.

She grinned back.

And rubbed her hand over my crotch.

We were parked at a spot overlooking the Missouri River. No other cars around. The sky above us was like an immense sheet of black glass punched through with stars. Below us, we could hear the sound of water going past.

Lorry had her head against my shoulder and I could smell the fresh-washed scent of her hair. I would have been enjoying it, except for what was building up inside me.

The compulsion.

You picked the wrong guy to travel with, I finally said. My voice was soft and sad.

Lorry raised her head to look at me. Her eyes burned like jewels in the darkness. I picked the *right* guy, she said.

If you knew me — really knew me — you wouldn't say that, I told her honestly.

So what should I know about you?

The darkness roiling up inside me was blacker than the sky. A whole universe of pressure was engulfing me, commanding me. I couldn't fight it anymore.

I'm him, I said softly.

Him? She shifted in the seat, sitting up straight. What are you talking about?

The one they're looking for. The one on TV and in the papers. I'm him.

There was a long, strained moment of silence. Lorry's eyes got real intense and I could feel her muscles tighten underneath her clothes. She edged back from me.

Why are you doing this? she asked. Why are you trying to scare me? I don't like it and it's not funny.

I'm not trying to be funny, I said in the darkness.

Her eyes were wide now. She blinked rapidly. This is for *real*?

For real, I said.

You're ——

—— the Big Sky Strangler. I finished the sentence for her.

Lorry threw open the Mazda door and jumped out. She began to run along the grass toward the main highway, about a half-mile from where we were parked.

She wasn't hard to catch. Most women aren't. They just don't run the way a man does. Besides, I'm fast. I can move like a lizard when I've a mind to. I caught her before she'd gone five hundred yards.

I grabbed her by the throat, my thumbs in place, ready to dig in. She was shaking and sobbing. Killing her would be easy.

But Lorry was a surprising woman. Suddenly she brought up her right knee in a hard, swift arc and got me in the balls. I doubled over, gasping, as waves of pain rippled through me.

You sick bastard! she screamed. She ran towards the Mazda.

By the time I got there, still dizzy with pain, she'd managed to start the engine and was about to drive off. I grabbed through the open window, fumbling for the ignition key, as she tried to slap my hands away.

Then she lashed out with a fist, catching me a good one across the face. I felt blood running from my mouth. It tasted salty.

Bastard! Bastard! Bastard! She kept screaming the word at me as I got the door open and dragged her out. I got her arms pinned, but she was kicking wildly.

I really like you, I told her, spinning her around and punching her in the stomach. Her breath puffed out in a grunt as she collapsed forward.

I mean it, I said. I think the two of us share a very special chemistry. And you're great in the sack.

She used the "f" word on me, which kind of ruined things. By then I had my thumbs in her throat. She began clawing at me, but I was a lot stronger and it didn't take long to kill her.

I felt the power.

I was just sorry that it had to be Lorry.

I dumped her in the Missouri River with the idea that she'd be carried to the bottom and that no one would find her body. To make sure, I tied the Mazda's heavy iron tire jack to her waist. I guess I didn't do such a great job of it because when her body hit the water

I saw the rope come untied. The tire jack sank while she floated on downriver with the current.

I'd botched the job. I'd been nervous and too hasty and I'd botched it.

I knew one thing: I had to get out of Great Falls. Fast. Before anybody found Lorry Haines.

I drove the Mazda out of town a few miles and left it in a wheat field. I couldn't keep driving it because I didn't know when Lorry's body would be found. When it was — when Lorry's picture was printed in the paper — Fred Farley would remember he'd sold her the Mazda and then the police would be looking for it. Better to be on the safe side and get rid of it early.

I mourned Lorry. I missed her. We'd had a really good relationship, the best of my life up to now. But I'd given in to the compulsion and killed her. I didn't want to do that. I wanted us to have a life together. But I went ahead and killed her anyway.

Which meant I didn't have any real control left at all.

Not any at all.

I am not a baseball fan. Never watch it on TV, and was taken (dragged is a better word) to just one ballgame, which I found totally boring. Thus, up to "The Ex," I had never written a word about our National Pastime.

This story was generated by a question inside my head: "Do you want it in the elbow or the knee?" That's all I had, just this odd question. I fashioned my one and only baseball story around it.

I'll never write another.

The Ex

*I*t was late afternoon on a weekday. Clear and sunny. Not a cloud in the sky. Perfect baseball weather. When the door chimed I walked from the den to answer it. No servants. Not since the divorce. So it took me a while to reach the front door. The chime was kicking echoes off the hallway when I got there. Whoever it was lacked patience.

I peered through the barred square in the door's center panel. Two young men in neat gray suits. Neat and smiling, both of them. One tall, one short. The short one was carrying a leather case. "Who is it?" I asked.

"We'd like to talk to you, sir," the tall one said.

The short one unzipped the case and took out a baseball bat. He waved it in the air, still smiling. Nice teeth.

"I don't sign those anymore," I said. "No gloves or balls either. Sorry."

The short one nodded. "That's okay, sir. It's a real privilege, just being able to meet you in person. My son Bobby, he's seven. Thinks you're great. Rates you just below Spider-Man."

I grinned. Kid must be a big fan.

"Is it possible we could talk to you, sir?" asked the tall one. "I mean, just for a few minutes maybe?"

"Be a real honor," said the short one.

I shrugged. Well, why not? I'd been dealing with ball fans for most of my adult life. In fact, now that I was retired, things were a little empty. I missed the ego-boost that fans can provide. Hell, I might even sign their damned bat!

"Step inside," I said, unlatching the door and swinging it back. "You fellas ever watch me play?"

"Me, I did!" said the tall one. He had a high, girlish voice, sandy hair, and a bland, unremarkable face. "I saw you homer in the ninth, with the bases loaded, in the last World Series game. Boy, you really smacked the old apple! The crowd went apeshit!"

I nodded, leading them into the den, chuckling at the memory. "Yeah, that was one of my better days. After we won the Series I decided to hang it up, leave on a high note. I'm just too frigging old to compete with all the young Turks. Man has to know when to quit. I've seen ballplayers go on for years past their prime and I've watched them lose the magic. It's a damn sad sight. When the magic's gone you've hit bottom. I quit while my name still meant something."

"Well, it sure means a lot in our family," said the short man. "My Dad, he used to talk to me about Babe Ruth all the time —— the same way I talk to Bobby about you."

I was flattered. "Want me to sign that bat?"

The little guy was amazed. He had a round, pumpkin face, and now it lit up. "But I thought you didn't ——"

"I'll make an exception," I said as he removed the bat from its case. Handed it over. I hefted it, swung it lightly. "Nice balance."

"Made the case myself," he said. "Custom leather. Special grain. Wanted to be sure it was protected."

I looked more closely. Pro model 125, an H&B Louisville Slugger 35-incher. Nice.

"DiMaggio used a Slugger," the little man said. "Early in his career. A model D 29. Me, I used to have a Spalding, but it cracked. They don't make 'em anymore."

"Not since the Second World War," I said, signing the H&B with a felt tip and handing it back to him.

"Hey —— I'm really very appreciative," he said. "You know, my sister-in-law *hates* baseball! Can you imagine anyone hating baseball?"

"To each his own," I said.

"I just can't figure it," the little man continued. "Women! You can never figure out a woman." He snorted. "Alma —— that's her name —— she thinks baseball is stupid. Makes no sense to her, all these guys running around these bases. I took Alma to just *one* ball game. She liked the open stadium, and the clipped green grass on the field, and the smells of hot popcorn and peanuts — but when the game started she was bored silly. Dozed through most of it. Women! You can never figure a woman. Sometimes, I think they live in a different universe!"

The tall one had been admiring my trophy case. "Must give you a great deal of satisfaction, having earned these."

I nodded. "At least they prove I was out there. Sometimes, my whole career seems unreal, as if it all happened in a dream." I shrugged. "But I guess a lot of retired players feel that way."

"Yeah, I remember your saying that — about it all being like a dream — in the *Sports Illustrated* interview," said the short man. "The one with your picture on the cover."

"I was pissed about that interview. Copy editor cut it in half when they printed it. Made me sound like an idiot. The transcript I saw of the original was twice that length. But then again, my wife was always telling me that I talk too much."

The tall guy turned away from the trophy case to face me. His smile had faded, and he had a hard, intense look. "We didn't come here to get the bat signed."

"Oh." I met his steady gaze. "Then why did you come here?"

"Because of her," he said.

"Her?"

"You know," added the little guy. "Your ex."

I stared at them. "Are you saying that my *wife* sent you?"

"In a manner of speaking," said the tall one.

"But she's dead!"

"We know," said the short one. "That's why we're here."

"I don't understand."

"She wanted it this way," the tall guy told me. "Set it up before she died. Made all the arrangements personally. She seemed to get a kick out of it. Sort of chortled when she laid out what we were to do." He gave me a long stare. "Guess she didn't like you much."

"She *hated* me," I said. "Only stayed with me because of the money I was making — and because of who I was. She enjoyed being hooked to a celebrity . . . being identified as my wife. It made her feel important, since she had no talent of her own."

"Why did you put up with it?" This from the short guy.

"Because a divorce is costly, and I knew she'd blame the failure of our marriage on me. And I was right. She did. Hired a Beverly

Hills lawyer. Jeez, but I got burned by that bitch. I knew she hated me —— but until the divorce I didn't know how deep her hatred was."

"Yeah," piped the small guy, "you wouldn't have liked what she said about you. Not very complimentary."

In thinking about my ex, I'd lost focus on just why the two of them were here. They still hadn't told me. I was suddenly angry. They were working for the bitch! Even beyond her death, she was still hounding me.

"If you've come for money ——"

"No, we're being well paid," said the tall man. "Money isn't what this is about."

"Then, damn you, man! Why *are* you here?"

"To execute her orders," said the short guy. "To do our job."

I was distinctly uneasy. Whatever my ex had in mind would be negative. Something dark. Maybe even . . . I backed away toward the desk. "She sent you here to kill me!"

They both chuckled, shaking their heads.

"Naw," said the tall man. "Killing's not our line. The company has people who do that. Special people. But that's not us."

"Then I don't understand why you ——"

"Back up a minute," said the tall guy. "Let's not rush. We're enjoying ourselves here."

"That's right," said the short one. "This is very enjoyable."

"You still watch the games?" the tall one asked.

"Uh . . . yes, of course. Just because I don't play anymore doesn't mean that I ——"

"Bet you've got yourself a swell TV setup," said the short man. "I mean, big screen, Dolby sound . . . the works."

"It's adequate," I said.

"And that red silk robe you're wearing," said the tall one. "Must of cost plenty. The wife, she loves red silk. She'd look real snappy in a robe like you're wearing."

Despite my basic apprehension, they were making me angry.

"Quit stalling," I snapped. "My ex had a purpose in sending you here. I want to know what's going on."

"In due time," said the tall man, grinning at me. "We've got all day."

"Yeah," said the other. "Our schedule is very loose." He took up a hitter's stance in the middle of the room, legs spaced, bat to shoulder. "When I was a kid I dreamed of playing in the major leagues," he said. "I was pretty good, too. I could sock the old apple pretty good." He swung at an invisible ball. "But I was too short to make the school team, let alone any pro team. Just too runty, they said. God, but I hate being called a runt." He looked at me. "At least you're tall, like my buddy here. Tall guys they never call runts."

"The irony is, he gets to work with a bat after all," said the tall guy in his musical voice. "He's our official batboy."

The little guy grunted. "Not much like playing in the majors, but it's a living."

"Shall we tell him exactly what we're here for?" the tall one asked the runt.

"Yeah, let's tell him."

"It's like this," explained the tall one. "Because you're kind of an icon to our kids, and because we both respect you personally, we're gonna give you a choice."

The runt hefted his bat. "Just one good smash. Kneecap or elbow. Your choice."

"Christ!" I breathed. "You mean to cripple me!"

"Not really," said the tall man. "You'll get over it. I'm sure you've got a real good doc. He can set the bone, maybe replace the parts that are too smashed up."

"You'll be fine," said the runt.

"How much are you getting paid for this?" I asked them. "I'll *triple* your rate!"

"That's bribery," said the runt, shaking his head. "We can't be bribed. We're pros. We've got our pride. Doing a job like this, it's not as simple as it sounds. You have to know just where to hit, and exactly how hard. Requires a lot of time to master the craft. I take pride in what I do. Money can't buy pride."

The tall guy put his hand on my shoulder. "The good thing about this is that your ex didn't die while you were still a player. This would have ruined you for the game."

"He's right," said the short one. "I'm just glad we didn't have to do this earlier. Now it's okay, with you being retired and all. It won't be a big problem for you."

The runt walked closer to me, idly swinging the bat.

"I'd advise you to choose the right elbow, since you're a south-paw. Then you can still use the other arm."

"Yeah," nodded the tall guy. "Kneecap's a bitch to heal. The bones don't knit as well, and you spend a long time on crutches.

More pain there, too. I'd definitely go for the elbow. But..." He shrugged. "It's your choice."

"I'll phone the police." I said tightly. "They'll deal with this."

"Stay away from the police," the runt warned me, eyes flashing. "You try to call in Johnny Law and I'll *really* smash you. I mean, a bad scene for you. By the time the cops get here you'll be a bloody mess. Heck, I don't want to have to do that to you. *Especially* not to you — being a personal hero of mine."

"You bastards!"

They both smiled blandly. "You don't have to like us for doing our job," said the tall man, "but we're not vindictive like your ex. She was definitely vindictive."

"Definitely," said the runt. "She arranged all this so you'd have, to quote the lady, 'something to remember her by.' Unquote."

"Damn her!" I snapped. "Damn her lousy soul!"

"Well, let's get to it," said the tall one.

"You name it, sir," said the runt. "Kneecap or elbow. Left or right side."

I realized that I had absolutely no option. I couldn't call the police. I couldn't escape. There was no one else in the house to help me. So I made my choice.

"Left kneecap," I said softly. "I need to use both arms. For the keyboard." I flushed. "I'm writing a book about my career."

"Okay, then," said the tall man, walking quickly behind me and pinning my shoulders in a wrestler's hold. "Go ahead. Go for the leg."

The runt took his hitting stance, looking serious. The bat was on his shoulder.

"Play ball!" piped the tall guy.

The runt smashed me.

The pain was incredible.

When the tall guy let go of me I collapsed to the den floor, screaming through clenched teeth. I was gripping my smashed knee, in agony. I'd been hurt plenty of times on the field, but it was nothing compared to this.

"You should have gone for the elbow shot," said the runt. "Kneecap's always worse." He carefully replaced the bat in its custom leather zipcase. "Well," he said to his partner. "Game's over."

The tall one leaned down, his face close to mine. "If you try to do anything about this, like calling the police or anything, the company will send some other people over to kill you. And I know you don't want that to happen."

"Right," nodded the runt. "Life is precious. Nobody wants to die."

All this happened five years ago.

I've walked crookedly ever since.

The narrator of this story is just eleven years old, but he's a long-time victim of parental abuse. Anyone, under certain pressures, can be driven to a point of violence. Age is no factor.

"Mommy, Daddy, and Mollie" is a character study of a boy who is no longer willing to play the role of victim. It is also a ghost story.

Mommy, Daddy, & Mollie

My name is Bruce. I'm eleven years old and eleven-year-old people usually have older people to take care of them like a Mommy and a Daddy. But I don't have a Mommy or a Daddy. I used to have them before all the blood. But I don't anymore. I'm glad I don't because Mommy and Daddy were not nice.

The preachers on the TV talk about the Bad Place where there's always fire and brimstone (whatever that is) and people stick pitch-forks into you and I guess that's where they'll end up in the fire with the pitchforks.

I've been living here with Mollie, my baby sister. Last month she turned ten which is not really being a baby, at ten, but she cried and whined a lot and after what happened to Mommy and Daddy she wet the bed like a baby and so that's how I think of her. Mollie the baby.

We've been living in this old broken-down house outside of Redmond by the edge of the Oregon woods. It has old rotted furni-ture still in it like our rusting iron bed with springs poking through the mattress. Abandoned is what they call the house but we live here so I guess it's not really abandoned. It smells bad inside (dead rats) and there was no heat in the winter when we came here and it rained a lot through some holes in the roof.

Mollie said that the cold rain was all my fault and if what happened to Mommy and Daddy hadn't happened she'd be at home in our house in Redmond, warm and safe, and not here in the freezing cold with water leaking through the roof. I got tired of listening to her and told her to just shut up and quit whining like a baby and I got some dry wood from the barn where the rain hadn't come in to that part and made us a fire and we got though the winter okay.

This house is awful. There are big fat black spiders near the ceiling on sticky webs and nobody likes spiders. I know for sure I don't. Just looking at a spider creeps me out.

We've lived in this house for three months now since I killed Mommy and Daddy. I guess that was not a good thing to do, killing them. But they were not nice, like I said, so killing them was not that hard to do and I'm not sorry.

Want to know how I did it?

They were both in bed when I did it with the axe. And there was plenty of blood. Smells rusty, blood does. It soaked right through the floor boards. They were snoring when I came into their bedroom with the axe. They sounded like a couple of barnyard pigs. Mommy and Daddy liked to drink a lot of whiskey and get stinkin, as Daddy called how they got. And that's how they were in bed that night. Stinkin.

The moon was out and lots of yellow light came through the bedroom window making it almost bright as day. I killed Daddy first because he was the strongest and then Mommy who woke up yelling no, no, don't do it, oh god no no. But I did it anyway with the axe.

That's when my sister walked into the bedroom because she was having nightmares and saw all the blood and was very upset, moaning and crying and asking me why I'd killed Mommy and Daddy and I told her because they were not nice.

I remember things.

There was this summer when I was seven and we found a stray pup in the front yard. Had big sad eyes. He'd been lost in the woods and had leaves and twigs tangled in his fur. I combed them out and fed the pup who was hungry with his ribs sticking out. Guess he'd been a long time in the woods. He was black, with a big white spot over one eye and a stubby white tail that wagged a lot.

I asked Mommy and Daddy if I could keep him and they said that dogs smelled bad and had fleas. But they finally agreed to let the pup stay and I named him Buster. (It was the name of a friend I had in grade school from when we lived in Portland.)

When Buster peed on the hall rug Daddy got really upset and the next morning Buster was gone. Daddy said that he'd wandered off into the woods again and I never saw him after that. I missed Buster something awful and Mommy said it was all to the good. That was her exact words. Dogs were nothing but mess and trouble and with Buster gone it was all to the good and he would not be peeing on the hall rug anymore.

I was like Buster. I did things that upset Daddy. I don't mean peeing on the rug. But other things that upset him usually after he drank whiskey and was stinkin. He'd beat me with his leather rodeo belt that had a silver buckle on it that he won for riding a steer and it hurt a lot and Mommy didn't mind. She said I needed to be taught a lesson but I never learned what it was. She'd slap me hard across the face and made my ears ring when I spilled something at supper like the mustard jar I knocked over. Then Mollie would laugh seeing me get slapped and Mommy would pat her on the head.

She never patted me on the head. Mollie was her favorite and I was just somebody who got slapped. Mollie never got slapped or whipped with Daddy's leather rodeo belt. Just me, I was the one.

So you see, to me, Mommy and Daddy were not nice people.

The police who came to the bedroom after the neighbors found Mommy and Daddy with all the blood would have taken me to jail if I'd stayed around. That's what Mollie said, that I'd be taken right to jail and never get out. Even though I was only eleven I'd still go to jail. And maybe she was right.

So we left our house in Redmond with me pulling Mollie along behind me and her whining a lot and went through the woods till we found this old place. Part of the roof had caved in and all the windows were broken out like missing teeth. It's not fun living here but I'm not in jail and that's good.

On the TV when we had one and used to watch it they said that eleven-year-old kids were too young to go to jail but Mollie said they lied so I'd come back, so I believed her about going to jail and not the TV people.

But what I want to write about is the ghosts.

I never saw any till we came to this old house. Mommy used to laugh at people who saw ghosts and said they were crazy people to begin with or they would not say they saw them.

But I'm not crazy and late at night I see the ghosts. They are Mommy and Daddy. And sometimes they talk just like they were still alive. You little bastard, they say, why did you kill us? And I tell them I didn't want to get hit anymore with Daddy's leather rodeo belt (with the big metal buckle) and get slapped hard by Mommy.

You were not nice to me is why you're dead, I tell them.

Ghosts can't hurt you. They are all vapory and you can see right through them. Daddy raises his fists at me but they are like puffs of smoke and when he tries to hit me it's like nothing is there. So I'm not afraid of them.

You're a miserable little monster, Mommy tells me and that's not true. I'm a nice person. I just don't like being beaten or slapped. The two ghosts yell at me and I can see the hate in their smoky eyes. Mommys and Daddys are supposed to love their children but they never loved me, only Mollie.

I told Mollie about seeing the two ghosts and she said I was crazy like the people Mommy used to talk about and I told her, no, they're real all right and I see them every night.

She kept saying she was going to tell on me, what I did to Mommy and Daddy, that she was going to go to the police and tell them about it. I really got pissed when she said that and told her to shut up her damn mouth. I called her a bitch. That's what Daddy called Mommy sometimes when they had arguments after getting stinkin. So was my baby sister. A bitch.

On Monday she said she was tired of living in a smelly dirty old broken-down house with dead rats in it and she was going back through the woods and find the police and tell them I killed Mommy and Daddy. You better not I told her. You'll be real sorry if you do. But she just stuck her tongue out at me.

So last Tuesday she said she was going to the police so I still had the axe and I used it again.

Now I live here all alone and each night there are these ghosts who yell at me and threaten me. But I know they can't hurt me.

Three ghosts.

Mommy, Daddy, and Mollie.

This is the shortest story in the book, an ironic example of our inability to understand that which is alien to us. It has humor, but the humor is very dark indeed.

The Alien

Something wrong. Controls not . . . the ship shuddering . . . Earth rushing up. Impact. Unconscious. Then . . . awake. Fluid from nose aperture. Standing. Dizzy. The outer port opening. Into daylight from Earth sun. Woods. Sunflicker through trees. Walking (unsteady) from wrecked ship. Survived. Hurt, but survived.

Voice sounds ahead. Two men in Earth vehicle. Truck. Correct word for vehicle. Men in a truck. Jesus, looka that. What is it? Dunno. Well for Christ's sake it ain't human.

Reach them. Need help. Fluid dripping. Thing could kill us. Naw, cantcha see it's bleeding? Weak. Looka them weak little legs and arms. Bleeding. Green blood. Jesus. Worth money. Take it to town. Sell it. Where? Who's gonna pay us? Dunno. Worth trying. From another planet. Oughta be worth something.

The men gesture. Into back of truck. Drive over bumps in road. Hurts. Reach an Earth town. Small. Only one main street. Where to now? Sheriff Wilkins, he'll know what to do. Big man. Badge. Heavy belly. Lookit what we brung in from the woods, Ollie. Ollie Wilkins. Got us a alien. From out of space. I'll take him, boys. Nossir! Belongs to us. To sell. There's nobody gonna buy an alien. Just hand him over.

Argue. Voices loud and harsh sounding. Two of them drive away in the truck. Heavy man takes over. To a medical place. (Hospital?) People all in white. Probing. Onto a long white table with them looking down. Dissect it. Can't, still alive. Won't be for long. Need to find out what's inside.

Still dizzy. Fluid still seeping. Something (cloth) pressed over breathing area. Room getting dimmer. Just before black a silver blade. Coming down. No pain. Christ, this is gonna make us famous.

Blackness.

When the British decided to sell London Bridge to a rich American some while back, the historic structure was taken apart, with all the stones being shipped to Lake Havasu, Arizona. The bridge was rebuilt over a diverted section of the Colorado River and a simulated British village was constructed to surround it.

Very late one night, I visited the "new" London Bridge during a trip to Arizona. Standing in the darkness, looking up at the long arc of fitted stones, I thought: Jack the Ripper may well have crossed this bridge after the Whitechapel kills. What if, I asked myself, somehow the Ripper returned to begin the century-old cycle of murders all over again in Arizona? The result: this novella, marking the deadly return of Bloody Jack.

Ripper!

London Bridge Area. London, England.
November 15, 1888.
Three minutes past midnight:

A thick wash of milk-white fog veils a blowsy, middle-aged woman, wrapped in a shawl of frayed wool, as she exits the soot-grimed doors of Boar's Head Tavern. Her steps are weaving and uncertain as she moves over the fog-damp cobbles, muttering to herself.

She is very drunk.

The side street, dimly illumined by a flickering yellow gas lamp, throws the woman's inked shadow ahead of her as she staggers forward. She stops, draws the thin shawl tighter around her shoulders, and coughs raggedly — a harsh, hacking sound in the night. She spits phlegm, swears under her breath, and angrily resumes her unsteady journey.

As she reaches the mouth of an alleyway, a cloaked figure emerges from the fog, gliding rapidly toward her. A bladed object glitters in the figure's right hand.

Scalpel!

The woman screams as an arm encircles her throat. Her attacker raises the blade, but hesitates as the thud of a police club reverberates through the alley. At the far end: a uniformed police constable, alerted by the scream, is running toward the struggling pair, blowing his whistle.

The cloaked figure releases the woman, who slumps to the gutter, gasping for breath. A second constable joins the first, their whistles keening in the darkness. The fugitive sprints away, moving like a sinuous ghost over the slippery cobbles.

The first constable reaches the fallen woman, who gestures toward the fleeing assailant. "Ripper!" she cries. "It's him, by God! It's *him*!"

The fugitive runs toward London Bridge, up the cold stone steps, with the two police officers in swift pursuit. The Ripper gains the top, attempts to sprint across the long arched structure, but slips on the fog-slick pavement and falls back against the stone railing.

The pursuers close in, nightsticks raised. The Ripper struggles wildly, smashing one officer to the pavement. The second officer slams his nightstick against the Ripper's skull. The dark figure staggers under the blow and falls backward, dislodging a weathered section of parapet railing. A loosened stone gives way, and follows the Ripper's body down . . . down . . . down . . .

Into the dark, fog-shrouded waters of the River Thames.

"Get a look at 'im, did you? Couldn't see 'is face."

"Was it 'im, I wonder. Was it Bloody Jack?"

"If it was, we'll never prove it, mate. Best we keep our gobs shut about this."

The second officer stares downward. "Whoever he was, he's right dead now."

"That he is . . . whoever he was."

The two constables continue to stare down at the dark waters below London Bridge.

Near Lake Havasu City, Arizona.
August 7, 2004. 8:37 P.M.:

David Kelley was hungry and exhausted. He and Lia had been driving all day —— over five hundred miles according to the odometer. Their visit to Lia's sister in Santa Fe had been fun, but the drive back from her place had been a killer. His stomach rumbled, pleading for food, and he thought hungrily of the fragrant sopapillas and the green chile stew they'd eaten that morning, a perfect breakfast in the crisp New Mexico dawn. His legs were cramped and his back ached. At this moment all he wanted out of life was a hot meal and a cool bed. Tomorrow they could drive the remaining miles back to Los Angeles.

Dave glanced over at his wife, at ease behind the wheel of their Lexus. Lia was humming "Over the Rainbow" as she drove, in accompaniment to a Judy Garland recording on the radio. A San Francisco station, clear as next door on the long skip of a cloudless desert night. He leaned forward to switch it off.

"Hey, what're you doing?" she asked. "That's a classic. One of my favorites."

"I'm starved and I'm exhausted and I damn well don't feel like listening to Judy Garland. It's like I've been in this car for half my life."

"You'll perk up when we get to the Bridge," she said.

He stared at her. "What Bridge?"

"The one in Havasu," she said. "London Bridge. I've been dying to see it."

"You must be kidding," Dave said. "All I want to see tonight is a steak smothered in onions and a decent motel bed."

"They have a pub in the village near the Bridge," Lia told him. "We can eat there."

She drove off the highway into a wide parking lot, braked, cut the engine and lights. The Arizona night was peaceful, and the deep, star-drenched sky seemed as limitless as infinity.

"C'mon, sleepyhead," Lia said brightly. "You'll enjoy this. It's one of Arizona's top tourist attractions."

"I *hate* tourist attractions," said Dave, as he stepped from the Lexus and stretched. The area was nearly deserted. Only two other cars were in the lot, both parked near a spiked iron fence. "Besides, it's obvious the place is closed."

"Nope," said Lia. "I checked. They stay open till ten. We've still got time to eat *and* see the Bridge."

They faced a tall iron gate flanked by a pair of heraldic stone dragons. A red-metal sign on the gate announced:
VILLAGE HOURS: 10 A.M. to 10 P.M.

"See," nodded Lia. "What'd I tell you? We still have time."

Dave sighed —— and, hand-in-hand, they walked through the gate.

Despite his gnawing hunger, Dave agreed to have a look at the Bridge before they had dinner at the King's Pub ("An Authentic Olde English Dining Experience," according to the village directory).

"This is insane," Dave said, as they walked through tree shadows toward London Bridge.

"Just relax and have fun," said Lia. "The place is charming. It's like really being in London!"

A large section of Sonoran desert had improbably been converted into a simulated English village, complete with lush, green lawns, double-decker buses, red-painted glass telephone booths, and timbered Tudor-style buildings.

"Where's the damn Bridge?" asked Dave.

"Around the next turn, I think. Beyond those trees." She put her hand gently over his face. "Close your eyes. I'll lead you."

"Why in hell do I have to close my eyes?" he demanded, in hungry irritation.

"To get the full impact when we're there," she told him. "Don't be such a grouch."

Scowling, Dave closed his eyes as they rounded the last bend in the walkway.

"Okay," she said as she removed her hand. "There it is!"

London Bridge towered above them, rising up in nocturnal majesty. Thousands of tons of fitted stone. More than nine hundred feet of arched granite.

Despite himself, Dave was impressed. "Hey, that's really something."

"Imagine! They brought it all the way from England. This is the by-God-for-real London Bridge!"

They walked along the concrete path beneath the massive structure, staring upward at the giant, gray mass of cut stone.

"Not long ago, this was all Arizona desert," she told him. "Then some American named McCulloch bought the Bridge from the Brits when they wanted to replace it with something more modern. McCulloch had it taken apart, stone-by-stone. Numbered each one so they'd know where to fit it when the Bridge was rebuilt here in Havasu. Just think: thousands of cut stones — like a huge jigsaw puzzle."

"They built it over the Colorado River?"

"No," she answered. "They put up the Bridge first, on dry land, then they diverted part of the Colorado River underneath. Took them three years. When they were through, they built this Tudor Village. For atmosphere."

"Well, I gotta admit it's pretty damn impressive," nodded Dave.

"I can't wait to walk across," declared Lia. She gestured toward a steep flight of stone steps. "That's how you get to the top. We can —— "

"*Eat*," Dave said firmly. "First we eat. *Then* we walk across the damn Bridge."

"Okay," she agreed. "The pub is just ahead."

"So, what else may I bring you good folks?" The waiter —— a local kid in his late teens, dressed in period livery, who was trying hard to affect a British accent —— hovered over their table, smiling down at them. "Would you be interested in dessert tonight? We're out of chocolate mousse right now, but we have a nice frosted ginger cake, made with the same recipe the Queen favors."

Dave pushed his plate aside, shaking his head. After a meal of romaine and salmon salad, steak and kidney pie, boiled potatoes, and asparagus with hollandaise sauce, Dave had no room for anything else. "I'm stuffed," he said. "How about you, Lia?"

She was dabbing her lips with a white linen napkin. "Not for me. It's getting late." She turned to their waiter. "We'll have our check, please."

They were the only customers left in the pub. Burnished wood beams in the high ceiling reflected the candlelight from their table, but otherwise the King's Pub was dark and lifeless, with the dinner hour long past.

The waiter returned with a silver tray containing Dave's credit card along with the charge slip.

"Are you going to the dedication ceremony tomorrow morning?"

Dave looked up as he finished signing the charge slip. "Dedication?"

"Marking the final completion of the Bridge. Everybody's going to be there. All our local officials . . . even the Lord Mayor of London flew over."

Lia looked confused. "I thought the Bridge was completed back in 1971."

"Right you are," said the waiter. "Except for one missing stone. It was found a couple of months ago at the bottom of the Thames. Been down there for over a hundred years. It was shipped over here to fit back into the Bridge —— and tomorrow's the big dedication."

"Afraid we're going to miss it," said Dave. "I have to get back to Los Angeles. Got a business to run."

"Are you staying the night here?"

"If we can find a decent motel," Dave said.

"Try the Tower Lodge, across the street from the village parking lot," suggested the waiter. "Real nice. Good rates — and a complimentary English breakfast buffet in the morning that you'll enjoy."

Dave nodded. "Sounds fine."

"But first, we're going to walk across the Bridge," said Lia, rising from her chair.

As the couple left the restaurant, the waiter locked the heavy wooden door behind them.

"Just look at all those stars," Lia said, as they stood outside the now-darkened King's Pub. The Arizona sky was spangled with thousands of bright pinlights. "They say there are a billion of them just in our galaxy alone!"

"I hope you're not serious about wanting to walk across the Bridge tonight," said Dave.

"Of course I am! I've wanted to do this for *years*!"

"I'm sorry, honey, but I'm bushed. Why don't we walk the Bridge first thing in the morning?"

She turned and gently touched his cheek. "I really want to cross it tonight, when it's dark and empty and mysterious. Tomorrow it's all going to be bright desert sun and crowds of people — remember what the waiter said about the dedication." She thought a moment. "Why don't you go check into the motel for us. After I cross the Bridge, I'll walk over there."

"You saw the gate sign," Dave said. "They shut down the whole place at ten — and it's close to that now."

"There's still time. You go on to the motel. I'll be there before you know it."

Dave shrugged. "Okay, if it means that much to you. Promise you'll come right over."

"Promise," she said, kissing his cheek.

"I'll be waiting," he said, as he set off for the parking lot.

The Tudor Village was deserted at this late hour. A few widely-spaced, Victorian-era street lamps cast a pale yellow illumination over the immediate surroundings, but most of the village was shrouded in darkness.

Lia's heels clattered against the sprinkler-damp pavement as she moved through pools of shadow toward the Bridge. It was wonderful being alone here, without other tourists to spoil the mood. She felt privileged and special, almost as if all this belonged to her alone.

The tall stone edifice of London Bridge loomed above her. Lia mounted the wide steps, her heart pounding and her mouth dry with excitement. This was the very structure that Londoners had walked across since the 1830s. Now she was part of it. Part of history.

At the center of the span, she paused. Large containers of flowers — red, white, and blue, in honor of both the British and American flags — had been arranged on the Bridge walkway that overlooked the village. A heavy drapery of royal purple velvet had been laid over one of the railing stones, with the coat of arms of the city of London stitched across the velvet in golden thread. This was it, she realized — this was the stone found at the bottom of the Thames River! As she stepped forward for a closer look, her foot caught on the uneven walkway. Grabbing for the parapet railing, she dislodged the purple drapery and her right hand slammed down on the stone. The thin, soft skin on her palm resisted for an instant, then opened, allowing the rough granite to punch through.

A ragged wound appeared. Shocked, Lia looked on as her blood dripped onto the newly-laid stone, briefly darkening the gray surface, then sinking into its ancient, weathered fissures.

A swirling, pulsating mist began to rise, thick and malodorous. Time seemed to lengthen as a shape formed within the unnatural fog.

This can't be happening, Lia told herself. *Can't! Can't! Can't!*

The shape in the fetid mist assumed the physical bulk of a tall figure in a black woolen cape and London greatcoat. A wide-brimmed hat shadowed the face, and a bladed object glittered wickedly in the figure's right hand.

Scalpel!

Lake Havasu City. London Bridge.
A clear, hot, sun-dazzled morning:

London Bridge was awash in color: balloons, bunting, and bright flags from across the length and width of Great Britain. Temporarily closed to traffic for this historic ceremony, the span was jammed with townspeople and tourists, most of them clustered at the center of the Bridge. The Lake Havasu City High School band thumped out brisk tunes, and Anson Whitfield, mayor of Lake Havasu city, was present, along with the City council members and numerous Arizona VIPs. Their folding chairs faced the newly-placed rail stone, now once again draped in purple.

Lake Havasu City's most honored guest, the Lord Mayor of London, stood with pompous dignity on the wooden dais, dressed in his official robe of office. As the high school band finished the last rousing notes of "Rule Britannia!" the Lord Mayor imperially raised his hand for silence and began to speak in a high, fluting voice — completely absorbed in the importance of himself and his position.

"Mr. Mayor . . . honored members of the City Council . . . ladies and gentlemen. This is indeed a historic occasion for us. Indeed, the importance of this day can hardly be overestimated. From the City of London, founded in the mists of ancient antiquity, we have come as emissaries across an ocean and a continent, here — to this place — to express . . . "

As the piping voice droned on, police detective Steve Gregory shifted uncomfortably in his folding chair. A tall, muscular man who favored direct action, he disdained pretentious words. He was here because he had been informed by the Chief of Police that his attendance was compulsory. The Lake Havasu city Police department was small, and as the newest addition to the force, Gregory was required to make a proper public appearance.

But he didn't have to like it.

He sat next to his partner, Joe Nez — dark, several years younger, half-Navajo — who looked equally bored with the proceedings. They exchanged sour glances as the Lord Mayor's florid words echoed through the loudspeakers and bounced back hollowly from the walls of the village buildings.

" . . . and now I take great pride in officially unveiling this missing stone, drawn up from the dark waters of the River Thames, and dedicated here today to mark the true and final completion of London Bridge."

As he swept aside the purple drapery, the crowd burst into applause. Mayor Whitfield stepped forward to shake the Lord Mayor's hand, and joined him on the platform for the TV and news cameras.

"Thank you, my Lord Mayor. We of Lake Havasu City are indeed honored by your presence here today." His voice rose in fervor. "This historic stone, now officially fitted to its proper place, forms yet another link in the unbroken chain of friendship forged between our two great lands, with London Bridge itself symbolizing an enduring bond: a literal bridge between the Old World and the New. Let me say, here and now, how personally proud I am, as Mayor of Lake Havasu City, to be a part of this auspicious ceremony that is truly . . . "

Gregory sighed loudly, making no effort to hide his contempt.

"He must think this is an election campaign," he murmured to Joe Nez under his breath. "I can't take any more."

"No choice," said Nez. "Dawson has his eye on us. We have to stick it out."

Facing them, in the single row of folding chairs reserved for city officials, Chief of Police Peter Dawson glared at his detectives, all too aware of their undisguised discomfort.

At this moment Dave Kelley pushed his way through the crowd. He was unshaven, his face flushed and drawn. Heedless of the ceremony going on around him, Kelley strong-armed his way to Dawson's seat and stood directly in front of him. "Are you the Chief of Police?" he demanded.

"Yes," Dawson replied, unsure how to handle the situation.

"It's my wife . . . " Kelley's voice was strained, close to the breaking point. "Lia didn't show up at the motel last night. Something *bad* has happened to her."

A worried husband, Dawson thought with relief. Not some dangerous nutcase. "I'm on duty now," he told the man. "Come to the station later and we'll discuss your problem."

"We'll talk *now*, dammit!" Kelley reached out and grabbed Dawson's tie. "My wife is missing and I demand that you do something about it!"

The attention of the crowd was now focused on the police chief and the distraught stranger. Dawson knew he must respond, to avoid further disruption in the ceremony. Gesturing toward Steve Gregory, he told the man: "Talk to that detective. He'll take your report."

Kelley turned to Gregory who — grateful for the reprieve — guided the man down the nearest bank of Bridge steps.

Two women in the crowd, Lynn Chandler and Angie Shepherd, had been closely watching the action. Both in their twenties. Both fit and attractive. Lynn, with the deep brown eyes and thick dark hair that she inherited from her mother's line of Papago ancestors. Angie, with the bright blue eyes and natural strawberry blonde hair that had originally — more than two hundred years earlier — come from Scots-Irish immigrants.

"So whatdya think of him?" Lynn whispered to Angie.

"Who?"

"The new cop," said Lynn. "Steve Gregory. From Chicago. Been here less than a month. And he's *single*." She looked at her friend. "He's been giving you the eye — or haven't you noticed?"

Angie shrugged. "He's okay."

"You need to get back in circulation. And with him . . . you could really circulate."

Angie laughed as she lightly punched her friend's shoulder. "Lynn, you're impossible."

Steve Gregory, seated with Dave Kelley on the steps below the Bridge, had his notebook in hand and was jotting down the details of Kelley's story. "When was she due back at the motel?"

"Fifteen . . . maybe twenty minutes after we split up in the village," said Dave. His eyes were haunted and unfocused as he raised his hands in a gesture of helplessness. "However long it takes to walk across the Bridge and back."

"Why didn't you go with her?" asked Gregory.

"I was dead tired — really zonked — from all the driving we did yesterday. I just wanted to sleep. After I checked in, when I finally got to our room, I laid down to wait for her. I must have dozed off, because when I woke up it was daylight, and Lia wasn't back. I phoned the police department, and they told me to see Chief Dawson. So I came here."

"How much money did your wife have in her purse?"

"Uh . . . a hundred . . . maybe less." He looked hard at Gregory. "You think this was a robbery — that somebody robbed her?"

"It's possible," said Gregory. "Out here alone . . . late at night . . . "

"But if some guy grabbed her purse, why didn't she come back to tell me about it?" He shook his head in despair. "I have a gut feeling it's something worse . . . something much worse." He looked up at the police detective in agony. "I don't think she's alive anymore. I just don't think Lia's alive."

Along the Colorado River.
Late afternoon, that same day:

The commercial fishing boat, *Lucky Lady,* was moored at the marina on Thompson's Bay. A twin-diesel, 40-footer, its fresh blue-and-white paint gleamed under the blazing sun. Angie Shepherd, her blonde hair up in a high pony tail, emerged from the canvas-covered passenger cabin wearing grease-splotched overalls and carrying a toolbox. Selecting a steel wrench and a long screw driver, she removed the cowling from one of the diesels and began to adjust the engine timing.

Dusk settled over the marina as the sun dropped below the horizon, but the heat of the day did not diminish. The warm sundown breeze picked up, causing the palm fronds of the trees along the riverway to rustle with a dry, crackling sound as the boat gently rocked against its moorings.

Angie finished adjusting the engine and replaced the metal cowling. Then —— on her way back to the passenger cabin —— she hesitated, canting her head to listen. There was a sound she couldn't identify. Something was bumping rhythmically against the hull.

Walking to the edge of the deck, she peered over the railing, down into the wind-rippled water. "Oh, God! Oh, my God!"

A corpse floated in the river current, face up, dead eyes staring at the darkening sky. The body of a woman, with her throat cut in a macabre, bloodless smile.

The Marina on Thompson's Bay.
That same night:

Several police and emergency vehicles, the light bars on their roofs flashing red, yellow, and blue, were parked near the dock.

Steve Gregory, in the cabin of the *Lucky Lady*, jotted down a fact in his notebook. Then he looked intently at Angie Shepherd. " . . . and you'd never seen this woman before?"

Angie shook her head. "No. Never."

She was shaken, her voice unsteady. Gregory put a reassuring hand on her shoulder. "Take it easy, Ms. Shepherd."

"It's just that I . . . I've never seen somebody who's been . . . " Her voice trailed off.

"It's always a shock the first time," Gregory agreed sympathetically. "Do you own this boat?"

She nodded, head lowered. "Yes. I run river tours on weekends — and hire out for fishing during the week." She raised her eyes to him. "Who was she?"

"Her name was Lia Kelley."

"From Havasu?"

"No. Tourist. She and her husband were just here for the night. She wanted to see the Bridge."

"Why was she killed?"

"That's a question we can't answer yet."

Angie nervously removed the band from her pony tail, then pushed her falling hair back from her face. "There's nothing else I can tell you."

"I'll have my partner drive you home. I'd do it myself, but I have to talk to the victim's husband. This has been pretty rough on him."

"It must be horrible for him," she agreed. "Look, my car's here at the marina. I don't need a ride home."

"You *sure*?"

"I'm sure." She smiled wanly. "But thanks for your concern."

The Tudor Village.
Morning:

Based on Gregory's interviews with the victim's husband and the waiter who had served the couple at the King's Pub, the village — now designated a potential crime scene — was closed to the public. Several police officers were combing the ground around London Bridge, looking for possible evidence. As Steve Gregory knelt at the center of the span, scraping residue from the pavement directly below the new rail stone, and then putting it into a small evidence bag, Joe Nez approached him.

"The prelim report just came in on the deceased," Nez said. "They found a fragment of clothing under one of her fingernails. The Chief thinks you ought to have a look."

Gregory stood up. "Okay, I'll drop by the lab once I've finished here."

"Find anything?"

"Some stains. Could be blood. If so, they may prove that she was killed here. If that's confirmed, the killer probably pitched her body over the railing. Then the current carried it into Thompson's Bay."

Nez looked past Gregory.

"Uh-oh . . . here comes Whitfield. We've got trouble in River City!"

Anson Whitfield, recently reelected mayor of Lake Havasu City, was short and stumpy, with a bald head and eyes that bulged like chicken eggs behind thick-lensed glasses. He was scowling as he reached the two detectives.

"Mayor Whitfield," nodded Gregory.

Whitfield ignored the greeting. "I've just conferred with the City Council. They're very upset."

"About what?" asked Gregory.

"Closing the village! A fine time you picked to do it. We stage a major dedication ceremony — we get national media coverage to attract more tourists — and *you* shut down the Bridge!"

Gregory's tone was calm. "We're investigating a homicide. We can't have tourists stampeding through there while we're doing it."

"What do you expect to find? There's no mystery about this!"

Gregory made an effort to look interested. "How do you figure that?"

"We know the Kelley woman had cash in her purse," said Whitfield. "Along with credit cards. The purse is missing. Obviously, some passing transient killed her for the money and credit cards. Some road bum who's probably in Phoenix by now."

"It's possible," agreed Gregory. "But we won't know until the investigation is concluded."

Whitfield snorted. "I don't intend to stand here and argue with you. As mayor of this city, I *demand* that you reopen the village immediately."

"As soon as we finish our search —— but not until then."

Whitfield glared at him. "I'm going to Chief Dawson about this."

"Go ahead. But you'll find that I'm acting on *his* authority."

The little man walked abruptly away, his face dark with anger.

Joe Nez sighed heavily. "He's a mean one to have against you. That man throws a lot of weight around here."

"I wasn't hired to promote local business," Gregory said. "We've got a killer to catch."

Joe looked directly into Gregory's eyes. "Steve, I grew up in politics. My father is Chairman of the Navajo Nation, and in these parts that's a powerful position. You don't know how things work around here. You're still the new boy in town, so take it easy. Real easy."

The Main Tourist Area of the Tudor Village:

As police officers systematically searched each shop along the main street, Sergeant Tammy Bishop entered the Bucket of Blood Candle Shoppe and ran her flashlight around the dark interior, revealing a thousand candles in all shapes, colors, and sizes. At intervals, spaced between the display tables, antique wooden mannequins stood dressed in a variety of British period clothing.

Bishop moved deeper into the shop, methodically sweeping her flash left to right as she advanced toward the rear. Suddenly, underfoot, she felt a trapdoor in the plank floor. Lifting it, she saw stairs leading down into blackness.

An ideal hiding place for a killer.

Unsnapping her belt holster as she moved cautiously down the steps, she stopped before reaching the bottom. A musty odor, like old mildew, hung in the air.

"Anyone down here?" she called.

Silence.

Then, at the far wall, she made out a dim shape. Bishop swung her flash in that direction. A tall, cloaked figure in black was suddenly clear.

"Don't move! I've got a gun!" she ordered.

Weapon in hand, Tammy Bishop walked toward the dark figure. She was sweating, and she could feel her blood pressure spiking. She'd never shot anyone, and although her skills with a gun had consistently earned her top police qualification scores, she still hadn't proved to herself that she could pull the trigger against a human being.

The adrenaline rush continued as she walked across the basement floor. Then, under her breath, one word: "Damn!"

She suddenly relaxed, an amused smile on her face. The unknown shape was just another costumed wooden mannequin. She quickly beamed her light around the walls, then turned to climb the stairs.

But behind the mannequin, in much deeper shadow, a pair of dark eyes watched her exit.

The Ripper smiled.

Western Arizona Regional Crime Laboratory. The same afternoon:

"I've examined the cloth fragment found under the fingernail of the deceased," said lab technician Kenny Leuong to Steve Gregory and Joe Nez. "I can't ID it yet."

"What's the problem?" asked Nez.

"Dunno. The fibers don't match anything sold in a modern clothing store. I'm sending a sample over to the state lab in Phoenix for a more complete analysis. They have the latest equipment, and for this, we need the best."

"Okay," nodded Gregory. "We can wait."

"Then there's the blood fragment we found in the victim's throat wound."

"I hadn't heard about that," said Gregory.

"It's not the victim's blood," said Leuong. "Possibly came from the blade used by the assailant."

Nez pursed his lips. "The guy could have killed before, with the same weapon."

"Could be, but I don't make guesses. That, gentlemen, is your department."

"Thanks, Ken. We appreciate your work. Let us know when you hear from Phoenix."

"You got it."

Rio Vista Apartment Resort.
Day:

Gregory parked his Ford pickup in the covered garage and was walking to his apartment when an authoritative female voice suddenly stopped him.

"Detective Gregory?"

He turned to face a woman in a light tan pantsuit. Late twenties, slender, auburn-haired, with a spray of freckles across her nose. Her emerald green eyes were intelligent, direct, and penetrating.

"I'm Steve Gregory," he said.

"My name is Elaine Phillips," she told him, handing Gregory her business card. "I'm with the *San Francisco Dispatch*. I need to talk to you."

"How did you get my address?"

"From Detective Nez."

"Didn't I see you at the Bridge dedication?"

She nodded. "That's what brought me to Havasu — the Bridge story. But I'm ending up with a much better one."

"The Kelley murder?"

"Right. I'm looking for personal angles, and since you're the officer in charge . . . "

"There isn't much I can tell you at the moment."

She smiled, nodding toward his apartment. "Could we talk inside? I'd really appreciate getting your views on the case."

"Only if what I say is strictly off the record. I don't want to be quoted in the paper. Are we agreed?"

"Agreed," said Elaine Phillips.

Gregory turned and keyed open his apartment door.

The Tudor Village.
Bucket of Blood Candle Shoppe.
Past Midnight:

In the darkness, a shape moved.

The Ripper glided soundlessly up the basement steps, to the rear of the shop, where an exit door led to a small commercial alley in back of the building.

The Ripper moved up the lightless alley to a large metal trash dumpster and began rooting among the piled garbage, searching for discarded food from the pub. Hunger was a consuming fire.

Lake Havasu City Police Department.
The next morning:

"I think we screwed up," said Joe Nez, as Steve Gregory entered their office."

"How do you mean?"

"I should never have given your address to that reporter —— and *you* should never have talked to her."

"Why not? It was off the record."

Nez handed Gregory a faxed copy of a *San Francisco Dispatch* story from that morning's issue. The headline read:

ARIZONA DETECTIVE REJECTS TRANSIENT THEORY.

Scanning the story, Gregory groaned in frustration. "That's the last time I'll trust a reporter with green eyes."

"The Chief's upset," said Nez. "He wants to see you."

"Uh-huh."

"*Now*," said Nez.

Steve Gregory rapped lightly on the door at the end of the hall.

"In!" The harsh voice belonged to Pete Dawson.

Gregory walked into Dawson's cluttered office. A fax copy of the *Dispatch* article was on his desk.

Dawson leaned back in his swivel chair, scowling. He tapped a thumb against the fax. "What the hell is this all about?"

"I gave my view of the case —— off the record. The lady promised not to quote me. She lied."

"Sit down," snapped Dawson.

Gregory sat down on a cracked leather couch that had seen better days.

"Whitfield was in here earlier," said Dawson. "He and the City Council are satisfied that this was a random killing. Now you come out in this damn newspaper story, saying just the opposite."

"I told it the way I see it." Gregory drew in a long breath. "There's something weird about this murder. The coroner's report said there was no sign of sexual assault, and I don't think Lia Kelley was killed for the money in her purse."

"What evidence do you have?"

"Look, Pete . . . true crime is a hobby of mine. I've studied criminal behavior all my life, and I'm telling you: the MO is all wrong here. If this was some road bum out to score a purse, he'd club the victim and take off with the money. He *wouldn't* cut her throat. That's an entirely different crime . . . by an entirely different kind of criminal."

"Bullshit! You have nothing to support that theory!" He stood up to face Gregory, fists clenched in frustration. "From here on, you talk to *nobody* about this case. You're not in Chicago anymore. You're in Lake Havasu City, and here you do things *my* way. Do you read me, Detective?"

"Loud and clear," said Gregory.

"Then get the hell out of my office."

Nez was waiting in the hallway. "How'd it go?"

"Don't ask."

"I just got a call from Ken at the lab," said Nez. "He got the report from Phoenix. Says it's a little 'spooky.'"

Western Arizona
Regional Crime Laboratory.
Mid-day:

Leuong handed over his report to Gregory and Nez.

"Wow," said Gregory.

"They're absolutely *certain* this fabric came from the 1880s?" asked Nez.

"Absolutely," said Leuong. "The fabric sample has a characteristic pattern something like a fingerprint. The dyes found in it were Industrial Age products, used commercially only in the 1880s, and the fabric itself was woven by manufacturing equipment dating back to the 1870s. Around the turn of the century they began to use a new type of mechanical system to spin the wool fibers."

Gregory shrugged. "Your average, everyday killer doesn't go around wearing clothes that are over a century old."

"That's not all," said Leuong. "That foreign blood fragment that we found stuck in her throat . . . "

"What about it?" asked Nez.

"Judging from the texture, coloration, and general composition, the blood is also quite old."

Gregory looked intently at him. "*How* old?"

"No way to tell for sure," said Leuong. "You can't date blood the way you can cloth. The DNA in the foreign blood hasn't degraded to any great extent, but preliminary analysis indicates anomalous characteristics." The lab technician hesitated. "It's *possible* that the foreign blood is from the same period as the fabric sample."

Nez raised an eyebrow. "From the nineteenth century?"

"Looks that way," said Leuong. "Spooky, right?"

"Yeah," said Gregory softly. "Spooky."

The Queen's Rest Motel. August 31, 2004. Night:

Elaine Phillips walked to the reception desk. Martha Grimes, the hostelry's middle-aged manager, smiled at her with genuine warmth. She liked her energetic young guest, whose presence prompted Martha to think back on her own life. Forty years before, when Martha graduated from high school, if she had gone to the University of Arizona as she had planned —— instead of marrying the boy who lived across the street —— could her own life have turned out something like the adventurous, globetrotting life of this interesting young journalist?

"You're checking out?" she said.

"Not quite yet," said Elaine. "I'll be back for my things."

"Going home to San Francisco, right?"

"Yeah, I'm going to drive to Phoenix tonight, and fly back first thing tomorrow morning."

"I read that article of yours," said Grimes, pushing back a strand of prematurely gray hair. "Our local Havasu paper played it big on the front page."

"I'm not finished yet," said Elaine. "*Newsweek* just agreed to pay me for writing a feature story about the case."

"My, aren't we moving up in the world!"

"Gotta take full advantage of whatever opportunities come along if you want to build a writing career," the journalist responded. "So I'm going to prowl around the village again, before I leave —— I want to get one last impression for the *Newsweek* story."

"You won't be able to now," declared the manager. "Since the murder, the village has been closed down, day *and* night."

Elaine smiled. "I'll get in."

**The Tudor Village. At the gate.
Same night:**

Elaine checked the area to make certain no guard or police officer was in sight, then moved to the iron fence. She scaled it —— grateful for all those hours she'd spent in the gym —— and lightly dropped to the ground on the far side.

The village was silent and deserted. The regular guard must be making his rounds, Elaine figured. *All the better for me. I'll just keep an eye out for him.*

She walked toward London Bridge, her shadow gliding beneath the high Victorian gas lamps. *This is where Lia Kelley walked that night.*

Reaching the foot of the stone steps which led to the Bridge, Elaine removed a small recorder from her purse. Her voice was soft and steady.

"Here, at these dark stone steps at this place of violent murder, it is easy to imagine how Lia Kelley must have felt, with a killer stalking her in the darkness. I can *feel* vibrations of death here."

Elaine switched off the recorder and reversed direction, now moving toward the main shop area. She passed a London taxi from the 1930s, its black paint dark as old blood, forever immobile beneath a gas lamp. Suddenly she stopped and turned back to the taxi.

Was someone inside?

No, impossible. A trick of the dim light. The vehicle was obviously empty.

She continued toward the shops.

Switching on the recorder once again, Elaine spoke softly: "Walking these dark streets alone is akin to being part of another era, another century . . . a harsh time of disease, starvation . . . and murder."

A faint, scraping sound behind her. The guard? She turned.

No. Someone else. Someone tall and dark.

Too late she tried to avoid the long arm snaking around her neck, stifling the scream that froze in her throat.

Her recorder fell to the pavement.

And a silver scalpel flashed in the night.

Lake Havasu City Police Gymnasium.
Two days later:

Beams of afternoon sun slanted down on the boxing ring, striping the gym floor, as Steve Gregory and Joe Nez —— in protective headgear, trunks, and boxing gloves —— sparred with one another over the squared canvas.

"You're wide open," said Gregory. "Keep your gloves up." He hammered a right to Joe's mid-section, then drove home a hard left.

Nez hit the canvas, grunting in pain. "Okay, okay," he said, raising a gloved hand in defeat. "You're the champ. Where'd you learn to hit like that?"

"Chicago," said Gregory. "South side. You learn fast . . . or you don't survive."

After their showers, back in the locker room, the two sat on a long wooden bench, drinking bottled water.

"You were really *intense* in there," Joe said, rubbing the tender side of his jaw. "Something bugging you?"

"It's that reporter —— the one who got me in trouble with Dawson."

"What about her?"

"She left a message on my answering machine. Apologized for the story. Asked me to phone her at her motel."

"So?"

"So I did. The manager told me that two days ago Elaine Phillips left the motel, said she was going to take a last look at the village. Said she intended on driving to Phoenix that night so she could take a flight back to San Francisco. She never returned, and her suitcase is still in her room."

"Doesn't prove anything," said Nez.

"I contacted the paper in San Francisco. She hasn't returned, and hasn't phoned them, either."

"Probably got a hot tip and took off somewhere on another story."

"No. I called the car rental company. She hasn't returned the car, and they haven't heard from her." He hesitated. "Want to know what I think?"

"You think the same creep who nailed the Kelley woman did in the reporter."

"Exactly."

Joe shook his head. "You need to cool out. Relax." He smiled. "And as it happens, we have everything you need right here: a great river, beautiful mountains, a gorgeous desert. Since you arrived in Havasu, all you've seen is the back of a desk. Get out and live a little!"

Gregory thought a moment. "Okay, I guess I *could* use some R&R." He grinned. "And I know just who to call."

"Then *call*," said Joe Nez.

Saguaro View Apartments.
The Front Office.
Late night:

Mrs. Alma Bowers, the widowed owner, had been hunched over her computer, posting chat room messages with other lonely souls around the world, people who lived in places she'd never heard of. Now, intent on a spirited exchange suddenly developing on the Christian Believers Bulletin Board over the scriptural proofs of the resurrection of Jesus, she failed to hear the office door open.

An insistent tapping on the Formica top of the front desk caused her to suddenly look up at the dark figure who stood there.

He placed a small, black-leather carryall on the counter.

"May I help you?" said Mrs. Bowers.

"I am in need of lodging. I understand that you have short-term flats for hire." The voice was deep, with a pronounced — but peculiar — British accent.

"We call them apartments here," she told him. "How long do you plan on staying?"

"That has yet to be determined."

Mrs. Bowers handed him a registration card and a pen. "Okay, just fill in your name and address."

The man hesitated, then scribbled "Edward Latting" and pushed the card back across the desk.

She stared down at it. "No address?"

"I'm . . . from London."

"Here to see the Bridge?"

"Uh . . . yes, in a manner of speaking."

"First trip over?"

"Yes. My first."

"Well, you'll need to pay in advance," she told him. "Everybody pays in advance."

"I apologize," said Mr. Latting. "I cannot accommodate you in this regard until tomorrow, when I shall be able to exchange my funds for American currency. May I pay you later?"

"All right, then, later." She reached behind her and handed him a key. "It's apartment thirteen, at the end of the corridor."

Latting smiled, his thin lips pulling back from yellowed teeth. "Ah, thirteen," he said. "My favorite number.

He left Mrs. Bowers to stare after him as he shambled down the passageway. Judas, she suddenly remembered, had been number thirteen.

Edward Latting opened the door to his unit and entered. Placing his carryall on the bed, he looked around at the studio accommodation: one room, a tiny kitchenette in the corner, and a small bathroom near the closet. The flat had a worn, lived-in look to it: faded wall paint, transparent curtains, thin carpet and frayed chenille bed cover. The only decoration was a framed print of London Bridge on the wall above the pressed-wood dresser.

Latting sat down on the bed, opened his black-leather carryall, and removed several newspaper clippings. Each headlined the murder of Lia Kelley. He stared at the clippings for a long moment, then crumpled the pages into a tight ball, his face flushed and tight.

Angie Shepherd's Home on the River.
Morning:

Angie was making French toast when the telephone rang. Moving the griddle off the heat, she grabbed a kitchen towel as she answered.

"Hi, it's Steve Gregory. We met when —— "

"Of course," she interrupted. "Detective Gregory. Do you need to interview me again?"

"No. I actually wanted to make a reservation for your boat —— for Wednesday."

"You want to fish?"

"Right."

"Done much fishing?"

"Are you kidding? I'm an old Lake Michigan boy."

"Okay, then. Be at the marina at seven sharp. And don't be late. Okay?"

"Got it. See you Wednesday at seven."

And he clicked off.

Lake Havasu Library.
Noon that same day:

Lynn Chandler was at the front desk, stamping returned books. Although she was the city's only librarian, a series of budget cuts had eliminated much of her paid junior staff, and so she worked a three-hour stint at the front desk each day. A few of the regular library patrons, taking an air conditioned respite from the blinding heat outside, sat at scattered tables in front of the stacks.

A tall man walked up to Lynn. "Good afternoon. I assume you are the librarian at this institution?"

"Yes. I'm Lynn Chandler. How may I help you?"

"My name is Latting." He smiled without warmth. "I would like to see some of your books dealing with modern culture . . . with this present century. I am . . . *new* here, and know little of your country."

"Of course," said Lynn. "We have history, current affairs, sociology . . . why don't we start with history? Would you like me to show you?"

"How very kind of you," said Latting.

As they moved toward the stacks, two city residents glanced up curiously to study the newcomer, who was definitely not a regular.

"I hope you don't mind my noticing," said Lynn, "but you have a delightful British accent."

"Thank you." He drew in a breath and stared at her. "Do you work here at night?"

"That's an odd question," she said. "Why do you ask?"

"I would like to talk with you. When we would have time to talk."

"I see." She frowned. "The library closes at eight. Usually, things start to slow down after seven, so you might try then. If I'm not busy, we can talk."

"And it would be agreeable with you if I stopped by?"

"Uh . . . I suppose so. I'm the librarian, and this is a public library. Everyone's welcome."

"Then I shall indeed stop by," he said. "I very much look forward to talking with you."

As Latting left, Steve Gregory entered the library. From the front desk, Lynn beamed at him. "Detective Gregory! I'm glad you stopped by. The books you ordered from the university library in Tucson just came in."

"Good," he said. "I was hoping they'd be here by now."

Lynn reached under the counter and produced three volumes: *The Crimes of Jack the Ripper, Slaughter in Whitechapel,* and *The Ripper Mystery.*

Gregory tucked them under one arm. "I appreciate this."

"I hear you're going fishing with Angie in her boat."

"How'd you find out?"

"Angie's my best friend. She mentioned your call."

"Yeah, well . . . I'm going out this Wednesday . . . give it a try."

"You've fished before, right?"

"Me? Yeah. Lots of times."

The Marina at Thompson's Bay.
Seven A.M.:

As Gregory drove his Ford pickup into the parking lot, Angie was making final preparations for the departure of the *Lucky Lady.*

She looked up and frowned as Gregory approached. He was dressed in Levis, denim shirt, boots, and sunglasses.

"Where's your gear?" Angie asked.

"Back in Chicago," he replied. "You *do* rent equipment?"

"Sure. Everything you'll need . . . including the bait." She gestured. "Get the bowline and we'll leave."

He started toward the stern.

She smiled and pointed forward. "*That's* the bow."

"Oh, sure." He freed the line and Angie pushed forward on the twin throttles. Slowly, the boat eased away from the dock toward open water.

The Colorado River. On Board *Lucky Lady.* Morning:

They were trolling as the sun spangled the moving current.

Gregory struggled with a snarled line. "I can't get ⸺ "

"Here." Angie handed him a fresh pole. "Try this one."

He looked relieved.

"You'll need bait for that," she said.

"Oh, yeah . . . of course," nodded Gregory, reaching for the bait bucket. "It sure is hot."

"Always is, this time of year," she said. "You'd better be using sun screen, too, or you're going to regret ⸺ "

"Damn!" Attempting to bait the hook, Gregory had pricked his thumb. He sucked at the wound.

Angie idled the engines and sat down next to him.

"Old Lake Michigan boy, eh?"

"I lied," he said. "I've never fished before in my life."

"That's pretty obvious."

"Truth is, I just wanted to see you again."

"Are you married?"

He laughed. "Been close a couple of times." His mood suddenly darkened. "My fiancée and I broke up just before I left Chicago."

"You dump her or she dump you?"

He thought for a moment. "I guess a little bit of both. Something bad happened on my job . . . she couldn't handle it. How about you?"

"I was married. To a good man. I loved him. He died two years ago in a private plane crash."

"That's rough."

The boat drifted in the current.

"For a while, after Larry's death, I lived with my sister in Flagstaff," she continued. "Then I moved back here."

"How did you get into the fishing business?"

"My dad. He grew up near here, and this was his boat. He passed it on to me when he retired. He runs a tourist museum in Tombstone now, so I usually don't see him except on holidays."

"So you've adjusted to living alone?"

"Adjusted." She smiled. "That's a good way to put it. You live alone and you adjust. I'm used to it by now, I guess. But I still miss the closeness of married life."

Gregory mopped his brow. "This heat is killing me. How about heading for shore and a cold drink?"

"You've got a deal," she said.

Lake Havasu Library.
Late that afternoon:

As Angie walked in the door Lynn grinned at her. "So how'd it go?"

"How did *what* go?"

"Don't play coy. Your date with the hunk detective."

"Date? He *paid* me to take him fishing." Angie chuckled. "And he can't even fish."

"Which proves it was a date! He was fishing for *you!*"

"Maybe."

"Ah-huh. No maybe about it."

"He comes on strong, that's for sure. I guess things move faster in Chicago than they do around here."

"What's holding you back? Steve's a terrific guy."

Angie sighed. "I don't know if I'm ready for another heavy relationship yet. Especially with a Chicago cop."

"Correction," said Lynn. "*Lake Havasu City* cop."

"He asked me to go horseback riding with him."

"You going?"

"I'm thinking about it." She picked up a book from the desk and riffled its pages. "So how's *your* love life?"

"Lousy — but it could be about to improve."

"Really? Fill me in."

"I met this British gentleman, here in the library. He's a little odd, but not at all bad looking. He wants to see me again."

"Terrific. Maybe we'll both get lucky."

"Meaning you *are* going riding with Steve?"

"Did I ever tell you you're impossible?"

And they both broke into laughter.

Lake Havasu City Herald. Office of the publisher/editor:

Within the field of journalism, Cassie Nebel was a legend. She had lived an extraordinary life. Born in 1920 to a wealthy eastern Arizona ranching family, she had gone to Boston for her university education, and later had been able to work her way up to the lofty position of National Affairs Editor of the *Boston Globe* before the Second World War ended. She worked as the Washington, D.C. correspondent for several newspaper syndicates in the following decades, until she was finally forced into involuntary retirement on her eightieth birthday.

She returned to her home state and invested her "retirement" funds in the purchase of the struggling *Lake Havasu City Herald* — previously a tiny weekly newspaper of no import beyond the confines of Mohave County. But now, helmed by the energetic and savvy Cassie Nebel, the *Herald* enjoyed regular statewide and regional notice. No one who had ever known Cassie doubted for a moment that she would achieve her ultimate goal: to make the *Lake Havasu City Herald* a newspaper of importance among those of the national press.

After knowing and working with her for more than three years, Police Chief Pete Dawson now considered Cassie Nebel a friend. He radiated easy confidence as he talked with her, while Steve Gregory and Joe Nez — both uncomfortable — lingered near the far office wall.

" . . . and you can assure your readers," Dawson told Nebel, "that there is absolutely no reason to fear any further violence in Lake Havasu."

"You've *solved* the Lia Kelley murder?" Cassie asked.

"We're satisfied that Mrs. Kelley fell victim to a random act that will not be repeated."

"You've identified the killer?" Cassie's tone was deceptively casual; she knew when she was being worked.

"Believe me, Cassie, if he were still in the area, we'd have him by now," said Dawson. "This was clearly the work of a transient: the type who strikes, then runs."

Her eyes flicked over Steve Gregory. "The *San Francisco Dispatch* article quoted Detective Gregory rejecting the theory of a transient killer."

Dawson smiled, and looked at Gregory.

"I'm certain that Detective Gregory has changed his mind. Right, Steve?"

Gregory was plainly uncomfortable. "It's *possible* that a transient killed Lia Kelley," he admitted.

Dawson's jaw muscles twitched. His voice was firm. "It's the only logical answer." He forced himself to visibly relax before he turned back to Cassie, who was observing him with shrewd eyes.

"Well, I think that about covers it, Cassie," he said, bringing the meeting to a sudden close.

Outside, in the parking lot, Dawson faced Steve Gregory. "I had hoped that you would back me up in there with a little more enthusiasm," he said.

"Sorry, but I'm not much of a politician, Pete."

Dawson's jaw was tight. "I'm not asking you for political posturing. I'm demanding departmental loyalty. There's a big difference."

He turned abruptly and walked back to his car.

Joe Nez was behind the wheel of his Honda as Gregory got in.

"Dawson's got a right to be pissed," said Joe. "I see his point. There's no reason to rule out a random killing."

"I've got a reason," declared Gregory.

"The vanishing reporter," Nez asked.

"Nobody's heard from Elaine Phillips since the night she walked out of that motel. Her people in San Francisco are concerned. She always checks with them before taking off on a story. But they've heard zip."

"I think she's okay," said Joe.

"I think she's dead," said Gregory. "And I think the same perp who snuffed Lia Kelley is responsible."

A Deep Canyon
in the Sonoran Desert of Arizona.
Just beyond noon:

Gregory and Angie, on horseback, rode out of the deep canyon, toward a stand of high rocks, as the intense desert heat shimmered in waves around them.

Gregory was flinching from the sun, and he looked dehydrated. Still a tenderfoot in the desert, he obviously didn't understand the danger of heat stroke — or how to protect himself from it.

"Want to stop?" she asked.

"Thought you'd never ask," Gregory replied wearily.

He guided his mount toward the rocks as Angie followed. She removed her canteen as they both dismounted and handed it to Gregory. He drank deeply. They eased down in the shade cast by the high rockfall.

He groaned and shifted his weight. "Never knew riding could be so much *work!*"

Angie laughed lightly. "You're just out of shape, cowboy."

"Knocked Joe Nez . . . on his ass . . . in the gym," Gregory responded thickly, his tongue still swollen by dehydration. "Wanta box?"

Angie laughed, walked back to her horse, and took a blanket from the saddle. Unrolling it, she removed an ivory-handled, .22 target pistol and three empty tin cans. "I'm no boxer," she told Gregory, "but I'm not bad at target shooting."

Gregory winced. Clearly uncomfortable, he watched Angie carefully space the three cans on a weathered cottonwood log in the middle of the now-dry arroyo.

She returned to Gregory, adjusted her stance, and raised the pistol. "I say I can score three for three." She smiled at Gregory. "Care to bet?"

He shook his head. "No. Go ahead."

Aiming carefully, she fired three rounds. Gregory flinched at each explosion as Angie's bullets spun two of the three cans from the log.

"Darn!" she muttered. "I missed the last one. Glad you didn't take my bet." She offered him the gun. "Here. You try."

"No, thanks," he said unsteadily. "I'd . . . rather not."

She looked surprised. "What gives with the 'I'd rather not'? Cops and guns, they go together like bacon and eggs." Then she saw that he was trembling. "Look," she said, "if you really don't want to . . . "

She checked the gun for unused cartridges, then put it back in the blanket roll.

Head down, Gregory motioned Angie to sit beside him.

He paused for a long moment. "Do you remember when I told you that something bad happened on the job in Chicago?"

"Yes," she answered softly.

"Well, I kind of went haywire afterwards. Nothing seemed to matter to me anymore. It was the worst time of my life."

"What happened?"

Gregory's voice was flat and toneless. "I shot someone. Killed him."

She stared at him, saying nothing, waiting for him to release the pain.

"I've never really talked about this — at least, not to anybody who wasn't part of the official investigation."

"I think you need to talk about it now."

"Yeah, I do." He looked deep into the far horizon with unseeing eyes, remembering. "There was a robbery. Liquor store on Wabash Avenue. A night job.

"My partner and I were less than two blocks away when we got the call. He took the street door. I went around back. That's when this guy came running out . . . right at me. Had a plastic bag in his left hand, and what I *thought* was a gun in the other.

"It was dark behind that building . . . and raining hard. One of those blinding Chicago thunderstorms. I saw something flash in his right hand as he came at me. So I fired. Three times. Two of my rounds hit him in the chest." Gregory stopped, shuddered, then took a deep breath. "He died in the hospital that night."

"And he didn't have a gun?" Angie asked.

"It was a *can opener*. He'd sharpened one end to make a weapon out of it." Gregory took another deep breath. "Naturally, there was a big hassle. Chicago tabloids did a number on me. I was suspended for a month during the investigation — which is when Jan and I split up.

"Eventually, it was officially deemed a righteous shooting, but when I went back on duty, I wasn't worth much. Couldn't think straight. Couldn't function. I just wanted to get the hell out of Chicago —— out of police work altogether. So one day my captain calls me in and tells me that a place in Arizona called Lake Havasu City was looking for an experienced police detective who wasn't going to demand much money. Turned out, he'd already been in touch with Dawson, and the job was mine if I wanted it."

Gregory smiled grimly. "To my surprise, I realized that I *did* want the job. Quiet little town in Arizona. Sunny weather. Clean desert air. No snow. No freezing winters. A complete change. I thought I could forget what happened in Chicago." He sighed deeply. "But I can't."

"You made a mistake that night. And it was a big one. But cops make mistakes. We *all* do."

Gregory was silent for a long moment, then raised his eyes to hers. "I don't want to . . . to *ever* have to fire a gun again."

A much longer moment of silence before he resumed.

"Angie, that kid was only thirteen years old."

And his face was filled with grief.

The Vicar's Dirk Night Club:

The dance floor was laced by flashing pinwheels of multi-colored lights, and the local band onstage —— Havasu's English —— was rocking.

"You're a good dancer," Angie said.

"Well, I can dance better than I can fish," Gregory answered, spinning her out for a turn.

"Want to sit down?" she asked.

"*Now* who's out of shape?"

They moved to a distant table on the patio where the background music became a softened counterpoint to their conversation.

"Thank you," said Gregory.

"For what?"

"For letting me talk. I feel better, now."

"I'm glad," she said. She instinctively pressed her hand over his as they both realized that a bond had formed between them.

"I've been meaning to ask you: What made you become a cop?"

"My old man was a cop," Gregory said. "So was *his* old man. Guess it just runs in the family."

"Didn't you ever want to be anything else . . . when you were little?"

"Oh, sure, but I finally realized that I just didn't have what it takes."

"To be what?"

"A prima ballerina."

They were laughing as the waitress arrived with wine spritzers. Gregory raised his glass. "Here's to people who understand."

They clinked glasses and sipped their wine.

"I want to understand you," Angie said. "I think you're very much worth understanding."

"What about you?" he asked. "What did you want to be when you were a little girl?"

"Straight answer?"

"Straight."

"Well, I never got to college," Angie said. "Dad had this boat service, and when he retired, I ended up doing what he did."

"With a marriage in between."

"Yeah. Larry and I had known each other since we were little kids; we were high school sweethearts. When I was growing up, I *really* wanted to be a psychologist — I wanted to help others with their emotional problems. So many lives get screwed up, and I wanted to help."

Gregory touched her cheek. "And that's just what you wound up doing. Helping *me*. I sure have been screwed up since things went bad back in Chicago." He looked intently into her eyes. "I'm glad I found you, Angie. You're becoming very important to me."

"You *mean* that, don't you?"

"Yes."

He leaned forward, and their lips met with warm, gathering hunger.

Bank of the Colorado River.
Morning:

The group of boisterous fourth and fifth graders, happy to be out of the classroom on a field trip, were sitting around Mr. Hought

— the new teacher in town — whose still-boyish demeanor had made him the instant favorite of the elementary school set.

" . . . and that's one of the reasons why we're all lucky to live in Havasu: we have so many different kinds of birds that visit us each year," he said. Hought nodded to a bright-eyed ten-year-old. "Judy, can you tell me a kind of river duck that we sometimes see here in Havasu?"

"Mallard," she replied.

He beamed a delighted-teacher smile at her. "Correct! The mallard. And do you know how to identify the *male* mallard?"

"His neck is green."

"You're right! Now, we all know that a female mallard has a light brown head, with dark streaks along — "

Judy abruptly interrupted him, pointing toward the river current. "Look, Mr. Hought . . . a *floating lady*."

The children surged forward as Mr. Hought gasped in shock at the gruesome sight of a woman's corpse bumping the shoreline.

Her throat had been cut.

Elaine Phillips.

Lake Havasu Library.
September 8, 2004. Night:

Lynn Chandler yawned and stretched. The wall clock said 7:48. Twelve minutes to closing time. Except for the periodic chirp of the library's resident cricket, it was quiet as Boot Hill cemetery — and with every other overhead light out as an electricity conservation measure, the main room was deeply shadowed. The tall stacks loomed in the background, phantom-shapes in the deepening Southwestern night.

Lynn pushed aside a pile of books and eased back in her desk chair. She was tired, and looking forward to a hot shower and a full night's sleep. A tuna sandwich and green salad take out from Blimpie's, then home to feed Tabby and Crinkles (her cat companions of several years), and she could still be in bed before ten.

Tomorrow she would be up before dawn, for a six-mile walk along the river, which would end just as the sun came up over the eastern horizon. Then her great-grandmother's traditional Papago breakfast: eggs scrambled with tepary beans, fresh spinach, and onions. She'd add a slice of cantaloupe, a mug of white sage tea, and her many nutritional supplements. From her own family history Lynn knew the scientific fact that fifty percent of Papago and Pima Indians develop full-blown diabetes by the time they're adults. Half-Papago, she was meticulous about both her nutrition and her exercise program so she could avoid what so many medical authorities seemed to think was inevitable.

Her solo daily routine seldom varied, and this was beginning to depress her. By rights, she should be out on the town past midnight with a muscled hunk, instead of being tucked away in her bed before ten. Going with Angie to the occasional Friday night dinner, followed by a film at the multi-plex, just didn't cut it.

Ah, she thought — maybe I'll get lucky.

A faint sound between cricket chirps. Lynn raised her head. The sound came from the far end of the stacks. Near the back door. Had she locked it? Yes, she was certain she had; she could remember locking it after the late afternoon FedEx delivery. Now the library was silent again. Maybe she had imagined the sound.

She picked up her purse and was in the act of switching off the reading lamp on her desk when she heard the strange sound again. Louder this time. Distinct.

Someone was in the library.

Lynn pivoted in horror as a dark, swift-gliding figure rushed toward her. Before she could scream, a blade was buried in her throat.

Lynn would never scream again.

Lake Havasu City Police Department.
Office of the Chief of Police.
Morning:

Startled by the knock on his closed door, Pete Dawson looked up in irritation from the columns of figures on his budget proposal. "In!" he growled.

Steve Gregory entered, walked over to the desk, and put down a folder. "Figured you'd want to see these."

Dawson opened the folder and removed several 8x10 glossy photographs. On top: a boot print in soft earth; underneath: a picture of a woman's scarf in an intricately interwoven, geometric Hopi design.

The chief looked up at Gregory. "What about 'em?"

"The boot print is from the river bank, a spot close to the village. Where we think the killer dumped Elaine Phillips."

"How do you figure?"

"The scarf is hers. She bought it at Windsor Garden Fashions in the village. Antique, one of a kind — from Hotevilla. Paid almost five hundred dollars for it, but said she'd be wearing it for the rest of her life. Planned to make it a signature piece for photos on all the books she expected to write. When she was put into the water, the scarf snagged on the branch of a cottonwood tree."

Dawson grunted. "And since her throat was cut — just like the Kelley woman — there's a good chance it's the same perp."

"Same MO. And the lab report indicates that the murder weapon is probably identical." Gregory hesitated. "I want permission to close down the village. Both murders are directly tied to that area."

Dawson stood up, walked to the window, and stared out "If I shut down the village again, I'll catch hell from Whitfield and the City Council."

"And if you *don't* shut it down, more people could die at the hands of this maniac." Gregory's voice was intense. "He's *out* there, Pete. He's already killed two women, and I think he's going to kill more."

Dawson swung back to his desk. "Once the village is closed, we may as well close the entire city. Tourism is what keeps Havasu alive — or hadn't you noticed?"

"I know you'll get a lot of heat from Whitfield and his gang, but we can't risk any more lives."

Dawson sat down at his desk and looked at the photos again. He stared at Gregory. "Do *you* believe this creep is going to quit killing just because we close the village?"

"We won't know until we try," said Gregory. "But at least no more women will get their throats cut on London Bridge."

Dawson tapped his desk with tense fingers. "How long do you want the village closed?"

"As long as it takes to catch the killer."

The chief scowled and shook his head. "No good, Steve. We don't know when, or even if, he'll be found. The best I can do is post plainclothes police officers in the village — but I can't authorize a shutdown."

Gregory clenched his fists. "You mean *won't*, not can't."

"I'm responsible to the public. I have sworn duties to this community that go beyond strict police work."

"Sure . . . sure you do."

Steve Gregory's face was tight with anger as he walked out of Dawson's office.

Gregory's Apartment.
That night:

The grilled cheese sandwich he was fixing for dinner had just finished browning when the ringing phone broke into his reverie. "Gregory here," he said.

"It's Angie. I'm worried."

"What about?"

"Lynn. She didn't show up today at the library, and she *never* misses work. When I tried to call her, I couldn't get an answer. I have a key to her place so I drove over, but she wasn't there. And she hadn't been there for a while."

"How do you know?"

"Her cats were ravenous with hunger. Lynn would *never* leave Tabby and Crinkles unfed — and she'd never go away without first telling me to take care of them, either."

Gregory could hear the fear in Angie's voice.

"I think something awful has happened to her," said Angie.

Gregory cleared his throat. "Can I come over now? I'll take a formal statement from you about Lynn, and that will start the ball rolling on a missing person investigation." He paused for a moment. "I was going to call you anyway, because I'm working on a new theory, and I'd like to talk it over with you."

"I'll be here," she said.

Saguaro View Apartments.
Night:

Edward Latting carried a newspaper down the corridor to number thirteen. He entered, sat down on the bed, unfolded the paper, and scanned the headlined story:

SECOND MURDER SHOCKS HAVASU CITY
Body Discovered In River Near London Bridge

Latting's eyes narrowed. He tossed the paper aside, walked to the closet, and removed his black leather carryall. He ran his fingers slowly and carefully — almost lovingly — over the contents. The bag contained plastique explosives. Satisfied, he closed the carryall and stood in front of the framed print of London Bridge. He stared at the print, taking in all its pastel details. His eyes darkened.

Removing a knife from his coat, he leaned forward, then slashed viciously at the print, cutting a jagged "X" across the glass.

Angie Shepherd's Home on the River.
Night:

Angie and Steve Gregory sat across the table from each other in the kitchen nook. Her face was clouded, and she was clearly distraught. Her movements were mechanical and robot-like. She had given him all the relevant information about Lynn that she had — and he'd dutifully jotted it down in his notebook — but she realized that, in truth, she had very little of value to tell him.

"When I leave here," Gregory said, "I'll go straight to the department and file a formal missing person's report, then I'll authorize a statewide APB. If she's out there, there's a good chance we can find her."

"If she was alive, she would've contacted me," Angie said, very softly.

He put his hand over hers. "Don't go there, Angie. We don't know what happened. You can't make any assumptions right now."

"Well, I'm going over to Lynn's place and bring Tabby and Crinkles back here." Her eyes filled with tears. "I think they need a new home, and that's what Lynn would have wanted."

"We'll do everything we can to find her," he said.

An awkward silence between them.

Then: "I've been working on a new theory," he said. "I think it's important."

Angie visibly straightened her posture and took in a slow, deep breath. "Okay, tell me about it."

"We found a tiny fragment of cloth under one of Lia Kelley's fingernails. The lab determined that it was over a century old. I think the killer bought the coat from an antique shop — to match his assumed identity."

"What identity?"

"I'll get to that." He leaned toward her. "Next, take the way he killed his victims —— by cutting their throats. My supposition is that he did it with a scalpel. Probably an antique; old, like the clothes. A surgeon's scalpel."

Angie winced. "Steve, I don't think I'm up to this."

"It's important for you to know everything," he said.

She sighed. "Okay. Go on."

"Consider the vital dates: August 7th, when Lia Kelley was murdered on London Bridge —— and August 31st, the last night Elaine Phillips, the reporter, was seen alive."

"What's the connection?" she asked.

"Just wait," he answered. "Let's add a *third* date: September 8th."

"When Lynn disappeared," she said dully.

He put his hand over hers again. "It may be the night when Lynn became a victim of the same killer."

Angie shuddered, and tears formed in her eyes.

"But there's no *proof.* I mean, they haven't found her body . . . "

"The body of Elaine Phillips wasn't found until it washed ashore."

"Then you believe —— "

"I believe that *someone* was murdered on September 8th. I just don't know who."

Angie's voice was strained. "I've been telling myself that Lynn will show up, that she's really all right somehow, but —— in my heart —— I know I'll never see her again."

Steve Gregory waited a long moment for Angie to absorb the shock, then continued: "The three dates I've named match exactly the dates of a trio of murders attributed to Jack the Ripper, in London's Whitechapel district, more than a century ago. Between August 7th and November 9th, 1888, six women were slaughtered in that area. The killer vanished the same year. I've been doing a lot of research and I found this."

He handed her a Xerox copy of a newspaper article.

"Read the headline," said Gregory.

"Dying constable Reveals Possible Solution to Ripper Mystery."

Gregory leaned toward Angie. "Constable Jonathan Graham made a death bed statement in which he claimed to have killed Jack the Ripper at London Bridge on the night of November 15, 1888. He said he couldn't *prove* that the man who fell into the Thames that night was the Ripper, which is why he'd kept silent about it. But there were no more Ripper murders after that date."

Angie sighed. "You believe that the man who died that night was Jack the Ripper?"

"I do."

"But what has this got to do with —— "

"Our killer wears clothing from the same period. He probably uses a doctor's scalpel, very possibly an antique scalpel also from that era. He cuts his victim's throats. And he strikes in the vicinity of London Bridge."

Angie wasn't making the connection.

"In his deranged mental state," Gregory continued, "our guy identifies himself with this iconic killer from the past. This gives him a sense of invincibility. I believe we're dealing with a nutcase who actually *thinks* he's Jack the Ripper."

"That's a pretty wild theory," she said.

"It's the only one that fits."

"What will Pete Dawson say when you tell him?"

"I already have. He thinks that ex-Chicago police detectives have bizarre imaginations."

"Meaning he doesn't buy it?"

"No. Not yet. But he *will*."

"Why?"

"Because if the pattern continues, two more murders will occur on the night of September 30th . . . and then he'll be *forced* to believe me." Gregory ground his hands together. "But I don't intend to let two more women die just to prove I'm right. We've got to stop this guy before those murders happen."

"How?"

He looked at her. "That's a very good question."

Lake Havasu City Hall.
Parking Lot.
Early morning:

In the late 1960s, Anson Whitfield —— grandson of Arizona pioneers, a University of Arizona law school graduate, and newly admitted to the Arizona bar —— established his law practice in the brand new community of Lake Havasu City and began a career that eventually culminated in his election as mayor. So far as Havasu was concerned, Whitfield was "Old Money" — and he enjoyed the considerable local status that went with it. Now, when he exited his Mercedes sedan and walked toward City Hall, his attire — carefully-tailored gray suit, red bolo tie, and carved turquoise silver clasp — radiated the extreme confidence natural to small town bigwigs.

As he crossed the municipal parking lot toward City Hall, he saw a Honda drive into the other entrance. Steve Gregory jumped out of the passenger door and intercepted the mayor.

"Mayor Whitfield, we need to talk."

"Not now. I'm late for a meeting."

"This is urgent," said Gregory, blocking his path.

Whitfield scowled darkly. He hadn't approved of Gregory being hired — ex-Chicago cops with questionable backgrounds didn't belong here; it was entirely the wrong tone for tourist-oriented Havasu — and he'd had no reason to modify his opinion since, especially after he'd accidentally overheard his granddaughter refer to the new detective as "a hottie."

"What do you want?"

"We need to close down the village."

"For another useless search?"

"No, sir. For the safety of the public. The killer is still at large and we can't afford to —"

Whitfield cut him off, speaking sharply. "Did Chief Dawson order the village closed?"

"No. I'm asking you to do this voluntarily, as a gesture of public safety."

Whitfield glared at him. "Public safety is *your* job. That's what this city pays you for. And unless Chief Dawson personally orders the village shut down, it stays open."

"Your attitude stinks, Whitfield."

The older man glared with anger. "I'll tell you what stinks! Your record! You didn't fit in back east, and you don't fit in here, either. You're unstable, a misfit." He jabbed a finger into Gregory's chest. "I know all about you! I know about that thirteen-year-old kid you blew away in Chicago."

Gregory's eyes flashed. He grabbed Whitfield by his coat lapels and pushed him against the cement block wall. His fist was cocked for impact as Joe Nez rushed in to intervene. "Whoa, buddy!" He pulled his partner away. "Just ease down."

Whitfield backed toward the entrance, badly shaken. "You're finished in this city, mister! I promise you that. Your career is *over!*"

"We'll see," said Gregory.

Whitfield entered the glass doors of City Hall as Pete Dawson quickly approached the two detectives.

"What was *that* all about?"

"I almost decked Whitfield. He was way out of line on what he said to me."

Dawson's jaw tightened. "How could you even think about decking the mayor?"

"I'm sorry, Pete, but the guy's an A-1 jerk."

"I'll second that," said Joe Nez.

Dawson blew out a frustrated breath. "Okay, we'll talk about this later. Right now, we have business to take care of. Cassie Nebel phoned me. Said we needed to get over there right away." He gestured toward the Honda. "You guys follow me over to the *Herald.*"

Lake Havasu City Herald Building.
Same day:

The three men walked to the rear of the building. Inside her office, Cassie Nebel looked up from a story she was editing.

"What have you got?" asked Dawson.

Cassie handed over a sheet of paper. "Our first crackpot poem. Maybe I should frame it."

The words on the sheet were handwritten in old-fashioned script:

My dear editor:
    I have composed a small poem I would like to see printed in your paper. I'm sure it will amuse your readers.
        Three dead,
        soon four.
        The stone has told me,
        there will be more.

The letter was signed: *Jack.*

Cassie was troubled. "Whitfield has been pressuring me to keep news about the killings out of the paper," she said. "I haven't decided what to do with this, but whoever this guy is, he can't count. There've been two murders, not three."

"No," Gregory corrected her. "It's three."

Cassie Nebel's eyebrows rose. "How do you figure? Lia Kelley. Elaine Phillips . . . "

" . . . and Lynn Chandler," said Gregory. "The last line says it all: 'There will be more.'"

Office of the Chief of Police.
Later, the same day:

Dawson perched on the side of his desk and glared at the two detectives seated on the couch. "After what you almost did to Whitfield today, this letter is the only reason I'm not kicking your rosy butt off the case, Steve. At least it proves that we *do* have a copycat Ripper working in Havasu."

" . . . who just killed Lynn Chandler," added Gregory.

"Could be," said Dawson. "She's definitely missing. If she is dead, that would make it three."

"Think it's a good idea for Cassie to print the letter?" asked Joe Nez.

Dawson shrugged. "Why not? No point in keeping it under wraps. Let's give our resident weirdo all the publicity he wants. Might help draw him into the open." He fiddled with the pen holder on his desk. "Besides, the public needs to be warned. This way, we'll have the whole country watching for him."

"What do you make of that part about 'the stone has told me there will be more'?" asked Joe.

Gregory rubbed his fist along his jaw. "I can't figure the 'stone' part, but one thing's for sure: we gotta nail this scumball, and fast." He tapped the letter on Dawson's desk. "Because if he keeps to the Ripper's pattern, he'll kill again on September 30th."

Saguaro View Apartments. The front office.
Same day:

The latest issue of the *Lake Havasu City Herald* was spread over the front desk, in front of Alma Bowers.

ANOTHER JACK THE RIPPER
AT LONDON BRIDGE?

An outline of a man's head was featured under the headline. The features were blank, with a large question mark in the center of the drawing. Under it, the words:

WHO IS HE?
WHERE IS HE?

Hearing footfalls down the corridor, she quickly folded the paper and put it aside, then peered around the corner. Edward Latting was leaving the building, using the side door next to the office, and he was carrying his black leather bag. He walked down the street, and was soon lost behind a stand of palm trees. At the same moment, Steve Gregory's pickup arrived. Parking in front of the building, he and Joe Nez exited the vehicle and entered the office.

"Joe!" she exclaimed with delight. "How good to see you!" How's your grandmama doing these days?"

"Doing better, Alma," he answered. "Had to go to the hospital in Gallup last month, but she's back at the hogan now, and Aunt Jessie's having a terrible time keeping her from working too hard."

"Well, you tell both of them I can't wait till I can eat a slice of their peach pie again. When I try to make their recipe, it just never comes out right, no matter what I do."

Joe turned to Gregory. "Steve, this is Mrs. Alma Bowers, one of my family's oldest friends. Alma, this is Steve Gregory, our new police detective in town."

"We're here because we were told you wanted to see us, Mrs. Bowers," said Gregory.

"Yeah. Well, part of it was I thought they'd send Joe, and I wanted to say hello to him. But the other part is something I thought I ought to report. My tenant in thirteen: Mr. Latting. He's sorta strange. Keeps odd hours . . . mostly goes out at night . . . says how he thinks London Bridge has a *curse* on it, how it's a 'place of evil' and should be destroyed. Those were his exact words . . . a 'place of evil.'"

"Where is Latting now?"

"He just left, a little while ago, with that black bag he always carries." Alma Bowers shook her head. "A real odd one, he is. Talks funny. Like most foreigners do."

"He's from overseas?"

"London, he said. First trip over."

"Do you have a key to his apartment?" asked Gregory.

"Sure. Got 'em to all the apartments, right here in the office. In case of emergency, you know."

She opened a drawer and took out a key. "C'mon. I'll open up thirteen for you."

The apartment was empty, as Mrs. Bowers told them it would be. Gregory walked to the framed print of London Bridge and ran his fingers along the grooves of the deep "X" scratched in the glass.

The bathroom contained no personal effects. Nez opened the closet. Bare.

"Looks as if your Mr. Latting has just checked out," said Gregory.

Office of the Chief of Police.
Same day:

Anson Whitfield paced the small floor space, tight with anger. He spun around and faced Gregory, his voice sharp: "*Gone*? How could he be gone?"

"He left before we got there," said Gregory. "No telling where Latting is now. We put out an APB, but so far, nothing's come in."

From behind his desk, Pete Dawson looked up at Whitfield, trying to appear pleasant. "Latting won't get far, Anson. We've got the whole county bottled up: both ends of Highway 95, the airport, the river, and a Mohave County Sheriff's copter is covering the desert."

"He was at Alma's all this time," fumed the mayor. "Right under your noses . . . here in town! A psycho killer. An obvious madman."

"There's no evidence that Edward Latting had anything to do with the murders," said Gregory. "Yeah, he's a weirdo . . . but that doesn't mean he's our killer."

"That's bullcrap!" snapped Whitfield. "You just don't want to admit that you let this madman slip right by you." He turned to Dawson. "Your *Chicago cop* has been running this case like a damn fool."

Gregory's eyes narrowed. "I won't take any more from you, Whitfield!"

Dawson stood up. "Quit it, *both* of you."

Whitfield's jaw was set. "Detective Gregory hasn't finished his probationary period yet. He can be terminated without notice." The mayor took a sheet of paper from his coat. "This is an official request, backed by the City Council, to have Detective Steven Gregory terminated from his position. Immediately."

Whitfield tossed the paper onto Dawson's desk and stomped from the office, slamming the door behind him.

A moment of silence as Dawson scanned the document.

"Legally, this is a request," he said. "It's not an order, so I'm rejecting it." He looked hard at Gregory. "But you're walking a tightrope, Steve. A lot of important people are stirred up, and you can't afford another wrong move. Not *one* . . . or it's all over for you."

Gregory nodded. "I understand. I appreciate your keeping me on the force."

"Just walk soft," said Dawson.

As Steve Gregory moved down the hallway, Joe Nez joined him. "Heat's on, right?"

"Whitfield handed Pete Dawson an official request to have me canned. For now, I'm still on the force . . . barely. But I'm not worried about Whitfield."

"You're worried about *something*."

"I don't buy Latting as the killer. I think we're after the wrong man."

"What makes you think so?"

"His handwriting, for one thing," said Gregory. "The registration card at Alma Bowers' place. His signature on the card doesn't match the writing on the note the killer sent to the *Herald*."

"The note could be a phony," said Nez. "From some other weirdo who wants publicity."

"Maybe," nodded Gregory, "but I think we're missing a big piece of the puzzle. There's more involved here than a copycat killer. I just feel that there's another whole aspect to this, that we're on the wrong track."

"What other track is there?"

"I don't know," said Gregory, "but I'm driving to Phoenix to check out the Arizona State University library. Maybe I'll find something that will bring us a lot closer to the truth."

Angie Shepherd's Home on the river.
An hour before dawn:

Steve Gregory pulled the Ford pickup to a stop behind Angie's white SUV. Exiting the car with a briefcase, he moved toward the front door.

Deeply asleep, the sound of the front door bell awakened Angie. She studied the fluorescent hands of the clock on her night table and frowned. Slipping a robe over her nightgown, she moved to the door and checked the view-glass.

"Steve," she said. "It's near daybreak." Sudden shock registered on her face. "Oh, my God! Is it about Lynn?"

He shook his head, no.

"Then what are you doing here?" She stared at his unshaven face. "You look awful."

"Been up all night," he told her. "Just drove back from Phoenix." He sighed. "I could use some coffee."

He followed her into the kitchen, where she filled a coffee pot with water and put it on the stove.

"Sit down, for heaven's sake, before you *fall* down," she said. "Try the couch in the living room. I'll bring in the coffee when it's done."

Gregory nodded and headed for the couch. He sat down heavily, placing his briefcase beside him, scrubbing at his eyes to stay awake.

Angie came in with two big mugs of coffee. He took the one she offered and sipped at it gingerly.

"Ah . . . good and strong. Just what I need." He gestured to the sofa cushion next to him. "Sit down. We have to talk. Or, at least, *I* have to talk."

She sat down. "Okay. Talk."

He opened the briefcase and began spreading books and papers across the large coffee table in front of the couch.

"Has there been another murder?" she asked. "Is that what all this is about?"

"No. No more murders. Not yet." He shook his head. "I can't

tell anyone else what I'm going to tell you . . . and you're going to think I've flipped out. But — as insane as it sounds — I believe what I'm going to say is true."

"You've got me hooked," she said.

He laid an 8x10 glossy photo next to a Xerox copy of a magazine article. "Two photographs of a boot print," he said. "What do you see?"

She studied both. "Well, it looks like they were made by the same boot. At least, there's an identical heel-and-toe pattern."

"The glossy is brand new, taken at the spot where our killer dumped the body of Elaine Phillips into the river."

"And the other?"

"It's a photocopy of a police sketch made at the scene of a Ripper killing in 1888. And, just as you say, both appear to be identical."

She looked confused. "But, I don't —"

"Then we have *this*," he said. Gregory placed a sheet of paper next to another book photo. "A Xerox copy of the note sent to Cassie Nebel by what appears to be our killer. The book photo is of a letter sent to a London newspaper after a Ripper murder in 1888."

She leaned close to the table. "The handwriting . . . it's exactly the same in both!"

Gregory's voice was firm. "That's because the same man wrote them."

"What are you saying?"

"I'm saying — God help me — that there *isn't* any copycat killer. Never was." He paused to gather courage. "The man who butchered Lia Kelley and Elaine Phillips is the *real* Ripper."

She looked at him in shock. "Steve . . . that's totally impossible."

"Which is what I keep telling myself," he said. "But look at this line from the poem he sent Cassie Nebel: 'The stone has told me there will be more.'"

"That doesn't make any sense."

"Oh, but it does," Gregory countered. "I'm certain that he's referring to the lost stone found in the Thames."

"But what has that stone to do with —"

Again, he interrupted her, speaking with deep conviction. "The first murder here in Havasu occurred during the twenty-four hour period in which the stone was dedicated. It's the key to everything."

"How do you mean?"

"That stone is tied directly into the killings. When it was brought back from the bottom of the Thames River, *he* came with it. Now he's here, in Havasu, in our time — and he's repeating the same historical murder pattern all over again."

"Steve . . . " Her voice was calm and certain. "Whoever this psycho is, he's not Jack the Ripper. Not *the* Jack the Ripper. Stones don't bring dead people back to life."

"Okay, okay. Whether you believe me or not isn't important now." He reached out to grip her shoulders. "Will you at least help me?"

"To do what?"

"I've got a plan, but I need you and Joe to help." His face looked haunted. "We've got to stop him, Angie — because he's *out* there . . . " Gregory hesitated, looking past the patio window, deep into the thick Arizona darkness. " . . . and he's ready to kill again."

London Bridge.
The following night:

Two armed guards patrolled the Bridge as the waters of the Colorado River lapped softly against the stone supports, tracing a liquid boundary around the deserted Tudor Village.

At the far side of the span, a dark figure emerged from the shadows. Climbing along the base, and unseen by the passing guards, he attached plastique explosive to a granite column. He moved to another part of the column and attached more plastique. Then he repeated the process a third time. Three charges successfully in place, before a guard hailed him.

"You, there!" the guard shouted, as he drew his weapon. "Stand clear, with your hands up."

The dark man, moving spider-quick, sprinted for the grassy hill near the Bridge. The guard opened fire, but the man continued running.

As he neared the top of the slope, sirens blasted the night. Outdoor floodlights suddenly illuminated the area. Police vehicles converged. Steve Gregory and Joe Nez piled out of an unmarked car, as Pete Dawson — who had been staked out in a cable TV van — joined them.

"We've flushed out our killer," said Dawson as he ran beside the two detectives.

"Possible," answered Gregory.

The fugitive sprinted for a nearby park area.

"Block the park exit!" Dawson yelled into his shoulder radio. "We have to bottle him up!"

As the police perimeter began to tighten, the dark man removed a detonator from his coat and raised it in the air.

"Once I press this button," he shouted, "London Bridge will be destroyed. The Devil rules this place of darkness. His abode of evil must be eliminated from the Earth."

"Guy's totally wacked out," said Dawson. "We're gonna have to —"

At that moment, running quick and low through the shadows, Gregory tackled the dark man before the detonator could be activated. As Gregory wrestled the device from his hand, the man in black suddenly snatched up a heavy tree limb.

Joe Nez shouted a warning, but too late. The tree limb smashed into Steve Gregory's head. Before he could strike a second blow, the attacker was quickly subdued by Nez and several other officers. He was handcuffed, read his Miranda rights, and led toward a patrol car.

"This is an unclean place," the dark man declared, his voice shrill. "Beware — all of you — lest you be consumed by the powers of Satan!"

Joe Nez hurried over to his partner. Blood was dripping from the wound in Gregory's skull.

"An ambulance is on the way," said Nez. "Relax, Steve. Don't try to get up."

"We nail him?" Gregory asked dizzily.

"Yeah, we nailed him," replied Nez. "We've got our killer."

Gregory looked up at his partner and smiled weakly. "Don't count on it, Joe," he said.

Lake Havasu City Police Department.
Jail Section.
Night:

The dark man was huddled on a cot in one corner of the cell, legs drawn up against his chest, his head lowered in defeat.

Dawson and a bandaged Steve Gregory stood in the corridor

facing the bars. "There's your Ripper, Steve," said the chief. "Not so fearsome now, eh?"

Gregory's voice was strained, the pain he was experiencing obvious. "Sorry, Pete. That's not him."

"Are you serious?" Dawson asked in disbelief.

"He's *not* the killer."

"Hell he isn't!" snarled Dawson. "Alma Bowers IDs him as Latting, the guy we've been after. And he doesn't have an alibi for the killings . . . *and* he just tried to blow up London Bridge! Plus we found newspaper clippings about the murders in Alma's dumpster, and they have Latting's prints on him. Ran a check on the guy: Arrested and released twice for assault, once when he made an attempt to burn down a church. Born and raised in Liverpool, but he spent most of the last few years in mental hospitals in the south of England. Released last year — on medication, which I assume he stopped taking. Oh, he's our boy, all right."

"Latting may be a nutcase, but that doesn't prove he killed those women."

"You told me the murders were the work of a copycat killer," said Dawson. "And you were right. Latting fits one hundred percent."

"I was wrong on the copycat angle," said Gregory.

Dawson glared at him. "If Latting didn't kill 'em, who did?"

"There never was a copycat Ripper, Pete — only the *real* one."

Dawson stared at him, dumbfounded.

"You're talking about the guy from the 1880s?"

"Yeah. That one."

"Well, he sure is active for his age. I make it he's pushing maybe 150 by now? Must take a lot of vitamins, huh?"

"I knew you'd never believe me. Didn't expect you to. But Pete . . . " Gregory's voice broke as he swayed forward. "Pete . . . we need to . . . to…"

Dawson gripped Steve's arm. "You okay?"

"Dizzy. A little . . . dizzy."

"You look lousy. Didn't the doc tell you to stay in bed?"

"I had to see you . . . had to *convince* you . . . " Gregory's forehead was pearled with sweat. "Pete, listen to me. Three nights from now he's going to kill again . . . just before midnight . . . on the 30th. All part of the pattern. Gotta stop him, Pete. Can't let him . . . "

Gregory fell forward, clutching at the bars of the cell to stay upright.

"Got to catch him, Pete. Got to . . . "

Havasu Regional Medical Center.
Night:

Steve Gregory opened his eyes, the lids sliding back slowly. He blinked several times, then tried to raise himself.

"Where am I?" he mumbled.

Angie answered. "You're in the hospital. You blacked out at the jail, and the EMTs brought you here. You've been unconscious."

"Yeah, partner, you really had us worried," said Joe Nez, who was seated in a chair next to Gregory's bed. "How do you feel?"

"Like Rip Van Winkle." Gregory drew in a breath. "How long have you guys been here?"

"We hardly left," said Angie. "I went home to feed the cats; but mostly, we've been here."

Gregory nodded. "I had a dream . . . about both of you. We were trapped together in the village. Going to die there. Ugly nightmare."

"That blow you took was serious," said Angie.

Gregory touched his bandaged head. "How long have I been out?"

"Three days," said Joe.

Gregory pushed himself up on the pillow, shocked. "*Three days!* Then this is the 30th?" His voice was edged with panic. "Dear God!"

"What's wrong, Steve?" asked Angie.

"It's tonight!" breathed Gregory. "He's going to kill again tonight!"

"Hey, the killings are over," said Joe. "We *caught* the guy, remember?"

"No. It was the wrong man. We haven't caught the Ripper."

Joe and Angie exchanged a knowing look.

She spoke gently. "I told Joe about your new theory. He agrees with me that the case has put you under a lot of pressure, and that — "

"Don't patronize me!" snapped Gregory. "I tell you, he's out there, dammit! Whether you believe me or not."

There was a strained silence in the room. Then . . .

"Angie . . . Remember . . . you promised to help me — you and Joe. With a plan I worked out. A way to catch the killer."

"Hey," said Nez gently, "there's nobody to catch."

"I'll prove there *is*," said Gregory. "Look . . . I've got no one else I can trust, and we're out of time. We've got to act tonight." His eyes locked on theirs. "*Will* you help me? Both of you? Will you?"

Angie and Joe stared back at him.

Havasu Regional Medical Center.
Parking Lot.
September 30, 2004. The same night:

Joe and Angie argued as they sat in her SUV near the hospital's service entrance.

"We shouldn't be breaking Steve out against doctor's orders," said Joe. "If we do, we'll be acting crazier than he is."

Angie stared out the windshield, thinking. "It's not such a big deal, is it? Playing decoy for a killer who's *already* locked up." She sighed. "C'mon, Joe. Once Steve sees that nothing is going to happen tonight, he'll be able to shake this delusion of his."

Joe shook his head. "He's in no shape to go running around chasing ghosts. Pete Dawson will have pups when he finds out about this."

"I don't care what Dawson or anybody else thinks. We're Steve's friends. We owe him our help. Are you with me?"

Nez capitulated. "Okay, if you're game, then so am I." He opened the driver's door. "Let's break him out."

And they moved towards the service entrance.

Lake Havasu City.
That night:

The streets were nearly empty. An occasional vehicle passed the SUV. With Angie at the wheel, Joe listened while Gregory outlined his plan.

"I'm certain that the Ripper is somewhere in the Village," said

Gregory. "Angie —— you'll be the one to flush him out. Once you've let me off at the gate, you two head for the Marina. Take *Lady* over to the Bridge and dock her there. Pretend you're having engine trouble. Joe will be hiding inside the cabin, so you'll appear to be alone."

"And you believe this will attract him?" Angie asked.

"Are you kidding? A woman in trouble. Vulnerable. Alone. He'll go for you, all right. When he does, I'll be there to nail him from the shore side. Joe can pop out of the cabin with his .38 and we'll have him in a crossfire."

"What makes you so sure he's in the Village?" Nez asked.

"The Ripper would feel at home there. It's the logical place for him to hide. He's *there*. You'll see."

"Well," said Joe, "I've always been curious about Jack the Ripper. Should be fun, meeting him in person."

"I know you both think I'm around the bend on this one," said Gregory, "but tonight I'm going to prove that you're wrong. Believe me, he'll take the bait —— and this is *one* kind of fishing I'm good at."

The Tudor Village.
Same night:

With its lights extinguished, the SUV rolled quietly into the parking lot and braked in the shadows near the main gate. Gregory got out and looked around.

"I don't see the guard," he said in a near-whisper. "Probably somewhere inside. You guys go on to the Marina."

They nodded. Angie motored away into the darkness.

Gregory removed a police automatic from his coat, checked the clip, and snugged the gun into his belt. Quickly, he climbed the iron fence and dropped to the ground inside the Village. The area was utterly silent around him. Under a full moon, the trees cast spidery shadows across the cobblestones.

Gregory moved slowly, with catlike stealth, toward the dock area beyond the Bridge. There was no hurry. It would take some time for Joe and Angie to show up with the boat. His main job now was to avoid being seen.

Suddenly, Gregory stopped. Someone was standing inside one of the tall, red, glassed-in London phone booths, just past the entrance to the King's Pub.

Keeping to the shadows, Gregory moved closer. It was the female gate guard. Standing motionless inside.

Gregory couldn't figure it. Obviously, the woman hadn't entered to make a call since the booth was a landscape decoration; no phone lines were hooked up to it. Just a period piece. So what *was* the guard doing in there? Despite the risk, Gregory had to know.

He made a wide circle around the booth, keeping low in the shadows. Still no movement. Now he was able to peer inside. *Christ!* The guard was propped against the glass, her eyes staring out.

Her throat had been cut.

At that precise moment, just as Steve Gregory was dealing with his shock, the Ripper lunged. Like a great dark snake, scalpel raised high and glittering in the moonlight.

Gregory spun around in time to deflect the downward sweep of the blade, dropping to one knee. Before he could rise, the Ripper knocked him unconscious with a single, chopping neck blow.

Now there was time for the kill, time to use the blade properly. Gregory's head was tipped back, exposing the soft skin of his throat. One clean thrust with the scalpel and ——

The Ripper hesitated, startled by a sudden sound from the water. A boat was approaching, the strong beam of its deck light probing the area.

Police? A river patrol? The Ripper ducked quickly behind the tall bulk of a double-decker bus.

Angie cut *Lucky Lady's* power, as if the engines had abruptly failed, allowing the craft to drift into the dock. She secured the bow line, then removed one of the engine covers. Her heart trip-hammered her chest; even though she didn't believe in ghosts, and considered Gregory's fear of the Ripper to be a groundless absurdity, a small voice inside stubbornly continued to ask: *What if he's right?*

She smiled self-consciously at her own fears. What if Santa slides down the chimney next Christmas? What if the Easter Bunny brings me some colored eggs? Jack the Ripper, back after more than a century? Nonsense. Foolish nonsense.

But what if?

Hidden from sight in the below-decks cabin, Joe Nez vented his frustration. His voice was a muted whisper: "We gotta be nuts. I can't believe we're *doing* this!"

Angie was about to reply when she raised her head. There was a movement from the Bridge steps. A dark figure was gesturing to her, waving her forward.

"Someone's out by the Bridge," she whispered to Nez.

"The guard?"

"No, it must be Steve, but he's too far away for me to be sure. He wants me to come over there."

"Okay, go see what's up," said Nez. "I'll hold the fort."

Angie told herself that there was nothing to fear here in the late-night darkness. Once she reached Gregory, this charade would be over. He'd realize that the decoy idea was a joke, that the whole situation was simply ridiculous. He'd have to admit the truth.

She reached the Bridge steps. The area was deserted. "Steve," she called softly. "Are you here?"

"*I'm* here," said a voice directly behind her. A harsh voice. *Female.*

Angie whirled around to confront a tall figure dressed completely in black, face deeply shadowed by a wide-brimmed hat, with a gleaming scalpel in hand.

Angie's muscles locked in shock. She could barely speak "Who are you?"

"The Angel of Death," said the Ripper, as she raised the killing blade.

Suddenly, at that instant, Joe Nez came charging out of the darkness, pushing Angie to one side so he would have a clear shot. But before he could fire, the Ripper slashed down with the scalpel, disabling the detective's gun hand. Joe's .38 clattered to the pavement. Diving to retrieve it, he slipped on the cobbles. The Ripper delivered a swift, savage blow to Joe's head with a booted heel, and Nez was suddenly out of action. He lay face down, unmoving.

As she accepted the stunning fact that Joe Nez could no longer help her, and that Gregory might already be dead, Angie ran for her life. Down the lonely, shadow-haunted brick-and-cobblestone street, under the tall antique gas lamps, past the clustered Tudor buildings of Old London, she ran as a deer runs in panic from the hunter.

She darted across the main square into a narrow, dimly-lit alley behind the King's Pub. Pay phone there. Call the police!

Angie picked up the receiver to dial 911 but before she could get it to her ear the dial tone ceased.

A swift, down-slicing move with the scalpel had severed the phone connection.

The Ripper was there.

Without hesitation, Angie instantly reversed direction, sprinting for the Bucket of Blood Candle Shoppe. Its rear door was ajar and Angie darted through.

Once inside, she realized why the alley door had been open: this is where the Ripper had been hiding, here in the store. Angie had unknowingly entered the lair of the beast.

She looked around desperately for a weapon, running through the store, searching, passing rows of multi-colored candles. Here: a candle owl blinked from its perch. There: a candle leopard crouched; its red-glass eyes seemed to followed her progress.

Angie reached the focal point of the shop, where the exterior of Newgate prison had been atmospherically re-created. Above the simulated iron gate, two plaster heads were mounted on spikes.

Dizzily, she stared at them in shock as the severed heads of Lia Kelley and Elaine Phillips gaped down at her.

Angie gasped in horror as her trauma-induced illusion slowly began to fade. Once again, there were only painted plaster facsimiles on the spikes.

"Realistic, aren't they?" said a graveled voice behind her.

Angie turned, helpless now. Nowhere to run. An icy calm settled upon her. Her fate was inevitable and she accepted it. The running was over. The Angel of Death had won.

"Steve said you were here — in the village," said Angie. "He was convinced that you had risen from the past, that you were Jack the Ripper."

"That is what I have been called . . . and it is how I signed my letters. To confuse people. To make them believe that a man committed the Whitechapel murders."

"Whitechapel? But that was — "

"In 1888," said the tall woman. "Between August 7th and November 9th, 1888. That's when I murdered Martha Tabram, Mary Ann Nichols, Annie Chapman, Elizabeth Stride, Catherine Eddowes, and Mary Jane Kelly. It was all most satisfying. Much blood. I was in complete control."

"But how —" Angie tried to form a coherent question, and couldn't. She shook her head. "That was over a hundred years ago! No one can live that long!"

"I died at the hands of London police in November of 1888," said the woman. "On London Bridge. When I fell into the Thames, a stone fell with me. That stone and I rested together, at the bottom of the river, for more than a century. The Bridge stone somehow absorbed my physical essence, which allowed me to be reborn with the blood of Lia Kelley."

Angie heard the words, but her brain couldn't make sense of them. The woman's story had to be the disordered raving of a lunatic.

"You intend to kill me." Angie said it dully, acknowledging to herself that her statement was fact.

"No, not yet," said the tall figure. "On London Bridge, at the stroke of midnight, I shall draw your blood, but first I have something to show you. Something special. Come with me, dear girl."

Numbly, Angie allowed herself to be led out the rear of the Candle Shoppe, along the alley, to a square, concrete-block building next to the King's Pub. The Ripper swung back a heavy insulated door and a mist of frosted air escaped from the building's interior. A meat locker which served the culinary requirements of the pub.

"Inside, now," said the Ripper as she shoved Angie bodily into the structure.

The Ripper's flashlight cast a pale beam of light over rows of hooked and hanging slabs of meat, each wrapped in a covering of coarse gray canvas. The cold gripped Angie's body as she was prodded forward. They reached the last row at the far end.

"I promised to show you something special," said the Ripper. "Now I shall honor that promise."

The older woman jerked the canvas shroud away from a hanging figure.

Angie choked out a scream, hand to her mouth.

"I knew you would want to see your friend again," she said, "so I kept her fresh for you."

Swaying there on a metal meat hook, twisting slowly in the frosted air, with her throat slashed ear-to-ear, was Lynn Chandler.

London Bridge.
Near midnight:

Wrists taped behind her, Angie was forced to the center of London Bridge — to the place of the restored stone. The moon was a white ghost in the sky. Far out on the water, a night bird cried.

"The stone will receive your blood," said the Ripper. "My powers will be renewed through you. *Your* blood will allow me to return to my own century."

Angie was too numb to respond. She no longer had any hope of survival; she was simply living out the nightmare.

"The time has almost come, Angie," said the Angel of Death. "And is this not a beautiful night to die?"

The hands of the village clock, a scaled-down replica of Big Ben, were closing on midnight. When the hour tolled, the Ripper would use the scalpel.

The blade was poised at Angie's throat.

Steve Gregory sat up. His bandaged head throbbed with pain. He was dizzy. His thoughts whirled chaotically. What happened? Where was he?

Then, with a rush, his focus became clear. The Tudor Village. London Bridge. September 30th. The Ripper. And . . .

Angie! Where was Angie?

Using the phone booth as support, Gregory pulled himself to his feet, swaying with the effort. He squinted his eyes, trying to clear his mottled vision as he looked toward London Bridge.

Movement! They were *there*, on the Bridge —— Angie and the Ripper. Was it already too late? Could he still save her life?

Gregory pulled the automatic from his belt and staggered toward the Bridge, encountering the inert body of Joe Nez near the stone steps. Dead? No. There was a pulse, steady and regular. Joe would be okay.

Must get up the steps. Must save her. Must save Angie.

Gregory began to climb. Step . . . by step . . . by step.

His legs felt rubbery and waves of dizziness swept over him, blurring his mind. But he kept on climbing.

Just as he reached the top of the span the hands of the village clock closed on midnight. The clock's mournful bell began to toll out the hour.

"It's time, Angie," said the Ripper, as the tall figure raised the blade against the light of the moon.

"Let her go!" Gregory shouted, his automatic up and ready to fire.

He moved forward, to within a few feet of the pair on the Bridge.

"When the bell stops tolling," hissed the Ripper, "she will die!"

"Shoot!" Angie pleaded. "For Christ's sake, Steve, *shoot!*"

Gregory's finger locked on the trigger. In his mind's eyes a thirteen-year-old boy fell into rain-swept darkness as Gregory's two bullets ripped into his chest.

The bell continued to toll: eight . . . nine . . . ten . . .

"*Do it!*" Angie commanded. "*Shoot!*"

"Say good-bye to Angie," the Ripper ordered.

Gregory fired.

Kept firing.

Again and again.

Until the clip was empty.

The Ripper fell back heavily against the stone parapet, still alive, but blood gouting from a dozen wounds.

With a wheezing cry, the dark figure toppled from the Bridge.

Down . . . down . . . down . . . into the waters of the Colorado River.

And this time the stone did not follow.

AUTHOR'S AFTERWORD

My surprise revelation — that the Ripper was a woman — is not so far-fetched as it may seem. Throughout the last century, many researchers have speculated that "Jack" may have been a female who possessed surgical knowledge — which would help explain why the Ripper seemed to vanish after each attack. No one was looking for a woman.

In his book, The Harlot Killer, *Allan Barnard ends the Introduction with these words:*

William Stewart offered the thesis that the Whitechapel harlot slayer was not a man at all, but a woman . . . able to gain the confidence of her victims . . . Proof is lacking . . . still, it is most interesting to consider that the police may have been on the wrong track in searching for Jack the Ripper [when] they should have been seeking Jane the Ripper.

— W.F.N.

About the Author

WILLIAM F. NOLAN is a prime example of the Renaissance Man. He has raced sports cars, acted in films and television, worked as a cartoonist for Hallmark Cards, been a biographer and playwright, narrated a Moon documentary, has had his work selected for more than 300 anthologies and textbooks, taught creative writing at college level, painted outdoor murals, gone para-sailing, designed book covers, operated his own art studio, created Mickey Mouse adventures for Walt Disney, been the conductor on a miniature railroad, cited as a Living Legend by the International Horror Guild, published books of verse, served as a job counselor for the California State Department of Employment, prepared pamphlets on eye care, created his own TV series for CBS, written a dozen novels including the best-selling SF classic, *Logan's Run*, performed as a lecturer and panelist at a variety of conventions, handled publicity for Image Power, Inc., has had 700 items printed in 250 magazines and newspapers (including 165 short stories), won numerous awards, including the "2007 Silver Medal for Excellence" from the Independent Publishers of America, had 20 of his 40 scripts produced, and has functioned as a literary critic and commercial artist.

William Nolan lives in Bend, Oregon with a stuffed gorilla and 3,000 of his favorite books.

For more information, see:
www.williamfnolan.com and **www.nolansworld.com**

a decade of quality SF & dark fantasy

"An excellent mixed-genre magazine...well worth checking out."
—Ellen Datlow, *The Year's Best Fantasy & Horror*

Issue #36, Winter 2007

Cover Art by **Adam Hunter Peck**

8 issues for $44.00
4 issues for $24.00
2 issues for $14.00